CHARLOTTE LINK

is one of Europe's bestselling crime writers and has sold more than 15 million novels in Germany alone. Her atmospheric brand of psychological suspense made *The Other Child* a massive No. 1 bestseller in Germany and was greeted by rave reviews. Charlotte has been nominated for the Fiction Category of the German Book Prize and her work has been widely adapted for TV, with the adaptation of *The Other Child* transmitted in Germany in 2011.

THE
OTHER
CHILD

CHARLOTTE
LINK

Translated from the German by Stefan Tobler

WORLDWIDE ®

TORONTO • NEW YORK • LONDON
AMSTERDAM • PARIS • SYDNEY • HAMBURG
STOCKHOLM • ATHENS • TOKYO • MILAN
MADRID • WARSAW • BUDAPEST • AUCKLAND

Recycling programs
for this product may
not exist in your area.

ISBN-13: 978-0-373-18966-3

The Other Child

Copyright © 2013 by Charlotte Link

Translation copyright © 2012 by Stephan Tobler

A Worldwide Library Suspense/January 2015

First published by Pegasus Crime, an imprint of Pegasus Books LLC.

This edition published by arrangement with Harlequin Books S.A.

® and TM are trademarks of the publisher. Trademarks indicated with
® are registered in the United States Patent and Trademark Office, the
Canadian Intellectual Property Office and in other countries.

www.Harlequin.com

Printed in U.S.A.

THE
OTHER
CHILD

DECEMBER 1970

Saturday, 19th December

SHE KNEW SHE had to get away as quickly as possible.

She was in danger, and if the people who lived on the isolated farm caught sight of her she was lost.

Suddenly the man appeared out of nowhere in front of her, just as she got to the farmyard gate and was about to hurry down to her car. He was big and not as scruffy as she would have expected among these dilapidated buildings. He was wearing jeans and a jumper. His grey hair was cut very short. She could not see any glimmer of feeling in his pale eyes.

Semira could only hope he had not seen her behind the barn. Maybe he had spied her car and come to see who was snooping around. Her only chance was in convincing him she was harmless, even though her heart was pounding and her knees knocking. Her face was beaded with sweat, in spite of the biting cold on this already twilit December afternoon.

His voice was as cold as his eyes. 'What you doin' here?'

She tried a smile, but felt her lips quiver. 'Thank God. I thought no one was here…'

He looked her up and down. Semira tried to imagine what he saw. A skinny little woman, not yet thirty, wrapped up warm in trousers, fleece-lined boots and a thick anorak. Black hair, black eyes. Hopefully he did not have anything against Asians. Hopefully he did not re-alise he had an Asian in front of him who felt like she was going to throw up at any moment. Hopefully he had not realised how afraid she was. Semira had an awful feeling he could smell her fear.

He nodded towards the copse at the bottom of the hill. 'Yer car?'

It had been a mistake to park it down there. The trees were too sparse and bare—they concealed nothing. He had seen her car from one of the upper windows of his house, and put two and two together.

What an idiot she was, to come here and not tell anyone. And then to park her car in sight of the wretched farm.

'I'm…completely lost,' she stammered. 'No idea how I ended up here. Then I saw your house and thought I could ask if…'

'Aye?'

'I'm new to the area.' Her voice sounded wrong in her ears, too high and a little shrill, but he did not know how she usually spoke. 'Actually, I wanted—I wanted—'

'So where you goin', really?'

Her mind was blank. 'To…to…what's it called again?' She licked her dry lips. She was standing face-to-face with a psychopath. He should have been locked up, and the key thrown away, she was sure of it. She should never have come here on her own. There was no one here who could help her. She was only too aware of the absolute isolation and remoteness of the place. No other farm near or far, not another soul.

She could not afford to slip up. 'To…' Finally a name popped into her head. 'Whitby. I wanted to go to Whitby.'

'Yer right lost. T' main road is fair drive from hre.'

'Yes, that's what I was starting to figure.' She forced a

smile again. The man did not smile back. He stared fixedly at her. In spite of his impassive appearance, Semira could feel his mistrust, his suspicion, which seemed to grow with every second that he talked to her.

She had to get away!

She forced herself to stand there calmly, although she really wanted to run. 'Could you tell me how to get back to the main road?'

He did not reply. His glacial blue eyes seemed to go right through her. She really had never seen colder eyes. As cold as if there were no longer any life in them. She was glad she had a scarf wrapped round her neck; she could feel a nerve twitching away under her right jaw.

The silence lasted too long. He was trying to work something out. He did not trust her. He weighed up the risk that this little person posed for him. He examined her, as if he wanted to penetrate deep into her mind.

Then a scornful expression passed over his face. He spat on the ground in front of her.

'Black bastards,' he said. 'Fillin' up Yorkshire now, an' all?'

She flinched. She wondered if he was a racist or was just out to provoke, to draw her out of her shell. He wanted her to give herself away.

Act as if this were a completely normal situation.

She felt a sob rising in her throat, and she could not stop a hoarse sound escaping. It simply was not a normal situation. She had no idea how long she could still control her panic.

'My…husband is English,' she said. She never did that usually. She never hid behind John when she was faced with prejudice about the colour of her skin. But an instinct had led her to give that answer this time. Now he knew that she was married and that there was someone who would miss her if anything happened to her. Someone who was not a stranger in this country and who would know immediately what to do when someone disappeared. Someone whom the police would take seriously.

She could not tell if her reply made any impression on him.

'Ge'yerself away,' he said.

It was not the moment to be indignant about his rudeness, or to argue for equal rights for people of different colours. She had to escape and find the police.

She turned to go. She forced herself to walk at a measured pace and not to give in to the urge to run. He had to think she was insulted without knowing that she was going mad with fear inside.

She had taken four or five steps when his voice stopped her.

'Wait!'

She froze. 'Sorry?'

He strode over to her. She could smell his breath. Cigarettes and sour milk.

'You were over at t' shed, weren't you?'

She had a knot in her throat and broke out in a sweat all over her body. 'What…what shed?'

He stared at her. She could read in his emotionless eyes what he could see in hers: that she knew. That she knew his secret.

He no longer had any doubts.

She ran.

JULY 2008

THE FIRST TIME he saw the woman he had just left Friarage School and was about to cross the road to go home. She was standing in the open doorway, clearly hesitating to set foot outside in the pouring rain. It was almost six and already unusually dark for the time of year. The day had been oppressively hot, then a storm broke over Scarborough with mighty claps of thunder. The heavens opened and it seemed that the end was nigh. The schoolyard was deserted. Water immediately gathered in giant puddles on the uneven tarmac. Angry blue-black clouds massed in the sky.

The woman was wearing a calf-length, flowery summer dress. It was somewhat old-fashioned but quite suitable for the day, until the storm came. She had long, mousy-blond hair, which she wore in a plait, and was carrying a shopping bag in her hand. As far as he knew, she was not a teacher. Maybe she was new. Or on a course.

Something invited him to step closer and to consider talking to her. Maybe it was her unusually old-fashioned appearance. He guessed her to be in her early twenties, yet she looked completely different to other women of her age. Not that looking at her was going to send a man into ecstasies, but something would hold your attention. You would want to know what her face looked like. How she spoke. Whether she represented some kind of alternative to her era and her generation.

He, at any rate, wanted to know. Women fascinated him, and as he knew almost all kinds of women by now, the unusual ones exerted a particular fascination.

He walked over to her and said, 'You don't have an umbrella?'

It was not that he felt himself to be particularly original at this moment, but in view of the torrential rain outside the question was almost inevitable.

The woman had not seen him approaching and jumped. She turned towards him and he realised his mistake. She was not in her early twenties, but at least her mid-thirties, perhaps even older. She looked friendly, but plain. A pale face without make-up, not pretty, not ugly—the kind of face that you would not remember for more than two minutes. Her hair was drawn back from her high forehead in a rather loveless way. It was obvious that she was not consciously trying to embody a particular type, but simply had no idea what to do to look more attractive.

A nice, shy thing, he judged, and completely uninteresting.

'I should've known there'd be a storm,' she said. 'But when I left home at lunch-time, it was so hot that a brolly would've been silly.'

'Where are you going?' he asked.

'Only to the bus stop in Queen Street. But I'll be soaking by the time I get there.'

'When does your bus go?'

'In five minutes,' she said in a whining tone. 'And it's the last one today.'

She seemed to live out in the sticks. It was astonishing how quickly the countryside swallowed you up outside the town boundaries. Without much of a transition, you were suddenly in the middle of nowhere, among settlements of just a few scattered farms, which were barely served by public transport. The last bus just before six! Young people there must feel that they were still in the Stone Age.

If she had been young and pretty, he would not have hesitated an instant to offer her a lift home. He would have asked if she would like to go for a drink with him first, somewhere down in the harbour with its many pubs. He was not meeting someone until later in the evening and it was nothing important. He had no great wish to sit around bored until then in his lodger's room in a house at the end of the road.

Yet there was nothing enticing about the idea of sitting over a glass of wine in a pub and looking all evening at the colourless face of this elderly girl—for that was the impression you got: she was an elderly girl.

TV would probably be more entertaining. Yet he hesitated to just leave her and sprint across the schoolyard and up the road. She looked so…abandoned.

'Where do you live?'

'In Staintondale,' she said.

He rolled his eyes. He knew Staintondale, oh God! A main road, a church, a post office where you could also buy the most basic foodstuffs and a couple of papers. A few houses. A red phone box, which was also the bus stop. And farms, which looked as if they had been thrown into the surrounding countryside.

'You've no doubt also got a little walk from the bus stop in Staintondale,' he guessed.

She nodded unhappily. 'Almost half an hour, yes.'

He had not only made the mistake of talking to her. He had the impression that she had noticed his disappointment, and something told him that it was a painfully familiar occurrence for her. It might have been the case that she had awakened a man's interest often, only for it to immediately extinguish when the man actually approached her. Perhaps she guessed that he would have offered to help, if only she had been a little more interesting, and now she assumed with some certainty that nothing would come of it.

'You know what,' he said quickly, before his selfishness and laziness got the better of his sudden generosity, 'my car is just down the road. If you'd like, I can drive you home quickly.'

She stared at him in disbelief. 'But…it's quite a trip… Staintondale's—'

'I know the place,' he interrupted. 'But I don't have any plans for the next few hours, and there are worse things than a drive in the country.'

'In this weather…' she put in doubtfully.

He smiled. 'I would advise you to accept my offer. First, you probably won't catch your bus now anyway. Second, even if you do, you'll have a nasty cold tomorrow or at the latest the day after. So?'

She hesitated, and he could sense her mistrust. She was asking herself what his motives were. He knew that he was good-looking and a success with women, and she was probably realistic enough to realise that a man like him could not really be attracted to a woman like her. She probably had him down either as a sex offender wanting to lure her into his car because he took whatever he could get, or as a man overcome by pity. Neither alternative was appealing.

'Dave Tanner,' he said, holding out his hand. She shook it hesitantly. Her hand felt warm and soft.

'Gwendolyn Beckett,' she said.

He smiled. 'So, Mrs Beckett, I—'

'*Miss*,' she corrected him quickly. '*Miss* Beckett.'

'OK, Miss Beckett.' He glanced at his wristwatch. 'Your bus goes in one minute. I think that decides that then. Are you ready for a sprint, across the playground and a few yards down the road?'

She nodded, taken by surprise by the realisation that she didn't really have any choice but to clutch at the straw which he was offering her.

'Hold your bag over your head then,' he advised her. 'That will shelter you a bit.'

She dashed after him across the playground awash with puddles. Along the wrought-iron fence surrounding the premises, tall trees bent under the pouring rain. On the left the enormous Market Hall appeared, a building with catacomb-like underground passageways and vaults. In its galleries and shops you could buy mountains of kitsch, and even a little art. To the right was a little residential street lined with narrow red-brick terraced houses, each with a gloss-white door.

'Down here,' he said, and they ran past the houses until they reached the small blue, rather rusty Fiat parked on the left-hand side of the street. He unlocked the car, and they tumbled onto the front seats with relieved sighs.

Water was streaming off Gwendolyn's hair, and her dress stuck to her body like a wet cloth. Those few yards had been enough to soak her through. Dave tried to ignore his wet feet.

'I'm an idiot,' he said. 'I should have fetched the car and picked you up at the school. Then you'd be more or less dry still.'

'Oh please!' Finally she laughed. She had nice teeth, as he noticed. 'I'm not made of sugar. And it's definitely better to be driven to my door than to jolt about on a bus ride and then have a good little trek awaiting me at the end. Thank you.'

'Not at all,' he said. He was trying for a third time to start his car, and finally got it going. The motor wheezed to life, the car jumped forward. In two jumps it was in the street, spluttering as it drove off.

'It'll be all right,' he said. 'The car just needs to warm up. If I get through the winter with this old heap of junk I'll count myself lucky.'

The motor was now starting to hum more regularly. It was fine for now: the car would make it to Staintondale and back.

'What would you have done if you hadn't caught the bus or met me?' he asked. Not that Miss Beckett particularly interested him, but they would be sitting next to each other in the car for half an hour and he did not want the situation to descend into an awkward silence.

'I would have phoned my father,' said Gwendolyn.

He threw her a quick glance. The sound of her voice had altered as she spoke of her father. It had become warmer, less distanced.

'You live with your father?'

'Yes.'

'And your mother…?'

'My mother died young,' said Gwendolyn in a tone that revealed that she did not want to talk about it.

A daddy's girl, he thought, who can't break free. At least mid-thirties, and Daddy is still the Only One for her. The Greatest. The Best. No man is his equal.

He supposed she did everything, consciously or unconsciously, to be Daddy's dream daughter. With her thick blond plait and her old-fashioned flowery dress she was just like the women from Daddy's youth, which would have been in the fifties or early sixties. She wanted to please him, and probably he was not keen on mini-skirts, conspicuous make-up or short hair. The signals she gave out were completely asexual.

Well, she hardly wants her old man in her bed, he thought.

He was very atuned to people's moods and could sense that she was wracking her brains for a way to change the topic, so he helped her out.

'By the way, I teach at Friarage School,' he said. 'But not the kids. The school lets its rooms be used in the evenings and some afternoons for adult education. I teach French and Spanish, and that just about keeps the wolf from the door.'

'Do you speak those languages well?'

'As a child I lived in Spain and France for a long time. My father was a diplomat.' He knew that *his* voice did not show any warmth when he mentioned his father. Instead he had to take care not to show too much hate. 'But let me tell you, it's no fun to have to teach a group of totally untalented housewives a language whose sound and expressiveness you love, and whose complete mangling you have to bear three or four evenings a week.' He laughed in embarrassment as he realised he might have committed a *faux pas*.

'I'm sorry. You might be taking one of the language courses. Have I just offended you? There are three other language teachers giving classes.'

She shook her head. Although the wall of rain outside meant that it was rather dark in the car, he could see that she was blushing.

'No,' she said, 'I'm not taking part in a language course. I…'

She was not looking at him, but was staring out of the window. They had reached the road that led north out of Scarborough. Supermarkets and rows of terraced houses flew past outside, garages and dismal pubs, a mobile homes park, which looked like it was sinking in the floods.

'I'd read in the paper,' she said quietly, 'that in Friarage School… Well, on Wednesday afternoons there's a course, which…for the next three months…' She hesitated.

In a flash he understood what she was talking about. He did not understand why it had not been clear to him at once. After all, he taught there. He knew about the new course. Wednesdays. From half-three to half-five. Starting today. And Gwendolyn Beckett was just the kind of person who would attend.

'Oh, I know,' he said, and made an effort to sound casual about it. As if it were the most normal thing in the world to attend a course for…yes, for whom? Failures? Dead losses? Losers? 'Isn't it a kind of…assertiveness training?'

Now he could not see her face at all. She had turned to the window. He guessed that she had gone bright red.

'Yes,' she answered quietly. 'That's it. You're supposed to learn to conquer your shyness. To approach other people. To control your…fears.' Now she turned towards him. 'That must sound like a load of rubbish to you.'

'Not at all,' he assured her. 'When you think you have a weakness, you have to face it. That makes a lot more sense than just sitting around and not doing anything but complaining. Don't worry. Just try to make the most of the course.'

'Yes,' she said, sounding despondent. 'I will. You know…it's not as if I was particularly happy with my life.'

She turned to the window again, and he did not dare enquire further.

Neither said anything.

The rain eased up a little.

As they turned off in the middle of Cloughton towards Staintondale, a gap appeared in the clouds and the evening sun burst through.

He suddenly had a tingling of excitement, was on the lookout. It was a feeling that something new was about to happen in his life. It might have to do with this woman sitting next to him.

It could also be something else entirely.

He told himself to stay calm. And to be cautious.

He could not afford to make too many more mistakes in his life.

2

AMY MILLS NEEDED the money that her job as a babysitter brought in. That was the only reason she did it. But she had to pay for her studies more or less on her own, so she could not be picky. Not that it was unpleasant to spend her evenings in someone else's living room, reading a book or watching the telly, just keeping watch over a sleeping child whose parents were out. But it meant she got home late, and she hated the trip home in the dark. At least in the autumn and winter. In the summer the evenings were light until late, and often the streets of Scarborough were full of overseas students coming to the East Yorkshire coast for summer English courses.

This evening was different. The storm and the afternoon's heavy rain had driven everyone inside and cleared the streets. What is more, after a very hot day it had cooled considerably. It was unpleasant and windy.

No one will be out, thought Amy uneasily.

On Wednesdays she was always at Mrs Gardner's place, taking care of her four-year-old daughter Liliana. Mrs Gardner was a single mum, supporting herself and her daughter with a number of jobs, and on Wednesday evenings she taught French in the Friarage School. The class finished at nine, but then she always went out for a drink with her students.

'Otherwise I'd never get out,' she said to Amy, 'and at

least once a week I'd like to have some fun. Is it all right by you if I'm back by ten?'

The problem was it was never ten when she finally got in. Half-ten if Amy was lucky, a quarter to eleven more likely. Mrs Gardner apologized profusely each time.

'I have no idea where the time went! By eck, once we start chattin'…'

Actually Amy would have liked to ditch this job, but it was her only more or less stable work. She looked after the children of other families too, but only irregularly. She could rely on the Wednesday money, and in her situation that was priceless. If only she did not have that trip home…

I'm such a coward, she often said to herself, but that did not do anything to lessen her fear.

Mrs Gardner had no car in which to drive her babysitter home quickly, and she was over the alcohol limit in any case. She had also drunk a fair few this Wednesday and it was later than ever before —twenty past eleven!

'We said ten o'clock,' said Amy in annoyance as she packed up her books. She had spent the evening studying.

At least Mrs Gardner showed a rueful face. 'I know. I'm terrible. But there's a new lady in our class and she bought us a couple of rounds. She had a right few stories to tell. By time I thought 'bout leavin'—it were already so late!'

She handed Amy the money and was decent enough to give her an extra five pounds. 'Here. Because yer really had t' do overtime today… Everythin' OK with Liliana?'

'She's asleep. She didn't wake up once.' Amy said goodbye to tipsy Mrs Gardner and left. On the street she hunched her shoulders against the cold.

Almost like autumn, she thought, but it's just mid-July.

Thankfully it had not been raining for a few hours. The way home took her along the street, part of the way down

St. Nicholas Cliff, past the rather dilapidated Grand Hotel and then over the long iron bridge which connected the centre of town to South Cliff and went over a main road that was busy during the day. Now at this late hour, however, the road down there was deserted, although it was still bright under the blazing street lamps. The silent sleeping town was creepy, but Amy still had her fear under control. The stretch through the park would be worse. Down to her left was the sea and the beach, high up above were the first South Cliff houses. In between were the Esplanade Gardens, which snaked upwards along terraces. They were densely planted with bushes and trees and a multitude of little paths cut through them. The shortest way through it was up the steep steps that led directly to the Esplanade, the wide road on whose western side the hotels stood, one beside the next. This was Amy's way home, and the dark steps were the tricky stretch. As soon as she reached the Esplanade, she would feel better. Then she had to go a good little bit further up the road and just after Highlander Hotel she would turn into Albion Road. An aunt of hers owned a narrow terraced house here and had given Amy a place to stay while she studied. The aunt was old and lonely and happy to have company, and Amy's parents weren't well off and found the offer of a free place to live very welcome. What is more, from there she could easily walk to the campus. She was glad that some things had turned out better than she might have expected. Where she came from, a working-class estate in Leeds, no one would have believed that Amy would make it to university. But she was intelligent and hard working, and for all her extreme shyness and her fearfulness, she was determined. She had passed all her exams with good marks until now.

She was in the middle of the bridge when she stopped

and looked back. Not that she had heard something, but every time she got about this far she had the almost automatic reaction, before she plunged on into the creepily empty Esplanade Gardens, to check if everything was all right—without being exactly clear what she meant by *all right*.

A man was walking down St. Nicholas Cliff. Tall, slim, taking quick steps. She could not see what sort of clothes he was wearing. Only a few more yards and he would have reached the bridge, towards which he was obviously heading.

There was no one else to see near or far.

With one hand Amy held on tight to her bag of books, with the other hand to her front door key, which she had dug out of her bag at Mrs Gardner's house. She had got into the habit of holding it at the ready on her way home. Of course that was all part of her fearfulness. Her aunt forgot to turn the outside light on every night. Amy hated standing there rummaging around in her bag for the key, as blind as a mole. There were ten-foot-high lilac bushes to the right and left, and her aunt—with the typically unreasonable stubbornness of old age—refused to have them pruned. Amy wanted to get into the house as fast as possible. To be in a safe place.

Safe from what?

She was too easily frightened. She knew that. It just wasn't normal to see ghosts everywhere, burglars, murderers and perverts behind every corner. She guessed it had to do with her upbringing—as the sheltered, mollycoddled only child of her straightforward parents. *Don't do this, don't do that, this could happen, that could happen…* She had always been hearing things like that. She had not been allowed to do a lot of what her classmates did, because her mother was afraid that something could go wrong. Amy had not rebelled against the bans; she had soon shared her mother's fears and was glad to have a reason she could give her school friends:

I'm not allowed...

The long and the short of it was that she did not have many friends now.

She turned round once more. The stranger had reached the bridge. Amy walked on. She walked a little faster than before. It was not only fear of the man that made her hurry. It was also the fear of her own thoughts.

Loneliness.

The other students at Scarborough Campus, an offshoot of the University of Hull, lived in halls of residence for their first year of study, then they formed little groups to rent out the inexpensive houses that belonged to the university. Amy had always tried to convince herself that it was natural and sensible for her to creep under her aunt's wing, because no rent was naturally better than low rent, and she would have been stupid to decide otherwise. The bitter truth was that she had no clique to go in with. No one had ever asked her if she would like to share this or that flat with this or that group. Without the old aunt's empty guest-room things would have looked bleak, and not only from the financial point of view. But Amy did not want to think about that.

From the end of the bridge it was only a few more steps to the park. As usual, Amy turned right, towards the steps. There was a new building in the bend; it was in the last stages of construction. It was not clear whether it would be residential or used by Scarborough council for some other purpose.

Amy walked quickly past it and then stopped short. Two

of the tall metal mesh fences that surrounded the house were now blocking the steps and the nearby meandering path, which would normally have offered an alternative. The usual entrance was barred. You could squeeze through sideways, but Amy dithered. In the afternoon when she walked to the pedestrian zone in the stifling heat, to run an errand or two before she started babysitting for Mrs Gardner, the way had still been open. In the meantime there had been a violent storm and an almost apocalyptical flood of rain. Possibly the steps and the meandering path had been damaged. The earthworks and gravel had been washed away. It might be dangerous to take either route up.

Added to that, it was obviously prohibited.

Amy was not the kind of girl to just ignore a law. She had always been taught to obey the authorities, whether she understood their rules or not. They had their reasons; that was enough. In this case she was even able to understand the reason.

Undecidedly, she turned around.

There were other paths that led up into the labyrinthine Esplanade Gardens, but none of them led quickly and directly up to the road and to where people lived. The lowest path led in the opposite direction: down to the beach and the Spa Complex, a collection of Victorian buildings right by the sea, which the town used for all kinds of cultural events. At night, however, they were completely closed off, and not even a nightwatchman was around. Running up the cliff behind the Spa Complex there was a funicular railway, mainly to transport elderly ladies and gentlemen who were no longer willing to struggle up the steep gardens cut out of the rock. Yet about half an hour before midnight the cars stopped, and now there was no longer anyone on duty in the ticket office. Of course you could also go up on foot, but it was a long and difficult way up. The advantage of this lower path was that it was lit. Large curving lamps, also modelled on the Victorian style, gave off a warm orange light.

There was also a middle way—the narrowest of all three. For a good stretch, half-way up the steep slope, it ran almost alongside the drop before starting to rise so gently that even walkers who were not in the peak of physical fitness were able to proceed with some degree of ease. Amy knew that this path came out right in front of the Crown Spa Hotel on the Esplanade. She would get to the top more quickly if she took the middle way than if she went along the beach, but the disadvantage was that there were no street lamps there. The path lost itself between bushes and trees in blackest darkness.

She took a few steps back, and looked towards the bridge. The man had almost crossed it now. Was she imagining things, or was he really walking more slowly than he had before? More hesitantly? What was he doing here at this time of night?

Keep calm, Mills, you're here *at this time of night* too, she said to herself, although it did not make her heart beat any little bit less fast.

He could be on his way home, just like you!

But tell me, who was just going home now? It was twenty to twelve. Not the time when people normally return home from work, unless they were babysitting for an inconsiderate mum who always came in too late.

I'm going to quit. I can't put up with it any more. Not for any amount of money, she resolved.

She weighed up her options. None of them seemed particularly promising. She could walk back across the bridge to St. Nicholas Cliff and then take the long Filey Road up through town—but that would take ages. Then there was always the bus, but she had no idea if her bus was still running this late at night. And a few weeks ago she had used the bus one day when the weather was bad, and she had been picked on at the bus stop by some drunken, pierced youths with shaved heads. She had been scared to death and had sworn that in future she would rather be soaked to the bone and risk a cold than find herself in such a situation once again. Fear—yet again. Fear of walking through the dark park. Fear of waiting at the bus stop. Fear, fear, fear.

She was in charge of her life and it could not go on like this. She could no longer let herself stumble from one crisis to the next, trying to avoid one fear and so inevitably raising another. And in the end standing paralyzed in a cool, rainy July night at a crossing, listening to her own panting breath, feeling her heart pound like a fast and heavy hammer, and asking herself which of her fears was the least worst. In the end it was the infamous choice between the devil and the deep blue sea, and that felt terrible.

The man was now on a level with her. He stopped and looked at her.

He seemed to be waiting for something, maybe for what she would say or do, and as Amy was a girl who had been taught to meet people's expectations, she opened her mouth.

'The…path is closed,' she said. Her voice croaked a little, and she cleared her throat. 'The fencing…blocking the path.'

He gave a brief nod, turned away and took the path towards the beach. The lit path.

Amy breathed a sigh of relief. Harmless, it had been completely harmless. He wanted to go home, normally he would no doubt have taken the steps. Now he would probably walk to the Spa Complex and then up from there, and curse inwardly that the journey home took longer than expected. His wife was waiting at home. She would have a go at him. It had gotten late in the pub with his friends in any case, and now this detour. Not his day. Sometimes everything happened at once.

She giggled, but noticed herself how nervous she sounded. She had a tendency to dream up the details of the lives of people completely unknown to her. Probably because she was on her own too much. When you did not communicate enough with people of flesh and blood you had to dwell in your own imagination.

One more glance back at the bridge. No one to see there.

The stranger had disappeared towards the beach. The steps were closed off. Amy did not dither any longer. She took the middle path, the unlit one. The little bit of moonlight that trickled through the long veils of cloud was enough to let her guess where the path at her feet led. She would come up at the Esplanade without breaking any bones.

The closely planted bushes, whose full summer foliage was heavy with raindrops, swallowed her up within seconds.

Amy Mills disappeared into the darkness.

OCTOBER 2008

Thursday, 9th October

1

WHEN THE PHONE in Fiona Barnes' living room rang, the old lady jumped. She left the window, where she had been standing and gazing out over Scarborough Bay, and walked over to the side table the phone stood on, unsure whether or not to lift up the receiver. She had received an anonymous call that morning, and the morning before, and last week too there had been two of these harrassing calls. She was not even sure if what was happening could be called anonymous calls, as no one said anything on the other end of the line. She could hear that someone was breathing. If she did not slam the receiver down on its cradle again in annoyance, as she had done that morning, then the unknown person always hung up after about a minute of silence.

Fiona was not easily scared, she was proud of her cool head and that she held her nerve. Yet this story disturbed and unsettled her. She would have preferred to just let it ring and ring without answering, but then of course she would miss calls that were important or that meant something to her. From her granddaughter Leslie Cramer for example, who lived in London and was just going through the trauma of a divorce. Leslie no longer had any relatives except for her old grandmother in Scarborough, and Fiona wanted to be there for her now in particular.

So she picked up after the fifth ring.

'Fiona Barnes,' she said. She had a scratchy, rough voice from a life of chain-smoking.

Silence on the other end of the line.

Fiona sighed. She should get a new phone, one with caller display. At least then she could see when Leslie was calling and leave the rest.

'Who is it?' she asked.

Silence. Breathing.

'You are starting to get on my nerves,' said Fiona. 'You obviously have some problem with me. Perhaps we should talk about it. Your strange approach is not going to get us any further, I fear.'

The breathing became heavier. If she had been younger, Fiona might have thought it possible that she had caught the eye of someone who was now satisfying a primal urge as he listened to her voice on the phone. But as she had turned seventy-nine in July that seemed rather unlikely. Nor did the breathing seem to suggest a sexual stimulation. The caller seemed excited in a different way. Stressed. Aggressive. In extreme turmoil.

It was not about sex. What was it about then?

'I'm hanging up,' Fiona said, but before she could make good on her threat, the other person had already interrupted the call. Fiona could only hear the monotonous beeping of the phone.

'I should go to the police!' she said angrily, slamming down the phone and immediately lighting a cigarette. But she was afraid that the police would fob her off with excuses. She had not been verbally abused, showered in obscenities or threatened. Of course everyone would understand that repeated silences on the phone can also be considered a threat, but there were no clues as to who the caller might be. This case was so extremely vague that the police would not try to trace the calls. In any case, no doubt the caller was clever enough to use only public payphones and not to use the same one each time. People today had gained experience from detective series on TV. They knew how to do things and which mistakes to avoid.

What is more…

She stepped over to the window again. Outside it was a wonderful, sun-drenched October day, windy and clear-skied, and Scarborough Bay lay there, flooded with a golden light. The deep azure-blue sea was rough. The waves had shining white crests. Seeing this view, anyone would have been in transports of delight. Not Fiona at this moment. She did not even notice what was in front of her window.

She knew why she was not going to the police. She knew why she had not told anyone yet, not even Leslie, about the strange calls. And why, for all her worrying, she kept the whole story to herself.

The logical question of anyone hearing about it would be: 'But is there someone who might have something against you? Someone who you could imagine might be involved in these calls?'

If she was honest, she would have to say 'yes' to this question, which would have inevitably led to further questions. And required explanations from her. Everything would have come to the surface again. The whole of the horrific story. All the things she wanted to forget. The things that Leslie, more than anyone else, should not hear about.

If however she played dumb, claimed that she did not know anyone who could have something against her, who would torment her like this, then there was also no point in telling anyone about it.

She took a deep drag on her cigarette. The only person
to whom she could open herself was Chad. Because he
knew in any case. Maybe she should talk to him. It would
also be a good idea for him to delete the emails she had sent
him. The attached files in particular. It had been careless
of her to send them via the internet. She had thought she
could risk it because it was all over so long ago. Because
it was all so far behind her, behind both of them.

Maybe she had been mistaken about that.

Perhaps she should also remove the extensive material on her computer. It would not be easy for her, but
it was probably better like that. After all, writing it all
down had just been a hare-brained idea of hers in the first
place. What had she hoped to achieve? Some relief? To
clear her conscience? No, it seemed instead as if she had
hoped to work something out, for herself and Chad. Perhaps she had hoped to get to know herself better. But it
had not helped. She did not understand herself any better
than before. Nothing had changed. You could not change
your own life by analysing it afterwards, by trying to find
a form for it that would relativise events. Mistakes were
still mistakes, sins still sins. You had to live with them,
you would die with them.

She stubbed out her cigarette butt in a flowerpot and
went into her study, to boot up her computer.

2

THE LAST VIEWER was the worst. He had not stopped complaining once. The parquetry floor was worn, the door handles looked cheap, the windows were not double-glazed, the rooms were awkward shapes and did not fit together well, the kitchen was not modern, the view of the little park behind the house was charmless.

'Not exactly a gift,' he said angrily before he left, and Leslie had to force herself not to bang the door shut behind him. It would have done her good, but the lock was not in the best of conditions—like so much else in the house, to be frank—and the violent action might have been too much for it.

'Lousy bastard,' she said from the depths of her heart. Then she went into the kitchen, lit a cigarette and turned the coffee machine on. An espresso was just what she needed now. She looked out of the window at the rainy day. Of course the park did not look especially appealing in this grey drizzle, but this tree-covered patch in the middle of London was the reason why Stephen and she had fallen in love with the flat ten years ago. Yes, the kitchen was old-fashioned, the floors creaked, many things were a little shabby, but the flat had charm and character, and she asked herself how anyone could not see that. Swanky so-and-so. But they had all complained. The old lady who was the second person to look around had complained the least. Perhaps she would take over the tenancy… Time was short. Leslie was moving at the end of October. If she did not find anyone by then to take over her current tenancy agreement, then she would have to pay double, and she would not be able to afford that for very long.

Keep your nerve, she told herself.

When the phone rang, she was about to ignore it, but then she reconsidered. It could be another viewer. She went to the hall and picked up.

'Cramer,' she answered. She found it more and more difficult to say her married name. I should use my old name again, she thought.

A shy quiet voice on the other end of the line said, 'Leslie? It's Gwen here. Gwen from Staintondale!'

'Gwen from Staintondale!' said Leslie. She had certainly not expected a call from Gwen, her childhood friend. It was a pleasant surprise. She had not heard from her in ages. It might have been a year since they had seen each other, and at Christmas they had only spoken briefly on the phone, not much more than the usual best wishes for the new year.

'How are you?' asked Gwen. 'Is everything all right? I phoned the hospital first, but they said you had taken holiday leave.'

'Yes, I have. For three whole weeks. I have to find someone to rent out the flat, and get ready for the move, and… oh yes, and I had to get divorced. Since Monday I'm on the market again!' She listened to her own voice. She certainly did not feel as comfortable about it as she sounded. It was astonishingly painful. Even now.

'Oh, my goodness,' said Gwen in dismay. 'That…I mean, we all saw it coming, but somehow there's always a hope… How do you feel?'

'Well, we've been separated two years now. So nothing has really changed. But as it's still a turning point in my life, I've rented a new flat. This one is too big in the long-term, and anyway…somehow it has too much to do with Stephen.'

'I can understand that,' said Gwen. She sounded a little uncomfortable when she spoke again. 'I…I feel completely tactless now, but…I really didn't know that you had just got divorced, otherwise…I mean, I wouldn't have…'

'I'm fine. Really. So don't beat around the bush. Why are you calling?'

'Because…now, I hope you won't be offended, but… you should be one of the first people to hear: I'm going to get married!'

Leslie really did not know what to say for a moment.

'Married?' she then echoed, thinking that the amazement in her voice must hurt Gwen, but she simply had not managed to conceal her surprise. Gwen was an old maid if anyone was: an old-fashioned girl living in isolation in the countryside…Gwen, for whom time seemed to have stood still, to have stopped in a past century where a young lady would wait at home until a gentleman rode up on his horse and asked for her hand… Marry? Just like that?

'Sorry,' she said quickly. 'It's just—I always thought you weren't all that keen on marriage.'

That was a lie. She knew that Gwen had pined for the stories which she devoured in romance novels to become true in her own life.

'I'm so happy,' said Gwen. 'So unbelievably happy…I mean, I had just about given up hope of still finding someone, and now I'll be married this year! We thought the beginning of December would be nice. Oh, Leslie, suddenly everything is…so different!'

Leslie had finally got a grip on herself.

'Gwen, I'm overjoyed for you!' she said sincerely. 'Really, you have no idea how much! Who is the lucky man? Where did you meet him?'

'He's called Dave Tanner. He is forty-three years old, and…he loves me.'

'How wonderful!' said Leslie, but once again there was a slight feeling of amazement. Her first thought had been of a considerably older man, perhaps a widower, a sixty-year-old with no great expectations, who as much as anything was looking for someone to take care of him. She was ashamed to think it, but she really could not imagine anything other than a selfish reason for a man to get involved with Gwen. Gwen was a dear woman, sincere and warm-hearted, but there was little about her to make her desirable in the eyes of a man. Unless that person was only looking at her inner character, which in Leslie's experience was something few men did.

But perhaps I'm completely wrong, she thought.

'I'll tell you everything,' said Gwen, whose voice was trembling with joy and excitement, 'but first there's something I want to invite you to. On Saturday we're going to celebrate a kind of…engagement, and it would be the most wonderful present for me if you could be there!'

Leslie thought quickly. The journey north was too long and difficult just for the weekend, but luckily she was on holiday. She could drive up on Friday morning and then stick around for three or four days after the weekend. She was from Yorkshire. She had grown up in Scarborough and it had been far too long since she had last been there. She could stay with her grandmother, who would be glad to see her. Of course she did not really have the time, as she had to find a tenant soon. Yet it would be nice to pay the past a visit again. And if she were honest, she was burst-ing with curiosity about the man who wanted to marry Gwen (*her friend Gwen!*).

'You know what, Gwen, I think that could work,' she said. 'A divorce is…well, anyway, the trip would distract me and that wouldn't be a bad thing. I could come tomorrow. Would that be all right?'

'Leslie, you don't know how happy that makes me!' cried out Gwen. She sounded different to how she used to, optimistic. 'By the way, the weather here is great! It's all working out so well.'

'It's raining here in London,' said Leslie. 'Another good reason to take the trip. I'm looking forward to seeing you—and Yorkshire!'

No sooner had the two women stopped talking than Leslie's phone rang again. It was Stephen this time.

As every time when he spoke to her, he sounded sad. He had not wanted the separation or the divorce.

'Hi, Leslie. I just wanted to see…you aren't here again today, and…well, is everything OK?'

'I took three weeks' holiday. I'm moving house and searching like crazy for someone to take on the tenancy of our flat. You don't by any chance want it?'

'You want to leave our flat?' asked Stephen, shocked.

'It's just too big for me on my own. And also…I need a new start. New flat, new life.'

'It's not normally as easy as that.'

'Stephen…'

He must have heard the growing impatience in her voice, because he immediately conceded, 'I'm sorry. That's none of my business, of course.'

'Right. We should really try to keep out of each oth-er's lives. It's hard enough that we cross paths so often at the hospital, but apart from that our lives shouldn't touch at all.'

They both worked as doctors in the same hospital. Leslie had thought about looking for a new job for a long time, but she had found nowhere else that would be as ideal as in the Royal Marsden in Chelsea. And then her stubbornness had been awoken: should she also sacrifice her career to the man who had cheated on her and deceived her?

'Excuse me, Stephen, I've got to go,' she continued coldly. 'I have to sort out a bunch of stuff, and tomorrow I'm driving up to Yorkshire. Gwen is getting married and the engagement party is on Saturday.'

'Gwen? Your friend Gwen? Married?' Stephen sounded every bit as astonished as Leslie had been when she heard the news. She thought, how humiliating that must feel for Gwen. Everyone to whom she tells the news is flabbergasted and can't hide their surprise. Hopefully she does not fully grasp what hurtful thoughts are concealed by the surprise.

'Yes, she's over the moon. And wishes for nothing so much as to have me there for her engagement. And of course I'm keen to meet her sweetheart.'

'How old is she now? At least in her mid-thirties, isn't she? It's about time she left her father and started her own life.'

'She's just very attached to him. After all, she only ever really had him, so perhaps the close relationship is quite normal.'

'But not all that healthy,' replied Stephen. 'Leslie, nothing against old Chad Beckett, but it would have been better if he had given his daughter a firm push out into her own life a long time ago, rather than let her wither away on that isolated farm. It's nice that the two of them have a good relationship, but a young woman needs more in her life. Oh well, it looks like things are moving now. I hope the guy she's hooked is all right. She's so hopelessly inexperienced.'

'I'll know more by Saturday night at the latest,' said Leslie, before abruptly changing the topic. Stephen was no longer so close to her that she would want to talk about a friend's possible psychological flaws with him. 'By the way, my new flat is quite a lot smaller than this one,' she said. 'So I can't take all the furniture with me. If you'd like to take something, you're very welcome.'

When he had moved out he had not taken anything with him. He had not wanted anything.

'I have everything I need by now,' he said. 'What should I take?'

'The kitchen table, for example,' replied Leslie tartly. 'Otherwise it's going to the dump.'

The beautiful, somewhat wobbly old wooden table… their first joint purchase, back when they were students. She had been so fond of it. But it was at this table that he had admitted his slip-up—his short idiotic affair with someone he had met by chance in a pub.

Afterwards nothing was the same as it had been before. To this day Leslie could not look at the table without remembering with a knot in her throat the scene which had been the beginning of the end. The candle burning. The bottle of red wine. Darkness outside the window. And Stephen, who absolutely had to get it off his chest.

At times in the last two years she had thought that everything would improve once the table was gone. And yet she still had not managed to get rid of it.

'No,' said Stephen after a moment's silence, 'I don't want the table either.'

'Well then,' said Leslie.

'Say hi to Gwen from me,' said Stephen and without any further goodbyes they ended the conversation.

She looked at herself in the round mirror that hung on the wardrobe in front of her. She looked thin and rather weary.

Dr Leslie Cramer, thiry-nine years old, radiologist. Divorced.

The first social event that she would go to after her divorce was, of all things, an engagement.

Perhaps that was not a bad sign, she thought.

Not that she believed in signs. Foolish thought.

She lit her next cigarette.

3

THE OUTSIDE LIGHT shone on her as she walked up to him and he thought: Oh my God! She must have spent hours thinking about how to make herself pretty, but as usual the result was just horrific. He suspected that she had inherited the flowery cotton skirt from her mother. In any case, its material and its cut suggested it was from a different, long gone era. She was also wearing a pair of rather inelegant brown boots and a grey coat with an unfavourable cut that, although she was actually very slim, made her look fat. A yellow blouse could be glimpsed underneath the coat. With yellow she had managed to choose the only colour not present in the garish skirt. It meant that when they got to the restaurant and she took off the coat, she would look like an Easter egg.

On the spur of the moment he abandoned the plan to drive to Scarborough with her. It would be too embarrassing if they met anyone who knew him. Some country pub or other would be better… He wracked his brains but could not think of one—and it had to be cheap. As always he was completely broke.

She smiled. 'Dave!'

He walked up to her, forced himself to envelope her in his arms and give her a peck on the cheek. Luckily she was so naive that until now she seemed not to have missed frantic petting or even sex. He knew that her favourite books were cheaply produced little romances and suspected that his reserve corresponded pretty much exactly to the romantic image she had already created in her head of her future husband. Sometimes he found her almost touching. And then he would ask himself again if it was all worth it.

'Do you want to say hi to Dad before we go?' she asked.

He pulled a face. 'I'd prefer not to. He never hides the fact that he doesn't really like me.'

Gwen did not try to deny this. 'You have to try to understand him, Dave. He's an old man, and it's all just going a little too fast for him. Whenever he gets taken by surprise by something, he closes himself off even more. It's always been like that.'

They climbed into Dave's rickety old car, which as usual played up a bit before starting. He asked himself yet again how long the rust bucket would still keep going.

'Where are we off to?' asked Gwen as they drove down the drive and out. The large brown gate hung crooked on its hinges. For years it had not closed, but no one had repaired it. On the whole of the Beckett farm, which had been handed down from generation to generation of the family, it seemed as though no one repaired anything any more, either out of inability or a lack of money.

'Let me surprise you,' replied Dave mysteriously, although he himself still had no idea and hoped something would turn up spontaneously.

Gwen leant back, then sat bolt upright in her seat again. 'Today that policewoman was on the telly. Detective Inspector What's-Her-Name. The one who's investigating the Amy Mills case. You know, that girl…'

It was almost three months since the horribly mutilated corpse of the twenty-one-year-old student had been found in the Esplanade Garden in Scarborough, and people around here still talked about it almost every day. Nothing like that had happened here for a long time. The victim had been grabbed by the shoulders and her head smashed repeatedly against a stone wall. Leaked forensic details had left the public shocked. The culprit had repeatedly paused in order to let his victim become conscious once more, before then redoubling his violence. Amy Mills had suffered for at least twenty minutes, regaining consciousness again and again, before she finally died.

'Of course I know who Amy Mills is,' said Dave, 'but I haven't seen the news today. Has there been a development?'

'There was a press conference. There's a lot of pressure on the investigators, so they had to talk to the public again. But at the end of the day it looks like they don't have anything. Not a trace, not a clue. Nothing.'

'Must have been a real crazy, the guy who did it,' said Dave.

Gwen shrugged, with a shiver. 'At least she wasn't raped. She didn't have to endure that too. But that also means the police are completely in the dark about a possible motive.'

'I'll say one thing though: it wasn't too clever to walk through that empty place on her own at night,' said Dave. 'The Esplanade Gardens—what a god-forsaken place that late at night!'

'It can't have been about money,' stated Gwen. 'Or jewellery. Her purse was still in her handbag, and she was still wearing her watch and two rings. It's almost as if…as if she died for nothing.'

'Do you think it would have felt any different to her if he had smashed her head in for a thousand pounds?' asked Dave rather sharply. Seeing her shocked face he added soothingly, 'Sorry, I didn't mean to say that. Either way it's not a pretty thought that there's a madman running around in Scarborough and apparently killing women without any reason. But who knows? Maybe it was motivated by jealousy or something like that. A ditched boyfriend who couldn't deal with his anger… Some people lose it when they are rejected.'

'But if there had been an ex-boyfriend who could have done something like that, then the police would know about him,' replied Gwen.

They were driving through the dark October evening. The Yorkshire Moors began here. Under the pale light of the moon the landscape was hilly and bare. Wooden fences alternated with stone walls. Now and then the shape of a cow or sheep loomed out of the night. It was late for an evening meal, but Dave had had to give a Spanish lesson and had only managed to leave Scarborough after eight.

At least he finally had an idea where they could go: a simple pub not far from Whitby. Not exactly romantic, but cheap and certainly not a place where the people would go whose opinion mattered to him. He had already realised that Gwen never complained—she made no demands at all. He could have promised her a candlelit dinner and then taken her to Kentucky Fried Chicken. She would have accepted without a word. The only man in her life until now had been her father. Although she was devoted to her father, feeling love, loyalty and a need to care for him, she had no illusions—as Dave had found out—about their lives. Their monotonous existence, without any hope of a change, on an isolated and dilapidated farm in Staintondale was neither healthy nor fulfilling. She knew that and was thankful that Dave had turned up so unexpectedly in her life. Day and night she was tormented by the fear that she might lose him again. She made every effort not to annoy him with complaints, demands or even by quarrelling.

I'm a scoundrel, he thought, a real scoundrel. But at least I'm making her happy for now.

And he wouldn't hurt her. He would see the matter through. He had decided to do it, and there was no alternative.

Gwen Beckett was his last chance.

And I'm her last chance, he thought, and he only suppressed the dawning panic with difficulty. He would spend the rest of his life with this ageing girl at his side. That could be another forty or fifty years.

He often thought about her. She had told him some things about her life. Other things he had worked out for himself. Her father had always been very indulgent with her. She interpreted this behaviour as displays of his love, although Dave sometimes thought that it could also be an expression of his indifference. When she was sixteen she had left school, because it 'wasn't fun any more' as she said. Not even then did Daddy object. Gwen had never trained for a skilled job, but had considered that keeping house for her widowed father was her life's task. She contributed to the family kitty by turning two rooms in the farmhouse into B&B bedrooms. The little business pottered along without any real success, which was no surprise to Dave. The worn old house desperately needed renovation, if it were to attract people who wanted to spend their holidays on the North Yorkshire coast. After a number of decades, the region was again becoming popular as a holiday destination. However, people today wanted a decent bathroom, a shower with a boiler whose hot water had not run out after a few minutes, pretty and clean crockery for breakfast and a place which looked reasonably attractive as they rolled up for what would be the most expensive weeks of their year. Overgrown with weeds and decorated with muddy potholes, the Becketts' farmyard hardly invited people to stick around. Indeed, apparently there was only one couple who came back regularly to spend their holidays here. The main reason, as Gwen had admitted, was that they had two Great Danes which no one else allowed them to bring.

Who is this Gwen Beckett? he asked himself many times each day, much too often.

She was very shy, but he had the impression that this resulted largely from the fact that she led such a retiring life and had forgotten how to deal with other people. She spoke warmly and respectfully about her father, and sometimes she gave the impression that she could imagine nothing more wonderful than to spend them with him, letting her best years pass her by in the isolation of Staintondale. Yet then he had to remember her words from that July evening, when they had met: 'It's not as if I were particularly happy with my life.'

Off her own bat she had found a course that aimed to give people like her self-confidence and a winning appearance. She had registered and driven every week for three whole months to Scarborough, to not miss a single hour. She had done exactly what the agony aunts in women's magazines suggest to readers with the same problems as Gwen: do something! Go beyond your comfort zone! Meet other people!

Gwen must really have the feeling, thought Dave, that in the blink of an eye she had been as successful as they promised. Sometimes she herself seemed barely able to believe it. She had gathered her courage and driven to the Friarage School, and on her very first day there she had met the man whom she was now going to marry and spend the rest of her life with.

She was happy. And yet he also sensed her fear—the fear that something could still go wrong, that the dream could still burst like a bubble, that everything looked too beautiful to be true...

And when he thought of that, he felt rotten. Because he knew that her fear was justified.

As if she could guess that he was going over and over the relationship in his head and that his thoughts were not all completely happy ones, she asked out of the blue: 'The engagement is still on for Saturday?' She sounded apprehensive.

Dave managed to ease her worries with a smile. 'Of course, why ever not? Unless your father suddenly boycotts the whole event and doesn't let us leave the house. But then we can still find a restaurant.'

Please, not that! A friend of Gwen's was coming from London, then the married couple with their two Great Danes who happened to be holidaying on the Beckett Farm right then, and Fiona Barnes, the old family friend. He could not quite see how she fitted in with the Becketts. Seven people! He had almost no money left. He would not be able to afford a visit to a restaurant. If old Mr Beckett caused a ruckus, he would be in a real jam.

He tried to not let his worries show. 'Nothing will wreck our engagement,' he reassured her.

Gwen reached a hand out to him, and he took it in his. It was ice-cold to the touch. He turned it over, drew it to his lips and breathed warm air onto her palm.

'Trust me,' he said. These words always worked well, he knew that. They worked particularly well with women like Gwen, not that he had ever met such an extreme example of such a woman before. 'I'm not playing with you.'

No, it was not a game. It certainly was not.

She smiled. 'I know, Dave. I can feel it.'

Not true, he thought. You are afraid, but you know that you cannot give in to your fear. We have to go through with it. Both of us get something out of it. Each in our own way.

It had now grown completely dark around them. They drove on into the lonely night and Dave felt like he was driving through a black tunnel. His throat tightened. He would feel better after the first whisky, he knew that; after the second even better, and he did not care whether or not he would still be fit to drive by then.

Just as long as these thoughts stopped hammering so hard in his head. Just as long as his future started to feel more bearable.

Friday, 10th October

1

JENNIFER BRANKLEY WAS reminded of her school days—not so much of the years when she dressed in a blazer, pleated blue skirt and wore a big brown satchel on her back, but rather the years when she herself taught. Every morning she would arrive at school ready for action and looking forward to the day that lay ahead of her. It felt as if it were decades ago; sometimes it felt as if it were a memory of another life. And yet only a few years separated her from that time which she in private called 'the best time of my life'. A few years…and now nothing was like it had been once.

She had leant the plastic bags with the shopping—mainly dog food for her Great Danes, Wotan and Cal—against a tree just behind the high black wrought-iron fence which surrounded the Friarage Community Primary School. It was a large complex, with a number of one- or two-storey red-brick buildings. All with blue blinds in the windows. Up to the left behind the school rose the hill on which the Castle stood. In front of that was St Mary's Church, widely known because Anne Brontë is buried in its churchyard. The Castle and church seemed to protect the town, the school, the children.

A pretty place, thought Jennifer.

It was the sixth or seventh holiday that she and her husband Colin had passed on the Beckett Farm in Staintondale, and Jennifer, in particular, had come to love North

Yorkshire. It had high wind-swept moors and wide valleys; endless meadows with stone walls; precipitous cliffs which plunged straight down into the sea; and small little sandy bays nestling into the rugged rocks. She loved the town of Scarborough too, and its two large, semi-circular bays divided by a spit of land, as well as its old harbour, the fine houses up on South Cliff, and all the old-fashioned hotels whose façades had to stand up to the wind and the salt water and so were always peeling a little. Colin mumbled sometimes to himself that it might be nice to spend the holiday somewhere else, but that would have meant leaving Cal and Wotan in kennels, which was out of the question for such highly sensitive animals. Luckily it had been Colin's idea originally to have pet dogs, and he had been clear that they should be particularly big dogs. Jennifer could always remind him of that when he complained. The main point for Colin had been the daily need to take them for walks of several hours. 'A miracle cure for depression,' he had said, 'and healthy in every other respect too. One day you won't be able to do without the activity and fresh air.'

He had been right. The dogs and walks had changed her life. They had helped her to climb out of the trough. They might not have made her a really happy woman, but certainly one who found a meaning in her life once more.

The dogs had been given to her by a charity that tried to find new owners on the internet for Great Danes who needed a good home. Cal had been found tied up at the side of a country road as a one-year-old dog, while Wotan had been brought to the animal shelter by his owners, after they realised slightly too late that life with such a big dog was not easy on the eighth floor of a tower block.

People's stupidity is terrible, Jennifer often thought. It's often worse than intentional cruelty, because it's so wide-spread. Stupidity and carelessness. That's what causes so much suffering, particularly for animals.

Today she had left the dogs on the farm with Colin and driven to town with Gwen. Gwen had been taking part for three months in a course to conquer shyness. Its last class had been this past Wednesday and the course tutor had arranged a little leaving party on Friday afternoon. Jennifer had made sure she did not comment on the course. She did not believe in all that stuff. Were people who had become set in their ways over decades supposed to be trained in three months in how to change completely and take charge of their lives? In her opinion, this kind of thing was out to make money from the very real problems and issues of often desperate people—people who were willing to grasp at any straw and pay good money for it too. Gwen had admitted that she had spent all her savings on the course, but Jennifer did not have the feeling that Gwen had really benefited greatly from it. Of course, she was different now, but that had nothing to do with the mumbo-jumbo of those Wednesday afternoons, not in Jennifer's opinion. Instead it was down to the absolutely astounding turn her private life had taken. A man. A man who had fallen in love with her.

The engagement party was tomorrow. Jennifer had scarcely been able to believe it. Seeing as Gwen had met him here in this school, she had to admit that taking part in the course, and the sacrifice of her savings, had not been completely in vain.

Gwen was getting married! To Jennifer, who although she was only ten years older than her friend had always felt motherly towards her, this was sensational, a gift, an amazing turn of fate. And yet it was also something that filled her with unease: who was this man? Why had he chosen Gwen? She might be friendly and caring, but she had never yet managed to catch herself a man. She was so old-fashioned, so naive. She could only ever talk about her father, Daddy this and Daddy that, and which man would not be driven crazy by that sooner or later?

Jennifer wanted to be happy for Gwen, with all her heart, but she could not. She had caught a glimpse of Dave Tanner the day before, when he came to the farm to pick up Gwen for a meal out, and since then she was even more uneasy. Judging by the car that he drove, he barely had money, and how could he? He made ends meet giving French and Spanish lessons, and lodged in a single furnished room. That did not exactly suggest hidden wealth. However, he was good-looking and seemed sophisticated. She had seen that in the few short moments in which she had observed him from the window of her room. Without a doubt, he could have very different women to Gwen— younger, more pretty and clued-up women, even in his financial difficulties.

His obviously catastrophic personal situation might be the reason for his romance with Gwen, and the thought of this had not let Jennifer sleep that past night.

She had held her tongue. To Gwen, at any rate. She had talked about her fears with Colin, who warned her strongly against getting involved. 'She's a grown-up. She's thirty-five years old. It's time that she made her own decisions. You can't always protect her!'

Yes, thought Jennifer, as she looked at the school, peaceful under the afternoon sun of the quiet October day, he's right. I have to stop trying to save Gwen from all possible mishaps. She's not my daughter. She's not even related to me. And even if she were—she has reached an age when she has to make her own choices about her direction in life.

The door of the front building opened. The people coming out must be on the course that Gwen was on. Jennifer tried not to fall into easy prejudices, nor into an excessive curiosity. What do they look like, the people who see in such a course their last chance to change their lives? Were they like Gwen, blushing easily, somewhat old-fashioned, reserved and actually really nice? Or were they unpleasantly uptight, bitter, frustrated? Aggressive? So ugly that it took your breath away?

They looked pretty normal, Jennifer realised. Many more women than men. Ony two men, in fact. The women were wearing jeans and jumpers, light coats. It was not a cold day. Some were pretty. Not that any of them were stunning beauties, nor were any wearing very bright or provocative clothes. All in all, they were indeed rather retiring people, who would not want to be the centre of attention. They certainly did not give the impression of being at all disturbed, strange or disgusting.

Jennifer smiled when she saw Gwen, who was wearing a flowery calf-length skirt as always, and big boots. And where had she got that terrible coat? Hopefully her fiancé would be able to persuade her to do without it one day.

Gwen came over, in the company of a man and a woman who both looked to be between thirty and forty. At a first glance, the woman looked rather nondescript, but on a second glance you noticed that she was really rather attractive. Gwen made the introductions. 'This is Jennifer Brankley. Jennifer—Ena Witty and Stan Gibson.'

Ena Witty smiled shyly and mumbled a hi. She had a very quiet voice. Stan Gibson, on the other hand, beamed at Jennifer. 'Hi, Jennifer. Gwen's told me a lot about you. And about your dogs. Are they really as big as she says?'

'Even bigger,' replied Jennifer, 'but as gentle as lambs. I shouldn't really say this, but I'm afraid they'd probably wag their tail even at a burglar, then lick his hand.'

Stan laughed. 'I wouldn't want to try.'

'I like dogs a lot,' said Ena.

Jennifer thought that Ena Witty was just the type of person she had expected to find on this course, not so Stan Gibson. He was not a particularly good-looking man, but he had an engaging, friendly bearing and did not seem shy or fearful. What had he been doing on the course these last few months?

As if reading her thoughts, Gwen explained: 'By the way, Stan wasn't in our course. In August and September the school was re-building some rooms, and Stan works for the company that did the work. He was still here every Wednesday at the time our course started. That's how he met Ena.'

Ena looked shyly at the floor.

Quite a matchmaking service, the Friarage School, thought Jennifer. Gwen found the man of her life here. Ena Witty found a boyfriend… If it continues like this, the school could turn it into a little money-spinner!

'Because I'm with Ena, I got to tag along to the leaving party,' said Stan. 'And in the last few weeks I've talked a lot to Gwen too. What do you think, Ena, shouldn't we invite Gwen and Jennifer over to our place sometime?'

'To *our place*?' asked Ena, caught unawares.

'Darling, now don't look so surprised. Sometime you'll move to my place, right? And then of course we'll invite good friends to *our place*!' He laughed long and loud and then turned to the two other women. 'It's probably all hap-

pening a bit quick for Ena. Tomorrow we set off early for
London and stay at my old folks until Sunday. I want them
to get to know Ena.'

Gwen and Jennifer glanced quickly at each other. Both
had the impression that Ena was not all that happy with
Stan's plans, but that she did not dare to voice her unease.

Then Ena smiled suddenly. 'It's great not to be on my
own any more,' she said, and Jennifer recognized the woman's loneliness, and realised that was what everyone in the
group shared in common, much more than problems with
shyness, self-doubt or any phobias. People who met on
courses like this one suffered above all from loneliness.
They were women like Ena, who remained alone because
no one noticed them and they had not learnt to show the
world their talents, gifts and qualities. Women like Gwen,
who had slipped into roles which then blocked them in,
and who at some point realised that the world was zooming
past them. They longed to escape their long, quiet, melancholic weekends and their endless evenings with only the
television for company.

'We'll call again about the invite,' said Stan.

They said their goodbyes and Jennifer and Gwen started
off towards the bus stop. The dog food was heavy, but
Gwen did not complain as she helped to carry it. They
could have borrowed Chad's or Colin's car, but Gwen—
although she had a driver's license—did not like to drive
if she could at all help it.

And Jennifer...

'What about just trying again?' Colin had asked at
lunch. 'It might be easier than you think.'

She had shaken her head. 'No. I can't. It won't work. It's
just...I don't think I can do it any more, anything could
happen...'

He had not insisted. She knew that he wished she would be more proactive in building up her old self-confidence, but sometimes she had the feeling that she had waited too long already and now would never pluck up the courage to do so. Anyway, she thought her life was more or less normal. She no longer dared to get behind a steering wheel, and she was a little unsociable and suspicious sometimes, but she was not lonely. She had Colin and her dogs; the holidays at Chad and Gwen's place; she was content. She had her depression under control. When it did flare up again, she just swallowed a pill, once a week at the most. She was far from being dependent on medication, as they had tried to imply.

But she was not to think about that, or about all the dirt they had dished on her. That was long ago—another time, another life.

She had found a new space for herself.

She just had to manage to leave the old one behind, completely, and to no longer explain it away or think back with longing to that time. This was a slow process, as she had found out at her cost, but one day she would be there.

And then everything would be better.

2

'You've a visitor,' said Mrs Willerton, the landlady, as soon as Dave had opened the front door and stepped into the narrow hall, which was hung with twee animal drawings. 'Miss Ward, your...well, is she your ex-girlfriend now or not?'

'I told you not to let anyone in while I was out,' replied Dave in annoyance and climbed the steep stairs two at a time before Mrs Willerton could ask any more questions. It was the pits: being a lodger and having to squeeze past his curious landlady all the time. Mrs Willerton was extremely curious about his love life, probably—he surmised—because her own was many decades in the past. As she had once admitted to him in embarrassment, Mr Willerton had made off twenty years ago with a motorbike bride he had met through a Harley Davidson fan club.

Dave could understand him only too well.

He was tired. He had been giving French lessons for two hours, having to bear a dozen middle-aged North Yorkshire housewives' ghastly pronunciation of a language he loved for its sound and melody. His longing was becoming stronger and stronger to leave all this behind. His life was far too difficult at the moment—crazily complicated and with the added burden of worrying that he was making an enormous mistake. Karen Ward, the twenty-one-year-old student, who he had been in a relationship with

for the last year and a half, was the last person he wanted
to see tonight.

He went into his room. As always, he had left it in quite
a mess. The bed was not made. A few of his clothes had
been thrown over the back of a chair. The remains of his
lunch were still on the table at the window: a paper car-
ton with the left-over rice from an Indian takeaway. Next
to it stood a half-empty bottle of white wine with a cork
quickly jammed in. Karen had always made a thing about
his sometimes drinking at lunchtime. At least he would be
spared those talks in future.

Karen was sitting on a little stool at the end of the bed.
She was wearing a dark-green turtleneck sweater and her
beautiful long legs were in tight jeans. Her blond hair
fell in a carelessly messy way over her shoulders. Dave
had known her long enough to know that she spent ages
every morning working on this casual look. There was
not a strand that was not exactly where she wanted it. Her
make-up too, which you didn't notice, was the result of
hard work.

She had really fascinated him once. But it had never been
more than that—an appreciation of her appearance, which
was obviously not the basis for a long-term relationship.

Added to that, she was just far too young.

He closed the door behind him. You could bet on Mrs
Willerton being downstairs in the hall with her ears
pricked.

'Hi, Karen,' he said, as casually as possible.

She had stood up, obviously in the expectation that he
would go up to her and at least for a moment take her in
his arms. But he just stood there at the door. He did not
even take his coat off. He did not want to give her any indication that he was prepared to have a long talk with her.

'Hi, Dave,' Karen replied after a long silence. 'Sorry that I just…' She let her words hang in the air. Dave did not do her the favour of accepting her apology for her unexpected appearance—she did not mean it, anyway, he knew that.

He did not say a word.

Karen looked around the unwelcoming room with a helpless expression.

'It looks worse here than last time I visited,' she remarked.

Typical. She always had something to complain about: his drinking too much wine, not tidying up enough, sleeping in too long, or not showing any ambition, or…or…or.

'It's been a while since you were here last,' he replied, 'and since then no one else has been tidying up after me.' Thank God, he added in his thoughts.

His reply was a mistake. He realised as soon as Karen replied tartly, 'Depends on how you see things, doesn't it, Dave? As far as I remember, I was last here exactly one week ago.'

What an idiot he was. Last week he had slipped up, although he had resolved not to let that happen with Karen again. He had met her by chance late one night on a pub crawl down at the harbour, in the Newcastle Packet, where she had just started to pull pints some evenings. He had waited until she came off work, had drunk a couple of beers with her, and had then taken her back to his room. Then slept with her. It had been pretty wild and uninhibited, as he vaguely remembered. Since he had broken up with her at the end of July, they had met a couple of times, just because it was always good to chat and have a laugh, and sleep with her, and because sometimes he needed a distraction from the dry times with Gwen. But it was not fair on Karen, and he was annoyed that he had been weak. No wonder that she thought their relationship could be on again.

'So, why were you waiting for me here?' he asked, although he knew the answer.

'Can't you think why?'

'Frankly: no.'

She looked really hurt, as if he had slapped her. He pulled himself together. 'Karen…I'm really sorry about last week. If it…is that why you're here. I'd had a few pints too many. But nothing's changed. Our relationship is over.'

She flinched a little at his words, but kept calm. 'When you dumped me in July—out of the blue—I just wanted to know one thing. Do you remember? I wanted to know if there was another woman.'

'Yes, and?'

'You said there wasn't. That it was just about the two of us.'

'I know what I said. Why do you have to bring it all up?'

'Because…' She hesitated. 'Because I've been hearing from various people that there's someone else in your life after all. In the last few weeks you've often been seen with another woman. Apparently she's not that young and nothing special.'

He hated this kind of conversation. It was like an interrogation.

'And what if I have?' he retorted. 'Did we sign an agreement that I can't start something with any other woman after our affair?'

'One and a half years is not an affair.'

'Call it what you will. In any case—'

'In any case I don't believe that you didn't know this…

new acquaintance before. You broke up with me on the 25th July. It's the 10th October today.'

'Yup, almost three months have passed.'

She sat there, waiting. He felt cornered and realised how angry he was getting. With everything he already had on his plate—as if his life were not enough of a hassle already.

'I don't owe you any explanations,' he said coolly.

Her lips trembled.

Please, God, don't let her cry now, he thought, annoyed.

'After last week—' she started in a shaking voice, before he immediately interrupted:

'Forget last week! I was drunk. I said I'm sorry. What else do you want me to say?'

'Who is she? Apparently she's quite a bit older than me.'

'Who said?'

'People who have seen you together. People studying with me.'

'So what? So she's older than you.'

'She's almost forty!'

'And what if she is? Suits me. I'm in my forties, after all.'

'So there is someone.'

He did not say anything.

'You've always had such young girlfriends,' said Karen in despair.

Youth. That was all she had to offer.

'Maybe I'm changing some things in my life,' he replied.

'But—'

He slammed his briefcase down on the table. He had been holding it all this time.

'Listen, Karen. Stop putting yourself down. Tomorrow you'll be bitterly sorry. It's over between us. There are any number of men who would walk over hot coals for a girl as beautiful as you are. Just forget me, and don't dwell on it.'

Her first tears fell and she sank back down onto the stool where she had sat and waited for him. 'I can't forget you, Dave. I can't. And I think...you can't actually have forgotten me either, otherwise last week you wouldn't have—'

'What? Screwed? Bloody hell, Karen, you know how things go!'

'Your new girlfriend isn't fit. Maybe you don't enjoy sleeping with her, like you do with me.'

'That's my business,' he said. He was getting more and more angry, because she had hit upon a sore point. He just could not imagine having sex with Gwen, and he was already fearing the day—or night—when it would be unavoidable. Probably the only thing that would help then would be to get completely plastered and to try to imagine Karen's beautiful body.

Better for Karen not to hear about this plan.

She was crying hard now. 'And today Detective Inspector Almond came by again,' she sobbed. 'About Amy Mills.'

Dave took his coat off, resigned. It was going to take a while. Now she had got to the topic that would really bring on the waterworks. At least it had nothing to do with him. A little progress. If only he were not so tired, and did not have so many problems.

'What did she need to see you again for?' he asked, beaten. And when Karen, instead of replying, just started sobbing more violently, he fetched a bottle of the hard stuff from a cupboard and two more-or-less clean glasses. 'Here, have a sip.'

She rarely drank alcohol and had always complained

when he did, but this time she put the glass to her lips and knocked it back. She let him pass her a second glassful and emptied it as quickly as the first. Then at least her tears subsided.

'Oh, she basically just asked again about everything we'd already gone over,' she said. She was just as distraught as in July, when Amy Mills' murder had shaken the whole of Scarborough. 'I'm the only person Amy was even a little in contact with, so she wanted to talk once more about all her daily habits and routines with me. But I don't know all that much about them. I mean...' she bit her lip '...I always found Amy a little...odd. So uptight. I felt sorry for her. But I certainly wasn't a close friend of hers.'

'You can't blame yourself for that now,' said Dave. 'You did more than the others. After all, you went for a coffee with her once or twice and listened to her problems. She obviously had real issues with making contact. That's not your fault.'

'The police have no idea who did it. There's not a single lead,' said Karen. 'At least, that's the impression I get.' She added: 'Do you know Mrs Gardner well?'

'You mean...'

'Mrs Gardner, the woman whose child Amy was looking after that evening.'

'Linda Gardner. Of course I know her. She teaches languages too, and we've always made sure our teaching matched up. But I don't know her more than that.'

'She was teaching the evening Amy was murdered.'

The evening he had met Gwen and driven her home. How well, how very well he remembered that evening!

'Right. That's why Amy was babysitting.'

'Detective Inspector Almond is looking for people who

knew that. Who knew that Amy babysat for Mrs Gardner. She asked me if I knew. I said I did.'

'You're hardly a prime suspect.'

'She wanted to know if I knew other people who knew too.' She looked at him, waiting for his reply.

He thought impatiently that she should just say what she was getting at. He hated the way she always beat around the bush.

'Yes? And?'

'I didn't tell her that I thought that you knew.'

'And why not?'

There was something sly about how she waited, at least he thought he sensed that. 'I…didn't want to make life difficult for you, Dave. It was your evening off. And if you remember, a day later we had a massive fight because you had stood me up and didn't want to tell me what had happened.'

Of course not. Should he have told her of the drive to Staintondale? And then be obliged to tell him about everything that had followed on from that?

He forced himself to stay calm, although she was really getting on his nerves. 'I always had a problem with the way you wanted to control me. Maybe that was a reason why our relationship broke down.'

'Did you know? That a young student used to babysit for Mrs Gardner?'

'Maybe she did tell me. And? Do you think I was lying in wait for Amy in the park and smashed her head in?'

Karen shook her head. 'No.'

She looked sad and tired. No doubt this was not primarily because of the fate of a fellow student who had only been a fleeting acquaintance, nor because the police were having obvious difficulties in solving the crime.

Rather, because her relationship to Dave had gone wrong. He started to feel traces of guilt, which annoyed him. He did not want to feel guilty.

'So...' he said.

She reached for her handbag.

'So...' she said too. Her voice sounded hoarse.

He pulled a face. 'I'm really sorry about how it's all turned out. Really I am.'

Tears started to well up in her eyes again. 'But why, Dave? I just don't understand.'

Because I'm crazy, he thought, because I'm doing something completely crazy. Because it's finally time for a different life. Because I can only see one way, just *this one way*, to go.

He knew that she hated it when he answered in clichés, but he did it anyway.

'Some things you can't understand. You just have to accept them.'

He held the door open for her. A floorboard creaked down in the hall. The landlady, who had been standing at the foot of the stairs the whole time, quickly made herself scarce.

'I'll come to the door,' Dave said.

She was crying again. He could at least try to treat her politely now at the end.

THEY WERE CATCHING up over a bottle of mineral water. Innumerable packets of cigarettes lay on the table. Leslie realised once again that she would never get used to some of
the contradictions in her grandmother's character, least of
all the fact that Fiona smoked like a chimney—up to sixty
cigarettes a day. She seemed completely oblivious to the
packets' warnings, which in ever more drastic words and
pictures foretold a painful death for those who enjoyed
the pleasures of smoking. And yet she refused to drink a
single drop of alcohol, or even to have any in her home.

'So unhealthy,' she would always say. 'It makes you stupid. I'm not going to willingly kill my brain cells!'

After the long drive up North from London, Leslie
would have liked to relax with a couple of glasses of wine,
not to mention that at the end of a week which had begun
with her divorce on Monday, she would really have liked
to numb herself with alcohol. She was peeved because she
had forgotten about this eccentricity of Fiona's, and had
not brought a bottle or two with her.

The two women sat at a little table by the window in the
living room. Outside it was completely dark, but between
the clouds over the South Bay a star shone now and then.
Sometimes even the moon came out. With its light you
could just about see the dark, turbulent mass of the sea.

'And what's your impression of Gwen?' asked Leslie.

Fiona lit a cigarette, the fifth since her granddaughter had turned up and moved into the guest-room with her bags.

'She seems quite overwhelmed by what's happening. And happy? I don't know. She's tense. I don't think she really trusts her fiancé.'

'How do you mean?'

'Maybe she doubts his seriousness. She wouldn't be the only one. Her father does. Me too.'

'Do you know Dave Tanner?'

'Know—not exactly. I've met him a few times at the Beckett farm over the last few months. And once I invited Gwen and him to come here. He didn't enjoy that at all. He doesn't like meeting the people around Gwen—not that there are many of us. He's probably afraid that they'll see through him.'

'See through him? You're talking as if he...'

'Were a crook? That's just what I think he is,' said Fiona forcefully. She took a nervous drag on her cigarette. 'We can be frank with one another, Leslie, between ourselves. I like Gwen. She's friendly. Sometimes she's a little too anxious to please people, and that can get annoying, but it's certainly not a sign of a bad character. She's thirty-five and, as far as I know, never yet in her life has there been a man who has had a real interest in her, and we both know why!'

Leslie made as if to object. 'Well, she's...'

'She's as plain as it gets. She bores people to death. She sometimes looks like a real country bumpkin. She wears the most unbelievable clothes. She is hopelessly old-fashioned and marked by those trashy novels she always reads. She lives in a world that doesn't exist any more. I can understand why men give her a wide berth.'

'Yes, but why can't there be someone who can see how she is inside and—'

Fiona gave a scornful laugh. 'And what would he find there? Gwen isn't stupid, but she hasn't tried to learn anything new since school. She hasn't really been interested in the wider world. Wait until you meet Dave Tanner! I just can't imagine that he could, for long, bear to be with a woman he could practically not talk to.'

'You mean…'

'He's educated, intelligent and interested in everything in life. What's more, he's good-looking and would have many doors open to him. But he's made a complete mess of his life. And that, I'd say, is the nub of it.'

'You mean…' Leslie said again.

'Do you know how the man makes ends meet? He gives adult education language courses for housewives. But he did A levels and he studied Politics, even if he did drop out. Instead of finishing, he got involved in the peace movement and did a whole lot of stupid things that didn't lead anywhere. Now he's forty-three years old and lodges in a furnished room, because he can't afford anything else. And he's bloody well fed up with it.'

'You know a lot about him.'

'I like to ask direct questions. And from the answers I get, and the ones I don't get, I can put together a picture, which is often not too far from the truth.

'University drop-out, pacifist, eco-warrior, that might all feel good when you're still pretty young. It might be a kick, certainly more exciting than a middle-class life. But at some point things swing around. When you get older. When living in a shared flat and endless protest marches are no longer "you". I bet you Tanner has been unhappy for a good while, but now he's got a classic midlife crisis on top of it all. He's frightened that he's only got one last chance to settle down to a normal life with a secure and regular income. I'd go further: I'd say he's pretty desperate. Even if he acts cool.'

'Do you know what you're saying, Fiona?'

'Yes. And really Gwen should be told too.'

Leslie bit her lips. 'You can't, Fiona. She'd be…it's just not possible!'

'But do you see what's awaiting her?' exclaimed Fiona. 'The guy will make himself at home on the farm and calmly wait until Chad departs this earthly life. Nor will he have to wait an eternity for that. I don't doubt that he'll bring all sorts of good ideas about how to make the farm into a really attractive place for people to spend their holidays. I expect he will have the drive to put his plans into action and really make something of the property. It's pathetic, how Chad and Gwen have run the B & B until now, and of course he could pep things up. But a marriage is about more than that, surely? I bet he would cheat on her right and left. He'd take advantage of the students on the Scarborough campus and at some point Gwen would find out, and her world would collapse! Should we let it get to that?'

'*She* decided to let it get to that.'

'Because she thinks she doesn't have a choice. She's been waiting for years for Prince Charming to come galloping along on his white horse and whisk her away. Now he's come, even if not on a white horse but on just about the most dilapidated old rust-bucket I've ever seen. But no matter. He's the only man near or far. So he's important to Gwen. So important that she silences all alarm bells—and I'm sure that they are ringing inside her.'

'She sounded different on the phone. More at ease. More cheery. I felt really happy for her.'

'She's certainly blossoming, no question. God, Leslie.' Fiona stubbed out her cigarette aggressively. 'Do you think I'm keen to tell Gwen the truth? Of course not! No one is. It's a difficult situation.'

'Maybe it's not our job to tell her, Fiona. We're not even related to her.'

'But we're the only people she has. Her father isn't happy about Tanner, but he isn't going to get involved. He was always too weak with Gwen. Never in his life would he manage to say no to her, especially not now. But I…she always saw me as a kind of mother to her. She's always relied on me. I wish—' She broke off abruptly and did not say what she wished, perhaps because the impossibility of it was all too apparent to her. Instead she looked penetratingly at her granddaughter. 'And how are you? How do you feel—freshly divorced?'

Leslie shrugged. 'I've got used to living on my own already. The divorce was just a formality.'

'You're not exactly beaming.'

'What do you expect? I wanted to spend the rest of my life with Stephen. We wanted to have children…. I hadn't foreseen that at thirty-nine I'd be moving into a little flat, perfectly laid out for a working single person, and be starting from scratch again.'

'I never understood why you separated! You two were so good together. God, because he drank too much once and jumped into bed with some young thing whose name he could barely remember the next day? You threw it all away for that?'

'The trust was gone. Until it happened, I wouldn't have thought it could be that serious. But that loss of trust af-

fects everything else. Everything had changed. I couldn't…
I couldn't bear *him* any more.'

'Everyone has to know for themselves,' said Fiona.

'Exactly,' said Leslie. 'Gwen too. Fiona, it's her life.
She's grown up. Dave Tanner is the man she's chosen. We
have to respect that.'

Fiona muttered something to herself. Leslie leant forward. 'And what about you, Fiona? You don't look great.
You look so pale. You've lost weight. Is everything all
right?'

'Of course it is. What shouldn't be? I'm an old woman.
You can't expect me to look fresher and more rosy-cheeked
every day. I'm on the downward slope of life. Pity that it is.'

'It's not like you to be pessimistic.'

'I'm not pessimistic, I'm just realistic. Autumn's come.
The days are often humid and cool. I feel it in my bones.
It's normal, Leslie. It's just normal that I'm no longer the
woman you once knew.'

'You're sure that nothing's troubling you?'

'Quite sure. Listen, Leslie, don't you start worrying
about me. You've got enough worries yourself. And now,'
she said getting up, 'let's get to bed. It's late. I'll need my
strength tomorrow if I'm going to survive the heady engagement party on the idyllic Beckett farm tomorrow—
especially as I know it's the start of a tragedy!'

'You *are* pretty pessimistic,' said Leslie smiling, watching her grandmother as she left the room. She knew Fiona.
She knew her better than anybody else in this world.

She was sure that something was bothering her.

Saturday, 11th October

1

'BUT YOU'VE ALREADY asked me about all of that,' complained Linda Gardner. She sounded not so much irritated as exhausted. She had been just about to go shopping with her daughter when Detective Inspector Almond called and asked if she could pop by. The wiry little policewoman she had talked to for hours in July. The whole nightmare came back to her in an instant. Not that she could often free herself completely from it.

'I know,' said Valerie Almond. She sat opposite Linda in her living room. She could see how how difficult her appearing again in the flat was for the young woman. 'I have to tell you, Mrs Gardner, that we're completely in the dark about this terrible crime against Amy Mills. That's why we're working our way through everything we have—and that's not much—one more time. In the hope that we've overlooked something. Or that one of the people we interview remembers something extra. Something they'd forgotten to say until now. Doing that's given me real breakthroughs sometimes.'

Linda looked out the window, as if there was something to see there, something to hold her attention. A brilliant blue sky, a golden October day. 'It's just that…I always blame myself for it,' she said quietly. 'If I hadn't been so set on having a good time, if I hadn't lost track of the time… maybe Amy would still be alive. Do you know, since my husband left, my day can be such a grind. As a single mum with a kid, I don't have many opportunities. I often feel chained to the flat. And to my child. The evening French classes were something special for me. Men and women my age, whom I could go to the pub with afterwards, drink some wine with, have a laugh, chat…and know that my little girl is in Amy's good hands. I could afford a baby-sitter once a week. Those Wednesday evenings were…I looked forward to them all week.'

'You're talking about them in the past,' said Valerie. 'Don't you teach any more?'

'Oh yes. But I don't go out afterwards with my class. I just couldn't.' Tears welled up in her eyes. She pursed her lips, trying to calm down.

Valerie looked at her sympathetically. 'Don't be too hard on yourself. We don't know that things would have been any different if you'd been back at the time you said.'

'But that…fiend was at the Esplanade Gardens just when Amy got there. If she'd have been there earlier—'

'That's just one of the alternatives,' interrupted Valerie. 'A criminal who was lurking in the park grounds and then found his victim by chance. The other possibility is that someone was out to get Amy Mills in particular. There's still no plausible explanation as to why the way up was blocked by two mesh fences. Right after the incident we talked to the workers from the construction site and they swore that none of them had placed the fences there. Nor had the park rangers. There was no reason to block the path. It was usable. Of course it could just have been some stupid boys' little prank. But it could also have been that someone was blocking Amy's shortest and quickest way up on purpose. She had no option but to take the long way round, deep in the park. Her murderer waited for her there—maybe after he saw her cross the bridge. That could have happened two hours earlier too. Maybe you being late only meant that the guy had to wait longer than he expected.'

'If it was planned...'

'We certainly can't rule out the possibility. That's why I asked about who knew that Amy babysat for you.'

Linda Gardner looked confused, 'But...what did this person want? I mean, it wasn't a sex crime, was it? And nor did the culprit take any money. Apart from that, Amy didn't have much.'

'If someone is crazy enough, they could have many reasons for killing someone,' replied Valerie. Seeing Linda Gardner's troubled expression, she did not want to mention it, but after she had seen the horrifically mangled corpse of Amy Mills, she was convinced that hatred was the culprit's motive. Either a personal hate directed at Amy Mills, or a general but no less violent aggression against all women.

She returned to her original question once more. 'Who knew that Amy Mills babysat for you?' She threw a glance at her notes. 'When we talked in July you named the students on your French course. At the time you said that you had eight students in total on Wednesdays. Six women and two men. They were all at the lesson that Wednesday.'

'Yes. But...'

'We've talked with all of them. It doesn't look as though any of them could be in any way involved in this, although I'm not going to exclude any possibility for now. Is there anyone else?'

Linda thought about it. 'The old lady in the flat below me might know. I'm not sure. I mean, I've never told her, but she might have realised, what with Amy coming and going. Amy has to go past her flat.'

'What's the lady's name?'

'Copper. Jane Copper. But it would be crazy to suspect her. She's small and weak and almost eighty.'

'Does she live on her own? Does she often have relatives or friends over? A son? A grandson? Anyone?'

'Not as far as I know. She seems pretty lonely.'

Valerie made a note of Jane Copper's name, but did not hope much for a lead there.

'My ex-husband knows,' said Linda suddenly. 'Yes, I told him.'

'Where does he live?'

'In Bradford. So not around the corner. He doesn't know Amy though, not even her name. One time on the phone I told him that I was teaching French to put a little extra money in the kitty, and he asked what I did with our little girl. I said that I'd found a girl who was studying to look after her. But I don't think he even knew that the class was on a Wednesday. We don't have a lot of contact, you see.'

'I'd still like his name and address,' said Valerie.

Linda gave her both.

'Why did you break up?'

Linda's face contorted into a bitter grimace. 'Young girls, very young girls. He just couldn't keep his hands off them.'

'Minors?'

'Not that young.'

Valerie jotted something down in her notepad. 'We'll talk to your husband. Anyone else you can think of?'

'I don't know…'

'Anyone else from Friarage School, perhaps?' dug Valerie.

Linda wracked her brains. Who at the school did she really talk to? She was not close to anyone there. She did not have the time or flexibility to strike up any kind of friendship.

But there was a vague memory… After Amy Mills' murder she had talked with any number of her colleagues about the tragedy, had owned up to being the person for whom Amy had babysat and who had been so careless about the young woman's leaving time. But *beforehand*… She thought that she had mentioned it *beforehand* in some context. At the school.

Suddenly she remembered. A good-looking guy who also taught French. With whom she compared notes before the beginning of each course. The first time she had been questioned she had not even thought of him.

'Dave,' she said, 'Dave Tanner, I think, knew.'

Valerie leant forward. 'Who is Dave Tanner?' she asked.

2

FROM THE VERY first moment the evening was heading for the catastrophe it ended in. Everyone agreed on that later, and everyone said that the atmosphere was as if they were sitting on a keg of gunpowder.

As usual it was Fiona who could not hold her tongue. Looking at Gwen, she had raised her eyebrows. Gwen was wearing an unusually pretty dress of peach-coloured velvet, drawn in at the waist with a black, plastic belt which revealed what no one present had known: Gwen had a much more slender figure than anyone could have guessed as long as she wore her usual baggy clothes.

'Lovely dress,' said Fiona finally. 'Is it new? It suits you!'

Gwen smiled, happy to receive the compliment. 'Dave found it for me. He says it wouldn't do any harm if I let my figure show a little more.'

'He's quite right,' Fiona agreed gently, before getting her claws out: 'And did he pay for it too?'

Gwen froze.

'Please, Fiona, that's not your business,' mumbled Leslie in deep embarrassment.

Dave Tanner pressed his lips together tightly.

'No,' said Gwen, 'but I didn't want him to.'

'A man could do worse than give his future bride something special as a present,' said Fiona, 'but that's just my opinion, of course.'

Her words were followed by an uneasy silence. In the end Jennifer Brankley saved the situation. She had helped Gwen to cook and lay the table, and so she had something of the status of a co-hostess.

'The food's ready,' she said with forced cheer in her voice. 'Would you all please come through to the living room.'

The living room served as a dining room too. They had all sat round the large table and struggled painfully to find things to talk about. Colin Brankley, who barely took part in the stunted conversations, was observing everyone. He thought that everyone wanted one thing: to be far away. Especially Dave Tanner. Colin Brankley was the branch manager of a bank in Leeds. He knew that people would not have thought of him as imaginative or as someone who understood people well. They saw him more as a grey, boring pen-pusher, someone who lived for his files and balance sheets. As it happened though, books were his passion. He read in every free minute and plunged more than other people into his own dream worlds. He spent a lot of time pondering the characters he found in novels, and behind his round face with its thinning hair and thick-lensed glasses, he understood more about what went on in people than anyone would have imagined.

As he ate his lamb roast with peppermint sauce, not really noticing what he was eating, in his mind he was making notes on the other guests.

Chad Beckett, Gwen's father. As reserved as he always was, so you could not really see what he thought about his daughter's sudden engagement to this rather opaque Dave Tanner who had appeared out of nowhere. Maybe he was worried, but he was not the sort of person to express his worries, not when alone with his daughter and certainly not in a larger group. And he had never tried to oppose his daughter—not even when it would have been good for her.

Fiona Barnes. As up for a fight as ever, and as usual she felt herself responsible for the Beckett family—for both the daughter and the father. She was sitting next to Chad and at the start of the meal she had cut the rather tough meat into bite-sized pieces for him. Colin also knew her well from their summer stays. She often came to the Beckett farm. There she would either sit with Chad in the sun in front of the house, or cajole him into a walk over the meadows. The two of them would often fight, but in the same way that an old couple do, where the wrangling is almost a ritual they love and a special kind of conversation. Fiona Barnes was called an *old friend of the family*, although no one had ever said how the friendship had sprung up or how long it had been there.

Colin could have sworn that Fiona and Chad had been lovers at some point in their lives. Since Chad had married rather late in life, Colin surmised that the affair between him and Fiona must have happened before that. He did not know why it had not led to a stable relationship. Gwen had long confided in Fiona, and Colin always had the impression that Fiona was very dear to Gwen, who valued her opinion highly. As far as her planned marriage went, however, Gwen was not likely to budge from her decision, however much Fiona might warn her.

Leslie Cramer, Fiona Barnes' granddaughter from London. Colin had met her for the first time this evening. He had sometimes heard about her from Gwen. So he knew that her marriage had broken down not long ago. She worked as a doctor. After her mother's early death, her grandmother had brought her up and she had often gone along with her to the Beckett farm. So Leslie and Gwen had become something like friends, although you could hardly imagine two more different women. Leslie looked quite the part of the classic modern career woman—somewhat cool, disciplined and out to succeed. In the old-fashioned, run-down rooms on the Beckett farm she looked completely out of place. For a start, her chic light grey trouser suit just did not suit rural Yorkshire. Yet Colin could sense that Gwen's engagement was not some obligation to her, something for her to sit through with gritted teeth. She had a genuine connection to Gwen, which had grown stronger over the years, and even to Gwen's taciturn father and to the dilapidated farm. Behind her well dressed and skilfully made-up appearance, she seemed lonely and even almost sad.

Gwen, the happy bride. Dave Tanner had been right. The peach-coloured dress did suit her. It put a rosy shine on her pale cheeks. She looked prettier than usual, but also tense. Gwen was not stupid. She knew that her fiancé was being watched suspiciously by all. She felt Fiona's aversion, the reserve in Leslie, and the unease which lay behind her father's silence. This evening was certainly not the engagement party she had hoped for. She tried to revive the faltering conversation, mainly—it seemed—out of the fear that too long a pause could allow Fiona to make a cutting remark or ask an inappropriate question. It pained Colin to see the strain she was under. He smiled encouragingly at her, but she was far too nervous to notice.

Dave Tanner, her future husband, sat beside her. Colin had seen him briefly once before when he had picked up Gwen with that unbelievable car of his. He was a good-looking man, who did not really manage to hide his mate-

rial poverty from people. His hair had long been in need
of a good hairdresser's attention, and his jacket, judging
by the cut and material, came from a cut-price clothes'
chain. Colin thought that the shabby chic look suited him
well. It made him look like an artist, a bohemian. It was
clear, however, that Dave Tanner himself felt very umcom-
fortable like that. Colin, who possessed the ability to look
deep into people, was sure he sensed something desperate
and panicky in his manner. The man was under enormous
pressure. Was he in love with Gwen? Colin doubted it. He
had other motives for this marriage. Nonetheless Dave
Tanner had clearly decided to make the best of it. Not a
bad man, Colin judged.

Fiona Barnes saw things very differently.

Colin's gaze drifted to Jennifer, his wife. She was sitting at the far end of the table, so that she could keep an
eye on her two dogs, who were lying on their rugs by the
door and sleeping. Cal snored quietly, while Wotan's hind
paws were twitching wildly as he dreamt. Now and then
his claws scraped on the stone floor. Jennifer looked…
contented. Colin found this remarkable, for seldom could
he really say she was contented. She suffered badly from
what has been called helper syndrome, had a real struggle
with her depression, was at a loss as to how to re-start her
career and could not get over what she insisted on calling
her *failure*. At the same time she was a good-hearted person who did not seem to know what bad traits like envy
or spite were.

From the first day on the farm she had felt responsible
for Gwen's wellbeing. She was not free of suspicions about
Dave Tanner, but she appeared resolved to ignore any hint
of fear. Jennifer seemed to have reached the conclusion
that Gwen should not be hurt or discouraged in this phase,

whatever would happen in the end. No doubt she secretly wished Fiona Barnes would be a million miles away.

Once Jennifer had served dessert—lemon sorbet with home-baked ginger biscuits—Fiona turned suddenly to Dave Tanner. The way she fired off her question, suggested she had been waiting all evening for this moment:

'Do you have any proper occupation?' she asked. 'I mean, apart from those few evening classes where you try to teach Scarborough's housewives French and Spanish?'

The colour drained from Gwen's face, then she went red. She looked over at Jennifer, pleading for help. Jennifer had frozen, a spoonful of sorbet half way to her mouth. Colin saw how Leslie Cramer closed her eyes briefly.

Sometimes she finds her grandmother excruciatingly embarrassing, he thought with some amusement.

'At the moment,' said Dave, 'the courses are my only occupation.'

Fiona acted surprised, although of course she had already known the answer.

'And that's enough for a man in the prime of his life? You're forty-three aren't you? You want to marry, start a family. You and Gwen might have children. What are you going to tell these children about your work? That you give some evening classes, and then only…how many evenings a week?'

'Three evenings at the moment,' said Dave. He remained polite, but seemed tense. 'I'd love to teach more,' he continued, 'but unfortunately there isn't enough demand to put on more courses, especially as there's a second French teacher, Linda Gardner—'

Gwen saw an opportunity to change the topic.

'Linda Gardner has become a bit of a celebrity in Scarborough,' she interrupted her fiancé, 'for a rather sad reason. She was the woman whose daughter Amy Mills was looking after, the evening she was killed.'

Leslie sprang to her friend's aid. 'There was a murder here in Scarborough?'

Before Gwen could reply, Fiona got a word in. 'At the moment,' she said with an unmistakeable edge to her voice, 'I'm more interested in Mr Tanner than the unfortunate Amy Mills. Chad…' She turned to the old man who was staring suspiciously at his lemon sorbet, as if he could smell some danger there. 'Chad, I'm asking the questions that you should be asking. Have you ever had a serious discussion with your future son-in-law?'

Chad looked up. 'About what?'

'Well, about his plans for the future, for example. After all, he wants to marry your only daughter.'

'All but nowt I can do 'bout it,' said Chad tiredly. 'And why should I? Gwen's grown-up. She has to know for herself.'

'He's got no money, and no proper job. That should at least *interest* you.'

'Fiona, you're going too far!' shouted Leslie. Her voice was so loud that Cal and Wotan both woke and raised their heads. Cal gave a low growl.

'You're absolutely right,' said Dave. He stared at Fiona. Neither his eyes nor the expression on his face revealed what he was feeling inside. 'You're right, Mrs Barnes. I don't have a proper job. Unfortunately I didn't finish my studies and didn't work towards any other qualification. And I struggle to make ends meet from the courses. But I have never claimed to Gwen that things were any different. I've not made a pretence of anything with Gwen, nor with any of you.'

'I think you have, Mr Tanner,' replied Fiona calmly.

Gwen let escape a low, indignant sound.

Jennifer hid her face in her hands.

Leslie looked ready to kill her grandmother.

Even Chad felt the need to say something. 'Fiona, perhaps we shouldn't get involved, especially us two?'

'What do you mean, *especially us two*?' snapped Fiona. His usually rather helpless expression changed. He looked directly and unflinchingly at her. 'You know what I mean,' he said calmly.

'I think—' said Leslie, but she was interrupted by Tanner, who suddenly pushed his chair back and stood up.

'I don't know exactly what you are implying, Mrs Barnes,' he said. 'But frankly, I'm not prepared to let you carry on treating me like this, even though this harmonious evening is supposed to be my engagement party. I think we've all had enough for this evening.'

'Please, don't go, Dave!' pleaded Gwen. She had gone as white as chalk.

'I'll tell you what I'm implying, Mr Tanner,' said Fiona. Colin thought that this old woman really did not have the slightest feeling for when to just keep quiet. 'I'm implying that you don't love Gwen Beckett, that you don't even particularly treasure or respect her. I'm implying that by marrying you want to get your hands on the Beckett farm. I'm implying, Mr Tanner, that you are in a spot of bother, and the only way out you can see is marrying a well-off woman. You know perfectly well what could be done with this farm and this land, so near the sea. Marrying Gwen is like winning the lottery for you, and you want to win at any price. As for Gwen's feelings and her future, you couldn't care less about that.'

When she finished, there was a shocked silence.

Then Dave Tanner marched out.

Gwen sobbed convulsively.

In the warmth coming from the hearth fire, the sorbet slowly melted in the bowls. No one touched their dessert any more.

Sunday, 12th October

1

SHE RETURNED TO her grandmother's flat a little after midnight and was still livid, and somewhat drunk. Rather drunk she feared, in fact, as she had struggled to open the building's front door. Then she had been at the wrong flat's door. Luckily she had noticed that she was on the wrong floor in time not to get a sleepy neighbour out of bed. Now she was in Fiona's flat and knew that she needed to take at least two aspirin, else she would feel rotten the next morning.

The door to Fiona's bedroom was closed. Probably the old woman was already in a deep and peaceful sleep. Leslie weighed up for a moment whether she should have a peek and check that everything was all right, but then she decided not to risk it. Fiona would probably wake up, and then anything could happen. No doubt they would get into such a terrible argument that it would be impossible, she thought, to talk normally to each other for months afterwards.

By the next morning perhaps the worst of the storm would be over.

LESLIE CREPT INTO the bathroom and rummaged around in the medicine cabinet, finding an open packet of aspirin with two tablets left. She filled a toothbrush cup with water and dropped the tablets in. She watched them slowly dissolve.

She could see the images of the terrible evening in her mind's eye.

After Dave had run out of the house, they had all heard how it took him four or five attempts to start his car.

Maybe he won't manage and he'll come back, Leslie had thought, although it was obvious that after such a humiliation he *could not* return, even if the alternative was walking to Scarborough.

In the end the car started and raced out of the yard, the engine screaming unhealthily. Gwen had not said a word. She stood up and left the room. They had heard her steps on the stairs: tired, slow steps.

Leslie also got up, but Jennifer was already at the door. 'It's OK, I'll talk to her.' Jennifer threw Fiona a cold glance. 'It might be good if you took your grandmother home now.' Then she went. Cal and Wotan got up, whining, and followed her.

'Fiona, how could you—' started Leslie, but Fiona interrupted immediately:

'I don't want to go home now. I've got to have an important chat with Chad. You go. I'll take a cab.'

'You'll be waiting a long time for a taxi out here…'

'I told you: I have to talk to Chad about something. It might take a while. So, either you can wait, or let me catch a cab.' Then she stood up and beckoned for Chad to follow her. Leslie could only watch in helpless anger as her grandmother, having just turned things upside because she felt like it, and without so much as sparing another word on the subject or showing any remorse, simply moved on to her own business. As if nothing had happened. That was so typical of her.

'No, I don't think I'll be waiting,' Leslie had replied irately. 'I don't think I can stand being here for another moment.'

Fiona had shrugged her shoulders. Leslie loved her grandmother, but she also knew that her grandmother could disappear behind a façade of untouchable iciness and arrogance when she did not want to deal with people or situations, and Leslie had suddenly remembered how often she had been confronted with that behaviour when she was an adolescent. It had really made her suffer. Old hurts resurfaced, painfully, and she thought this was perhaps the reason why she had said she could not stay on the farm another second.

She just could not have endured another moment in her grandmother's company. And so it was clear that she could not return to Fiona's flat right now, especially as she would not even find a drop of something nice and strong there. She needed something to take the edge off her anger and sadness.

She had said goodbye to Colin (a strange, difficult-to-read guy, she had thought), and he had assured her that he would get Fiona a taxi. She knew Gwen was in good hands, with Jennifer. She got into her car and roared off. In Burniston she saw a well-lit pub up ahead. She slowed down, turned into the car park and got out. There were almost only men in the Three Jolly Sailors. Their surprised or lewd gazes followed the unknown woman as she strode over to the bar and sat on one of the leather-covered bar stools. In rural Yorkshire women did not go to the pub on their own, but Leslie did not care two hoots. She ordered a double whisky, then another, then another, and thinking back now she thought there might well have been another one too. She remembered the smell of disinfectant wafting from the toilets, and the friendly old barkeeper who at some point had put a plate of chips covered in grilled cheese in front of her.

'You should eat something too,' he had said, but the sight of the soggy chips and melted cheese almost made her sick. A man tried to strike up a conversation with her, but she replied with such venom that he hurriedly backed off. When she walked back to the car park around midnight, swaying slightly, she knew she should on no account be driving, but she did not care about that either. She made it back home to her grandmother's place without the police stopping her or any other incident occurring.

Back home…right now that was the showy, giant white block of flats in which her grandmother lived. Prince of Wales Terrace, South Cliff, one of the best addresses in Scarborough, with a view of the whole of South Bay. And yet Leslie had never felt at home there. And nor did she this night.

The tablets had dissolved. Leslie drank her water in little sips. She did not want a hangover, which would only make everything worse.

What would it make worse? She looked at her reflection in the mirror over the sink. It was terrible how Fiona's complete lack of consideration had ruined Gwen's evening, and she only hoped that Dave Tanner had not disappeared forever. But was that the only, really the only reason why she felt so terrible now?

It's because she's so cold, so bitterly cold, she thought, meaning Fiona, and because I really just want to get out of here, tonight if possible, and because I'm afraid to go back to my own flat.

The flat was so empty since Stephen had left. The flat in which everything reminded her of him. The flat in which her life had broken down two years ago—love, happiness, the feeling of being together, of being secure, plans for the future.

She saw Stephen's slightly reddened face in front of her. She heard his quiet voice. 'I have to tell you something, Leslie...'

And she had thought: Don't tell me, just don't tell me! For a split second she had sensed that it could only be something that would change her whole life. She had felt it and wanted to stop it, but it could not be stopped, and until this day she had sat in the ruins of that evening and still could not believe it.

She drank the glass of water. You're drunk, Leslie, she told herself, and that's why you're so sentimental. Stephen didn't go. You threw him out. It was the right thing to do. Anything else would have been a slow death. You've been living alone in the flat for two years now, and coping, so you'll be fine going back tomorrow. Not tonight. In the state you're in, you'd smash into a bridge.

She came out of the bathroom and tiptoed past Fiona's bedroom. Once she had closed the door of her own room behind her, she breathed out with relief. The room was turning a little, and she had some difficulty in focusing on individual objects.

The final whisky had definitely been one too many, she thought sleepily and: maybe I should have had those chips.

Somehow she managed to get her clothes off, dropping them on the floor carelessly. She slipped into her pyjamas and under the covers. The sheets felt cold. She pulled her knees up, like an embryo.

Dr Leslie Cramer, a thiry-nine-year-old divorced radiologist, lay three sheets to the wind in an ice-cold bed in Scarborough with no one to give her warmth. No one.

   She started to cry. Then she remembered her empty flat
in London and cried even more. She pulled her sheet up
over her face, as she had as a child. So that no one could
hear her crying.

2

HE HATED SCENES like the one tonight. He hated it when feelings boiled over, when emotions went haywire, when women cried, when his daughter locked herself in her room, when people went in all directions, and when on top of everything he had the impression that people were looking at him accusingly, because they had obviously expected him to do something to contain the chaos. It was an expectation he could not live up to, but perhaps he had never lived up to expectations, and that might be the real problem with his life.

Chad Becket was eighty-three years old.

He was unlikely to change now.

It was five o'clock Sunday morning, but that was not an unusual time for Chad to get up. When it had still been a working farm, his father had often got the whole family out of bed at four, and Chad was no longer able to change the rhythm by which his whole life had run. Nor did he want to. He liked the hours before daybreak, when the world was quiet and sleepy and seemed to belong to him alone. He had often used the time to wander down to the beach in the half-light, sometimes in the thick fog that pressed inland from the sea. On those days he had been forced to go down the steep cliff almost blind, but it had never been a problem. He knew every stone, every branch. He had always felt safe.

Now he could no longer risk it. For the last three years his bad hip had made every step painful. He still refused to go to the doctor about it. He was not against doctors per se, he just did not believe that anyone could help him with his hip. At least, not without an operation, and the thought of hospital filled him with dread. He had a feeling that if he ended up in one, he would never return to his farm, and as he had the firm intention of dying in his bed, he was not going to leave his own patch of land now, not on the final stretch.

He preferred to grit his teeth.

The day was going to be sunny and bright again. That meant that his hip would not play up too much. The wet days were bad, when the clammy cold crept into his bones. The house was hard to heat and the rooms were always damp in the winter. His mother used to heat bricks for hours in the range in the kitchen, before putting them in the beds in the evening. At least that way you could warm up, seeing as the sheets were normally damp too. But his mother had been dead for ages, and Gwen had never known that trick. He himself thought, as did so many others too, that for his pleasure alone it was not worth reviving the habit. He found the damp linen unpleasant in the evening, but you would fall asleep in the end, and then you did not notice any more.

He listened carefully. Everyone seemed to be sleeping. Not a sound came from Gwen's room, nor any sign of life from the Brankleys or their dogs. Just as well. After a night like last night they would only get on his nerves.

He shuffled into the kitchen to make himself a coffee but did a double take when he saw the mess in the room. As Jennifer had been taking care of Gwen all evening and then later gone out with her dogs, it must have been Colin who had cleared the table. He had obviously seen his job as done once he had put the dishes, glasses and food in the kitchen. The crockery was piled high on the table, sideboards and in the sink. No one had covered the leftover soup, the roast or the vegetables stuck to the pans. It did not smell good.

Chad decided to do without a coffee for now.

He slowly moved over into the little room beside the living room, which served Gwen and him as a kind of study. Not that the farm required an actual functioning study or office, but they had the computer here. In spite of Chad's refusal to move with the times, it had found its way into the house in the end at Gwen's insistence. Files from years past, when the Beckett farm had still made modest profits, lined the wooden shelves along the walls. A few catalogues lay on the desk. Fashion, as Chad saw it, the stuff that Gwen ordered now and again. He lowered himself with a groan into the office chair and booted up the computer.

Unbelievable that he had learnt to use the thing! He had fought against it for long enough, but in the end Fiona had convinced him to set up an email address. In fact, she had set one up for him, and set up his password. 'Gwen often uses the computer. She doesn't have to read your mail, now does she?' Fiona had said.

He had replied, 'What mail? Don't even get normal post. Who's goin' to send me news by computer?'

'Me,' replied Fiona, and then she had explained slowly and patiently how it worked: how to open his mailbox, how to enter the password (*Fiona* of course), how to open each email, and how to reply. Since then they had corresponded via this strange medium that Chad was just as suspicious of as before, although he could not help being fascinated by it. It was nice to get a letter from Fiona now and then.

And then to answer with a few meagre words. Not that he had dared to explore this *modern madness*, as he referred to computer technology, in any more depth. It would never have occurred to him to surf the internet. In any case, he would not have known how, nor did he want to know.

Fiona had been pretty nervous yesterday. Probably that was why she had not stopped until she caused a scandal. The attack on Dave Tanner had let her blow off steam, although Chad was convinced that her aversion to Gwen's fiancé was genuine enough, and that she harboured serious reservations about him. She might well be right in what she suggested about his motives, but Chad could not get worked up about it. It was Gwen's life. She was over thirty. If she got hitched now, it was none too early, and maybe she would be happy with Tanner. Chad did not think that love should be the only reason for people to marry. Perhaps Tanner was trying to change his life, so what? At the end of the day, it would do the Beckett farm good. Perhaps he and Gwen would have children, and Gwen would blossom in her new role as a mother. She was a very lonely person. Chad took the pragmatic view on things: better to have Tanner than no one. He could not really understand why Fiona was so worked up about this.

After she had completely ruined the evening, she had sat here on a folding chair next to the desk and lit one cigarette after another. He had known her since her childhood. He knew her better than anyone else in the world, and he had known something was worrying her. After she had moaned a good deal more about Gwen's marriage plans, she had finally come out with it.

'Chad, I've been getting strange calls lately,' she had said quietly and hastily. 'You know…anonymous calls.'

He did not know. He had never received such calls. 'Anonymous calls? What kind? Threatenin'?'

'No. No. I mean, the caller doesn't say anything. He—or she—just breathes.'

'Is it...?'

She shook her head. 'No. Not *that* kind of breathing. Not dirty, I'd say. It's a very calm breathing. I think the other person is just listening to me getting bothered, and then hangs up after a while.'

'An' how d'yer get bothered?'

'I ask who's there. What he wants. I tell him—or her—that staying silent doesn't get us anywhere. That I want to know what it's all about. But I never get a reply.'

'Maybe you should do summat like 'im. Not speak. Just hang up when you hear 'im breathin'.'

She had nodded. 'I should never have reacted. I've probably done exactly what he expected. Still...' She had lit her next cigarette. Chad asked himself, not for the first time, how someone could smoke so unrestrainedly for decades and still be in such rude health.

'I can't get away from wondering who the caller is,' she said after a few nervous drags on her cigarette. 'If you do that, you have a reason. Why have they targeted me?'

He had shrugged his shoulders. 'Chance maybe. Found a name in t' phone book and called up. Probably got lots of victims. Maybe 'e do it all day, one after another, and 'e do it a lot with you because you get so bothered.'

'That's sick!'

'Aye, suppose so. But it might be 'armless. Just a hopelessly uptight person somewhere on end of line, someone who don't dare go out and would never dare talk t' a stranger. Feels powerful when 'e makes the calls, nowt more than that.'

She chewed her lower lip. 'And you don't think that it has…something to do with the stuff back then?'

He knew at once what she meant. 'Nay. Why d'yer think that? That's ages ago.'

'Yes, but…that doesn't mean it's over, does it?'

'Who'd phone up 'bout that now?'

She did not reply, but he knew her well enough to know that she was thinking of someone in particular. He could guess which name was knocking around in her head.

'Don't think so,' he said. 'Why now? After all these years…Aye, *why now*?'

'I don't think she ever stopped hating me.'

'Is she still alive?'

'I think so. Up in Robin Hood's Bay…'

'Don't upset yourself,' he warned her.

'Don't be ridiculous,' she replied as gruffly and sharply as she could, but the hand holding her cigarette had shaken a little.

Then she came out with what she really wanted to ask. 'I want you to delete the emails. All the ones I wrote to you. The ones I wrote *about that thing*.'

'Delete? Why?'

'I think it would be safer.'

'No one can read them.'

'But Gwen uses the same computer.'

'Thought that's why I got that thing, that password. Not any good, is it? Rubbish it is, all this computer technology…

'Anyroad, don't think Gwen would nose around in me things. She's not that interested in me.'

For the first time in the conversation Fiona had smiled, not happily so much as wryly.

'Then you judge her wrongly, I'd say. You are second

to no one in her eyes. But you never did have much of a feeling for the subtleties of human interaction. Still,' she was serious again, 'I'd appreciate it if you would delete the emails. I'd feel safer.'

The computer was ready now and Chad opened his mailbox. Fiona had sent him five emails over the course of the last half year—five, that is, with an attachment. Between each of them there had come a flurry of her usual messages.

She would write something to pep him up when the weather was bad and she feared that he was in pain; something sharper when she was annoyed that he had not been in touch for a while; something ironic when she had once again met someone they both knew and she could be nasty about the acquaintance. Sometimes she wrote about a film she had seen. Sometimes she complained about growing old. But she never mentioned old times, the past which they shared.

Until March of this year. Then the first file arrived, along with her instructions on how to open it.

'Why?' he had asked in his reply—nothing else, just *Why*, in bold italics, followed by at least ten question marks.

Her answer had been: 'Because I have to straighten things out for myself. I have to tell someone. And as no one else can know about it, it can only be you!'

His reply: 'I know it all anyway!'

And she in turn: 'That's why you're no danger.'

Then he thought: She's can't handle it.

He remembered asking her the previous evening what had triggered her writing it all down, all the things that no one was supposed to know, only him. He knew it anyway and was not keen to be reminded of it.

She had considered his question as she smoked, then said, 'Maybe what triggered it was realising that my life won't last much longer.'

'Are you ill?'

'No. But old. It can't be too long now. No need to pretend.'

He had read some of what she had written, but not all of it. Often he had felt it was asking too much of him. He would get angry at her for bringing it all up again, for picking at the scab. She was unearthing something dead and buried.

He clicked on the first email. It was dated 28th March. It was in Fiona's typical style.

'Chad, hi, how are you? It's dry and warm today so you must be doing well! I've written something that you should read. It's just for you. You know the story, but maybe not every detail. You're the only one I trust. Fiona.
PS: Double-click on the file. Then just click on Open!'

He opened the file.

The Other Child.doc

1

AT LEAST WE did not have to look after a relative back then, at the end of the summer of 1940, when all our lives changed. Many of my girl friends' fathers were at the front and their families were trembling at the thought of receiving bad news. My father on the other hand had already died before the war, in the spring of 1939. He got into a fight with another drunk on one of his infamous pub crawls, in which he would drink away the little money he earned as a street cleaner. It was impossible to tell afterwards who had started the fight and what it had actually been about. Probably nothing in particular. In any case, my father was badly injured and had to go into hospital, where he contracted tetanus—a disease that people were not really able to deal with in those days. He died very soon after. Mum and I were left on our own and had to get by with the widow's pension from the state. Actually we were better off financially than before, because no one took all the money down the pub. And Mum found two jobs as a cleaning lady, so increasing our income. We managed as best we could.

In the summer of 1940 I turned eleven. We lived in London's East End, in a little flat up under the roof. I remember how stifling hot that summer was. Our flat was like an oven. Germany was getting the world involved in the war. France had been occupied, and the Nazis had pocketed our Channel Islands while they were at it.

People here were getting nervous, even if the government was exhorting us to remain firm, appealing to people's fighting spirit and talking of an imminent victory over Nazi Germany.

'What will we do if they come here?' I asked Mum. She shook her head. 'They won't come, Fiona. You can't take an island as easily as that.'

'But they occupied the Channel Islands!'

'They were small, and undefended, and they're right off the coast of France. Don't worry, darling.'

The Germans themselves did not come, but from September they sent their bombers. The Blitz began. Night after night London was attacked. Night after night the sirens wailed, people gathered in air-raid shelters, houses collapsed and whole streets disappeared under ash and rubble. The next morning a previously familiar area could look completely different, because a house was missing or only smoking away as a ruin. On the way to school I would see people searching in the ruins for belongings that might have survived the inferno. One time I saw a dirty, thin young woman who was burrowing around like a madwoman among the stones of a collapsed house. Blood ran down her hands and arms. Tears streamed down her face and left bright, shiny tracks in the layer of dust.

'My child is down there!' she screamed. 'My child is down there!'

No one seemed to be concerned. That shocked me deeply. When I told Mum about it that evening, the colour drained from her face and she took me in her arms. 'I'd go crazy if anything happened to you,' she said. I think that was the day the idea started to grow in her that I should leave London.

Evacuations had started before then. On 1st Septem-

ber 1939, the day Hitler invaded Poland and two days before England declared war on Germany, evacuations had
begun of hundreds of thousands of people from the large
cities. There was already a fear of attacks from the air, especially the fear that the Germans might launch poison
gas attacks. Every citizen had to carry a gas mask with
him at all times, and everywhere in the city there were
warnings reminding us of how real the danger was. *Hit-
lor will send no warning*, they said in giant black letters
on a bright yellow background. In other words, we could
be the victims of his cunning at any time.

Most evacuees were children, but pregnant women, the
blind and people with other disabilities were also evacuated. Mum had asked me in passing if I also wanted to
leave, but I had objected violently and so she had dropped
the idea. I was extremely relieved, because the whole
thing flooded me with fear, almost horror. For some odd
reason the first evacuation had been named *Operation
Pied Piper*, and like most children I knew the legend of
the Pied Piper of Hamlin, the rat-catcher of Hamlin who
led a long train of children into a mountain, never to be
seen again. That was not exactly reassuring. Somehow
I had the idea that we were all to be taken away and
never return.

In addition, from what we heard it was pretty chaotic.
England had been divided into three types of zones:
into evacuation zones, neutral zones and zones where
the evacuees were to be received. There were reports
of chronically overcrowded trains, of traumatised young
children who could not cope with being separated from
their parents, and of a lack of organization when it came
to receiving the evacuees in other towns and other families. East Anglia reported it was full to bursting, while
in other areas hundreds of families who had offered to

take someone in were left waiting. People cursed the government for not having allocated enough money for the whole operation. And then the bombs did not fall as expected. At the end of the year most of the evacuees returned to their families and their hometowns.

'You see how good it is I didn't go,' I had said to Mum.

But then came the summer of 1940, and now everyone realised that the war was going to last longer than they had hoped and that the Nazis had moved dangerously close. From June large-scale evacuations took place once again. Parents, particularly those who lived in London, were asked again and again by the government to send their children away.

Once more posters covered the centre of London. This time they carried a picture of children and in large letters the words: *Mothers! Send them out of London!*

However, no one was forced to do it. Parents could decide for themselves what they wanted to do. So for a while I managed to talk Mum out of her notions of getting me somewhere safe.

Now in the autumn my position started to weaken, which made me uneasy.

At the start of October our house had taken a direct hit. We were sitting in the air-raid shelter with other people from our house when there was a deafening boom above us. We thought our eardrums would burst. At the same time the ground trembled and quaked, and dust and plaster fell from the ceiling.

'Out!' screamed a man. 'Everyone out at once!'

Some people swarmed to the door in panic. Others called out for calm. 'It's hell out there! Stay here. The roof will hold!'

Mum was for staying. There were so many bombs landing in quick succession nearby that, she thought, we would be more likely to die on the street than to be buried here in the cellar. I would have preferred to go outside. The fear of suffocating down here was making it difficult for me to breathe. Not that I was going to do anything that Mum had not given me the OK for. So I stuck it out, shivering and trembling, with my head in my hands.

In the early hours of morning the 'all clear' sounded and we crept out, fearful of what we would find up above. Our house was a pile of rubble. The one next to it too. And the one next to that one. In fact, apart from a few houses, the whole street was. We rubbed our eyes and stared incredulously at the sight of the devastation.

'Now it's happened,' Mum said in the end. Like all of us, she had swallowed a lot of dust. Her voice sounded as if she had a cold. 'Now we don't have a home any more.'

We poked around in the ruins for a while longer, but did not find anything that was still in a usable state. I found a bit of cloth which had been part of my favourite dress, on whose red linen yellow flowers were printed. I took the scrap. The rest of the dress was not to be seen.

'You can always use it as a hanky,' Mum said.

Then we set out to find new accommodation. My father's sister and her family, our only relatives, lived a few streets further on. Mum was sure they would take us in for a while. Auntie Edith's house was indeed still standing, but they were not at all pleased to see us. The family of six was squeezed into a two-bedroom flat on the ground floor and had already taken in a friend who had also become homeless.

In addition, Edith's husband had just been sent back from the field hospital and was not—as Edith confided in a whisper—quite right in the head at the moment. He would sit and stare out of the window all day, now and then starting to cry for no reason. It was clear that Mum and I were all that was needed right then.

And now Mum spoke again about us separating, and she sounded serious. I heard her talk to Edith about it.

'I'm thinking of sending Fiona to the country. They're taking more and more children away. Fiona's not safe in London.'

'Good idea,' said Edith relieved. It meant one less person in the overcrowded house. Not that she wanted to send her own children away just yet. She claimed she would not be able to bear their leaving.

Unfortunately my mother was less sentimental. Although I cried and screamed and showed my complete despair, she did not back down. She arranged everything so that it could go ahead.

Soon I was on the list to go to Yorkshire with a group of children at the start of November.

2

THE TRAIN WAS to leave Paddington Station at nine in the morning. The morning of 4th November was foggy, although we could see that the sun was trying to penetrate the grey.

'You'll see. Today will be a glorious autumn day,' Mum said to cheer me up.

My mood could not have been blacker. I did not care whether the sun shone or not. I trotted along beside my mother with the obligatory gas mask over my shoulder and a little board suitcase in my hand, which Edith had lent me. The government had put together lists of what the children should take with them, down to the number of handkerchiefs considered necessary. As we had been bombed and had little money, Mum had not nearly managed meet all of these requirements. Auntie Edith had plundered her children's old clothes for a dress that was too short for me, a sweater whose sleeves did not nearly reach to my wrists, and a pair of boots that was actually made for a boy. Mum had sewn a nightie for me and knitted two pairs of socks. I was wearing the checked dress that I had been wearing on the night of the bombing, as well as my old cardigan and my red sandals—they were the only belongings of mine that I still had. It was really too cold for those clothes. Mum warned me that I was bound to catch a cold. I insisted stubbornly. I had lost everything I possessed, my own mother was sending me away—I needed at least *my* dress and *my* shoes to have something familiar to hold on to. So let me catch a cold. Maybe I'd catch pneumonia and die. It would serve Mum right if no one from her family was left alive.

We had to walk down the street we had lived in until that October night. It was the most ruined street in London, it seemed to me. Right at the end of the street a single house had been standing since the raid, but already from a distance we could see that it too had fallen victim to the air attacks.

'I think they don't want to leave a single stone standing in London,' Mum said in disbelief, and with *they* she meant the Germans.

As we approached, we noticed the intense smell of burning that hung over this last bastion in our street—now finally vanquished. We saw that smoke was rising from the rubble. The house must have lost the battle with the bombers in one of the past few nights. We had known the families who had lived in the house a little, as you know each other when you live not many yards from each other in the same street. We knew who was who, exchanged pleasantries, knew a little about everyone's lives but not in detail. The Somerville family had lived on the first floor. Father, mother and six children. I had played with their second oldest daughter sometimes, but only when I was bored and could not find anyone else to play with. The Somervilles were considered anti-social. Although no one spoke about this in front of a child, I had gained an inkling of this. Mr Somerville drank, and much more than my Daddy. He drank from morning to night. You could never catch him sober. He was abusive to his wife, which had led to his wife, Mrs Somerville, who apparently also drank more than was good for her, walking around with a grotesquely crooked nose. It had been broken in a fight with her husband and mended wrongly. He was also abusive to his children. People said that some of them were a little soft in the head because of how often he had hit them, and that their mother's excessive consumption of alcohol during her pregnancies had caused them damage. Whatever the truth of the matter, there was always the fear of appearing rather suspect yourself if you were too close to the Somervilles, and so for that reason too I had kept contact with the children to a minimum.

We stood in front of the smoking ruins for a moment and were wondering to ourselves with some apprehension what had become of all the people who had lived here, when young Miss Taylor came out of the neighbouring house. A small section of its ground floor was still there, and roofed. She came from a village in Devon and had come to London to try her luck. She worked at a laundry. She was leading a small boy by the hand, who I recognized as Brian Somerville. He was seven or eight years old and was reckoned to be rather dense.

Miss Taylor's face was chalk-white.

'That was an inferno these last three nights,' she said, and I saw her lips were trembling violently. 'It was…I thought…' She wiped her free hand over her brow, which in spite of the cold morning was wet with sweat. Mum said later that she had been suffering from shock.

'I'm going to see if I can doss at a friend's place,' she explained. 'She lives a little further out, and I hope they aren't being bombed as much there. Anyway, it's going to be too cold to stay in this ruin. And I can't bear it all any longer. I can't bear it any longer!' She started to cry.

My mother gestured to little Brian who was staring at us with giant, shocked eyes.

'What about him? Where are his parents?'

Miss Taylor sobbed loudly. 'Dead. All dead. Even the sisters. All of them.'

'All of them?' exclaimed Mum, shocked.

'They dug them out,' whispered Miss Taylor, who had probably just realised what an effect this conversation might have on the already traumatized child holding her hand. 'Yesterday, all day long. Everyone who was living in the house...or rather, what was left of them. The house was hit the night before last. They said nobody could survive it.'

Mum pressed her hand to her mouth in horror.

'And then last night he suddenly appeared at my place.' Miss Taylor nodded at Brian. 'Brian. I don't know where he came from. I can't get a word out of him. Either he was buried in the rubble, but managed to survive and free himself, or he wasn't at home that night. I mean, you know...'

We knew. Sometimes when Mr Somerville was completely out of it, he just did not let his children into the flat. Often one of them had asked to kip in a neighbour's flat, and on summer nights they had sometimes camped out on the street. When I was younger and more foolish, I had sometimes envied them their freedom.

'Where should I take the little tyke now?' wailed Miss Taylor.

'Can you take him to your friend?' asked my mother.

'Never. She works all day too. Neither of us can look after him.'

'Does he have any relatives?'

Miss Taylor shook her head. 'I chatted with Mrs Somerville sometimes. She always wanted to leave her husband, but she said she had no family she could go to. I'm afraid Brian...is now alone in the world.'

'Then you have to hand him over to the Red Cross,' Mum advised and looked pityingly at the pale boy. 'Poor boy!'

'Oh God, oh God,' moaned Miss Taylor. It seemed the situation was too much for her.

And then my mother did something that was to have far-reaching consequences, something that was not like her at all. She was not by nature someone willing to lend a helping hand. She would always say that it was hard enough keeping our own heads above water, and that we could not afford to take on other people's problems too.

'All right, I'll take him,' she said. 'I'm just taking Fiona to the train station. She's being evacuated. I'm sure I'll find someone there who can help me, one or other of the Red Cross nurses for example. Then I can hand Brian over to them.'

Miss Taylor looked as if she wanted to hug my mother. Before you could say Jack Robinson, Mum had two children at her side: her own eleven-year-old daughter in a thin summer dress with a board suitcase in her hand and an eight-year-old boy in trousers stiff with dirt and a formless, sack-like sweater which, to judge by its worn condition, had already served whole generations of children as an all-purpose item of clothing. The boy moved as if in a trance. He did not seem to take in what was going on around him.

In this formation we arrived at the train station, at the very last minute as we discovered. Either Mum had got the times wrong, or we had been dawdling, held up by Brian's ambling along. In any case, most of the children were already on the train. Clusters of them were squeezed at the windows, waving to their parents standing on the platform. Many of them were crying. Many mothers looked as if they would really have liked to climb onto the train themselves. Various children were screaming that they wanted to get off the train and go home. All of them had little badges, on which their names were written. Red Cross nurses and other helpers were scurrying here and there with clipboards and lists in their hands, trying to keep track of everything in the chaos.

Mum approached one of the Red Cross nurses determinedly. 'Excuse me. My daughter was registered for this train.'

The nurse was a tall, large woman. She had such an unfriendly face that I felt quite afraid. 'You're early!' she barked. 'Name?'

'Swales. Fiona Swales.'

The nurse looked down her list and ticked off something, no doubt my name. She fished a little card badge out from under her clipboard.

'Write your daughter's name on this. And her date of birth. And your address in London.'

Mum found a pencil in her handbag and squatted down to rest the name-badge on her knees as she wrote. The nurse stared at Brian.

'And what about him? Is he going too?'

Brian reached for my hand, frightened. I felt sorry for him and did not pull my hand away, although I would have liked to.

'No,' said my mother. 'He's an orphan. I don't know where to take him.'

'And I'm supposed to know?'

Mum stood up and fixed the badge to my cardigan's lapel.

'You are from the Red Cross!'

'But I'm not responsible for orphans! Can't you see all that I have to do here?' And with those words she hurried onwards, to snap at a little girl who, in tears, was trying to get off the train and was screaming for her mother.

'You have to get on the train, Fiona,' insisted Mum nervously.

Brian held onto me with both hands.

'He's not letting go, Mummy,' I said, surprised at the strength in Brian's little hands.

My mother tried to separate Brian from me. The conductor blew his whistle. In the blink of an eye, a wave of people had carried and pushed us to the carriages. There were children who had not been able to tear themselves away yet, parents who wanted to reach through the windows one last time and touch their children's hands or cheeks. The farewells around me were heart-rending. I was determined mine should not be. I was angry with Mum for sending me away, and I was sure that I would never forgive her. I had reached the iron steps of the carriage. Brian was still clinging resolutely to my hand, although I was trying quite brutally by now to shake him off. A wall of people pressed us onwards from behind.

I turned around. 'Mummy!' I shouted.

I had lost her in the turmoil. I heard her voice coming from somewhere, but I could not see her. 'Get on, Fiona! Get on!'

'Brian's not letting go!' I screamed.

A father standing right behind us lifted his daughter up into the carriage. Then with one arm he grabbed hold of me and with the other arm Brian, and in a second we were both on the train too.

'Close the doors!' shouted the conductor.

I pushed my way down the passageway, pulling Brian behind. He did not let go for a moment.

Well done, Mummy! Now I'll have to see how to get rid of him!

'I can't believe how stupid you are!' I snapped at him. 'You're not supposed to be here! They'll send you back straight away!'

He stared at me from his huge eyes. I noticed how white his skin was and how clearly you could see the web of blue veins under his temples.

He had no badge, no suitcase and no gas mask. He was

on no list. They would send him back in no time. It was not my fault that the man had just lifted him into the train.

I found a free seat on one of the wooden benches and squeezed on beside the other children. Brian tried to sit on my lap, but I pushed him away. In the end he stood nearby.

'Don't be so mean to your little brother,' said a girl of about twelve who was sitting opposite and eating a delicious smelling pâté sandwich.

'He's not my brother,' I replied. 'I don't even know him!'

The train started to move. I had to swallow hard in order not to break into tears. Many children were crying, but I did not want to be one of them. We slowly left the train station. The sun had still not managed to break through the fog. The day was grey and dark. My future did not look any brighter. Grey, dark and uncertain, as if the damp, impenetrable fog lay over it too.

I felt that the end of my childhood had come. Without any tears, but with my heart as heavy as lead, I said goodbye to it.

IT WAS LATE afternoon by the time we reached Yorkshire. The train timetable had been thrown into disarray, because our train had unexpectedly come to a stop a few miles outside of London, where it had to wait three hours. The previous night's bombs had caused two large trees to fall on the tracks. The clean-up work was already underway when we reached the spot. The nurses and teachers accompanying us on the train made an effort to keep us calm and in good spirits. Some organized games in little groups, others distributed paper and colouring pencils. The sun did finally break through, scattering the banks of mist and bathing the autumnal landscape in a gentle light. We were allowed to get off the train and stretch our legs. Some of the children started to play 'it' immediately. Others squatted down, leaning on trees, and began to write their first letters to their parents. Some of the children were still crying. I kept to myself, unpacked the sandwiches my mother had made for me, and started eating.

Brian stuck to me like my shadow. He looked at me fixedly from his large, horrified eyes. I found him creepy and tiresome, and although on the one hand I was happy that he was not—to top it all—chatting away to me, I found his complete silence rather irritating.

'Can't you say anything?' I asked.

He looked at me fixedly. Somehow he awoke my pity. After all, he had lost his whole family and now by a big mistake he was stuck on a train for Yorkshire. He seemed like a lost little animal to me. But I myself was only eleven, and was confused, scared and in pain at having just been separated from my mum. Where was I to get the energy to look after this helpless being? I did not even have a clue how to cope with my situation.

I gave him a piece of bread, which he ate, chewing it slowly. Even as he did so, his eyes did not leave me for a moment.

'Can't you stop staring at me?' I asked, irritated.

As was to be expected, he did not reply, nor stop staring at me. I poked out my tongue at him. It did not seem to make any impression on him.

When we arrived in Yorkshire, darkness was already falling. Soon pitch-black night would hide the countryside from view. The sun was long gone. We rolled into Scarborough station, got out of the train with stiff joints and shivered in the cold as that autumn afternoon drew to its end. The lively chat, which the more robust of the children had kept up for most of the journey, had now petered out. Now that it was dark, everyone's fear of what was coming, and of which they knew nothing, gained the upper hand. And people felt how homesick they were. I think that every one of the children would have had nothing against further nights in an air-raid shelter under a shower of bombs, if they had been allowed to stay with their parents. Later, as an adult, I read essays on the topic of the evacuations. There are academic articles and PhD theses that deal with them. Almost without exception they suggest that the traumatisation which many children suffered as a result of sudden separation from their parents and maltreatment in the host families was worse and had a much more damaging effect on their further lives than the considerable trauma of the nights of bombing.

Personally, I have never in my life felt more miserable and wretched, more unprotected and helpless than I did arriving in this unknown place with an uncertain future ahead of me.

A man was waiting on the platform. He talked to the nurse whom I had found so unpleasant in London and who was obviously in charge of our group. We had to line up in twos. The question of whose hand I should hold was quickly solved. No sooner had we got out than he latched onto me again. We looked like brother and sister: a big sister and somewhat younger brother. Well, I thought, not for long. Tomorrow morning at the latest they would send him back to London.

I almost envied him, but then reminded myself that he did not have a mother waiting for him like I did. If what Miss Taylor said was true, and he had no living next of kin, then he would end up in an orphanage.

Poor devil, I thought.

We followed the man through the station to where a number of buses were parked and waiting. We were asked to get into the buses. It did not seem to matter who ended up in which bus. Only a very few children, whose names were on a separate list, were assigned individually to particular buses. As later became clear, they were the lucky ones who were to be put up in their relatives' homes. Their destinations were already clear, while the destinations of the rest of us were still undecided. The buses left for various villages, many deep in the countryside. The bus I was in—and Brian, still holding my hand—was the only one that stayed near the coast and dropped its passengers off in the area around Scarborough. The town of Scarborough itself was no longer a *Reception Zone*, but the villages around it had been approved. Their beds were needed urgently.

No one checked us as we got on the bus. No one noticed that the little boy holding my hand did not have either a badge or luggage. We were shooed onto the bus in a hurry, so I did not dare to speak to one of the adults. It might sound surprising that I was not able to act sensibly, but you have to think how scared and unsure of myself I felt.

Once we had left the town behind and were driving through the countryside, there was absolute silence in the bus, except for the quiet sobbing of two little girls who tried in vain to suppress their sobbing. No one said a word. Everyone was afraid, tired and hungry. I believe all of them felt like I did: we were afraid that if we opened our mouths we would burst into tears.

I pressed my face against the glass. I could still see some of the outlines of the landscape. No houses, rolling hills, few trees. The sea must be somewhere. I was very far from London.

The bus stopped abruptly at the side of the road, and when the instruction came to get off the bus I was confused. Here, in the middle of nowhere? Were we to spend the night on the ground between one meadow and the next?

After we had got off the bus and again lined up in the obligatory twos, I saw a beam of light some distance away. The nearer we came to it, the clearer the silhouettes of buildings could be made out against the night sky. They were two- and three-storey houses that seemed to have been dropped here in the middle of nowhere. Nevertheless, they promised light and—more importantly—warmth. It had grown unagreeably cold, and I was freezing in my summer dress, cardigan and socks that slipped down.

In front of the buildings we had to stop and wait. They

appeared to be a tiny shop and two residential houses, as far as I could see. One of the nurses motioned for us to wait outside, and we spread out on a meadow opposite the shop. Although we had not walked far, most of us sat down immediately in the stubbly grass, which was already covered in the night dew. We were exhausted. Our fear had exhausted us.

I could not stand the cold any longer. I opened my little suitcase and fished out the sweater with the sleeves that were too short and pulled it on. I also put one of the pairs of socks my mother had knitted for me on top of my other socks in the hope that my icy feet would warm up a little. I saw that Brian did not have any socks on, and reluctantly sacrificed my second pair of new socks. They were too big for him, but as he did not fill his shoes we could fit the extra wool in too. I suspected that he had inherited the shoes from one of his older brothers and, as I expected of the Somervilles, there had been no attempt to see that they fitted him. For the first time since we had left London, he looked away from me. He looked at the socks, and stroked them again and again with an almost reverent look on his face.

'Listen, they aren't a present! I want them back!' I warned him.

He did not stop stroking the wool.

The door of the little shop opened, as did the doors of the buildings next to it. A crowd of adults rushed out. They all seemed excited and angry. They were talking frantically at our escorting nurses. From what I could gather, they were angry about our late arrival. They had reckoned with us arriving much earlier by train in Scarborough and also earlier there. They were annoyed that they had spent half the day waiting here with nothing to do.

A girl sitting next to me poked me with her elbow.

'Those are the families we are going to live with,' she hissed, 'the host families!'

'I worked that out already,' I replied haughtily.

She gave me a short sideways glance. 'I'm going to be picked up by my aunt. What about you?'

'I don't know who's picking me up.'

Now she looked sorry for me. 'You poor thing!'

'Why?' I asked. I tried to sound curt, but my heart was beating hard.

'Well, one hears such terrible stories,' the girl next to me replied with palpable pleasure. 'One can end up in quite awful families. You might have to work hard all day and barely be given any food. And they treat people badly. Very badly. I heard that one time—'

'Rubbish!' I interrupted, but inside I was much more shocked than I let on. What if she were right? And some hell were awaiting me? Then I would run away, I decided, even if I had to walk to London. I was not going to stay in a place where I was treated badly!

The adults assembled in front of us and one of the nurses began to read out names on her list. The children who were named had to come to the front and were handed over to their new families. In most cases, they were obviously related, while in some cases there seemed to have been another reason for agreement and allocation beforehand. I dearly hoped that these people had honourable motives such as pity and a wish to help, but I had my doubts. Auntie Edith had told me that families who took in evacuees were given money from the government. I remembered that my mother had been annoyed with Auntie Edith and told her off for 'her big mouth'. My mother had not wanted me to hear about the money. It put a question mark over the pure intentions of the host families.

The girl next to me was called up. She rushed forward and with a happy squeak fell into the arms of a young woman who held her tight and seemed close to tears. Her aunt. I envied the girl bitterly. In the past I had never thought about why—apart from Auntie Edith and her brood in London—I had no relatives, but now in this circumstance it suddenly seemed like a painful gap in my life. How nice it would be to cuddle up to someone who knew me and loved me.

Instead I was sitting in a field somewhere in Yorkshire, in the dark except for the weak light cast by oil lamps that had been brought outside. I was far away from everything I knew and had no idea what my future would hold. A small traumatised boy was at my side, continuously stroking the socks I had put on his feet. He seemed determined to never leave my side again. And now those people who had not been allocated a child yet came towards those of us who had not been called up yet. They went down the rows slowly, shining torches or stable lamps in our faces and choosing whom to take with them. We were examined and assessed, then either rejected or picked out. Even today, as I write this, I can feel how small, humiliated and helpless I felt. Today such a procedure is unthinkable. In twenty-first century England it is unimaginable to think of children sitting in a field and more or less auctioned off like animals at a country fair. But it happened in the exceptional circumstances of those years. The virulence of the German air raids on London had taken everyone by surprise, and the number of victims exceeded people's fears. The aerial defence of London, undertaken with a woeful lack of equipment, had proven to be inadequate. The aim of bringing children to the safety of the countryside was a top priority, no matter how. There had not been time to organise everything perfectly. One could not worry about the children's psychology. They would have to cope.

A woman stopped in front of me, bending down towards me. She did not look much older than my mother and had a friendly face with finely chiselled features. She smiled.

'So, what's your name?' she asked and then answered her own question as she read my name badge: 'Fiona Swales. And you were born on 29th July 1929. So you are eleven.'

I nodded. For some reason I could not say anything. She held out her hand. 'I'm Emma Beckett. I live on a farm not far from here. I heard about the evacuation from London on the radio and wanted to help. Would you like to live with us for a while?'

Again, I nodded. She must have started to think I was mute. She seemed really nice, and I realised I could have had it much worse.

A farm…I had never been on a farm in my life.

She looked at Brian. 'And this is your little brother?'

Brian, who was still fixated by his socks, knew that we were talking about him. He clung to my arm. I tried to shake him off, but he would not let go. 'No.' Finally I had found my voice again. 'I don't have a brother. This is a neighbour's child. He is…he shouldn't be here.'

'No? Do his parents know he's here?'

'His parents are dead,' I explained. 'And his brothers and sisters. The whole family is, except for him. The night before last a bomb fell on their house.'

Emma Beckett looked deeply distressed. 'But that's terrible! What are we to do with him?' She turned around and beckoned for a young woman to come over, to whom she explained the situation in a few words. The woman began to breathe heavily in panic and seemed completely out of her depth with the situation. She leafed through her lists wildly.

'He's not on the list?' she asked. 'What's his name?'

'Brian Somerville,' I replied.

She leafed through them again and shook her head. 'He's not listed!'

I had just said that. I told her how he had been given to us and how he then suddenly ended up in the train with us. The young woman beckoned for a Red Cross nurse to come over. I stood up. I did not want to crouch down so small in front of the three excited adults who were now surrounding Brian and me. Brian stood up immediately too. He held onto my arm tightly.

As was to be expected, the nurse could not find his name on her list.

'He shouldn't have got on the train,' she stated, although it was rather too late to put that into practice.

'What's to become of him?' asked Emma Beckett once again. Brian started to shake. His little hand clasped mine so hard that it hurt.

'He should really go back to London with us,' said the nurse.

'But he obviously has no one to go back to!' cried Emma.

'There are orphanages.'

'And bombs too! He's much safer here!'

The nurse hesitated. 'I can't just take an unregistered child from London. I'd get in trouble and…'

'We could take him to the home in Whitby,' the young woman suggested. 'That's where the children are going who don't find host families here tonight.'

Emma Beckett squatted down and looked closely at Brian. 'He's in shock,' she said. 'I don't think he should be separated from Fiona right now. He's only got her right now.'

Oh, wonderful! Somehow I had guessed it during the journey: Brian Somerville and I would continue to stick together. The adults debated back and forth, but in the end our escorts agreed to Emma Beckett taking Brian to her farm too.

'We'll sort things out in London,' said the nurse and scribbled Emma's name, address and a few more notes down on her notepad. 'You'll hear from us.'

'Fine,' said Emma with relief. She took my suitcase. 'Come on, children. We're driving home.'

Her friendliness and attempt to make the situation easier for us annoyed me a little. *We're driving home!* Did she seriously believe I would see her farm in the middle of nowhere as home, just because she wanted me to? My home was with my Mummy in London. Nowhere else.

Brian and I trotted along behind her, Brian holding my arm tight. I had almost grown used to this weight that I had been dragging around for about twelve hours now. We went back down the path, then turned left along the road for a stretch until we saw a church on the left. An all-terrain vehicle was parked by the side of the road. It had two open benches at the back. A large stable lamp on one of the benches provided some light for the scene. As we approached, a shadow peeled away from the driver's door. Someone had been leaning against the car, waiting for us. A big boy, maybe fifteen or sixteen years old, stepped into the circle of light thrown by the lamp. He was wearing long trousers and a thick sweater, was chewing something (a blade of grass, as I saw when I was right next to him), and had a crabby expression on his face. Unlike Emma, he did not seem to be pleased with our sudden appearance.

'This is Chad, my son,' said Emma, swiftly stowing my suitcase on the floor of the back part. 'Chad, this is Fiona Swales. And this is Brian Somerville.'

Chad stared at us. 'I thought you wanted to take in *one* child. Now it's *two*!'

'I'll explain later,' said Emma.

I stretched my hand out to Chad. After some hesitation he shook it. We had a good look at each other. There was something dismissive in his look, but also interest.

'Chad doesn't have brothers or sisters,' Emma explained. 'I think it could be nice for him to have other children in the house for a while.'

Clearly Chad did not think so, but the topic must have been discussed so often and heatedly already between his mother and him that he did not dare to be too vocal about his opinion right now. He mumbled something and then swung himself up onto the bench.

'Take the two little ones up front, Mum,' he said.

I was annoyed that he called me 'little', and incensed that he lumped me and Brian together. In my eyes Brian was still almost a baby.

'I'm eleven,' I said defiantly, jutting out my chin to look a little bigger.

Now Chad grinned. He looked down at me from the height of the car.

'Already eleven? Fancy that!' he said and even I realised that he was making fun of me. 'I'm fifteen and I don't want to have anything to do with you or the little boy holding your hand. All right? You leave me alone, I'll leave you alone, and we'll just wait for the Germans to lose the war and for everything to go back to normal!'

'Chad!' said Emma, in an admonishing tone.

We got into the car. Although Chad had been so rude to me, he was the first person that day who had managed to lift my mood somewhat. I did not know why. As we drove off from the church and into the darkness and uncertainty ahead, my heart was a little lighter. I felt some curiosity about what was awaiting me.

Sunday, 12th October

3

LESLIE WOKE WITH a banging headache and wondered, once she had collected herself enough to remember the night before, how wretched she would be feeling now, if she had not taken those two aspirin.

She forced herself to get up, and swayed out of bed. She was terribly thirsty. Her mouth and throat were dry and burnt. She went into the kitchen, turned the tap on, bent down and let the ice-cold water run into her mouth. Then she splashed water on her face, to wake up.

When she straightened up, she was feeling a little better.

A glance at the kitchen clock showed her it was almost midday. She must have slept like the dead. That was not like her at all. She normally got up very early, even if the night before had been a late one. Just like her grandmother. Fiona was always up at the crack of dawn. Leslie remembered how often as a teenager the old woman's energy had left her feeling completely shattered.

At the moment, however, there was no sign or sound of her. The flat seemed deserted.

Maybe she had gone out for a walk. Leslie looked out through one of the windows. Another beautiful day. The sun was casting its rays over the bay, causing the foam on the dark blue waves to glisten. The sky was infinite and glassy. A few sailing boats were out. No doubt it would be really warm again.

It was just odd that nothing in the kitchen suggested Fiona had eaten breakfast, nor that she had prepared anything for her granddaughter as she normally did. At the very least, she would have left the coffee to keep warm on the coffeemaker's plate. But when Leslie had a closer look, she saw that the glass jug still contained the rest of yesterday's coffee. When she picked up the jug, the brew splashed around inside and left brown marks on the inside of the glass. No one had touched it for over twenty-four hours.

Leslie frowned in irritation. There were two things her grandmother could not do without in the morning: at least two cups of strong coffee and one cigarette. It was almost unimaginable that she would have gotten up and gone for a walk without having had those two things.

Leslie went to the living room. Empty and silent. No ash in the ashtray. Could Fiona still be sleeping at half past eleven?

Without a moment's hesitation, Leslie went over to Fiona's bedroom and quietly opened the door. She could see the bed, neatly covered with a bedspread. The curtains were open. Fiona's slippers lay in front of the wardrobe. The room looked just as it always did during the day. It was not clear whether someone had slept here the previous night or not.

Maybe Fiona had spent half the night talking to Chad and decided in the end that she would spend the night on the farm. Probably she was just as loathe to talk to her granddaughter as her granddaughter was to talk to her. Leslie was still angry, but her aggression had been dissipated to some extent by her painful hangover. She thought she would do best to leave Fiona to her own devices. Fiona had acted unreasonably, and it would not do her any harm to notice that the people nearest to her had been put out and were not going to be easily appeased. Colin or Jennifer could give her a lift back to Scarborough, or she could take a taxi. She should make herself a coffee, and a few sandwiches for the journey, and set off for London. What with her move coming up, she had enough on her plate. Why should she waste her time here arguing with the old dear.

In spite of her resolution, she went back into the living room and picked up the phone. Better to check that everything was all right. She did not want to worry all the way home.

It was a while until someone answered on the Beckett farm. Then Leslie heard Gwen's voice. It sounded as though the young woman had cried for hours—not surprising in the circumstances.

'Hi, Leslie,' Gwen said, and just those two words sounded so desolate that Leslie's heart went out to her. 'Did you get home well?'

'Yes. Fine. I just took a little detour via a pub, and now I feel as if my head is in a vice, but that will go. Gwen, Fiona was out of order yesterday. I want you to know that I'm one hundred per cent on your side.'

'Thank you,' said Gwen quietly, 'I know you didn't want things to turn out like that.'

'Have you…has Dave phoned since then?'

'No.' Now Gwen started to cry again. 'He hasn't. And he's not answering his phone. I tried to reach him a dozen times. I texted him four times, but he hasn't replied. Leslie, he's done with me. He's had enough. And I can understand!'

'Just wait,' consoled Leslie. 'Of course he's smarting. Fiona laid into him in front of everyone. No wonder he's disappeared. But I'm sure he'll come out again sometime.'

Gwen blew her nose noisily.

'Do you think she was right?' she then asked.

'Who? Fiona?'

'With what she said. That Dave is only…after the farm? That he's not interested in me?'

Leslie hesitated. The conversation was threatening to head into a minefield, and today of all days, with this headache plaguing her.

'I don't think Fiona can be a judge of it,' she said, simultaneously silencing the inner voice that told her that Fiona had always been a pretty good judge of character. 'She doesn't know Dave well enough. And nor do I unfortunately. Yesterday evening was too short to get a proper impression of him.'

This was a little white lie. Of course she had not really got to know Dave Tanner. However, she had shared her grandmother's suspicion all evening. Tanner was too good-looking and cosmopolitan for her to imagine that he had fallen in love with Gwen. The two of them were too different, and not in the 'opposites attract' way, but rather in a way that ruled out attraction. In addition, Tanner's whole appearance revealed his blatant lack of money. Leslie could see how and why Fiona had reached her conclusions.

'I wish you could go and talk to Dave,' said Gwen, 'to show him that not everyone in the family is against him. And maybe you could find out what he…really feels about me.'

'Actually I'm about to leave for London,' Leslie replied in some discomfort. She did not at all like the thought of becoming more entangled in this whole baneful affair.

'But you wanted to stay in Scarborough for a few days!' exclaimed Gwen in surprise.

Leslie explained that she was rather angry with her

grandmother and so had no wish to stay any longer. 'I'm so relieved that I didn't have to see her this morning. Did you have the questionable pleasure of having breakfast with her, or have you been able to avoid her so far?'

At the other end of the line there was a confused silence for a moment. 'Sorry?' asked Gwen. 'She's not here. Did she want to come over?'

Leslie felt a tingling in her fingertips. 'Didn't she sleep at your place?'

'No. As far as I know, she ordered a taxi to get home.'

'But it doesn't look like…she slept here.'

The tingling in Leslie's fingertips increased. 'Listen, Gwen, I'll phone you back. Let me go and check.'

She hung up, went to Fiona's bedroom and opened the wardrobe. She looked through the dresses, skirts and blouses carefully, until she was sure that the dress Fiona had worn the night before was not among the other clothes. Nor was it in the bathroom or in the laundry basket. Fiona's shoes and handbag were also missing. As Fiona was certainly not out for a walk in her silk dress and high heels, it was clear Fiona had not changed clothes, at least not in her flat.

She was definitely not home.

Leslie ran into her room and quickly got dressed. Although her body was crying out for a nice long shower and a strong coffee, she could not bring herself to waste another moment. She brushed her hair hurriedly, grabbed her car key and the key to the flat, and ran outside, pulling the door closed behind her.

Three minutes later she was on the way to the Beckett farm. The low, bright sun shone in her eyes and made her headache worse. She ignored it.

4

'I CALLED A cab for her,' said Colin. 'She had been with Chad for a long time, maybe two hours. Then she and Chad came out of the study and she said she wanted to go home. I had been watching telly and was about to go upstairs to bed. I offered to call the cab. She said she wanted to walk for a bit, as the night was quite bright, and could I please order a cab for Whitestone Farm. So I did.'

'For Whitestone Farm?' asked Leslie astonished. 'To get there you need to go through the wood, over the little bridge and up the hill. It would take her at least fifteen minutes!' Leslie, Colin and Gwen, who looked pale and teary, were standing in the kitchen. Gwen was doing the dishes and Colin, who had been sitting at the table earlier and frowning into a pile of closely typed papers, had stood up and was drying the dishes.

'But that is just what she wanted to do,' he said. 'Have a walk.' He thought for a minute. 'I had the impression that she was quite worked up. Either about the thing with Dave Tanner or something unpleasant she had been talking to Chad about. In any case she was agitated, and I could see that she needed to stretch her legs.'

'I wonder where she might have gone,' said Leslie. 'Maybe she didn't want to go home, to keep out of my way. Although that's not like her at all. She's not a person who avoids confrontations.'

She turned around, hearing steps behind her. Chad appeared from the living room. He seemed as introverted as always.

'Hi, Leslie,' he said. 'Fiona here too?'

'Fiona seems to have disappeared,' said Colin.

Chad looked from one to the other in confusion. 'Disappeared?'

'Colin called a cab last night,' said Leslie, 'for Whitestone Farm, because she wanted to have a walk first. But she didn't come home. Did you see her leave, Chad?'

'Saw her at door,' replied Chad, 'when I were 'bout t' go t' bed. She were puttin' on her coat and said she wanted t' walk a stretch t' cab. Then I heard door close behind her.'

'I'm going to call the cab office,' said Colin and put the dishcloth down, 'The trip must be registered with them. Then we'll know more.' He went off into the study to make the call.

Gwen stopped doing the dishes and dried her hands. 'Don't worry, Leslie. It'll soon be cleared up.'

Leslie tried to smile. 'Of course. She's hard as nails.' She put a hand to her brow. 'I've got a terrible headache. Could I have a coffee? As strong as possible?'

'Of course,' said Gwen immediately. 'I'll just put the kettle on.'

They heard padding and panting and the two Great Danes came round the corner and into the kitchen. Jennifer followed close behind. Her cheeks were ruddy and her hair tousled. 'It's gorgeous outside,' she said. 'Sun, wind and crystal-clear air. You should have come, Gwen. Oh, hi, Leslie! How are you?'

'Fiona has disappeared,' said Gwen.

Jennifer looked as confused as Chad had a couple of minutes ago.

'That's to say, she obviously left here last night, but she never arrived home,' added Leslie. 'I only noticed late this morning. Colin is just calling the cab office.'

Colin appeared behind his wife. 'They're just checking,' he said. 'They'll call right back.'

'Mighty odd,' remarked Chad.

'We can rule out any idea that Dave Tanner gave her a lift,' opined Leslie.

'Dave had been gone for two hours by the time Fiona thought of leaving,' said Colin. 'Unless he had stayed around here somewhere, and why would he do that?'

'Maybe to talk to his fiancée again once everyone else had left or gone to bed,' suggested Jennifer.

Hope shone in Gwen's eyes. 'Do you really think so?' she asked.

'But why would he then have picked up Fiona? Her of all people!'

Jennifer shrugged. 'He would have had every reason to talk to her. To convince her of his good intentions, to show her how he saw things. It wasn't his duty to try to clear things up, but he might have wanted to, anyway.'

'And why wouldn't he then have driven her home?' asked Chad.

'They went to his place, talked all night and then went somewhere for breakfast!' Jennifer looked from one person to the next. 'I can imagine them doing that, Tanner as well as Fiona.'

'I don't know, I —' started Leslie, but then the phone rang. She did not finish her sentence but waited in silence like everyone else until Colin returned from the study.

'How very mysterious,' he said. 'They talked to the driver. He was at Whitestone Farm as agreed. He'd been told to wait but on no account ring the bell, but he couldn't see anyone near or far. He waited a good long while, then he slowly drove further down the road, but there was no one there either. So he drove home in the end, without a customer and pretty annoyed. He had phoned the office to say it must have been a mistake.'

Everyone looked at each other. Suddenly the atmosphere was tense. There was fear in the air.

'So, first of all let's walk along the path to Whitestone Farm,' decided Leslie. 'She might have fallen, or had an attack of dizziness.... She's so old!' She looked at the two men. 'Neither of you considered accompanying an old woman in the middle of the night? Or talking her out of it?'

'Can't talk Fiona out of anythin',' growled Chad, quite correctly.

Colin ran a hand through his hair. He looked sheepish. 'Right,' he said. 'Of course I should have walked with her. It was…late, and I think…I didn't think it was my responsibility. And I was annoyed…*everyone* was annoyed with her…' He broke off uncertainly.

Leslie did not pursue it. He was right. Everyone had been mad with Fiona. She more than any of them—so mad that she had gone home without waiting for her grandmother.

'Gwen, please try one more time to reach Dave. Maybe he knows something. If he still doesn't reply, I'll go and find him.' Leslie turned to go. 'Who's going to come and help search the road?'

Colin and Jennifer joined her, Jennifer taking the dogs along. The narrow road was peaceful in the sunlight. It was lined with six-foot-high hedges which shone in all the colours of autumn. A few fat blackberries still hung between the branches. A calm October Sunday that could almost be late summer… In the distance the blue sea glistened.

The gate to the neighbouring farm appeared a little way ahead. A footpath led across the farm along the side of wide sheep pastures. The road made a sharp bend to the right and then led downhill in a gentle curve before disappearing into a copse of ferns, bushes and tall trees which still had their leaves on. The sun only penetrated parts of it. The light was dim and bathed everything in a soft green. A narrow bridge made of stone led over a deep, wooded gorge. This dry autumn there was only a trickle of water in the stream below. After the bridge the road corkscrewed slowly up the opposite hill.

At night it must be pitch black here. At least it was almost impossible to get lost, because you could not leave the road. And you were protected from the gorge by the walls. Someone completely drunk might still manage to fall to their death, but Fiona had been sober as a judge, as always.

A deep fear was creeping up on Leslie. Something here was just not right.

They walked to Whitestone Farm and then a little farther, peering into the roadside bushes and letting their gaze wander over the pastures behind them. Wotan and Cal would leap on ahead happily and come back, not appearing to sense anything at all unusual.

'Could the dogs follow a scent?' asked Leslie. 'For example, if we gave them something Fiona had worn?'

Jennifer shook her head. 'A dog has to be trained for that. The two of them wouldn't know what to do.'

Frustrated, they went back to the farm. Whatever had happened to Fiona, there was no trace of her on the path she had wanted to take.

At the gate to the farm Gwen was waiting for them. She had tried to call Dave Tanner a number of times. 'He just doesn't answer his phone,' she said, 'it's as if he's been swallowed up by the earth!'

'Just like my grandmother,' replied Leslie and pulled her car key from her trouser pocket. 'So I'm going to drive over to him. Do you want to come, Gwen?'

Gwen hummed and hawed, in the end deciding against it. Leslie thought it typical of her friend: she never took the initiative. She didn't risk things. This had led to a life where little happened, and for long periods nothing at all.

Leslie had Gwen give her the address, and was soon sitting in her car again. Still plagued by a headache and driving along the sunlit country road she felt an intense need to call Stephen, to tell him that something terrible had happened, to let him console her and give her advice, to hear his warm voice which had always had a calming effect on her. But then she forbade herself this sudden weakness. Stephen was no longer the man at her side. And also: nothing terrible had happened.

At least, there was as yet no reason to think so.

5

DAVE TANNER LIVED in the town centre, only a few steps away from the pedestrian zone with all its department stores and small shops, right by the Market Hall and the Friarage School where he gave his lessons. Friargate Road was lined with two rows of terraced houses of red brick and white-painted front doors. Most of the houses lay a little lower than the road and were accessed via downward-leading steps, giving a certain dark, subterranean feel to them.

When Leslie stopped and got out of her car, parked just behind Dave Tanner's bucket of rust, she could smell the sea in the light wind, and that blew away some of the trepidation in her. You could not see the water from here, but it still conveyed a sense of freshness and purity and managed to make even this monotonous road something special.

She looked at the houses. She noticed that signs had been put up in almost all the front gardens and on the walls saying that ball games were prohibited on this road. It seemed that so many windowpanes had been broken already, no doubt because the school was nearby, that the residents were unanimously trying to eliminate this constant danger.

In the house where Dave Tanner lived, a faded yellow curtain twitched almost imperceptibly on the ground floor. Leslie guessed that she was already being watched. A little further up on the other side of the road a young woman rushed out of her house with a child on her arm. She looked around nervously before heading towards St Helen's Square and the pedestrian zone. She threw Leslie a suspicious glance.

Either, thought Leslie, unknown people are rarely seen in this street or my relatively new car makes me look very exotic.

She had just decided to ring the bell when she saw a figure approaching out of the corner of her eye. She turned around.

Dave Tanner came strolling up the street. He was quite relaxed, or at least gave the impression of being so. When he saw Leslie, he started to walk faster.

'Well, well,' he said, when he reached her, 'what gives me the honour of your visit today? Are you here to represent the Beckett family and examine my living conditions and social milieu?'

As he had not greeted her, Leslie also omitted to wish him a good morning. She asked him directly: 'Why don't you answer Gwen's calls?'

He looked at her in surprise, then he suddenly laughed. 'That's why you came? To ask me that?'

'No. Actually I'm looking for my grandmother. Fiona Barnes.'

This was just as astonishing to him. 'Here? At my place?'

'Did you drive straight here yesterday evening?'

He looked amused. 'Is this an interrogation?'

'Just a question.'

'Yes, I drove straight here. I have no idea where your grandmother is, and frankly, meeting her is the last thing I want to do.' He gestured to the front door. 'We needn't talk on the street. Would you like a coffee?'

Leslie had asked Gwen for a coffee, but now she realised that she had not found time to drink it. It was almost two in the afternoon, and she had not eaten or drunk anything yet all day. She felt a little wobbly on her feet and her stomach gave signs of being a little upset.

'A coffee would be great,' she said gratefully.

Dave went down the steps to the front door ahead of her. Leslie could now clearly see the outline of a person behind the curtain. Dave had seen it too.

'My landlady,' he explained. 'She takes an active interest in other people's lives—to put a positive spin on it.' He opened the door. 'Please. Come in.'

Leslie stepped into the dark narrow hall and almost collided with an elderly woman who was just coming out of the living room: the landlady. She examined Leslie from head to foot.

'Well?' she said. 'A visitor?'

Leslie held out her hand. 'I'm Dr Leslie Cramer. Mr Tanner and I need to have a quick chat about something.'

'Willerton,' said the landlady. 'It's my house. I rent out an upstairs room, since my husband is no longer around.'

Dave squeezed past the two women to get to the stairs. 'Watch the stairs, Dr Cramer,' he said. 'They're worn and steep, and it's rather dingy.'

'Find a room somewhere else if you think it's lousy here!' exclaimed an offended Mrs Willerton.

Leslie followed Dave up the stairs, which were indeed a hazard to life and limb. At the top Dave opened a door. 'I'm afraid I have to invite you into my bedroom,' he said. 'It's the only room at my disposal.'

The room was complete chaos. There was a wardrobe, but whatever Tanner used it for, it was not for his clothes. Trousers and sweaters lay strewn over the backs of chairs and armchairs and in piles on the floor. The bed was un-made and the sheets rumpled. There was a bottle of min-eral water next to the bed. The whole of the small table in the corner was covered in crumpled newspapers that had obviously been much read. Leslie spied a lipstick on the windowsill and scrunched-up black tights under the chair at the table. She was surprised to find signs that Gwen had often stayed the night, but she said to herself that Gwen was obviously not quite the vestal virgin her aura suggested. Of course she had the right to have fun here with her fiancé. Anything else would not be normal. And yet she had not thought that Gwen used lipstick—she had never seen her made-up in fact, and nor had she sus-pected Gwen would use ultra-thin tights. But who was to know, maybe Gwen became a vamp when she went out with Dave and the puzzle of the two wildly different peo-ple had its solution here: in sex. Maybe they had crazy, fantastic, heavenly sex.

Although that was, as Leslie had to admit, extremely hard for anyone who knew Gwen to imagine.

Dave brushed a few T-shirts off a chair. 'Please. Sit down. I'll make us coffee.'

At a sink in a kind of small wet room by the door, he ran water into a kettle and then turned it on. He took a jar from the cupboard—instant coffee, thought Leslie in res-ignation, I feared as much—and spooned the brown pow-der into two cups. He pushed the newspapers to the side and placed a little bowl with powdered milk and sugar cubes on the table.

'Voilà!' he said. 'Everything's ready!'

'You've been out walking already?' asked Leslie.

He nodded. 'The weather is too nice to spend the whole day sitting in this room, don't you think?'

'Did you go to bed straight away yesterday? I mean, after everything that happened, you must have been a little agitated.'

'No. I wasn't too worked up. And yes, I went straight to bed.' He brought over the boiling water and filled their cups. 'Dr Cramer, what's this all about? You're asking again and again what I did last night. Why? What's up with your grandmother? And what's it got to do with me?'

'I drove back to her flat last night without her. I was angry with her and had no wish to talk to her. She stayed on the Beckett farm for a good while, and then she asked Colin Brankley to order a cab for her, to pick her up at a farm fifteen minutes' walk from the Beckett farm. She was over-excited, Colin says, and wanted to have a walk. The cabbie didn't find anyone at the agreed meeting place, circled around for a while and then drove back to Scarborough. Fiona neither showed up at her flat nor back at the Beckett farm. She just disappeared, and I'm pretty worried.'

'Naturally. But why do you think I might know where she is?'

Leslie took a sip of coffee and burnt her tongue. An awful brew. She reached for the sugar, although she did not usually take any.

'I just hoped you might know something. Fiona might have gone looking for you, because she had acted so badly to you. I was just…looking for answers.'

'Unfortunately I really have no idea where she could be,' said Dave.

And why should he lie to me, thought Leslie. She felt tired and scared. Nevertheless something in her refused to really consider that anything serious could have happened to her grandmother. Fiona was not the kind of person something could happen to. But then she asked herself if there was a kind of person nothing happened to? Wasn't that what was so eerie about fate, that anything could happen to anyone anywhere?

She looked around the room and wondered how a grown man could live like this. A student, yes, but a man in his forties? What had gone wrong in Dave Tanner's life? His eyes were restless, perhaps even a little despairing. He hated this room, and did nothing to make it nicer. On the contrary, he had let it become a complete tip. The room embodied his anger at his life—at the poor, run-down terraced house and his intrusive landlady, at his car which was always letting him down and finally also at his job which did not even start to satisfy or fulfil him. He seemed intelligent and educated to her—why had he ended up in this hole of a room under the same roof as that awful woman?

'I think it must have been about half-eight yesterday evening, when I left the Beckett farm,' said Dave. 'I reckon I was here by about nine. I drank a little wine and then went to bed. I didn't see or talk to Fiona Barnes. That's all that happened.'

'You must have been pretty mad.'

'I was mad, because she had attacked me in front of everyone. Because she ruined the evening. Even if she had never expressed them that directly till then, her opinions about me were not exactly a surprise. I had always felt her suspicion.'

'She looks after Gwen.'

'With what right?'

'What do you mean?' asked Leslie surprised.

He stirred his coffee so violently that the coffee splashed over the side. 'What I said. With what right? She's not

Gwen's mother or grandmother. She's not kin. Why does she feel called to meddle in Gwen's life?'

'She's been friends with Gwen's father forever. Gwen is very attached to her—has always seen her as a second mother. So Fiona feels responsible. And she's suspicious.'

'Why?'

Leslie chose her words carefully. 'I suppose you know you are a rather attractive man, Dave. And you probably don't have any difficulty in attracting young pretty women. So why Gwen? She's…'

He looked at her, waiting for her continue. 'Yes?'

'She's not exactly a beauty,' said Leslie. 'That wouldn't necessarily be a problem, if she was witty and a sparkling conversationalist. Or if she had a remarkable intelligence, or a fascinating self-confidence, great ambition, cleverness…something. But she's shy, rather naive and not very…not very interesting. My grandmother doesn't understand what attracts you to her.'

'Your grandmother understands it all perfectly. The farm. All those acres of wonderful land that will be Gwen's in the not too distant future. And she says quite clearly that I'm only interested in that. In the property.'

'And is she right?' asked Leslie, challenging him.

'How do you mean?' replied Dave.

'I don't want to be rude, but…'

'No, do.'

'OK. I can't imagine that you're satisfied with the life you lead here. I think you're looking for an opportunity to escape all this.' She made a gesture that took in the room's chaos. 'You are a man who makes a strong impression on women, but you have nothing to offer them, and that limits your options of marrying someone better off quite considerably. A woman of your age would be horrified to see this room. Young women would be less shocked, but they tend not to own anything and so can't help you out of your mess. From that perspective, Gwen is an extraordinary piece of luck—and moreover, one that you're not going to let slip away, as you won't be given another one like it any time soon, if ever.'

He listened to her in silence. If her words annoyed him, his face did not betray it. He gave the impression of being calm.

'I'm listening,' he said when she paused. 'Carry on, now you've started.'

'Gwen is lonely,' continued Leslie, feeling surer of herself. 'In spite of her love for her father she feels so alone. She senses that her life, as she leads it now, doesn't have a future. She is dreaming of a prince and would be prepared to make a lot of compromises, if only she could find one to whisk her up onto his horse and ride into the future with her. She would throw caution to the wind and ignore everything that might make other women hold back.'

'And that would be?'

'Your circumstances. That you lodge in this room. Your job, which really can only be called a *job*, and not a *career*. Your car, which threatens to give up the ghost at any moment. You're no longer a student. Why do you live like this?'

'Maybe I like it.'

'I don't believe that.'

'But you don't know.'

'Then let me re-phrase my question,' said Leslie. 'If your life is fine and dandy, and if Fiona is wrong and it's not the Beckett farm that attracts you to Gwen, then what is it? What do you like about Gwen? Why do you love her?'

'Why do you love your husband?'

Leslie flinched, and to her annoyance she felt her cheeks were burning. 'I'm divorced,' she said.

'Why? What went wrong?'

She slammed down her coffee cup, which she had just put to her lips. Now she had a brown puddle in front of her. 'That's none of your business,' she said brusquely.

He remained calm. 'True. And nor is it your business, or Fiona Barnes', what Gwen and I feel. When people interrogate me I feel just the same as you felt just now at my question. It's nobody's business. And one more thing.' His voice had taken on a dangerous edge. 'You should let Gwen lead her own life. All of you. Let her finally grow up. Let her make her own decisions. In the worst case: the wrong decisions. The wrong man. Or whatever. But stop trying to make her happy. You're not helping her get over her lack of experience and inability to deal with life—you should all think about that!'

She took a deep breath. 'You egged me on to be impolite, Mr Tanner.'

'Yes. So that you finally understand.'

She was angry, but she was not sure what she should be angry about. She felt like he was treating her like a schoolgirl, telling her off, but she also realised that he was right. Fiona and she had meddled in what was not their business. They were treating Gwen like a little girl and Dave like some con artist. It had only caused confusion and unhappiness. Dave had left his own engagement party early, Gwen was sitting at home bawling her eyes out, and Fiona seemed to have disappeared from the face of the earth. In all, a pretty crushing set of results for the weekend.

The thought of Fiona brought Leslie back to the really pressing issue. She finished her coffee quickly, leaving just a pile of undissolved sugar and coffee powder at the bottom. She stood up.

'I didn't want to offend you,' she said, 'and thanks for the coffee. But now I really have to look for my grandmother. I'm afraid that if she hasn't appeared by this evening, I'll have to inform the police.'

He stood up too.

'Not a bad idea,' he said. 'But maybe she's already home now, waiting for you.'

Leslie doubted that somehow. She felt her way down the steep dark stairs. The landlady was standing in the hall at the bottom of the stairs, wiping the frame of a mirror with a cloth. It was obvious that she had tried to hear every word spoken upstairs.

How could Dave put up with her, thought Leslie, and she immediately knew the answer: he could not. He is a deeply unhappy person.

Dave went down to her car with her. Getting in, she said, 'Do me a favour would you, and call Gwen? What happened yesterday isn't her fault. Don't take this as further meddling—just a friend's request.'

'Let's see,' he said vaguely.

Driving off she looked in her rear-view mirror, but he was not watching her. He had turned around immediately and gone back inside. With a little shudder Leslie imagined what a long, quiet Sunday in that wretched room must be like. She would not have wanted to swap places with Tanner.

Fiona's flat was as empty as it had been that morning. There was no sign that anyone had been here in the meantime. Leslie felt ravenously hungry. She got a frozen meatloaf out of the freezer and put it in the microwave. Then she called the Beckett farm, to see if there was any news, but Chad told her he had not heard anything.

'I'll wait until five,' said Leslie. 'Then I'm calling the police.'

'Right,' said Chad.

She sat down by the living room window to eat and looked at the sun-drenched bay, the beach full of walkers and of dogs playing crazily, the harbour, the castle above it. After only a few mouthfuls, it felt like her stomach was in a knot, although a few minutes earlier she had thought she would faint for hunger. The growing feeling of foreboding was almost overpowering, and she could only hope that it came from her overwrought state and was unfounded.

Maybe Fiona in her anger had wanted to be awkward, and had taken a room in a hotel, to let them all stew.

Would she do that to me? Leslie wondered.

She knew the answer, because she knew the woman who had raised her only too well. Fiona did not care too much about other people, not even her own granddaughter.

If she felt like disappearing for a bit, she would not worry about the effect it would have on her only relative and on her friends.

6

THE GORGE ON the edge of a pasture up by Staintondale was bathed in a blinding light. The hurriedly erected spotlights lit the scene in a horrific, unsparing clarity. People, police cordons, cars. Somewhere further off sheep were bleating.

Detective Inspector Valerie Almond had been called away from a family party. She hated her job in moments like this. Without any gentle transition, she had been taken from the warm, cheery atmosphere of a living room full of people she loved and saw much too infrequently, and plonked in this dark pasture. Her colleague had picked her up, as she had been out without her car. She was wearing a suit and stiletto heals, not the most suitable attire in which to traipse along a grassy verge towards a cliff. To make things worse, it was dark and a cold wind was blowing inland from the sea.

'Where's the woman who found her?' she asked.

Sergeant Reek, who was accompanying her, led a figure out from the shadow of a parked car and into the spot-lit area. A young woman, Valerie guessed she was not yet twenty-five. She was wearing jeans, wellies and a thick sweater. She looked frighteningly pale and shocked.

'You are...?' Valerie asked.

'Paula Foster, Inspector. I live down there on the Trevor farm.' She made a vague gesture downwards into the night.

'I'm working there for three months, as an intern. I'm studying agriculture.'

'And what time was it when you came here?' asked Valerie. 'And why?'

'Around nine. I wanted to take a look at one of the sheep,' Paula replied.

'What was the matter with it?'

'It's had a puss-filled wound on its leg for two days now. I spray the wound in the morning and evening with a disinfecting spray. Normally I'm here around six o'clock.'

'Why only nine today?'

Paula lowered her head. 'My boyfriend was here,' she said quietly, 'and somehow…we lost track of the time.'

Valerie did not think that was something she needed to be ashamed of.

'I understand. And how did you know the sheep would be here? The animals are spread over a massive grazing area.'

'Yes, but there's a shed over there.' Again she gestured into the impenetrable darkness beyond the cordons. 'Not far, but you can't see it now. We're keeping the injured sheep in there for now. But today…'

'Yes?'

Paula Foster was the personification of a bad conscience.

'When I got here, the door was open. I probably didn't close it properly this morning. I was all excited and rushing, because my boyfriend was coming. And then I saw the sheep was gone.'

'And so you went looking for it?'

'Yes. I had a torch with me, and I shone it in wider and wider circles, starting from the shed. And then I heard it. From down there in the gorge.'

She paused. Her lips were trembling lightly. 'I heard it bleating quietly,' she continued, 'and knew that it had slipped down the slope and couldn't make it up on its own.'

'So you climbed down into the gorge,' deduced Valerie.

'Yes, the slope is pretty steep, but it's only earth and leaves. It wasn't hard to get down.'

'And then you saw the dead woman.'

Paula went even paler. She had difficulty in continuing. 'I almost slipped down onto her. I...I was scared to death, Inspector. A dead woman...right at my feet. I was stunned...' She put both her hands to her head. She was obviously still stunned.

Valerie felt for her. A terrible situation: a dark autumn evening, a desolate place, a terribly mutilated corpse at the bottom of a gorge. And a young woman who was only expecting to find a lost sheep. She tried to go on as gently as she could, to give the woman time to gather herself.

'Did you call the police immediately?'

'First of all, I climbed back up as fast as I could,' said Paula. 'I might...I might have been screaming, I'm not sure. Once I got to the top, I wanted to call, but I didn't have reception. It's bad around here. I ran towards the main road, and somewhere there I got a weak connection.'

'Then you waited for us? Or did you go down again, to look for the sheep?'

'I went back down,' said Paula. 'But I couldn't find the sheep. I'm afraid it's gone further up the gorge. Probably I did scream, and it got scared. And now with these lights, and all these people...there's no way it'll come back now. I have to go and find it.'

'I understand,' said Valerie. She turned to Sergeant Reek. 'Reek, can you climb down there with Miss Foster and help her to find the sheep. I don't want her wandering around on her own.'

Reek's face expressed anything but enthusiasm, but he did not dare contradict her. He and Paula were about to start clambering down, when Valerie thought of one more thing.

'Miss Foster, you said you come here in the morning and evening. So you were in the shed this morning?'

Paula stopped. 'Yes around six o'clock.'

'And you didn't notice anything? Something different to usual... Maybe the animal was agitated, something like that?'

'No. Everything was just the same as always. It was still dark of course. Even if someone had been around'—she swallowed, as the unpleasant idea dawned on her—'then I wouldn't have seen them.'

'Right. Sergeant Reek will take down your details. We'll have to talk to you again.' With that Valerie ended the conversation and started down into the gorge herself, a risky undertaking with her completely unsuitable footwear, and she cursed more than once. At the bottom she found the doctor. He had been squatting down by the body of the woman. It lay deep in the leaves. He straightened up.

'Compelling conclusions, Doctor?' asked Valerie.

'Nothing which would really help,' said the doctor. 'Female corpse, between seventy-five and eighty-five years old. She was beaten to death with, I think, a stone at least as big as a fist, with which she was hit more or less at random on her temples and the back of her head, at least twelve times. She must have fallen unconscious quickly, but the perpetrator didn't stop working her over. I'm assuming she died of a brain haemorrhage.'

'Time of death?'

'Roughly fourteen hours ago, so around eight this morning. Before that she lay unconscious for at least eight hours. From what I've been able to ascertain so far, she wasn't yet dead when her murderer left her. The post mortem will tell us more, but I would guess that the crime was committed between ten p.m. and midnight.'

'Anything thrown up by forensics? Where she was found—is it the scene of the crime?'

'From what I gather, she was attacked up at the top of the gorge. Then she rolled down here. The perpetrator apparently didn't follow her down.'

Valerie chewed on her lower lip.

'At first sight, there seems to be a certain similarity to Amy Mills' case.'

The doctor had been thinking about this too. 'Both were battered to death, although in different ways. Amy Mills' head was rammed again and again into a wall, while this woman's skull was smashed in with a rock. In both cases great brutality and strength were used. But major differences are also blatantly obvious…'

Valerie knew what he was about to say. 'The extreme difference in the victims' age. And then of course the scenes of the crime.'

'It's not unusual for a perpetrator to be lurking in a particularly empty part of a city for a possible victim,' said the doctor. 'But who hangs around on a godforsaken dale expecting someone to come along?'

Valerie thought about it. Of course, someone might have been waiting for Paula Foster. She was not much older than Amy Mills, and she often came here. If she was meant to be the actual victim, then the old woman's murder happened by accident. She was at the wrong place at the wrong time and literally ran into the waiting killer. But then there was the question of why the perpetrator would have been waiting for Paula here at night. And what was an old lady doing at night on a narrow, unlit farm footpath between a gorge and a field, almost a mile from the main road, when she was—as far as Valerie could see—well dressed, even dressed for a special occasion? What was she looking for?

Or was she the intended victim from the start? Had the perpetrator brought her here and then set about executing her?

A young policeman approached. He held a handbag in his plastic-gloved hands.

'It got caught in a tree on the slope,' he said. 'It's probably the victim's bag. According to her cards, diary and what have you, the owner is a Fiona Barnes, née Swales, born on 29th July 1929 in London. Resident in Scarborough. There's a photo which seems to be of the victim.'

'Fiona Barnes,' repeated Valerie. 'Seventy-nine years old.' She thought of the young Amy Mills. Was there any connection?

'And one more thing,' said the enthusiastic young officer. He was new, trying to make a name for himself. 'I phoned the station in Scarborough. Around 17:20 this afternoon a Fiona Barnes was reported missing. By her granddaughter.'

'Well done,' Valerie praised him. She wrapped both her arms around her freezing body. The wind blew ever colder, it swept across the moor and whistled down into the gorge.

Right after being found, the corpse already had a name. That was quicker and easier than usual. It often took weeks to find out the dead person's identity. But Valerie was wary of a premature optimism. Amy Mills had been identified quickly too, but that had not helped one jot.

'Then I'd like to see the woman's granddaughter right away,' she said.

The young officer beamed as he realised he would get to drive his boss. Sergeant Reek was tramping around somewhere out there in the dark looking for an injured sheep.

Sometimes you just got lucky.

Monday, 13th October

1

'ARE YOU AWAKE?' whispered Jennifer. She poked her head through the door of Gwen's room. 'I saw the light was on.'

Gwen was not in her bed. She had not even got undressed. She was sitting in a chair at the window, staring into the pitch-black night that still hung over the land. It was half past four in the morning. As yet, nothing announced the day which was about to begin.

Cal and Wotan squeezed past Jennifer, bounded over to Gwen and licked her hands. Lost in her thoughts, Gwen ruffled their big heads.

'Come in,' she said. 'I haven't slept a wink.'

'Me neither,' replied Jennifer, coming into the bedroom and closing the door quietly and firmly behind her.

They were all in shock. Everyone on the farm was — since Leslie's call late last night. After a police officer had visited Leslie.

Chad had disappeared into his room without a word, bolting the door behind him.

Colin had paced back and forth between living room and kitchen.

'Impossible,' he said again and again, 'that can't be!'

Gwen and Jennifer had sat motionless on the sofa, stunned and speechless.

Fiona was dead. Brutally murdered. At the edge of a meadow, not all that far from the Beckett farm, but far from the path Fiona had wanted to take on Saturday night. No one knew how she had got there.

Long past midnight everyone had gone to bed, although obviously no one had managed to sleep.

'I wanted to talk to you about something,' said Jennifer. She seemed tense, but that didn't surprise Gwen, whose nerves were highly strung. Her eyelids were heavy with exhaustion, but she was wide awake. She was sweating and shivering simultaneously. It was like the flu, only much, much worse.

'Yes?'

Jennifer sat down on the bed. 'I've been thinking,' she started cautiously. 'It might seem strange to you that I've been worrying about this, now of all times, but…I know you feel terrible and…'

Gwen felt like she had a mouth full of cotton wool. It was hard to speak. 'I can't believe it,' she said with some effort. 'It's just…like a bad dream. Fiona was always… unbreakable. Strong. She was…' Gwen looked to find the right words to describe what Fiona had been to her, but she did not find them. Finally she said, 'She was always there. She was always there and it felt like she'd always be there. That gave so much…security.'

'I know,' said Jennifer gently. She stroked Gwen's arm briefly. 'I know what she meant to you. I know too that you want to be left in peace, but we have to talk about something. It's important.'

'It is?' asked Gwen indifferently.

'Today the police will come and question us all about Saturday night,' said Jennifer. 'They'll want to know about every little thing. And we should think about what we'll tell them.'

In spite of her lethargy, Gwen was annoyed. 'Why? We can just tell them what happened.'

Jennifer spoke slowly, choosing her words carefully. 'The problem is the fight between Fiona and Dave. It was a big one.'

'Yes, but…'

'The police will latch onto it. Look: Fiona attacks Dave so viciously that he leaves the house angrily, even though the evening meal is his engagement party. A few hours later she's dead. Murdered. They'll put two and two together.'

Gwen sat up straight. 'You mean…'

'They are bound to suspect Dave first of all. How do we know whether he drove straight home? He could also have hung around outside. He could have intercepted Fiona as she walked towards Whitestone Farm.'

'But that's ridiculous! Jennifer—I know Dave! He'd never do such a thing. Never!'

'I'm just saying what the police will think,' stressed Jennifer. 'Dave had a motive, you see? He could have killed her in the heat of the moment, out of anger. He might have been scared that Fiona would ruin all your plans by constantly sowing doubts in your mind. She was in the way of all that he hoped for. He certainly would have had his reasons for wanting to silence her for ever!'

'The way you're talking—it's as if you've already decided he's the perpetrator.'

'Rubbish. But you and he, the two of you must be prepared for the fact that the police will confront the two of you with these suspicions.'

'The two of us?'

'They could suspect you too,' said Jennifer slowly.

Gwen stared at her in astonishment. 'Me?'

'Well, you were of course angry with Fiona too. And you were afraid she could destroy your dreams for the future. You still don't know whether Dave might not be so sour that he never turns up again!'

'But, Jennifer, that's no reason for me to go and…that's completely crazy!'

'What did you do after Dave left?' asked Jennifer.

Gwen looked at her numbly. Her friend's train of thought paralysed her. 'You know. We both sat here in my room. I was crying. You were here for me.'

'But then, later, I went for a walk with the dogs. You didn't want to come with me.'

'No, but…'

'Listen, Gwen, it's just a suggestion. You don't have to accept it, but…why don't we just say you went with me? We took the dogs for a walk together. Then you'd have an alibi for the crucial time and wouldn't have to defend yourself against any insinuations.'

'I don't need an alibi!' said Gwen, horrified.

'No, but it won't do any harm to have one.' Jennifer got up, turning towards the door. 'You can think about it. I'm going out with Cal and Wotan. When I get back, you tell me what you've decided. If you want to do it, then we should just agree on our story, so you know exactly where we were walking at the time in question.'

She opened the door and stepped out into the hall. 'All right?'

Gwen did not look all right. 'Yes,' she said nevertheless. 'I understand. I'll think about it, Jennifer.'

She stared at the door closing behind her friend and suddenly thought: and Jennifer would not have to worry any more, either.

2

'Do you know this woman?' asked DI Valerie Almond and held a photo up in front of Dave Tanner's face. Not yet completely awake, he nodded.

'Yes.'

'Who is she?'

'Fiona Barnes. I only know her a little.'

'And do you know this woman?' Another photo.

'I don't know her personally, just from the papers. It's Amy Mills, the girl who was murdered here in July.'

'Fiona Barnes was found murdered yesterday in Staintondale,' said Valerie.

Thunderstruck, he felt all the colour drain from his face. 'What?'

'She was killed with a rock. In some ways the murder is similar to that of Amy Mills.'

He had sat down on a chair. Now he stood up. He ran a hand down his face. 'Good lord,' he said.

To Valerie, he seemed thoroughly shaken.

But in the course of her career she had seen and experienced too much to take anything at face value. Dave Tanner might really be completely shocked and surprised, but it could just as easily be a show he was putting on. Valerie would reserve judgment.

She had turned up at Dave's landlady's property with a rather sleep-deprived Sergeant Reek. He had spent half the night looking for the sheep, found it in the end and dragged it back out of the gorge. She asked to speak to Mr Tanner. The name Tanner had electrified her the previous evening when she had given Leslie Cramer the sad news of her grandmother's death and carried out a cautious first conversation with her. Like Amy Mills' employer Mrs Gardner, Tanner gave language classes at the Friarage School, and now here he was being mentioned in connection with a murder for a second time.

It could be the connection they needed. In any case, at the moment it was the only connection between the two immensely different women.

Dave Tanner had still been in bed when the landlady knocked on his door and told him the police were there. She had snorted with excitement. Tanner had been surprised, but was prepared to talk then and there. He had pulled on a pair of jeans and a jumper and shown the officers into his room. He offered them coffee, which they declined. Valerie had taken a good look at him. His puffy eyes told her that he drank too much, but that did not make him any more or less of a suspect. Valerie was annoyed that she had not investigated him right after talking to Mrs Gardner. She had tracked down Mrs Gardner's ex-husband first. He had turned out to be a harmless fellow and, moreover, he could prove where he had been at the time of Amy Mills' murder: on holiday in Tenerife. The hotel he named confirmed his visit.

'We've spoken to Dr Leslie Cramer, Fiona Barnes' granddaughter,' said Valerie. 'According to her statement, you had a very heated argument with Mrs Barnes last Saturday evening.'

'It wasn't an argument. Mrs Barnes attacked me—you

no doubt already know what she said. In the end, I'd had enough and I left. That was all.'

'Dr Cramer said that by your own account you drove straight back here and went to bed.'

'That's right.'

'Witnesses?'

'No.'

'Your landlady?'

'She was watching TV. She didn't hear me come back.'

'How do you know?'

'Because *when* she does, she always jumps out and intercepts me.'

'Where were you on 16th July of this year? In the evening?'

'I…had a date.'

'You know that just like that? I wouldn't spontaneously know what I had done three months ago.'

He looked at her with hostility.

He is starting to realise that his situation is rather precarious, thought Valerie.

'I met my fiancée for the first time on 16th July. That's why I mentioned a *date*, and why the date is fixed in my head.'

Valerie looked in her files. 'Your fiancée—Miss Gwendolyn Beckett, is that right?'

'Absolutely.'

'Where did you meet your fiancée?'

'In Friarage School. I don't teach on that day, but I had gone over to collect some files that I had left there. Gwen Beckett was attending a course there. It was tipping it down when she was about to leave, so I offered to drive her home, and did.'

'All right. What time was that?'

'We drove off around six. I was at home by half eight.'

'That's early.'

'We got to her farm at around half six. But we sat in the car talking for over an hour. She told me about her life, I told her about mine. Then I drove back.'

'You were here at home then? On your own?'

'Yes.'

'Can your landlady confirm that?'

He ran a hand through his hair helplessly. 'No idea. I mean, unless the 16th July was a special day for her too, I doubt she'll remember whether I was at home that evening or not. But perhaps you can explain what this is—'

'Did you meet Mrs Fiona Barnes for the first time last Saturday?' Valerie changed the topic abruptly. 'Or did you know her already?'

'I knew her. I had met her a couple of times on the farm, when I was picking up Gwen. She invited Gwen and me to her place once. She's a friend of Gwen's father.'

'Was there ever any conflict between you on those occasions?'

'No.'

'She never let show that she mistrusted you?'

'She showed that she didn't like me. She was cool and distant and always looked at me quite aggressively. But I really didn't care.'

'And the evening before last it started to bother you?'

'She laid into me without holding back at all. Yes, it bothered me, that's why I went. But I didn't kill her. God! I wasn't that bothered by the old lady and what she thought!'

Valerie let her gaze drift around the room. Like every other visitor to Dave Tanner's room, she was surprised by the mess, the tattiness and unmistakable signs of poverty. Dave Tanner's language, his bearing and behaviour all pointed to a good upbringing and education, and to a family background that must have been upper middle class. Tanner did not belong in this house, in this room. Almost inevitably Valerie came to the same suspicion which Fiona Barnes and Leslie Cramer had not been able to ignore. The farm which Gwen Beckett would soon inherit—wouldn't it be a life-saver for Dave Tanner? How scared was he that Fiona Barnes' venomous comments, which perhaps hit the nail squarely on the head, would dissuade Gwen from marrying him as planned? He might have thought his future livelihood depended on silencing the old woman by any means necessary?

Valerie changed tack once more.

'You knew that your colleague Mrs Gardner employed a young woman to look after her daughter when she taught?'

'Yes. She had mentioned it.' Tanner spoke carefully now, although you could sense that he was struggling to keep calm. Valerie could see that he had seen through her attempt to confuse him with the abrupt jumps from topic to topic. 'But I didn't know her name. I didn't know the girl herself.'

'You knew where Mrs Gardner lived?'

'No, we had very little to do with one another.'

'But you could have found out her address via the school office at any time, of course.'

'I could have. But I didn't. There was no reason to.'

Valerie looked around the room again, with an obvious scorn which Tanner could not help but see.

'Mr Tanner, I think I'm right to assume that your financial circumstances are not all that rosy. You have no other income apart from your earnings from the language classes?'

'No, I don't.'

'So you just about get by, I suppose.'

'Yes.'

Valerie let the answer hang in the air. She got up. 'That will be all for now, Mr Tanner. We will most certainly have further questions for you. You don't have any plans to travel in the near future, do you?'

'No.'

'Good. We'll be in touch.' Valerie and Sergeant Reek left the room. In the hall they bumped into the landlady.

'And?' she asked breathlessly. 'Has he done something?'

'We just had a few routine questions,' replied Valerie. 'Tell me, you don't know what time Mr Tanner came home on Saturday evening?'

Mrs Willerton regretted that she really did not know. 'I nodded off in front of the telly,' she explained. 'When I woke up, it was almost midnight. I don't know if Mr Tanner was home or not.'

Valerie found that regrettable too. A landlady as curious and nosy as Mrs Willerton was a gift to any investigating officer. Such people knew only too well the details of the lives of everyone around them. It seemed like a cruel trick of fate that Mrs Willerton had slept through that crucial Saturday evening.

'Can you remember 16th July of this year?' asked Valerie.

You could see the cogs in the landlady's brain turning. '16th July you said? 16th July?'

'That was the day Amy Mills was murdered. You must have heard about the case.'

The landlady's eyes opened wide. 'Was Mr Tanner involved in that?' she whispered in horror.

'There is no evidence to suggest that at present,' said Valerie, playing things down.

'You will want to know if he was home that evening,' deduced Mrs Willerton. She had a despairing look. 'No idea. Oh, good Lord, I don't know!'

'Not a problem.' Valerie smiled at her. 'It's three months ago. It's not surprising that you can't remember such details.'

'I'll call you if anything springs to mind,' promised Mrs Willerton. Reek handed her his card. The woman took it, her hand shaking.

Valerie did not count on anything. Mrs Willerton was old, lonely and bored. She would probably phone in with information, but it would have to be considered with the utmost scepticism. She might not lie, but she would dress events and incidents up in a way that strained common ideas of truth. She longed for attention, and to be taken seriously. Tanner would be her victim.

Valerie and Reek stepped out onto the street. It was a glorious day once again, promising to be really warm.

'Now what?' asked Reek.

Valerie glanced at her watch. 'The Beckett farm,' she said.

3

SHE STARED AT the phone, waiting for it to ring, and knowing at the same time that it was fatal to wait for a phone to ring. She listened to the sounds of the flat: the quiet hum of the fridge in the kitchen, the ticking of a clock, the dripping of a tap that was not properly turned off. Someone walked around upstairs. Now and then a floorboard creaked. Outside the late summer presented itself in all its glory once more, spilling its light on the waves, causing the leaves on the trees of the Esplanade Gardens to catch flame. The sky was a crystal-clear blue. That morning on the radio they had said you should take full advantage of the day, rain and fog were coming.

Leslie tried to understand that her grandmother was dead.

That her grandmother would never come home to her flat.

That everything Leslie saw around about, all the familiar furniture, the pictures on the walls, the curtains, a jumper thrown carelessly onto an armchair, they were all relics—objects that had been left behind, earthly possessions for which their one-time owner now had no need. It was impossible to take in, because Fiona's life was expressed so clearly in all these things. Her favourite cheese in the fridge, the stash of packets of cigarettes, the roses on the table, which Fiona herself had been the last person to water. And under the wardrobe the wellies in which she had always trudged off when it was rainy. Her toothbrush, comb and hairdryer in the bathroom, and the few cosmetics she had used.

She would not return to any of them.

She won't return to me, thought Leslie.

Fiona had been a mother to her. She had seen Fiona as a mother. Now she had lost her mother.

When she had lain in bed in the early hours of last Sunday morning, and had tucked her knees up to her chin and cried, so cold and alone, her mother had either already been killed or was dying.

And she had not died peacefully in her bed. She had not been able to say goodbye to anyone. A crazy man had murdered her, had lain in wait for her and smashed in her skull, had left her at the bottom of a wooded gorge.

It was unimaginable. It made the mind reel. It was beyond what she could understand. Leslie knew that she was suffering from shock. Although she understood with absolute clarity what had happened, although she had understood every word that Detective Inspector Almond had said to her the night before, she still did not grasp the full horror of it. There was still a barrier that shielded her from the terrible realisation that what had happened would have an effect on the rest of her life. She would never really be able to come to terms with the death of her grandmother, who was the only person in her childhood and youth to whom she had been deeply attached emotionally. The thought of the brutal, wild crime would also be linked to her grandmother's death. She would never be able to visit Fiona's grave without thinking about the old woman's last hours. There could never be consoling phrases such as: *She didn't suffer* or: *It was a blessing she died* or: *At least it happened quickly.* One thing was sure: Fiona had suffered. The only way in which her death was a blessing was that it ended the torture she had suffered at the hands of a criminal. And it had not happened quickly. She had been dragged, driven, forced to go to the isolated pasture by that person, whoever it was. She must have had a sense of what was to come. Had she called out to her granddaughter when she feared death?

At least the shock had meant that Leslie had been able to have a surprisingly calm conversation with Valerie Almond. The officer had told her of her grandmother's violent death with careful, gentle words.

'Unfortunately I'll have to ask you a few questions,' she ended by saying. 'But they can wait until tomorrow.'

Leslie had sat numbly on the sofa. Shaking her head, she said, 'No, no. Ask me now. It's fine.'

The conversation had helped her to cope with the first hour. She had run through every detail of Saturday evening in a rational and concentrated way. It did her good to make her mind work hard, trying to remember every little thing.

In the end she asked, 'Will I have to identify my grandmother?'

Valerie had nodded. 'It would be helpful. Not that there's really any doubt about the identity of the dead person, sadly, but it would make things one hundred per cent certain. First the post mortem needs to be completed, but… it would be good if someone could go with you. Do you have any other relatives here in Scarborough?'

Leslie had shaken her head. 'No. Fiona was my only relative.'

Valerie felt for her. 'There's no one you can go to now? It might not be good for you to spend the night alone in the flat.'

'I want to stay here. It'll be all right. I'm a doctor,' she added, and although her job really was not relevant right now, somehow the remark seemed to convince Valerie Almond.

Valerie had said she would go to the Beckett farm in the morning to talk to everyone there.

'That will be about ten o'clock. It would be good if you would come too. Should I send a car for you?'

'I'll be there. I'll drive myself, thanks.'

The officer had said goodbye and given Leslie her card with the request that she get in touch if anything else occurred to her which could be connected to her grandmother's murder.

'Even if it seems trivial to you,' she had added, 'it might be vital to us.'

Leslie had called the farm and told a stunned Gwen what had happened. Gwen had asked question after question, had said how horrified and shocked she was, had asked more questions. Gwen went on so long that Leslie thought she would lose it and start to scream.

'Listen, Gwen, as you can imagine, I need some peace,' she had interrupted her friend. 'We'll see each other tomorrow, all right?'

'But don't you want to come over now? You can't be alone now! I mean, it's not good for—'

'See you tomorrow, Gwen!' Then she had hung up.

How had the night passed? She could not have said. Had she wandered aimlessly from room to room? Had she sat on the sofa and stared at the wall? Had she lain on Fiona's bed with insomnia and her eyes wide open? Had she leafed through old photo albums? Only hazy images remained the next morning. She had done all of those things in that terrible night, as the hours dragged by so painfully slowly,

as if it would never be morning again. She remembered
that at one point she had got into her car and driven to a
garage. She had come back with a bottle of vodka and
drunk a good lot of it. She was ashamed of that, but why
the hell didn't Fiona have even a drop of alcohol at home?

She did not manage to eat breakfast. She had not eaten
anything but a few mouthfuls of meatloaf since that supper
two days ago. But she had poured litres of alcohol down
her throat. Never mind.

At half past eight she had not been able to bear it any
more and had called Stephen in the hospital. She was told
he was carrying out an operation, but they'd pass on the
message. Then she just sat by the phone. She ground her
teeth, because two years ago she had sworn never again
to go to Stephen for help, for company or for his support.
She had held firm, even in the blackest, saddest hours after
the separation. Even on weekends that seemed to last forever, which she had spent with a bottle of wine in front of
the television, feeling like she was the most lonely person
in the world. She had known that he would come flying
back into her arms if she gave him so much as the small-
est sign. But she had gritted her teeth.

Until today. Until this incident, which she did not know
how she would survive once the paralysis wore off.

The phone rang.

She forgot her pride and picked it up at once. 'Yes?
Stephen?'

The other end of the line was silent.

'Stephen? Leslie here.'

She could hear someone breathing.

'Who's there?'

Breathing. Then the person hung up.

She shook her head and also hung up. Immediately afterwards the phone rang again. This time she heard Stephen's voice.

'Leslie? The line was busy just now. It's me, Stephen.'

'Yes, hi, Stephen. I just had a strange call.' She dismissed the thought of it. Someone had misdialled or been playing a prank.

'I've just come out of the operating theatre, else I'd have called earlier. Has something happened?'

'Fiona is dead.'

'*What*?'

'She was murdered. On Saturday night.'

'That can't be,' exclaimed Stephen horrified.

'She was found yesterday. It's…I can't believe it, Stephen.'

'Do they know who did it?'

'No. At the moment they don't have any idea.'

'Was she robbed?'

'Her handbag was still there. Her purse too. No, it wasn't…about money.'

She talked in a monotonous tone of voice.

Stephen needed a few seconds to compose himself and gather his thoughts. 'Listen,' he said. 'I'll find someone to cover for me. Then I'll come up to Scarborough as fast as I can. To you.'

She shook her head violently, although Stephen could not see that. 'No. That's not why I called. I just wanted…' She paused, and took a deep breath. What had she wanted?

'Maybe you just need someone to hold you,' Stephen said.

It sounded tender, sensitive, understanding, warmhearted. Actually, he was exactly what she could do with now. Someone to hold her, someone whose shoulder she

could lean on, someone who she could pour out her heart
too and talk about her feelings of guilt.

A rock. That's what he had been for her at one time.
She had believed he would always be a rock for her. Until
the end of time.

In spite of her misery and her helplessness, her anger at
his betrayal rose up in her again. She remembered vividly
the shock and pain of that moment. He wanted to take her
in his arms? He was the last person she wanted that from.

'You can keep that skill of yours for your pub acquaintances,' she said, ending the conversation by slamming
down the receiver.

Perhaps it was not fair of her, not after she had made
him call her. The conversation had not been his idea, after
all.

But it was what she felt.

'ANONYMOUS CALLS?' asked Valerie Almond sharply. 'What kind?'

Chad Beckett thought for a minute. 'It were that nothing were said. The phone rang, someone breathed, didn't answer questions an' then 'ung up.'

'And how long had that been going on for?'

'She didn't rightly say. *Recently*, she said, I believe.'

'Fiona Barnes told you about this on Saturday evening?'

'Aye. After Dave Tanner had left and my daughter had taken t' room cryin'. She asked t' talk. An' that's when she told me 'bout calls.'

'It must have affected her.'

'Distressed her a little, aye.'

'And did she have any idea who could be behind the calls?'

Chad shrugged his shoulders again. 'Nay, lass.'

'Not the slightest idea? Someone who couldn't stand her? Someone she had once had a massive fight with? A fallout, something like that? Everyone has things like that happen in their life.'

'But they don't normally lead t' anonymous calls. Anyroad, Fiona couldn't work it out.'

'And you?' Valerie looked attentively at the old man. 'Can you work it out?'

'Nay. I told Fiona what I suspect. Someone disturbed,

who found random victims in t' telephone directory. A
harmless madman who enjoyed this strange power game.
Mostly it's types like that who're behind such calls.'

'Of course. Except that their victims do not normally
find themselves murdered soon afterwards in a gorge in a
wood. We have to take this seriously as a lead, Mr Beckett. If anyone springs to mind, who you think could be the
caller, you should let me know their name.'

'Of course,' said Beckett.

His face was grey, and his skin glistened slightly. It
looked as though he was not well. Talking to him, Valerie
had discovered how long he had known Fiona Barnes:
since he was fifteen. She had arrived at the Beckett farm
as an evacuee during the war. They had become friends
for life. The way his friend had died seemed like something out of a nightmare to Beckett, but he was the kind of
person not to talk about it. He would deal with the whole
thing on his own, and whatever sleepless nights he suffered, whatever horrific images filled his days, he would
not open up to anyone.

Valerie said goodbye and stepped out of the study. She
met Leslie and Jennifer at the front door. They had been
talking quietly. Valerie decided to bring up the calls right
now.

'Dr Cramer, I'm glad to see you again. Did your grandmother mention anything to you about receiving anonymous calls for a while?'

'No,' said Leslie, 'she didn't, but—' she remembered,
'this morning I got a strange call. Someone was just breathing down the line and then hung up. I didn't think anything more about it.'

'That is pretty much exactly the way Fiona Barnes
described the calls to Mr Beckett on the evening of her

death,' said Valerie. 'No words, just breathing. You were
called in your grandmother's flat, were you?'

'Yes,' said Leslie.

Valerie thought for a moment. She had gathered all the
people on the farm in the living room to talk about the fatal
Saturday evening. She had then talked with each one of
them individually too. She had asked about enemies that
Fiona Barnes might have. No one had thought of anyone.
It really seemed as though the only claimant to the title
was Dave Tanner. By all accounts, Fiona had humiliated
him deeply. However, everyone declared that they could
not imagine it had caused him to murder her.

'He's just not that kind of guy,' Jennifer Brankley had
said. Valerie had avoided saying that you could rarely see
who was or was not likely to commit criminal acts. She
had come across brutal murderers who seemed so lovely
you could easily have entrusted yourself to them along
with everything dear to you.

'But if this strange anonymous caller was Fiona's murderer, then he wouldn't have called this morning,' said Jennifer. 'He'd have known she was dead.'

Valerie listened to her absentmindedly. The problem
was that at this point she could not exclude any options,
and yet nor did she have anything that really seemed like a
likely lead. An anonymous caller who wanted Fiona dead?
How would the caller have known that late on Saturday
night she would be walking along a lonely road that led
to the Beckett farm? No one could have foreseen that circumstance. Only the people who had taken part in the
unfortunate engagement party could have known of it.
But which of them could have gone and murdered the old
woman so brutally, and why?

She said goodbye to Leslie and Jennifer and stepped out

into the farmyard. In spite of its rundown state, it looked almost idyllic in the light of this glorious day. The wind blowing from the sea brought the smell of seaweed and the taste of salt.

Valerie started to think.

Leslie Cramer, the granddaughter, had by her own account left the farm a good while before her grandmother and had gone to the Jolly Sailors in Burniston, to drown her sorrows with a few whiskies. That would be easy to check up on. Valerie knew that around here a woman who went into a bar on her own and got plastered would stick out more than a sore thumb.

Chad Beckett had chatted to Fiona in his study, and she had told him of the calls which were obviously troubling her. Chad had reassured her. According to Chad, they had then talked about this and that before she had decided to go home and he had gone to bed. Of course it was possible that he had followed her, but Valerie doubted it. Firstly, she saw no sign of any motive, and secondly she saw how difficult it was for him to get around. It was rather painful for him to walk. He was an old man struggling more and more with his body. Fiona Barnes, on the other hand, had been described to her as unusually fit and mobile for her age. It was hard to imagine that he could have made it to the gorge and then found the strength to beat a woman to death who could easily have run away from him.

Colin Brankley. The holidaymaker who had called the cab. He had said good night to Fiona and gone to bed. His wife could not confirm this, as she had taken the dogs for a walk. Mentally, Valerie put a question mark by Colin's name. He was an intellectual, a bookworm, for years he had spent his holidays on this wretched farm.

'My wife is very attached to the dogs,' he had explained.

'So we don't have much choice about where to go. Besides, Jennifer and Gwen are friends.'

All right. That did not sound implausible. However, two facts remained. Colin was in his mid-forties, strong and agile; he certainly had the physical ability to kill an old woman. And he did not have an alibi. Valerie decided to check what he had done and where he had been at the time when Amy Mills was murdered, although she already guessed that it would not lead to much. He would say that he had been asleep in his bed at home, and his wife would confirm that.

His wife. Jennifer. Valerie could not have said why exactly, but there was something inscrutable about her. Her eyes darted about restlessly. It was as if she was under great pressure, ready to blow her top, and only her extreme force of will kept a lid on it. Something was not right. And the name Jennifer Brankley rang a bell with Valerie. She had come across it once before, but she could not put her finger on when.

She would find out.

Jennifer Brankley had spent the first hour and a half after the dinner's sudden end in Gwen's room, consoling the distraught young woman.

Then she had persuaded her to go for a walk with her and the dogs. They had gone walking for a good hour and a half, Jennifer had said.

Unfortunately they had taken the opposite direction to the road, and gone over the hills and down another gorge to the sea.

'Wasn't it too dark?' asked Valerie, raising her eyebrows questioningly.

'The moon was shining,' replied Jennifer, 'and I know the path well. The dogs too. When we're here, I go that way two or three times a day. I've got a torch with me for emergencies.'

Gwen Beckett had confirmed the story. She had not wanted to go, but Jennifer had said the exercise would do her good. She could not, however, say how long they had been out.

'I was…somehow numb,' she had said quietly. 'I had been looking forward to the evening so much, and then it all went wrong. I was in despair. I thought everything was over.'

Valerie took a few steps across the farmyard and sat down on a pile of firewood, letting her gaze wander over the eastern horizon. The farm lay at the foot of a gently rising hill, which was crisscrossed by old stone walls. Here and there were a few trees, shining fiery red and golden yellow in the sunlight. According to Jennifer a path, a dirt path, went part of the way up the hill and then straight south, ending at a gorge which a wooden hanging bridge crossed. Beyond the bridge there were steps which wound their way down into the gorge. You had to walk along the bottom for a bit. There was a path but it was very overgrown. Then the gorge opened out onto the beach and you found yourself in the little bay that belonged to the Beckett farm.

'Can you swim there?' Valerie had asked.

Gwen had said you could. 'But it's pebbly. A long time ago my father planned to have sand brought in, to make a little bathing beach for our visitors. But it never happened.'

The farm is a gem, all it needs is for someone to make use of it and its possibilities, thought Valerie, not knowing that she was following the exact same train of thought as Fiona. Tanner, she thought, must have seen this when he started to woo Gwen Beckett. How far would he go to

stop a meddling old woman from trying to pull his fiancée and her property away from him?

And Gwen had felt threatened too. No longer the young-
est of women, suddenly an interesting man had appeared
in her life and wanted to marry her. Valerie had sensed
immediately that Gwen saw Dave as her only chance, and
she might be right. That made Fiona a danger to her. If
Fiona had continued to stir things up at every opportunity
without showing any tact, when would the moment have
come when Tanner would not take any more and would
give up? But would someone like Gwen Beckett go and
kill a woman she had known all her life, whom she loved
and was attached to? Gwen seemed to be suffering and in
shock. Unless she was a very good actor, then the news of
Fiona's death had surprised her and thrown her off kilter.

I'm going round in circles, thought Valerie. She felt that
she did not yet know the real motive for Fiona Barnes'
murder. She only knew about the fight with Tanner, the
scandal at the engagement party. But that was not enough.
The murder was carried out with a brutal violence that far
surpassed the venom of Fiona's aggression. She had ruined everyone's evening, but she was an old woman who
would have been eighty on her next birthday. Who seriously thought she had the power to influence other people's
lives in a major way and possibly even to destroy them?

And how did all this relate to Amy Mills' murder?

Forensics, next, thought Valerie. I have to know whether
both crimes were committed by one and the same person.
Then the argument Fiona started would be completely irrelevant.

And Tanner would have to become the centre of her investigation again. He was the only person she knew who
was connected to both cases, even if the connection to

Amy Mills' case was rather labyrinthine and elaborate, as she had to admit.

It would be interesting to know whether Amy Mills had also received anonymous calls. And then there was Paula Foster, who had perhaps been intended as the victim. Someone might have known that she came to the shed every evening. Just as someone had known that Amy Mills walked late at night on her own through a deserted park every Wednesday evening. Two young women, not dissimilar types. That would mean Fiona's death was not planned. Because she had disturbed someone? Why would she have taken the path to the gorge instead of going to Whitestone Farm? Or had she met her murderer on the road, recognised him and so he had not been able to let her live? Although it was a puzzle why someone out to get Paula Foster would have been around at half past ten. Paula was out at different times.

Valerie stood up and walked to her car. She had to talk to the pathologist. When she had time, she wanted to put Jennifer Brankley's name into the police computer. It might not be relevant to this case, but she wanted to find out where she had come across the name before.

She opened the car door. She was tired. All the pieces of the puzzle were mounting up in her head in a confused pile, and she was afraid that she would never manage to order them.

She forced herself to heed the old rule of thumb she had once worked out: not to look at the mountain of pieces, but just the next step. Then the next one. And the next one. She had a tendency to panic when everything piled up too high above her and became too confused and unfathomable.

And she harboured a terrible fear of failure.

Not exactly beneficial in her line of work, and she only hoped her colleagues did not suspect anything.

Valerie turned her car around and drove off.

5

'Dr Cramer? Can I talk to you for a moment?' Colin Brankley appeared at the door to the kitchen. He was holding a pile of papers in his hand and looking around uneasily, as if he wanted to be sure that no one was around.

Leslie was at the sink and running water into a glass. She was thirsty, tired and numb, and at the same time excited. Her nerves seemed to be humming under her skin. She wondered to herself when she was going to cry or scream or break down. She must seem strangely calm to other people, as if it had not touched her. But she knew that all the emotions relating to her grandmother—to her violent death, but also to her life—were working away deep inside her. Images kept popping into her mind, scenes, episodes, moments, which she had not thought of for ages, which had been completely forgotten. It was like a fever.

Probably that was why she needed water so much—and as cold and fresh as possible.

'Leslie,' she replied. 'Just call me Leslie.'

'All right.' Colin stepped into the kitchen. 'Leslie. Do you have time?' He pulled the door to behind him.

'Yes. Of course.' She put the glass to her lips, realising as she did that her hand was trembling slightly. She put the glass down. She did not want to spill it on her with Colin watching, even though it was just water. 'There's probably a lot I should be doing, but I don't know…' She paused, undecided. 'At the moment I don't know what to do next.'

Colin looked at her, feeling for her. 'I can understand. It was a terrible shock. For all of us, but especially for you. None of us…can really believe it.'

His friendliness was what she needed. She felt a choking in her throat and swallowed, painfully. It would be good to cry, but not now. Not in this kitchen, not in front of Colin. She barely knew the man. She did not want to break down in front of him.

'Do you have something for me?' she asked calmly, pointing to the papers in his hand.

'Yes.' Hesitantly he laid the pile on the kitchen table. He looked around again, as if he were expecting someone to come in at any moment. 'It's something which…well, it probably should be handed over to the police but…'

'But?'

'But I think it's not up to me to decide. You are Fiona's granddaughter. You have to decide what to do with it.'

'What is it?'

He lowered his voice. 'Text files. Attached to emails that Fiona Barnes sent to Chad Beckett.'

She looked at him in surprise. 'Chad Beckett can work a computer? And has an email address?'

'Well, "work the computer" might be an exaggeration. But he has an email address, yes. Because Fiona insisted, Gwen said. The two of them kept in touch by email. Not infrequently.'

'And?'

Colin seemed unsure of how to express what he had to say. 'Fiona and Chad have known each other since childhood. And—it seems out of the need to make sense of certain events for herself—Fiona wrote down their story. At least the main points. And gave it a strange title, although that riddle is solved as you read it. *The Other Child*. She immerses herself in the past, describes their first meeting—you know: the evacuation, her arrival here at the Beckett farm…'

Leslie was now fully alert and increasingly irritated. 'I know the story. Fiona often told me it. How touching, that she wrote it down for Chad and herself. But what I don't quite understand…is how you have a print-out of it? Aren't they files which were meant only for Chad?'

'Absolutely. And that becomes even clearer when you read it. Their story. When you read what really happened.'

'What really happened?'

'I'm fairly sure,' said Colin slowly, 'that you heard a censored version from your grandmother. Just as Gwen only knows part of the truth. And with her, all of us too.'

Leslie had a thought, and in spite of her sorrow she had to laugh. 'Do you mean that Fiona and Chad had a relationship? Does my grandmother describe wild orgies in the hay? You know, of course she never said anything of the sort, but I was always convinced something had happened between Chad and her. And that doesn't really shock me. I don't think it would help the police any.'

He looked at her in a strange way. 'Read it. And then decide what to do.'

She looked back at him icily. 'Where did you get this? How did you get access to Chad's emails?'

'Gwen,' he said.

'Gwen?'

'She uses the same computer as her father. She tried to…spy a little. It wasn't hard to find the password he used. *Fiona*. That was it.'

Leslie gulped.

He had loved her. She had always thought that.

'And then she snooped around in his emails?'

'She opened the files and read the story. When she finished, she was so shocked that she printed it all out. As soon as we arrived last week, she gave it to Jennifer to read. Yesterday morning Jennifer gave me the pages, with Gwen's permission. At that point of course none of us knew anything about the crime. I read all of it, yesterday and last night.

'OK. So three people now know all about things which are actually only Fiona and Chad's business?'

'Read it,' he asked again.

She felt anger rising inside her. What a betrayal of two elderly people who were nostalgic for the old days. She could just about see why Gwen, once she had found the beginning of her father's life story, had not been able to stop herself from reading it. But why had she shared it with two outsiders? She might have had a close friendship with the Brankleys for many years, but they were not family. She would have liked to protect her grandmother, but she knew that it was too late now.

'I'm not sure if I want to read it,' she said. 'You know, I always respected Fiona's private life.'

'Fiona is the victim of a horrific crime. This story could throw some light on her death.'

'Why didn't you give all this to Detective Inspector Almond while she was here?'

'Because the story also throws light on Fiona. If what she describes here—' he said pointing to the pile of paper, 'is made public, which is more than likely if it lands in the hands of the police, and it arises there's a direct link to Fiona's murder, then it could be that Fiona won't be remembered at all fondly here in Scarborough.'

Leslie now made no effort to hide her annoyance. 'So what did she do? Rob a bank? Was she a kleptomaniac, a nymphomaniac? Did she have perverse desires? Did she cheat on her husband? Did she and Chad cheat behind Chad's wife's back? Did they support the IRA? Was she a member of a terrorist organisation? What did she do?'

'Read it,' he said for a third time. 'Take the sheets home. Gwen and Jennifer don't need to know for now that you have them.'

'Why not?'

'On no account does Gwen want the police to know their content. For her, it's mainly about her father. Jennifer is on her side, as always. Both of them would be angry with me if they knew I was letting you have them. But I think...'

'What do you think?' asked Leslie after he had paused.

'I think you have a right to know the truth,' said Colin. 'And that you, and only you, have the right to decide whether the truth is made public. I would completely understand if you didn't want that. But the solving of the crime might depend on this. And that's for you to decide too: whether your grandmother's murder should remain unpunished. You might prefer that.'

She was scared. She knew she would not get an answer, but she still asked, 'What, Colin? What, for God's sake, does it say?'

He did not need to say *Read it* a fourth time. He just looked at her.

It was almost a pitying look, it seemed to her.

4

Life on the Beckett farm proved not to be all that bad. Quite the contrary, in a short time I had settled in surprisingly well.

Emma Beckett was as nice and kind as she had been when we arrived. She was more gentle than Mum, nor as strict. You could always ask her for something delicious: a little bit of bread and ham to keep you going between meals, a glass of homemade apple juice, sometimes even a piece of chocolate. She was convinced that I must be dying of homesickness, and I did nothing to dissuade her from the belief, as there was more in it for me that way.

Her son Chad, though, saw right through me. 'You're a cunning little thing,' he said to me once. 'You play the lost little sheep to my mother, but you don't want to go back to London one little bit!'

Not one little bit—that was not true. I missed our old house, the street, the children I had played with. Sometimes I missed Mum too, although she had always nagged so much. But after the night of bombing I had lost my home in any case. I certainly had no fond memories of Auntie Edith's overcrowded flat. I do remember bawling one night when I thought of my father. Although he had drunk so much and had never given Mum any money, he was my father. I would see Mum again, London too, I was sure. But my father was lost forever.

Emma's husband Arvid was no substitute father to me.

He was not out-and-out unfriendly, but he acted as if I were not there, and that is how things remained. From the beginning I had the impression that he had not agreed with his wife's idea to take in an evacuee. Probably it had not been easy to persuade him. Perhaps the money the government gave host families had been an incentive. But now a second child, *the other child*, as he called Brian, had turned up, more or less by mistake, and there was not even money for him. That did not exactly improve the situation.

'The Red Cross will soon take charge of Brian,' Emma said whenever Arvid moaned about another mouth to feed. In fact, no one came for Brian and I thought I sensed Emma's relief. She did not want Brian to go to an orphanage. She herself would do nothing to put his stay on the Beckett farm at risk.

I liked life on the farm. You could not imagine a greater contrast to life in London. The empty spaces that seemed to go on forever, the wide stone walled pastures dotted with hundreds of grazing sheep. The scent of the sea. I loved to clamber down to the bay which belonged to the farm. It was a dangerous, secret path that went along a deep gorge and almost disappeared as it went through a primeval wood at the foot of a rock face. I fought my way through grasses and ferns, which were dark in the winter and bathed in a strange green light in the summer. I imagined that I was one of those great discoverers I had heard about in school: Christopher Columbus or Vasco da Gama. The natives could be lying in wait for me anywhere, cannibals—on no account could I fall into their hands. I jammed a stick between my teeth. It was my knife, my only weapon. Every snap in the undergrowth, every shrill cry of a bird made me jump and gave me goose bumps all over. The only thing I missed in these moments was other children. In our street in London, in the maze of its backyards, we had always gone around in a crowd of ten, sometimes even fifteen or twenty children. I was all alone here. Of course I went to school in Burniston and got on with my classmates, who found me a rather exotic creature, but unfortunately we all lived far too far apart to meet outside of school hours. For miles there was nothing but sheep pastures, punctuated by the odd farm. You would have had to walk for hours to get from one to the next.

I was a child who liked to play, and who took advantage of the freedom and endless possibilities of life on the land. I was also a girl just entering puberty. Mum had always said I had matured early. That might be true, at least for the forties. I found a few rubbishy novels in my bedside table and devoured them, red with embarrassment. They were old and worn, and I wondered if Emma had devoured them with the same passion as me. 'Passion'—that was the word which best described the books' content too. That is all they were about. Beautiful women, strong men. And what they did together made my cheeks burn. I wanted nothing more so much as to grow up quickly and to experience for myself everything that I was hearing about here. It was an almost inevitable development for me to imagine Chad Beckett as the man at my side, a strong, good-looking hero.

I had an immense admiration for him. I think I was even in love with him. Unfortunately he only saw me as some uninteresting girl his mother had brought home and who would hopefully disappear again soon. He treated me with almost more indifference than his father did.

The only male who was around me, whenever he could be, was Brian. *Whenever he could be* meant whenever I did not manage to shake him off. Over time I

perfected the art of disappearing. Each time he would
wander around like a lost lamb, crying quietly to himself, as Emma told me each time with a gentle rebuke.

I countered that by saying that he just got on my
nerves. 'He's so much younger than me. And he doesn't
say a word! What should I do with him?'

It was true. Brian still could not speak. Emma always
wanted to know if he had spoken in the past. She thought
I should know, after all he had lived in my neighbourhood.

With the best will in the world I could not remember.
Had any of us in the street really paid attention to little
Brian? I could only tell Emma that people had always
said the Somerville children were all pretty thick. This
expression made Emma angry—and it was the first time,
by the way, that I had really seen her angry. 'How can
people just declare that?' she exclaimed. 'About children
who can't stand up for themselves? How can people make
such sweeping statements?'

I did not want to make things worse, otherwise I would
have pointed out that it did seem to be true in Brian's
case. An eight-year-old—or perhaps he was already nine,
no one knew when his birthday was—who could not
speak? That was not normal. The children in my school
said the same thing once, when Emma came by on her
bike to bring me the breakfast I had forgotten to eat. Brian
was sitting on the bike's rack. It was break time and he
slid off the bike and rushed over to me making indefinable noises. He babbled something which no one could
understand.

'Your brother's got a screw loose,' the class represent-
ative said to me later.

'He's not my brother!' I shouted, and I must have

been looking daggers at her, because she stepped back in surprise.

'It's all right,' she said gently, as you would talk to an angry dog.

It was incredibly important to me that no one thought I was related to the little moron. That's what I called him in my head: little moron. I could not say that out loud, at least not in Emma's presence.

That sounds very cold and harsh. And perhaps that could be said of me; that I did not behave in a particularly nice way to this disturbed little boy. But you also have to think about who I was in 1940 and 1941. I was a child who liked adventures, and at the same time a girl who read romances and was experiencing confusing emotions about a fifteen-year-old boy. From one day to the next I had lost London, where I was at home, and was suddenly on a sheep farm in Yorkshire. My father had died, my mother was far away. I had sat in the cellar of our house when it had collapsed above us, hit by a German bomb. I had a lot of things to come to terms with, I realise that now.

It was not as clear to me at the time. I only felt that Brian's clinginess, his love, was suffocating me. I felt completely overwhelmed by him. The presence of this silent, traumatised child was too much for me somehow. I fought it tooth and nail. Maybe that was not so unusual considering my age.

What would have been normal would have been for Emma to take him to a doctor. It was clear that the little boy needed help, whether medical or psychological. And no doubt Emma saw that too. I never had the opportunity to speak to her about it, but I now believe that she was simply afraid she would wake sleeping dogs if she took the child to any official institution. No one had got in touch from London. Probably Brian had been lost somewhere between the nurses, who had noted down his name that dark November evening after his arrival in Staintondale, and the authorities responsible for him in London. Emma was convinced that he would not cope with a transfer to an orphanage, so she was happy that no one seemed to have remembered him. She did not take him to the doctor. Nor did she send him to school, for which she did not need to feel bad, as it would have been immediately clear to anyone that Brian was in no way able to keep up with children of his age or even younger.

Although the whole story irritated her husband Arvid, Brian's wellbeing was a matter that held no concern for him whatsoever, so she could do as she wished. Nor did Chad get involved. He was at an age when he had very different things in his head. For my own part, I soon had eyes for Chad alone, and only noticed Brian because I often had to find all kinds of cunning tricks to throw him off my trail.

Apart from Emma, he had become a kind of *nobody* for everyone. After a while that is what Chad started to call him: *Nobody.*

In February 1941 Mum visited me in Staintondale. She had wanted to come for Christmas, but the family for whom she did the housekeeping rather needed her help, and she could not do without the extra money. It had not been a problem for me. Christmas on the Beckett farm was lovely. It had even snowed a little. I had surpassed myself in helpfulness. Whenever I could, I had made myself useful on the farm or in the house, and had saved up a tidy amount of pocket money. With it I bought Chad a sheath knife. I knew he had long dreamt of having one. When he unpacked it, his eyes shone, and when he thanked me something had changed in the way he looked at me. It was as if he no longer just saw a stupid little girl from London who just got on his nerves, but a person you could almost take seriously. That look and his smile were the most beautiful part of the Christmas festivities. And the book he gave me:

Little Women by Louisa Alcott.

'Because you like reading so much,' he said with some embarrassment.

I would have liked to give him a hug, but I did not dare. So I just held the book tight.

'Thank you,' I said quietly and swore to keep the book forever. I managed. I still have it today.

Christmas passed in a flurry of church visits, singing and good food, and there was really no need for Mum's long, guilty letter in which she explained and justified her absence. Indeed, her letter made *me* feel guilty. Mum seemed to think that I was missing her terribly and probably it would have been completely normal if I had. I asked myself why I was not homesick and why I had settled in to life on the Beckett farm within just a few weeks. I think I know the answer now. It was not just the fact that I had fallen in love with Chad Beckett. Nor was it because my mother and I had so often had run-ins, and Emma was gentler and easier to get on with. I think I had found *my home* there on the Yorkshire coast. I'm not a city person. Although I was born in London and lived there for the first eleven years of my life, I did not see its streets, its many people and high houses as my home. Whereas Yorkshire's endless fields, its dreamy little villages, the way the earth and sky merged on the distant horizon, the nearness of the sea, all the animals and its clear air gave me the feeling of being home. Even if I did not realise that at the time.

When my mother finally did come one weekend in the middle of February, she could see that I looked well. Yorkshire was not showing itself to its best advantage, but which landscape does manage that in February? There was a constant cold grey drizzle. The farmyard was muddy, and the top of the hill behind the farm had been swallowed up in the low-hanging clouds. I would still have liked to show Mum the bridge, the gorge and the beach, but she refused to follow me outside.

'Much too cold,' she said and rubbed her arms, shivering, although we were sitting right by the living room hearth. 'And too wet. I'm not going to go clambering over rocks, my dear, sorry. Last thing I want is to break an ankle.'

I was under the impression that she did not particularly like the Beckett farm, that she would not be able to stay half a week here. Nonetheless, it was better than the bombs in London.

'The Germans are still attacking,' she said. 'Not as bad as at the start, but I'm still happy you're here. Safe. So many people's children have been evacuated by now.'

She still lived with Auntie Edith, which was horrible, as she told me.

'Just too many people and not enough space. And you know Edith. She really shows you that you're getting on her nerves. She treats me like a beggar. I mean, I'm her dead brother's wife! I'm not just anybody!'

Her gaze fell on Brian who, as always, was near me. He was sitting at our feet and pushing around a little wooden car that had once belonged to Chad. As usual his play did not seem to have any recognisable sense to it.

'Does he understand us?'

I shook my head. 'I don't think so. He can barely speak.'

Brian had actually tried to form words in early January, for the first time since he had arrived. Emma had reacted euphorically, but I thought it was a rather limited success. To my annoyance, what he did manage to say rather clearly was the word *Fiona*. He could also say something that sounded like *come!* and *hoby*. Emma wracked her brains to think what the last word could be. Chad and I were sure that he was trying to say *nobody*, the name we used when we were alone with him. But we did not let on. We knew Emma would have got rather angry if she heard.

After Mum was sure that Brian would not repeat what he might hear, she came out with the news which was probably the only reason for her trip north.

'It might be that I won't be at Auntie Edith's much longer,' she said.

'Is our house being rebuilt?' I asked.

'No. That will take a little longer. They're clearing the rubble from the streets, but there's not much point in starting to rebuild while the Germans are still bombing.'

'And so where will you go?'

She hummed and hawed a while before saying quietly and hastily, 'I've met someone…'

I did not understand right away. 'And?'

'He's called Harold Kane. He is…he works in the docks. As a foreman!'

'A man?' I said, not believing my ears.

'Yes, of course a man,' Mum replied somewhat sharply. 'Who else?'

I was stunned. I had barely been gone four months and my mother was already going courting. I was old enough to put two and two together. When she said she had met a man, and in the same breath said she would not be living with Auntie Edith for much longer, then that meant she had fallen in love with this Harold Kane and would soon move into his flat. How could it happen so quickly? Daddy was dead. England was at war. Hitler was out to conquer the world. They had needed to evacuate me. And yet even with all this happening, Mum had nothing better to do than look for a new man. I found that embarrassing and a little undignified.

What is more, I realised I was a little envious. My love affair with Chad was just as one sided as it had ever been. It had not started. In the meantime, Mum had snagged herself a guy who was probably ready to marry her. It was *my* turn. I was young. Mum seemed ancient to me; she was thirty-two. She had already lived through the most important part of her life.

'Why is he working in the docks?' I asked with a poisonous and challenging tone to my voice. 'Why isn't he fighting in the war?'

Mum sighed. She had understood my provocation and saw future difficulties. 'He is exempt because his work is essential to the war effort,' she explained.

I would have liked to murmur something like *shirker*, but I did not dare. I had a feeling that Mum would react very angrily if I did. It probably was not true, either. Arvid Beckett was exempt too, because he was needed on the farm, and I would never have thought of judging him for it. I would have not minded in the least if no man had to go to the front. I shared Emma's deep worry that Chad might get called up too, if the war did not end soon. No doubt Mum was worried about her Harold and happy that he had been able to stay in London.

'Well, then I won't have much of a role in your life any more,' I said darkly—a comment which Mum of course objected to in no uncertain terms.

'You're my child!' she exclaimed and hugged me. 'Nothing between us will change!'

She no doubt meant what she said. But although I did not yet have much life experience, my instinct told me that something would change. A new member joining a family always changes something. And who knew how this Harold would act towards me? I could not imagine that he would be all that enthusiastic about the fact that his bride was bringing a twelve-year-old daughter into the relationship too.

Accompanying Mum the next morning on the rather long walk to the main road where the bus to Scarborough drove past once a day, I wished with all my heart that my stay on the Beckett farm would be long, really long. I felt the need to return to London less and less. The paradox was that the period of my stay in Yorkshire was dependant on the length of the war, and no sensible person would hope for that to continue for long, especially as Chad was going to turn sixteen in April and then the situation for him would become critical.

Standing at the side of the road and waving Mum off, the tears started to flow. My life seemed confusing and difficult. It was dark and frightening. No one in the world gave me a feeling of security, perhaps my mother least of all.

And the following summer it happened. A few days after my twelfth birthday I received a telegram from Mum. In it she told me that she and Harold had married.

6

It was a dry hot day. The sky was that crystal-clear blue which is so typical of August. The apples were ripening on the trees. The wind carried the smell of the sea and the freshly mown grass. It was a perfect day. Holidays. Freedom. I should have been lying under a tree and reading, dreaming and lazily watching the clouds drift by above me.

Instead I was sitting on a boulder on the beach, falling apart. In my hand I held the telegram which in a few meagre words told me that the previous day I had gained a stepfather. *Stepfather!* I knew stepmothers from fairy tales. Stepfathers could not be much better.

I cried my eyes out.

Of course I had somehow known that it would come to this, but strangely I still went into shock. I felt betrayed, taken unawares. Mum should have talked to me first, instead of presenting me with a fait accompli. She should have introduced me to Harold, to find out whether he was nice to me, and whether we got on. What if he hated me at first sight—and I him? What if he ordered me about, made my life difficult, shouted at me? Perhaps she did not care. Perhaps she was so euphoric about her conquest that she was no longer interested in whether or not her child was doing well.

And at the word 'child' I had another horrible thought: what if Mum and Harold had a child together? I supposed

Mum was not too old, otherwise Harold would probably not have married her. If that happened, I'd really be only on the edge of their lives. Mum would spend all her time caring for the crying baby, and Harold would adore his little offspring, and I would just be in the way. They would put me in an orphanage with Brian. Harold would go on at Mum until she agreed.

I was too taken up with these dark thoughts, and my crying and railing against my fate, for me to notice someone approaching. When I suddenly saw a movement from the corner of my eye, I looked up in surprise.

It was Chad. He was a few feet from me and did not seem at all happy to see me.

'You're 'ere?' he said slowly. 'Thought I could be alone 'ere.'

'I often come here,' I admitted.

Luckily he did not seem annoyed. 'Right. A good place for a cry, in't it?'

I fished out a handkerchief and wiped my nose, although I knew I had swollen red eyes and a blotchy face. Probably I looked uglier than ever before.

'Mum married again,' I said, waving the telegram in my hand.

Once again he said, 'Right.' Then he looked around suspiciously. 'Is Nobody somewhere around?'

He was all I would have needed right then!

'I lost him. Don't worry. He wouldn't dare come down here on his own.'

Chad took a few faltering steps towards me. No doubt he would rather have been alone, but something held him back from just shooing me away like a tiresome fly. He had done that at first. But now I was twelve. You could not act as dismissively and impolitely to a twelve-year-old girl. Realising this, I started to feel a little better.

'Is he disgustin'?' Chad asked, pointing to the telegram.
I swallowed. Just don't start crying again.

'I don't know him,' I had to admit. 'He and Mum met
since I've been here with you. I haven't been back to
London since.'

'She coulda brought 'im with 'er, when she came t' visit.
If she knew 'im then.'

'He didn't have time. His work is essential to the war
effort.' At least something about Harold she could be a
little proud about.

Chad did not seem to hold such work in high esteem.
He harrumphed. 'Like me Dad and t' stupid farm! There
be only one place for a man in a war, at t' front!'

I felt a cold chill down my back as he said this, although it also impressed me deeply. The way he said
it sounded so brave, so determined. Chad had finished
school that summer and now he had to help out more
on the farm. It was work which did not appeal to him.
He and Arvid were always having run-ins about it. I had
heard Arvid and Emma talking about it a month earlier.
Emma would have liked Chad to go on to the sixth form
and then perhaps university.

'He can do it,' she had said, almost pleadingly. 'His
teachers think so too. He gets good marks.'

Arvid had cut her down.

'Sixth form! University! What ever for, woman? Our
boy'll inherit t' farm. Don't need a Higher School Certifi-
cate for that. He'll grow into the job. One day I'll pass it
all on t' him. He's lucky. Not many who get a property
like this just thrown int' their lap!'

However, at the moment I did not have the impression
that Chad was interested primarily in a sixth form education. His goal lay elsewhere, and I found that unsettling.

'I've just talked to me parents,' he said. His cheeks were

red, probably not just from the climb down the gorge. 'I'm sixteen. I could enlist if me Dad gave me permission! Can't understand why he's refusin'!' Sitting down beside me on the boulder, he picked up a few small pebbles and flung them angrily into the sea.

'Enlist? You mean…?'

'For t' front, of course. I'd like to fight. Like t' others!'

'There aren't many sixteen-year-olds who are going,' I mooted.

'Some do,' he insisted. He threw some more pebbles. I had rarely seen him as angry.

'Your father needs you on the farm.'

'My country need me at t' front. Others 're dyin' for England! And 'ere I am sittin' and shearin' sheep. Can you imagine what that means for me?' He turned his face towards me. I could see in his eyes that he was not just angry, he was also sad—almost despairing.

Maybe he was feeling much the same as me in that moment.

'D'you know what kind of a guy Hitler is?' he asked.

I only had vague ideas. 'Not really…'

'He's crazy,' said Chad. 'Mad. He wants to take over the world. He's attackin' every country. He's even takin' on Russia now. Only a madman could do that!'

'But then he won't manage to conquer Russia,' I suggested, shyly. I knew that Hitler had attacked Russia that summer, but I had not thought any more of it. I hoped I did not look too silly to Chad.

'Imagine the Germans would invade England,' said Chad. 'Not just send their bombs, although that's bad enough. But imagine they were suddenly 'ere. *That the Germans were suddenly 'ere!*'

I did not see that the Germans could make my current situation any worse. Not even Hitler seemed as much of a bogeyman to me as Harold Kane. Naturally, I kept this to myself.

'That would be terrible,' I said compliantly.

'It would be a bleedin' catastrophe,' stressed Chad, before falling into a gloomy silence.

'Mainly it's Mum who's stoppin' me,' he said after a while. 'I think I could bring Dad round. But when I just start to say I want t' join up, she gets hysterical!'

'She's afraid for you.'

'Afraid! I'm pretty much a grown-up. It's time for her t' stop being afraid for me. Let her hold and kiss and suffocate Nobody with her care. That's not for me any more. I have t' go me own way. Follow me own convictions!'

I thought that what he was saying sounded very good. As always, I was so impressed by him. But I still did not want him in the war. Of course not, on no account! I did not say that. I wanted him to see me as his ally, not as a younger version of his frightened mother.

'Sometimes,' I said, 'things don't go as you'd like in life.'

It was not that I thought I was saying something particularly clever. It just seemed like the naked truth to me.

Chad looked at me.

'But then you don't have to accept it,' he replied.

'Sometimes you do.' I waved the telegram in my hand. 'Sometimes you're helpless.'

He kept on looking at me. Something had changed. The look in his eyes had changed. He—yes, he was looking at me as if he were seeing me for the first time.

'You've got beautiful eyes,' he said, and sounded almost surprised. 'Honestly, right beautiful. With golden flecks in them.'

I have green eyes with a little bit brown in them. Brown, not gold.

Maybe the light had changed the colour, or he just saw

what he wanted to see. I don't know. But to me it was as if the world had suddenly stood still. As if the waves had paused, the seagulls had gone silent and the gentle summer wind was waiting. My mouth was suddenly dry, and I swallowed. Suddenly the telegram with its earth-shattering news was unimportant.

'I…' I said, but did not have the faintest idea what else to say. 'Thank you,' I finally said and thought that I really did not have a clue about things. What should you say in a moment like this? *Thank you*, that sounded like what a schoolgirl would say, but however hard I tried, I could not think of anything else.

He will think I'm a little idiot, I thought, depressed. The special moment in which the whole world around me had held its breath was passing as quickly as it had come—for a girl who had been speechless when a man said something nice to her.

But he carried on looking at me with that new expression, and there was something in his gaze which gave me hope that he did not just see a schoolgirl in front of him.

He reached for the telegram. 'Give it t' me,' he said.

With a few quick folds he had made a paper aeroplane. He stood up. 'Come on,' he said, 'let's send it off!'

I stood up too. Chad checked the wind direction and threw the plane skilfully into the air so that the thermal caught it and carried it on. It flew for a good distance before plunging into the sea. For a while we carried on looking at it dancing around on the waves, then it disappeared from sight.

'Gone,' said Chad. 'Don't think about it again.'

I had to laugh. It was as simple as that. All at once Mum was gone. Harold Kane too. I suddenly did not care about the future or what was going to happen. The only real thing was the present, the beach, the sea, the sky. And Chad, who quite naturally took my hand.

'Come on,' he said. 'Let's go home.'

I remember thinking on the way home that it was the happiest hour of my life. I felt I would never be happier, my life would never be more complete. Even today, more than half a century later, I can still recall what was special about that afternoon. Maybe every life has these moments which cast us under a spell whenever we think back to them, however much time has since passed and however our lives have turned out. What was special about that afternoon was naturally the fact that I had more or less been given a declaration of love. That is how I understood Chad's comment about my eyes, and indeed the following months were to show that he was finally requiting the secret and rapturous feelings which I had been harbouring for him. Looking back, I know that it was more than that, more than a romantic meeting between a boy and a girl on a beach. It was—but I could not know that at the time—one of the few intense moments Chad Beckett and I were to share in innocence. I mean that literally. We had not yet made ourselves guilty.

That would change, and today I'm sure that was the reason why a life together—which would otherwise definitely have been possible—failed.

Because of our guilt.

1

SHE WOKE UP because her alarm clock rang. It took her a few seconds to realise it could not be her alarm, because she was in Scarborough and not her London flat, and she did not have an alarm clock here. She must have been dreaming, or have imagined something, especially as it was quiet now.

She sat up in bed. Outside day had broken. She saw fog pushing up against the windowpane. The weather sooth-sayers had got it right: it was autumn.

She wanted to sink back into the pillows, but then she heard the ringing again and it dawned on her that someone was at the front door. She felt for her watch. It was almost nine. She never normally slept this long. With a slight feel-ing of guilt she remembered the whisky she had bought yesterday and of which she had drunk a good deal in Fiona's living room that evening. Probably that was why she had slept so deeply and long.

Only tea tonight, she resolved, although she immedi-ately had a bitter premonition that she would not manage to keep her resolution.

She stood up and felt her way through the flat. When she passed the living room she saw, lying on the table, the pile of papers which Colin had given her and she had read all evening. *The Other Child.doc*. Beside it, her glass and bottle of whisky. The standing lamp was still burning, she had forgotten to turn it off.

She pressed the button to release the door to the street, and opened the door to the flat. A minute later Stephen traipsed up the stairs—a bleary-eyed Stephen carrying a travelling bag and wearing trainers.

'Did I wake you?' he asked.

She was stunned. 'Yes. No. Well you did, but it doesn't matter.' She stepped back. 'If you'd like to come in…'

He stepped inside, shaking himself, a little like a wet dog. He was wearing an anorak that shone wetly. 'I haven't been here for ages. I parked far too far away,' he said apologetically. 'Down at the Spa Complex. I had to walk up through the gardens…God, the paths are steep, and then you can't see a thing!'

Leslie was still struggling to wake up properly. 'Where are you coming from?'

'From London. I set off about four in the morning.'

'Why on earth?'

He shed the wet anorak. 'I managed to get time off. And I thought…'

'What?'

'I thought you might need me. Well, I can imagine you're feeling pretty terrible…'

She crossed her arms in a defensive gesture. 'I told you I didn't want you to come.'

'Still,' he replied. 'You did call me.'

'I'm sorry. It was a mistake.'

He looked hurt. 'Leslie, could you possibly…'

'I couldn't!' she hissed. Don't be weak. Think what he has done to you. How much it hurt when he told you about his slip-up. How you felt afterwards. The fear that he could do it again. The suspicion as to whether it was really just

one night. Fear and suspicion. She had been relieved when
she had found the strength to finally end it.

He carried on, not paying any attention to her objec-
tion. 'Could you possibly take into account that we were
married for ten years and together for fifteen? That your
grandmother was also part of my family? I've also lost
someone. I've got a right to mourn too. I've got a right to
know what happened.'

'All right. The last point: at the moment no one knows
what happened. If that's why you came, you're in for a
disappointment. No new leads. And the point before that:
of course you can mourn. But on your own please. Without me.'

They stood opposite each other. Leslie noticed that her
breath was coming in short, panicky gasps. She tried to
calm down.

Don't let him get you worked up!

Stephen looked at her pensively, then he grabbed his
anorak, which he had slung over the back of a chair.

'You made yourself clear. I'll look for somewhere to
have breakfast and...'

Suddenly ashamed, she brushed the hair from her face
embarrassedly. 'You can have breakfast here. It's fine.
I'm sorry if I...'

He smiled in relief. She disappeared into the bathroom
and heard him go into the kitchen. In the past they had
often spent their holidays with Fiona in Yorkshire. Stephen
knew his way round the flat. Looking at her swollen face
in the mirror, she thought she was almost relieved not to
be on her own. Maybe Fiona's death would be the start
of a new phase in her life, in which she could give up her
aggression and hurt. In the end it would be possible to be
friends with Stephen.

Having showered and blow-dried her hair, she put on jeans and a sweatshirt and went to the living room. It smelt of coffee. Stephen had set the table at the window, although it was rather meagre fare. A big piece of cheese lay plonked on a plate in the middle of the table, accompanied by a dish with crackers. Stephen, who had been looking out into the impenetrable fog, turned around. 'What do you live on?' he asked. 'The fridge is bare. The only thing I found in the kitchen, and plenty of that, is coffee and cigarettes!'

'That's it. The answer to your question,' said Leslie. 'Coffee and cigarettes. That's what I live on.'

'Not very healthy.'

'I'm a doctor myself.' She sat down, poured herself a cup of coffee and enjoyed the first sip. 'Just what I needed! Now I'm back in the land of the living!'

During what passed for breakfast Leslie brought him up to date with the modest progress of the investigation, as much as she knew it. She told him about the calamitous engagement party, about the holidaymakers Colin and Jennifer Brankley, about the fight between Dave Tanner and Fiona, and about Fiona's fatal decision to go walking on her own that night.

'Somewhere on that lonely road she must have met her murderer,' she said.

'This Dave Tanner must be the main suspect,' said Stephen. 'He might have still been in the area. And from what you've told me about the evening, he must have been dead angry.'

The pun was unintended but Leslie picked up on it. 'Not enough to want someone dead. That doesn't fit somehow. Yes, he was angry, but angry enough to want someone dead…I don't think so.'

'What kind of a person is he?'

'Hard to read. But not in the way that you'd think he could commit a crime. More like in the way Fiona suspected. He might really not be on the level with Gwen. He's good-looking. He's the kind of man young women flock to, and he's scrabbling around to make ends meet. Gwen, or more precisely: the Beckett farm, is a real chance for him.'

'A man ready to marry her and have children with her is also a real chance for Gwen,' said Stephen, thoughtfully. 'I mean, it's not the classic romantic love story, but the relationship could be good for both of them.'

'If he manages in the long run to keep away from the tempting offers of beautiful girls,' said Leslie, before adding tartly, 'And both of us know only too well how hard that can be for men.'

Stephen looked like he wanted to reply, but he refrained.

After a while he pointed to the little table where the computer print-outs, the glass and the bottle gave a clear picture of how Leslie had spent her evening. 'Exciting reading?' he asked.

'Fiona's life story. Or at least a part of it. She wrote it down for Chad and sent it to him via email. It was meant to be for his eyes only, but Gwen guessed the password and printed it all out. Colin Brankley gave me the sheets. He was very mysterious about it, but I'm not yet sure why. Fiona describes her evacuation from London during the war and her life on the Beckett farm. She often told me about it. What's new is finding out that she was really in love with Chad, but that's something I had at least suspected, and that they had some sort of relationship. I haven't got any further than that yet.'

She shrugged. 'As you can see, I drowned my sorrows drinking yesterday. So after a while I wasn't really taking in what I was reading.' She thought for a moment. Something surfaced from her alcohol-laden memories, a term...

'Guilt,' she said. 'She hinted at a guilt which Chad and she had burdened themselves with. But I haven't read about that yet.'

'What kind of guilt? Any idea?'

'Not really. The only thing I can imagine is that Fiona and Chad had a relationship, even once Fiona was married to my grandfather and Chad to his wife. Although... she wrote that Chad and she could not have a life together *because of guilt*. So it can't have anything to do with their later spouses!' She furrowed her brow. 'Did I tell you that Fiona had been getting anonymous calls?'

'No. What kind?'

'Silence. Breathing. Nothing else. She hadn't told anyone about them, except Chad, on the evening she died. They must have had quite an effect on her.'

'Did she tell Chad whether she suspected anyone?'

'No. She had no idea who it was.'

Stephen put down his cup, leant forward and looked at Leslie very seriously. 'Leslie, I think the story there,' he nodded towards the little table with the print-outs, 'should be in the hands of the police. A vital clue might be hidden in it.'

'So far it's just someone's life story. A love story.'

'She wrote about guilt.'

'But...'

'Don't play it down. She wrote about guilt. She was receiving anonymous calls. Then she's murdered. That means that anything which in any way can give an insight into Fiona's life should be made available to the police.'

'Her notes are very personal, Stephen. Even as her granddaughter I feel a little uneasy reading them. They are

memories she only wanted to share with Chad. Now Gwen,
Jennifer and Colin know them too. Soon me too. Frankly,
I'm disappointed in Gwen and her snooping around. She
certainly shouldn't have let Jennifer and Colin, who aren't
even family, read them. Do they have to know Fiona's
thoughts and feelings as a child and young woman?'

'Maybe there are things in it that Gwen couldn't deal
with on her own. Leslie…'

She reached for her cigarettes impatiently and lit one.
'Yes. OK. I'll read it. And if there is anything which might
be relevant, of course I'll tell the police.'

'I hope you can judge what's relevant,' said Stephen.
'And, Leslie, you know you are not allowed to keep things
to yourself, even if you read something which…'

'Yes?'

'If you read something which doesn't throw a good light
on your grandmother. The main thing is to find her murderer. That's more important than anything else.'

'Stephen, there's something you don't know. A young
woman was murdered here in Scarborough in July. In a
similar way to Fiona. So it's very possible that Fiona's murder had nothing to do with her own life. She might just
have had the bad luck of running into a psychopath who
is going around killing women.'

'Possibly. Anything's possible.'

She got up. Stephen was too close now. The room was
too small. And the coffee was cold, too.

'You know what,' she said, 'I'm hungry, and this breakfast really wasn't enough. Let's go into town and have
something proper to eat. Then let's do the shopping. Let's…
do something normal!'

In his eyes she could read what he thought: that there

would be no normality in their lives for a long time. That their escape into the fog could only bring them a momentary distance from events, nothing else.

2

THE MORNING HAD been a mixed bag for Valerie Almond, but she resolved to look on the bright side.

Jennifer Brankley? Bingo! Valerie congratulated herself on her good memory. Even if she had not recalled the details, the name had at least clearly rung a bell. Entering her name in the database had confirmed her hunch. Brankley had been involved in a scandal seven years ago.

She had been a teacher at a school in Leeds. She had been extremely popular with her pupils, respected by her colleagues and appreciated by parents. Jennifer was known for her very direct and intense relationship to the young people she taught. She did not see her job as only about passing on knowledge and helping the pupils obtain good grades. She had wanted to be their partner, their confidant, the person they would turn to. She had really wanted to be there for them, and it seemed that they accepted her offer. Jennifer Brankley was often voted the pupils' teacher of the year. You could not find a person in the school who did not have something good to say about her. At least, that was *before* the incident.

'That went too far,' as another teacher said anonymously in the internet edition of one paper. 'However much she understood her pupils and was ready to help them, she shouldn't have done *that*!'

'That' was to supply a seventeen-year-old pupil with

strong tranquilisers, and for several months no less. The girl had always suffered from a violent fear of exams, and as she neared her A levels the fears were becoming acute. She would become extremely scared and have panic attacks, and she confided in her teacher, Jennifer Brankley. Before an exam she was particularly dreading, Jennifer had given her some tranquilisers, and she had indeed been calmer and more relaxed as a result. Since the exams were stretched out over four months and the pupil was both enthusiastic about the effects of the tablets and felt they helped her to achieve better grades than normal, she did not want to be without the pharmaceutical support. The papers reported that Jennifer Brankley later said she had been absolutely aware of the balancing act of what she was doing, and that it had been clear to her she was on a collision course with the law. However, she had not been able to refuse the girl's heartfelt pleas.

The catastrophe snowballed when the pupil told one of her friends about the pills and this girl told her parents. They immediately told the first girl's parents. The headmaster and the police were informed, and the press. From one day to the next Jennifer Brankley had found herself at the centre of a storm and looked on helplessly as a wave of malice, scorn and anger hit her. Of course the papers had not been able to hold back from manipulating the story to their own ends.

Valerie found unbelievable headlines in the archives. The most harmless of them said *Teacher drives pupil into pill addiction* and: *Addicted: what did treacherous teacher Jennifer B want?*

At some point it came out that Jennifer Brankley herself sometimes took tablets to get through the working week. This would not normally have interested anyone, as it did

not affect her work nor was she in any way addicted to
the medicine. Yet once she was caught in the maelstrom
of suspicion, accusations and people's desire for sensation, then anything and everything could be used against
her. Naturally, her consumption of these tablets—which
quickly ballooned into a *dangerous pill addiction*—was
the first thing to be seized upon, although if there had been
anything in her marriage or previous life which had lent
itself to a spectacular front-page headline, it too would
have been taken apart. At least in the area around Leeds
and Bradford, Jennifer was put through the media mill.

After this ordeal she lost her job as a teacher.

Valerie got up from her desk and reached for her coat.

Sergeant Reek, who sat at the desk opposite hers, looked
up. 'Inspector?'

'I'm driving out to talk to Paula Foster,' explained Valerie. 'I don't actually think that Fiona Barnes was killed
by mistake, but I'd like to be sure. And then I might head
on over to the Beckett farm.'

On the way down to the car park she thought about the
less positive news that morning. The post mortem had not
come up with anything of use. It looked as if Fiona Barnes
had met her murderer on the road at night and then, either
attempting to escape or at the murderer's insistence, had
taken the small path that went through the Trevor farm.
The culprit had hit her repeatedly with a large rock on
the back of her head, with increasing force and brutality. As the doctor at the scene of the crime had suspected,
Fiona Barnes had still been alive when the murderer finally stopped hitting her. She had died in the early hours
of the morning of a brain haemorrhage, following a frac-
ture to the skull. The attack must have taken place between
eleven and half past eleven that night.

. Fiona had probably lost consciousness with the first blow, or at least lost the ability to react. There was no sign that she had defended herself from her attacker. There was no one else's skin under her fingernails, nor was anyone else's hair found on her.

The weapon used was not found near the scene of the crime. There was no shortage of rocks. This suggested that the culprit was not armed when he met his victim. He had spontaneously grabbed a weapon and been clever enough to either take the rock with him or to dispose of it far from the scene. There were a number of streams around here. If he had dropped it in one of them, it was unlikely it would ever be found.

This was also just like the Amy Mills case, thought Valerie, getting into the car. The murderer was not armed in that case either. He used the wall to kill his victim. Either he knew the place very well, or he was relying on coming up with something at the right moment. In neither case did there seem to be much forethought. Nevertheless, the places where the victims were intercepted might have been chosen carefully. In the Mills case, the attacker also wore gloves. Mills often went through the Esplanade Gardens on Wednesday nights. There was still no explanation as to why the mesh fences had blocked her usual route. They could well have been part of a planned murder.

However, it would have been impossible to predict that Fiona Barnes would walk down that road on her own that evening. Until her sudden decision to walk part of the way, she herself had not even known. What is more, she would normally have been driven home in her granddaughter's car.

Normally...

Valerie drove slowly out of the police compound. The

fog was so thick that you could only see a few feet in front
of you. She turned on the headlights and sadly remembered the sunshine of the day before. Then it had been fun
to get up and throw herself into the work ahead. Now the
whole world seemed to be moving slowly and heavily, as
if in a cocoon which swallowed all sound and made images blurry.

A shitty day, thought Valerie, as she crept up the street.

All the circumstances of Fiona Barnes' murder seemed
to lead to the conclusion that her murderer must have been
one of the people who took part in the engagement party
which ended up going so wrong that nothing could repair
it. Valerie's problem was that she could not really see a
motive. Only Tanner—and possibly Gwen—might have
had one, and that motive did not seem sufficient for such
a brutal murder.

She had talked to the coroner for a long time. 'Man or
woman? What do you think?'

The forensic doctor had hesitated. 'Hard to say. It was
definitely someone driven by rage, I'd say. He—or she—
got more and more angry. You need strength for the blow
which led to her death.'

'More strength than women normally possess?'

'Not necessarily. There was real hate behind this. Hate
doubles your strength. No, I wouldn't rule out a woman
attacker. One thing's for sure, the culprit is right-handed.'

Great, thought Valerie sarcastically, that narrows things
down. Right-handed, like at least three quarters of people, and it could be a man or woman. Now I'm getting
somewhere.

She felt a familiar pressure descending. She knew that
she would have to have a lead soon, or better yet: solve the
case—or both cases—if she did not want her superiors to

get involved. Then she would be out of it—pulled off the
case and a complete failure as far as clearing up crime.
If the suspicion grew that it was a serial killer whom this
relatively young officer was unable to track down, then
someone from Scotland Yard would be brought in. She
needed a clue urgently.

Jennifer Brankley. The woman had seemed strange to
her from the first moment. Not just because she spent her
holidays on this desolate farm and always had the two
giant dogs with her. It was something else. Now that she
had read the old press reports she knew what it was: Jennifer Brankley was a deeply bitter woman. She felt she had
been treated badly by life, by people and by fate. She had
never got over her dismissal. The incident was still eating
her up, years later.

What would her psychogram look like?

She has that so-called helper syndrome, thought Valerie, peering into the fog of a barely visible crossroads.
What she did for her pupil was not normal. She could have
done all sorts of things for the girl—talked to her parents,
or a doctor, asked a psychologist for advice, whatever. But
she wanted to help her herself, spontaneously and directly,
and so she risked everything. Her job—no, her career.
It could even have wrecked her marriage. All the filth
the papers printed would have destroyed many relationships. Colin Brankley worked in a bank. His bosses cannot have been pleased. No doubt the incident caused him
some trouble. Jennifer Brankley risked that too. As if the
only thing she had seen was her pupil's need. As if nothing else had mattered.

She still believed that she had been treated badly, un-
fairly, that a great injustice had befallen her. You could see
it: she only wanted the best; she was being punished for it.

What was her relationship to Gwen?

A strong relationship, you could feel that. Jennifer was a little like a mother, a big sister, a confidant. What would she not do for Gwen?

Could she have felt Gwen's future happiness with Tanner was so threatened that evening that she decided to wipe out the source of the danger—that danger being Fiona Barnes?

Or was nothing of the kind planned? Had someone—Jennifer? Dave?—confronted Fiona, wanting to have a talk or an explanation for her meddling? Had the situation got out of hand, and escalated into a fight and then violence?

Valerie slapped her hand on the steering wheel. Poking around in the fog, that was what she was doing. Desperate guessing, stumbling around in the dark, hypotheses, and dismissing them again. No clues, nothing.

Go through it all again with a fine-tooth comb, she told herself. Try not to miss anything. Why was Tanner the chief suspect?

Not only because he was the only one to have a motive—even if not a particularly convincing one—to attack Fiona Barnes, but also because he was the only one who could be connected to the Amy Mills case, however precarious the connection might be. Was there anyone else? Someone else who had known Mills?

She had now turned onto the road leading to Staintondale. Banks of fog lay on the ground like giant cushions. Tall wet blades of grass bent down towards the damp tarmac. Valerie took her bearings from the fog banks, in order to follow the course of the road.

Gwen Beckett. She had attended the Friarage School course. Linda Gardner had taught there. Amy Mills had worked for Gardner.

In any case, it was a connection. Even if it led to absurd conclusions. She could not imagine Gwen Beckett
as a cold-blooded double murderer. Nor was there any apparent motive in Amy Mills' case. As for Fiona—she had
messed up the engagement party, was that reason enough?

Valerie's instinct told her: No!

Amy Mills. She let the facts of the murdered young
lady's life pass through her mind and suddenly sat bolt upright. How could she have missed that…Amy Mills was
from Leeds. Had gone to school there. Jennifer Brankley
had taught in Leeds… It was a faint possibility, but still.

Using her car's hands-free radio, she immediately called
Sergeant Reek.

'Reek, please find out which school Amy Mills went
to in Leeds. And which school Jennifer Brankley taught
in—also in Leeds. There could be more than one school
in each case. Check if there was any overlap and if the two
knew each other.'

'I'll do that. But according to her statement, Mrs Brankley had never heard Amy Mills' name.'

'Statements can be true or false, Reek. It's up to us to
find out which.'

'OK,' said Reek.

Valerie finished the call. Her heart was beating faster
as she drove on. Excitement. The thrill of the chase. Whatever it was, it was a feeling she had been desperately waiting for. Finally a step forward, finally a lead. It could be
a hot one.

Just in time she saw the little lane leading to the farm
where Paula Foster lived. She yanked the steering wheel
round and turned up the lane. She had to concentrate on
the young woman now, had to eliminate the possibility that

she was the intended victim, otherwise she would still be in danger. Even if she had already crossed off this alternative in her own mind.

3

'REALLY, DAVE. NOTHING, absolutely *nothing* that Fiona said the other evening has changed what I feel for you. I'm still…I still love you. I believe in a future with you.' Gwen looked at him unflinchingly. She was sitting on a chair in his room, dressed as usual in a long woollen skirt and a jumper she herself had knitted in an indefinite colour. She was carrying a large bag. It had been quite a journey, by foot, then by bus, and then from the bus stop again by foot. The humidity outside had turned her hair into something that looked like candy floss and stuck out frizzily in all directions. Her dark eyes were like two pieces of coal in her very pale face. A little rouge might have helped to improve her general appearance, a dab of lipstick…

She would never learn how to make herself a little more attractive, thought Dave, looking at her. He was sitting on his bed and had just managed to slide Karen's scrunched up tights under the bed frame. Thank God Gwen had not seen them. She was so occupied with what she had to say, with convincing him, that he had even managed to make Karen's lipstick disappear discreetly as he moved around the room and made the tea. Gwen had not said she was coming. Suddenly there she was at the front door: a delicate creature appearing out of the fog. The landlady was not at home, which is why Dave himself had opened the door. At least he was dressed. That in itself was a miracle, for when he had woken up late that morning one glance out the window had been enough to convince him that it would be better to spend the day in bed. After all, he only had to teach in the school that evening. In the end a strange inner restlessness had got him up. It had taken him a while to work out that it was not at all unnatural for him to feel unsettled in his situation. He had no idea what would happen next. Above all, he had no idea what serious consequences the investigations into Fiona Barnes' death could have for him.

Of course he was the number one suspect, and he recognised that the short conversation the day before with DI Almond would not have changed that. They could not prove anything against him, but he was under suspicion. If they found no other leads, he would be firmly in their sights. The noose would tighten around his neck. He was a man without a great reputation, a man who lived in unusual conditions, and this would not help. The whole affair could prove tricky, he was well aware of it.

To hell with Fiona Barnes, the old lady, he had thought, drinking a strong cup of coffee to warm up. It was a cold day, but as usual his landlady was being stingy with the heating.

To hell with all that. Sod Gwen and her clan. It brought you bad luck, the Beckett farm and everything around it. Find another way to go.

Easier said than done. He could not see another way. He had not seen one for years. It was unlikely that one would suddenly appear in front of him now. When the doorbell rang, at first he had expected to see the police officer in front of him once again, ready to fire away questions. He had briefly considered not opening the door at all, pretending that no one was at home. But then he had given himself a kick up the backside. It was better to face the situation. Better to know what they had against him than for him to close his eyes to it.

But then it was not Almond at all. But Gwen. Now she had been sitting in his room for a quarter of an hour talking at him. She had got so cold and wet that the first thing he had done was to make her a hot cup of tea. At least she did not nag him about the mess, as Karen always had. Gwen had only been to his place twice and had never said anything about its calamitous disorder. Nevertheless he had never liked to have her there. His room was a den, a place to retreat to, away from Gwen. He needed some space without her, a place that was taboo for her.

Suddenly the thought crossed his mind that he would perhaps even have preferred receiving DI Almond into his room. Not his fiancée. That is, if they were actually engaged. After all, the party had ended rather abruptly. Maybe she was more like his almost-fiancée. Even that felt a little threatening to him.

'It's all right,' he said soothingly, realising that Gwen had stopped talking and was looking at him expectantly. 'Really, Gwen, I don't hold it against you. It's not your fault Fiona said all that.'

'In all honesty, I'm not all that sad she's dead,' admitted Gwen suddenly with a violence unlike her usual self. 'I know it's a sin and that you shouldn't think such a thing, but she went too far this time. She always meant well, but sometimes…I mean, you can't meddle in everything, can you? Just because my father and she once…' She did not finish her sentence.

Dave guessed what she had wanted to say. In any case, he had thought along those lines already himself. 'There was something between the two of them at one point, was there?' he asked. 'I don't think that's a surprise to anyone. You feel it somehow.'

'If only it were just that,' said Gwen. The disturbed look in her eyes did not escape him. 'My father and Fiona were…they…'

'What?' asked Dave, as she hesitated.

'It's a long time ago,' said Gwen quietly. 'Maybe those things are irrelevant now.'

Normally he would not have been interested in the lives of Chad Beckett and Fiona Barnes, for both of whom he harboured an equally strong dislike, but in view of the current situation, particularly his own situation, he should not ignore any such comments.

So he leant forward a little. 'Perhaps it is relevant, who knows. After all, Fiona was killed pretty brutally.'

Not a little astonished, she looked at him as if he had just confronted her with some new monstrosity, rather than an incident being discussed in all the streets and alleys of Scarborough. 'But…that doesn't have anything to do with her and my father,' she said. 'Or with what they shared. The murderer is probably the same person who killed Amy Mills, and there's no connection between her and them.'

'How do you know? That it was the same murderer, I mean?'

'That's what I understood from Detective Inspector Almond,' replied Gwen, now unsure.

Almond had thrust a photo of Amy Mills in front of his face too. He knew that there had been considerations along the lines that the cases might be connected, but he had been under the impression that although the officer had some clues which suggested a link, there was not a shred of evidence.

'Could be,' he said. 'But needn't be. Gwen, if you know anything that could help the police, then you should…'

'Dave, I…perhaps we shouldn't talk about it any more.' She had tears in her eyes.

So why start at all then, he thought angrily, if you don't want to talk about it.

'You do know that I'm one of the police's main suspects, don't you?' he asked.

She must have known, but it seemed to shock her, hearing it bluntly from him like that.

'But—' she began.

He interrupted her. 'Of course I didn't do it. I don't have either Amy Mills or old Barnes on my conscience. Amy Mills I didn't know, and Fiona Barnes… Good Lord, just because she's said some vicious things about me, I'm not going to go and smash her head in with a rock. I was mightily peeved on Saturday night, but I don't take an eighty-year-old woman seriously enough to murder her for some out-of-order insinuations.'

'They won't really believe that you did it, and if you haven't done anything, then you've nothing to fear,' she said in such a tone of voice that revealed her utter trust in police investigational procedures.

Only a few years previously Dave had thought of all policemen only as 'pigs', and he was not ready to share her faith in them. Things were clear to him: DI Valerie Almond wanted to work her way up the career ladder—of course, that is what everyone wanted. So she needed to solve the *Moors Murders* as a paper had already called the two crimes. To do so, a culprit needed to be convicted. The longer she stumbled around in the dark, the more stubbornly she would cling to the few tenuous clues she had, and unfortunately that meant: him. Thanks to the fact that

Barnes had torn him off a strip in front of a whole host of witnesses, he was now in the firing line. Of course he still had an ace up his sleeve, and he would play it if need be, but only if he had no other choice.

'Gwen, you know—' he started before stopping, seeing the naivety and blind submission in her face. He had wanted to explain to her about people who are wrongly accused and imprisoned, about ambitious policemen and corrupt judges, about the press's power to put officers under pressure and push them in false directions, about the shenanigans of high-level politics, how an important citizen might be sacrificed to the needs of an ambitious careerist. He would never have assumed that as long as you did not commit the crime, you would never be punished for it. He had never believed in the justice system. He had always considered it to be cynical and open to bribery, and this conviction had caused the irrevocable split with his father—a total servant of the *system*—twenty years ago. He had not had the slightest contact to his family since then.

He could have explained to Gwen that this was the reason for the life he had now, which others might see as a failure, and which he himself often enough saw as a failure—and that was the depressing nub of the problem for him. He was unable to make any kind of peace with his country, his state or any of the whole political and social structure. He would be unable to become part of the society of Great Britain as long as he rejected and scorned it. He could have talked to his fiancée about the predicament which had crystallised for him with the passing of the years. His predicament was that he recognised, in spite of everything, that he too was a part of the system and had to come to terms with it. He did not have the strength to reject it forever and in every way. Yet at the same time he felt that he was a traitor to his convictions and to his own nature.

He would have liked the woman he planned to marry to be someone to whom he could open up and share his internal contradictions, but he knew that Gwen would not be able to follow him. Her life was the farm, her wonderful Dad, her romance novels, cheesy television dramas and her waiting and hoping for a miracle. He did not think she was stupid. But her life had happened in its own particular space. Unlike most people nowadays, it had been marked all too strongly by seclusion, ignorance of the ways of the world, and shyness. He had told her about his youthful protests against the stationing of cruise missiles and she had stared at him as if he were talking about little green men from space. He had started a long and excited speech in which he had given vent to his unhappiness with the Thatcher years and how much that era had determined his later way of life against the system. She had listened with a despairing look on her face. He knew this was not because she had a different political opinion. He could have lived with that and found the intellectual friction in their differences interesting. The problem was that she had *absolutely no* political opinion. She was completely indifferent as to whether Labour or the Tories were in power. Indeed, neither party was going to change her personal situation one iota. That was probably true of many people, but they did not then simply ignore everything unrelated to their immediate environment. It was unusual to do that. It was disastrous that Gwen could obviously not do anything else.

'Oh, nothing,' he said simply and so refrained from another doomed attempt to let his future wife see inside him and to share with her some of the thoughts, fears and confusions he felt.

'Please just promise me that if you know something important about Fiona, you will tell the police,' he added. That was where they had started: that Fiona and her father had done something stupid, which Gwen had trouble digesting. It could be relevant.

Probably not, he thought.

She looked at him. She was somewhere else entirely. Where *she* had started.

'Will you still…are we still…I mean…has anything changed?'

Now, his inner voice told him, you could get out. With a pretty plausible reason. She would be in despair, but she would not have to blame herself for the break-up. It would all be Fiona's fault—the old cow with the evil tongue, and Gwen could hate her for all eternity and would not have to beat herself up about her own inadequacy. Do her the favour. Use this merciful opportunity.

He could not. Even knowing it was the right thing to do, he just could not. She was the way out of this cold room, out of this life on the breadline, out of sleeping all day and drinking all night, and above all out of the feeling of being a loser who would never sort his life out.

'No, Gwen,' he said with a voice raw with the effort of getting through this moment. 'No. Nothing has changed.'

She got up. She smiled.

'I want to sleep with you, Dave,' she said. 'Now. Here. I so much want to.'

Good Lord, he thought horrified.

4

THE PHONE RANG just as Colin was starting to think seriously about lunch. It was already half past two and he was starving. No one on the Beckett farm seemed to feel responsible for cooking today. Gwen had disappeared since the morning, no one knew where to, and Chad had barricaded himself into his room—literally: the door was locked. Colin's tentative query was answered with a rough growl.

Detective Inspector Almond was there. She had suddenly appeared and had said that she wanted to talk to Jennifer on her own. For the last half hour the two had been sitting downstairs in the living room while Colin waited upstairs with increasing unease. And hunger.

He hurried down to the study to get the phone. At least he now had an excuse to get closer to the living room.

'Yes?' he answered it, while simultaneously straining to hear something of the conversation in the next room—in vain.

'Hello.' A woman was on the other end of the phone. She was not easy to understand because she spoke so quietly. 'Excuse me, who am I talking to?'

'Colin Brankley. On the Beckett farm.'

'Oh, Colin! You're Jennifer's husband, aren't you? This is Ena. Ena Witty.'

'Colin did not have the slightest clue who she was. Right?' he said.

'I'm…I'm a friend of—an acquaintance of Gwen's. Is Gwen there?'

'Unfortunately not,' said Colin. 'She's not in. Can I take a message?'

Ena Witty seemed thrown by this news. 'She's gone?' she asked in disbelief.

'Yes. Would you like her to call you back?'

'Yes. It's that…I have to talk to her about something important. At least, I think it's important. But I'm not sure, so I…perhaps…I'll call her back…'

The woman sounded rather confused to Colin. He was keen to end the call. He had just heard the front door close and then a car engine start in the yard. Thank God the Almond woman was finally buggering off. He had to see how his wife was doing.

'Right then, Ms Witty,' he said impatiently. 'I'll let Gwen know you've called. Does Gwen have your number?'

Ena did not know. She dictated her number for Colin, and after a moment's hesitation as to how much she should confide in the stranger at the other end of the line, she added: 'I've got…you see, I've got a really big problem…I don't know what to do, and I have to talk to someone. It's urgent. But of course I know that…well, Gwen will have other worries. I read about the horrible crime at the Beckett farm in the paper. Apparently the victim was a good friend of the family? How terrible for Gwen!'

'We're all here for her,' said Colin. He did not want to go into it any further. He did not know this acquaintance of Gwen's and he had no idea how close the two friends were.

'So, Ms Witty…' he said and she finally realized he was in a hurry.

'I'm sorry to bother you,' she said. 'And please, do get Gwen to phone me. It's really very important.'

He promised her once again that he would pass on her request, and then he said goodbye and hurriedly put the phone down. He rushed to the living room, where Jennifer, very pale, was sitting on the sofa. Colin thought she looked pretty upset.

'Darling, finally! She's gone. Should I make us a cuppa? Or do you want something to eat?'

Jennifer shook her head. 'I'm not hungry. But if you…'

'I can't be bothered just for myself,' Colin said. He shivered. 'God, it's cold and clammy in this room! And so foggy outside…horrible day, isn't it?'

She did not reply. Resolved, he knelt down in front of the fireplace. 'Help me, will you,' he asked. 'If no one else is going to do it, we'd better do it ourselves.'

As they worked to get a fire started, Colin asked, as if by the by, 'What did she come back for? Almond, I mean.'

Jennifer, who was passing him a log, froze. 'She knows,' she murmured.

'What?'

'The whole affair from back then. That I was a teacher and…well, all of that. She told me.'

'What's that got to do with this case?'

'She wanted to know if I knew Amy Mills. You know, the girl who was murdered here in July.'

'Why should you?'

'She was from Leeds. Went to school there. She thought I might have taught her.'

He froze now, and stared at her. 'But you didn't, did you? You said you'd never heard the name, and…'

'No. I don't know her.'

He let the fireplace alone, although they still did not

have a fire to take the edge off the cold in the room and the bleakness of the foggy day. Jennifer was sitting on the rug next to the logs and staring in front of her. He squatted down in front of her and took her hands in his. They were cold as ice. 'You're sure you don't know her?'

'No.'

'That's just…' He was breathing heavily, trying not to get excited, but he could feel the anger rising in him. 'They don't have anything,' he said bitterly. 'Nothing at all. Not the slightest clue, and so they start to poke around in people's pasts. This policewoman is completely lost, if you ask me. And out of her depth. Now she's digging up old stories and trying to make something of them. Can't wait to see what she finds out about the lot of us!'

'She knows that I used to take pills sometimes back then.'

'And? Is that illegal?'

'She wanted to know if I still took them.'

'And what did you say?'

'I said the truth. That I sometimes take a tranquiliser, before going into town for example, or when I've got something on. But that I don't often.'

'Right. And a lot of people do that. Listen, she's got no right to ask you those things. And you don't have to answer. It's none of her business.'

'She didn't believe me,' whispered Jennifer.

'What didn't she believe?'

'That I…I have a normal life. She looked at me so strangely. I think she wants to pin an addiction on me, because then she could claim I'm unpredictable and possibly also dangerous. And her colleague is already checking my statement about Amy Mills. He's asking the schools in Leeds and Amy Mills' parents.'

'He won't find anything they can use against you.'

'Probably not,' said Jennifer, but she spoke in a monotonous, helpless tone.

Colin pressed her hand more firmly. 'Darling, what is it? What's worrying you? They haven't got anything on you, and that's how it'll stay. Don't let them get to you.'

She looked at him. He could feel her fear. Damn it, he was angry. Angry at this Almond, this thoughtless woman. He knew why Jennifer was so agitated.

'It drives you crazy having to talk about it all again, doesn't it?' he asked cautiously. 'Having it all brought up again? Churned up again. Is it the old feelings which are weighing on you?'

She nodded. Her depression had her in its grip. You could actually see how it paralysed her. During the first three years after *the affair* she had been like this permanently. Since then she had it under control, but he had never let himself be deceived. Her fragile state of mind could easily come undone, especially if that was what someone was aiming for.

He could have throttled DI Almond.

'It won't ever be over,' she whispered.

'That's not true. It's over. It's over, even if some stupid policewoman talks about it.'

'It was my life. The school. The girls. It was everything.'

'I know. That's how it felt to you. But so many things make life worth living. Not only work.'

'I…'

'We have each other. We have a happy and strong marriage. How many people would give an arm and a leg for that? We have a beautiful home. We have nice friends. We have our two darling, enchanting dogs…' He grinned, hoping to tease a smile from her. She tried, but did not manage.

'You see,' he said anyway. He reached out, brushed a strand of hair from her forehead. 'Listen, I don't think Almond will bother you again. She's just stumbling around in the dark—literally, just look outside! She won't get anywhere with Leeds, the schools and Amy Mills. She'll drop this lead and have to find other ones. And in any case: you were out walking with the dogs. Gwen was with you, she can vouch for you. You told Almond that too?'

Instead of a reply, Jennifer asked, 'Who just called?'

Colin made a dismissive gesture. 'Someone Gwen knows. Ena Witty, I think she said. Pretty confused person. She has some problem she needs to talk to Gwen about quite urgently. She sounded over-excited and uncertain. Asked for Gwen to call her back.'

Jennifer's gaze took on a far-away look, as if she were seeing a distant time. 'Oh yes. Ena Witty. With her extraordinarily loud boyfriend. She was on the same course as Gwen. I got to know her last Friday.' She shook her head.

'That seems like a different world now,' she murmured.

'Our world will go back to normal again,' Colin reassured her. 'Peaceful and simple and unexciting. No doubt about it.'

'Yes,' said Jennifer, and at that moment she sounded like a good schoolgirl, agreeing to something which she did not at all believe in.

For a long time she had no longer seen her world as normal.

5

OF COURSE STEPHEN had offered to accompany her. He had almost forced her to let him. She had felt how hurt he was at being rejected. As always, the chance to cause him pain gave her a feeling of satisfaction, although she knew that it would not be long before it would collapse and leave her in a deep emptiness. The opportunity to hurt him could not remove her own hurt, the broken trust and the disillusion he had caused her. She simply managed to numb them briefly, nothing more.

She had driven to Hull on her own to identify her grandmother's body in the morgue. She had not for a moment harboured the hope that it could all be a mistake, that some unknown woman would be lying in front of her and Fiona would return days later from some short trip, surprised at the excitement caused by her disappearance.

They had prepared her grandmother's body well. There was scarcely anything to see of the nasty injuries to her head. She did not look peaceful, as you always hope dead people will look, but neither like she was in pain. Instead she looked rather indifferent. She even looked down on her own death coolly, Leslie thought.

She nodded to confirm that it was her grandmother, and then she quickly left. She lit a cigarette in the foyer and smoked it hurriedly, her hands shaking. Valerie Almond, who had accompanied her, wanted to fetch a glass of water for her, but Leslie said no. 'Thanks. I think a whisky's what I need.'

Valerie smiled in sympathy. 'You still have to drive.'

'Of course. Just joking.'

Valerie had offered to have an officer fetch her and take her home, but Leslie had not wanted that. She felt better acting under her own steam, when she had to concentrate, navigate, then find a parking space. Sitting on the backseat of a police car, too many thoughts about her grandmother would have flitted through her head, and that was what she had to avoid at all costs.

'Are you all right getting home on your own?' asked Valerie.

Leslie hated looking weak. 'I'm a doctor, Inspector. Seeing a body is not going to throw me.'

'You were close to your grandmother, weren't you?'

'She raised me. My mother died when I was five. From then on, Fiona was all I had.'

'Why did your mother die?'

Leslie took a drag on her cigarette before replying. 'My mother was a hippie. A flower child. She was always going from one festival to the next. And always on drugs. That was just part of it. Hash, marijuana, LSD. Alcohol too. At some point a cocktail of all of them was just too much for her body to take. She died of heart and kidney failure.'

'I'm sorry to hear that,' said Valerie.

'Yes,' replied Leslie evasively.

After a moment's silence, a kind of tactful pause after Leslie had told her about her mother's early death, Valerie asked, 'How well do you know Jennifer Brankley?'

'Jennifer? Not at all. I only met her personally last Saturday, at the…engagement party.'

'But you had heard of her before that?'

'Yes. Gwen had mentioned her in her letters and calls. She seems to be good friends with her. The Brankleys spend their holidays on the Beckett farm at least twice, sometimes three times, a year. I'm happy that Gwen could earn a bit of money like that. And she was in dire need of a friend. Gwen was…is…very lonely.'

'Do you have the impression that Jennifer Brankley sees herself as Gwen's protector in some way?'

'Jennifer is ten years older than Gwen. She might try to mother her a little. What are you getting at?'

'I'm trying to understand the structures and find some order in them,' Valerie replied rather vaguely.

Leslie thought for a minute and then laughed. 'You don't mean that Jennifer Brankley killed my grandmother? To save the relationship between Gwen and Dave Tanner? Acting as Gwen's *super-mother* so to speak?'

'I don't mean anything, Dr Cramer. Above all, I don't want to draw any premature conclusions. There are two possibilities. Perhaps Fiona Barnes was killed by someone she didn't know, who just met her by chance—but given the late hour and the isolated location of the farm, that doesn't seem all that probable. So the second possibility seems more likely: it was someone from the engagement party—or rather, what should have been a party.'

'So, you suspect me, Colin and Jennifer Brankley, Dave Tanner, Gwen and Chad Beckett.'

'I haven't got that far. As I said, I'm just ordering things. I'm trying to look behind the scenes, as it were.'

'How absurd, Inspector. It's unimaginable that it would be one of us.'

'Can you say that with absolute certainty? You only know Gwen and Chad Beckett really well. All the others were—and remain—essentially strangers to you.'

Leslie thought about this sentence as she drove back. She drove up the coast road towards Scarborough. There were breath-taking views of the sea here, but today the fog hid everything from sight. To top it all, it was now growing dark. The fog, the darkness, the cold.

It suited a day for identifying the dead body of the woman who had been her last living relative.

From now on, I'm really on my own, thought Leslie. She was freezing, although she had turned up the heating and it was roasting in the car. When Stephen and I separated, I still had Fiona. Now there's no one else.

She clung to Valerie Almond's words, so that she did not get swallowed up in thoughts of her own loneliness. She had managed not to cry all day—she did not want to start now.

It was true that she did not really know anyone here apart from Gwen and Chad. Now that she thought about it, right from the start she had found Jennifer a closed book, Colin too. He looked like a respectable, slightly stuffy bank employee, but something about him told her that he was not. There was more to him than that, but perhaps he had not found a way to express it. Perhaps he was somebody who was never being challenged enough, never being valued for who he was.

But we all have our weak points, thought Leslie. That doesn't turn us into murderers. How would DI Almond characterise me? Frustrated, single, a successful career woman but privately a failure. Disappointed by men, perhaps disappointed by life in general. Difficult childhood with a drug-dependant mother. Then growing up with her grandmother, which is no real substitute for a proper, intact family.

I'd be the right material to go crazy and kill an old

woman. Valerie Almond might be wondering what I held against Fiona.

Now she was thinking of Fiona after all. She had to make sure she didn't get sentimental.

So, things to hold against her: *You were damn cold. I can say that, because if there's one truly strong memory of my mother I have, it's that she was so warm. So happy. Over-excited no doubt, and doped up to her eyeballs on some drug, totally high, but I didn't know that then. I just remember that she used to hold me a lot. Take me in her arms. Press me close. I would snuggle up close to her at night to sleep…*

Careful, Leslie. Don't idealise her. She had no end of men over. You know that from Fiona, but you also have hazy memories of a good many long-haired guys at the breakfast table in the mornings. So some nights she'll have thrown you out of her bed mercilessly, you'll have had to sleep somewhere else because she preferred to screw away happily than to cuddle her little girl. Tough for a child who is used to something else.

Fiona was the embodiment of stability. Everything had its place. She would never have let me sleep in her bed, but also not thrown me out when she felt like it. I had my room, and my own bed. Everything was predictable. Everything was cold.

She drove towards a lay-by that she could barely see in the fog. She parked and pulled out a cigarette. She had to stop thinking of Fiona and her childhood. It wasn't safe. One thing came fast on the heels of another, and before long there was no stopping the thoughts. She had good mechanisms for protecting herself. She could not allow herself to break down because of Fiona's death.

She was almost relieved to hear her mobile ring, although she suspected it would be Stephen calling, concerned for her. He had no right to be.

However, it was not Stephen. It was Colin Brankley.

'Sorry to bother you, Leslie…I tried to reach you at your grandmother's flat. A gentleman answered the phone and gave me your mobile number…'

She saw no reason to explain that the *gentleman* was her ex. She did not like Colin Brankley. She realised that in this moment. He was opaque. Maybe not even honest.

So just said, 'Yes?'

'It's that…my wife is worried. Gwen left the house this morning and still hasn't come back.'

'Is that so unusual?'

'Actually, yes. At least she always says where she's going—if she goes anywhere. And she doesn't often.'

'Maybe she's at her boyfriend's place. Couldn't she be?'

'Yes…' said Colin slowly. It did not sound as though he really thought it were possible.

'She'll be making up with Dave. I hope so, anyway. After that sorry party, they've certainly got a few things to clear up.'

'I don't have Dave Tanner's number.'

Leslie knew that Colin was probably acting under pressure from his wife, and that Jennifer in turn was guided by her concern for Gwen, but she could not help feeling annoyed. Gwen was thirty-five years old. She could stay out as long as she liked without needing to explain herself to anyone, let alone her paying guests. It was unacceptable for someone like Colin Brankley to be calling round after her.

Her voice sounded sharper than she had intended when she replied. 'I don't have Tanner's number either. And I don't think it's up to us to keep tabs on Gwen. She's old enough to know what she's doing.'

'Of course. It's just that after everything that's happened…'

'I can't see any reason to snoop on her.'

'Well, I didn't see Jennifer and myself as spies,' replied Colin coolly and hung up without a goodbye.

He was miffed. So what. What had the Brankleys to do with her?

She drove on. Whether or not she wanted it, she was rather unsettled by the conversation. Gwen was a grown-up, she had a steady boyfriend who she wanted to marry, and normally there would be nothing unusual in her wanting to stay away from home for a day and a night. What was normal about Gwen? Could she and her behaviour be measured by the usual standards?

And was the wider situation at all normal? A young woman brutally murdered in a lonely part of Scarborough. An old lady bludgeoned to death on the edge of a pasture. And Gwen's fiancé among the suspects the police had their eye on…

Leslie was tempted briefly to drive over to Dave Tanner's place. Just to pop in and check that everything was as it should be. But with what reason?

Hi, Gwen, I just wanted to check everything was OK. We were worried…

Gwen's big problem in life was that she had never really grown up. She might finally manage to do that with Dave. Shouldn't she be supported in that, rather than treated like a child?

She rejected the idea of dropping by Tanner's flat and drove straight to her grandmother's flat instead.

She had to admit that it was nice to see the lights on in the windows. She had just taken leave of her grandmother on a foggy autumn day—a cold, dark flat could have been rather depressing. Unlocking the upstairs door to the flat, she could smell that Stephen had been cooking. Curry, coriander…it smelt warm and enticing. Through the open living room door she could see that candles were burning on the dining room table. Stephen stepped out of the kitchen. He had a dishcloth tucked around his waist and a glass of white wine in his hand.

'There you are!' For a moment it seemed as if he were about to put the glass down and give her a hug, but something held him back. So he stood there uncertainly. 'How was it? How are you?'

She took off her coat. 'Well, it wasn't exactly lovely. And I'm not doing great. But I'm all right.'

'You sure?'

'Yes!' She took the glass from his hand and had a large sip. 'Good thing we went shopping.'

'I cooked your favourite dish.'

'That's nice of you. Thanks.'

He smiled.

Suddenly she thought: he's so gentle. Tries so hard. He…curries favour. It would have gone wrong between us anyway. He's not the man I need, who suits me, whom I want.

This realisation was completely new. It came to her like a flash that moment in the kitchen door. It was a big surprise to her. Stephen and Leslie—weren't they a dream couple, made for each other? They had only broken up because Stephen had fallen for the flattery of another woman in a moment of weakness; he had destroyed what was indestructible—that was what she had always believed in her anger and desire for revenge.

Maybe she had got it wrong. Maybe he had only speeded

up something which one way or another was bound to happen.

He saw the changing expressions on her face and could see that something was moving her deeply. 'What is it?'

'Nothing.' She gave herself a shake, like a dog, and in a few quick gulps emptied the glass. Now just don't think about it, not about her and Stephen.

'Anything happen here?' she asked instead.

'A Mr Brankley called. From the Beckett farm. They're worried about Gwen. I gave him your mobile number.'

'I know. He called. I think his worries are over the top. Gwen's probably in bed with Dave having a good time.'

'That'd be good.' He paused. She felt there was something else.

'Yes?'

'Someone else called,' said Stephen awkwardly.

Leslie was immediately alarmed. 'Not the…?'

'It was an anonymous call,' said Stephen. 'Just like the one you described. Silence. Breathing. And then hanging up.'

She stared at him. 'But Fiona's dead!'

'Maybe the caller doesn't know. It might not be the murderer.'

'Or,' said Leslie slowly, 'her death isn't enough for him. He's got it in for all of us. The whole family.'

'That's crazy,' retorted Stephen.

He did not sound completely convinced of what he said.

The Other Child.doc

7

WHEN DID EMMA'S health start to fail? Or when did we notice? I cannot say for sure now. I was only thinking about Chad. At times in the autumn of 1941 and spring of 1942 a German bomb could have fallen on the Beckett farm and I would not have noticed a thing. I was in love, head over heels incurably in love, and there was nothing else which would have interested me. I was not even thirteen yet, but I think there were many elements in my biography which made me mature early—as my mother did not tire of telling me. There was my father's drink problem, our continual worries about money, then my father's early death, the war, the bombs, and that night in the air-raid shelter when the house collapsed above us...plus the sudden separation from my mother and lastly the feeling that she had betrayed me in favour of a completely unknown man. All of that had taken much of my childhood, had robbed me of my childhood innocence. I felt grown up. I was wrong of course, but I was more mature than my twelve years suggested. Mentally and physically I was well into puberty.

Chad and I stole time together whenever we had the opportunity. That was not always easy. I had to go to school and lost a lot of time walking there and back, and Chad's father had him working from morning until night on the farm. But again and again we managed to steal away. Our rendezvous was the barren, stony patch of beach down in the bay, even in the winter when the easterly wind would whip in from the sea and freeze our noses blue. But I liked the grim cold, maybe because it made Chad's hugs all the warmer and gave me the feeling that I had found a safe haven.

At that time we did not have sex. I think we did not dare to. My feelings were more romantic in nature. I did not yet sense physical desire, or only the start of it under layers of fear and uncertainty. No doubt it was different for Chad, but he kept his head and simply found me too young. When spring came, and with it warm days and long, light evenings when we could have made love on our 'secret' beach, he was tempted more than once. Each time he quickly untangled himself, pulled himself away as much as he could.

So we normally just talked, and actually always about the same things. Today I wonder why we did not get tired of those topics after a while, but at the time it was all so exciting, even repeating the same old stories. To be precise: Chad's eternal lament about the war and the fact that he could not take part. It vexed him no end, made him angry at times, at times almost depressed. I remember that I once interjected shyly: 'But if you went to the front, you wouldn't be able to be with me!'

'The one has nothing to do with the other,' replied Chad.

'They do. Either you're in the war, or here with me. I'd miss you like mad if you weren't here any more!'

'Maybe you don't understand yet. It's about more than just my feeling or yours. It's about England. It's about a crazy dictator who is attacking foreign countries. He has to be stopped!'

Secretly I could not see how Hitler's demise was dependent on Chad going to the front or not, but I saw what he meant and said no more about it. Nevertheless it did make me sad. I felt the difference. Chad had a second passion in his life and it was very big, perhaps even bigger than his feelings for me.

I, on the other hand, only had him.

In any case, I think I remember that Emma was often sick that winter and into the spring. We were aware when she was sick, but we did not realise that her sick periods were becoming alarmingly frequent. One throat infection followed the next. No sooner had she recovered from a violent cold than she got bronchitis. The winter was very cold and tough, and no doubt she had thought she would get better when it warmed up again. But in May 1942, an unusually hot and dry May, she had a cough which seemed almost to suffocate her. After she had dragged herself wheezing and panting out of bed day after day to do her chores, she came down with such a high fever that Arvid, who normally took little or no care of his wife, finally called a doctor. The doctor diagnosed the start of pneumonia and ordered complete bed rest.

'Really you should be in a hospital, Emma,' the doctor said, 'but I hardly dare to suggest that as I can already guess your answer.'

'I'm not leaving home,' Emma croaked promptly.

He turned towards me. I had let him in and led him upstairs, and was standing somewhat fearfully in the doorway. To answer my own question at the start of the chapter as to when we noticed Emma's health had started to fail: I think that was the moment. Rather late, I'm ashamed to say.

'You will have to look after Emma,' the doctor told me. 'You will cook lovely, strong, meaty broth for her, and make sure she eats it. She has to drink lots of water. And she's to stay in bed, understand? I don't want to hear that she's dragged herself downstairs to make a meal for the family or to tidy up the house. She needs a complete rest.'

I promised to do everything he asked. I was afraid. I really wanted to care for Emma.

After the doctor had gone, she let me know whom she was most concerned about: Nobody of course.

'You have to take care of Brian, while I'm sick,' she whispered. 'Please, Fiona, he has no one else. Arvid is none too fond of him, and Chad doesn't even know he exists. The poor little boy…' She had to cough and fought for air, her face contorting with pain.

I would have liked to say that both of those things applied to me. I could not stand Nobody either, and my answer to the problem was to treat him as if he were nothing. But I knew that I could not let Emma get excited right now. So I only said, 'But I'm away at school half the day!'

'I have to make sure Arvid keeps an eye on him then,' croaked Emma. 'But in the afternoon you could…'

'Why don't we take him to a home? After all, he can't stay here forever,' I said sullenly.

Emma closed her eyes, exhausted. 'He'd be lost in a home,' she murmured. 'Please, Fiona…'

What choice did I have? The following afternoons Nobody clung to me like a burr. Arvid looked after him in the morning, cursing about it like a fishwife. He acted as if the farm business would go to wrack and ruin because he had *the other child*, as he still called him, clinging to him. As soon as I got back from school and he saw me, he would dump Nobody on me, before I had even put down my bag and washed my hands. Nobody beamed when he saw me coming and held onto me. I had him with me the whole time, and I had lots on my plate as it was. I had to do my homework, had to cook dinner, had to keep the house tidy, feed the chickens, collect the eggs, and tend the vegetable patch. I just could not shake off Nobody. When I had been plucking weeds and stood up I bumped into him, standing right behind me and devouring me with his eyes. When I fed the chickens, he ambled around in my way. And in the kitchen he would drive me crazy. I hated cooking in any case, and his strangely observant gaze, trying so hard to understand my overly uncertain movements, made me even more nervous than I was already.

Of course I was in a foul mood because I barely saw Chad now apart from at mealtimes. Even when I had finished my chores at the end of the afternoon, how was I to meet Chad in the bay as long as Nobody was following me like a shadow? Once I locked him in his room and went off, but I regretted it when I returned. Nobody had got himself into such a state that he had made a mess in his pants and thrown up. He and the whole room stank, and his face was swollen from crying. It was just lucky that Emma had not noticed. I had to get rid of the clothes without getting caught, put him in the bath and then mop the floor. Angrily I asked myself why Emma did not finally look for a suitable place for the boy. By now it was clear that he was mentally disabled and that nothing could change that, and he was turning into a real burden.

To pay him back for all the extra work he was giving me, I scrubbed him down with ice-cold water. He did not do me the favour of whining or bursting into tears. On the contrary, I almost had the impression that he was so thankful for this attention that he would also have let me pack him in ice or hold him underwater for minutes on end. Although he was shivering from the cold and his lips were turning blue, he looked at me with beaming eyes in which I could see his devotion and adoration.

'Fiona,' he stammered smiling, 'a-and Boby.'

'Your name's not Boby,' I snarled. 'You're *Nobody*! Do you know what a Nobody is? Nothing! Nothing!'

He seemed not to have understood anything I had said, because he smiled broadly, as if I had given him a declaration of my love.

'Boby,' he repeated, and then again, 'Fiona!' He reached out his hand and tried to grasp my hair.

I quickly turned my head away. 'Stop it! And now get out of the bath. I have to dry you.'

He climbed out obediently and stood there on the rug, shivering and his teeth chattering. I looked at his thin, freezing body and felt something like a prick of conscience. It was cruel and mean of me to stick him in ice-cold water for so long. After all, he had not dirtied himself on purpose, only out of despair because I had locked him in and left him alone for at least two hours. I suppose he had fears I had no idea about, but, bloody hell, I was almost thirteen, I was in love, I just wanted to enjoy my life a little. I was out of depth being asked to care for a mentally disabled nine- or ten-year-old boy.

Looking back now, and without wanting to belittle what I did, I have to say that my behaviour was probably pretty normal. If Brian had been a little brother who I had been made to look after, I would also have tried everything to get out of it, and I would probably have not treated him any more kindly. Most girls my age would have done the same. The problem was that unlike a normally developed child Brian could not defend himself. Other boys would have shouted so the whole farm heard if they were locked in. They would have hammered and kicked the door and been freed a few minutes later by an adult. Nor would they have allowed me to pour icy water over them. Even if I had been older than them, they would have found ways and strategies to stand up to me.

Brian, though, was different. And I was too young to really understand his helplessness. I swayed between pity and intense irritability. The irritability won out easily. If he had not been so clingy, so fixated on me and yet at the same time so unable to take part in a sensible conversation, I might have had a more friendly tone for him. Instead I bounced off his shell and did not have the patience or peace of mind to make more of an effort with him.

Nevertheless I was shocked enough about my behaviour that day to try harder in the following weeks. The consequence of this was that Nobody clung to me even more closely and I could barely ever be alone with Chad. This did not exactly endear the little boy to me.

In June Emma was able to leave her bed. She had become frighteningly thin and looked a shadow of her former self. Although she often needed my support in the first weeks, she could look after Nobody again, and I managed to escape to the bay and be alone with Chad almost every day. The hot May was followed by a hot June, and an even hotter July. Cloudless days with the scent of grass and flowers. A sapphire-blue sea at our feet. And long evenings when the setting sun lit the western horizon in a glorious blaze. The war was far away and I did not care about it. If Chad had not kept harping on about his wish to go to the front, I think I would almost have forgotten that somewhere there were massacres and bombs, misery and tears. I felt secure because Emma would not let Chad go. I had the most wonderful summer of my life. That is not just how I felt at the time. I still know that they were the best weeks of my life.

On 29th July 1942 I was thirteen. The letter I received from my mother on that day put an end to all of that—

to the easygoing summer days, to the joy of puppy love, to the endless freedom of the Beckett farm, which had now become my home, in the part of the world where I felt at home.

Mum wrote that the air raids on London had diminished considerably and that there was no reason why I should be a burden on the Becketts' pocket any longer (that is how she expressed it, although my stay in Yorkshire was paid for!). She would come at the end of August and fetch me back to London. It was also high time, she said, for me to meet my stepfather.

My world collapsed. Although I have just written that the summer of 1942 was the most wonderful of my life, that was only true until that sunny Wednesday at the end of July. From then on I was trapped in the deepest despair.

The following August was the worst of my life.

8

I ARRIVED BACK in London on 1st September. I had not said a word to my mother for the entire train journey, making her so mad that she had bitten her fingernails right down and would no longer look at me. It was a sunny late summer day, but to me London looked ugly, miserable and absolutely unbearable. Here you could see and feel the war which had been so far away in Yorkshire. Broken houses, piles of rubble and burnt-out streets. People hurried along the pavements. Many of them were poorly dressed and looked hungry. We had to walk from the train station to our flat—which in fact was Harold Kane's flat, and which I had sworn to reject as a home forever. Instead of the smell of salt and hay on the breeze, I was surrounded by the stench of petrol and dust. Mum carried my suitcase. I lugged along the bag in which Emma had packed bread, meat and cheese. It contained mountains of food. She said that things were getting harder to come by in London, and she was right, as I would soon find out. Mum had half-heartedly offered to take Nobody with us and *hand him over to the relevant authorities*, but as was to be expected, Emma refused, horrified at the idea. I had never felt such a burning envy for Nobody as I did that day. He was to stay in the paradise to which I had to say a painful goodbye. He had cried when Mum and I left for the train station, and I saw Emma popping sweets into his mouth to comfort him.

Chad had been tending the sheep and had not showed his face. That was what we had agreed the evening before, and I preferred it like that. I did not want to cry, but I would have if he had stood next to his mother and Nobody and waved me off. I could only get through the day by sinking into an icy rage. Seeing him would have broken down all my inner defences.

When I saw the half destroyed city I did say something to my mother. 'There aren't any more bombs? It looks like they're falling every night!'

'Well fancy that!' said Mum. 'So you can speak!'

I looked daggers at her.

'That's the damage from the air raids at the end of forty and start of forty-one,' Mum explained. 'At the moment not much is happening. No air raid sirens for weeks.'

'Aha,' I replied sullenly. It was not exactly mature of me, but in that moment I wished for dozens of German planes to dump tons of bombs on London that night. Then Mum would see her mistake and send me back to Yorkshire in a panic.

My mother stopped, wiped the sweat off her face. My suitcase was heavy. The late afternoon was very warm. 'Fiona. We're a family. You, Harold and I. It's not good for us to become strangers.'

'I can hardly become a stranger to Harold. He's never seen me.'

'The more's the pity. For a year now he's been your father—'

'My stepfather.'

'Right, your stepfather. It's important for you to get to know each other, for the three of us to find a good way to live together.'

'And what if we don't?'

'We'll find one. Fiona, be happy you still have a family! Some children have lost everything in this war! Think about poor Brian Somerville who has no one in this world!'

'I'd rather not,' I replied angrily. 'Else I'll burst with envy. He could stay, I couldn't.'

Now Mum looked really hurt, but she had brought it on herself, I thought. We did not say another word for the rest of the walk. Conversation just could not happen between the two of us that day.

Harold Kane's flat was in Stepney, in one of the ugliest houses that I had ever seen. A miserable grey building set back from the street and hidden behind two other buildings which were considerably higher and so stopped sunlight from reaching this hidden away house. Only one house in this street had been completely destroyed by a bomb. However, the blast had obviously blown in the windows of a number of other houses. I could see hideous and crazy makeshift repairs of tarpaulin and boards. The street was very narrow and dark, even on this sunny day. In the winter it must have been as bleak as anything. By now I was used to the wide freedom of Yorkshire's countryside. I could have bawled my eyes out.

Harold Kane was already home. I had hoped that he would still be at work, and so I would have a little breathing space to get used to the new flat. Instead, he opened the fourth-floor door after we had panted up the steep dark stairs with my suitcase and bag. He was big and heavy-set and had an unhealthy red colour in his face. At the time I did not know this marked him out as a drinker. I thought he was ugly and unpleasant. I hated him at first sight.

'So you're Fiona,' he said and held out his hand. 'Welcome to London, Fiona!'

He tried to be friendly, but I didn't trust him. My feeling said that the idea of fetching me back was not his but my mother's. How was he to deal with this thirteen-year-old girl suddenly landing in their comfy coupledom? Mum and he had settled into their new life a year ago. To him I could only mean trouble.

The flat was very small and rather sparsely decorated. Even without ever having had much money, we had lived better than this. There were two rooms and a small additional chamber. They all faced out the back onto another house, which was so close that you could stretch your arm out the window and touch its walls. Although the late afternoon sun was still shining outside, there was no sign of it here. It could just as well have been an overcast November day instead of the sunny first day of September.

The first room was used as a living room and kitchen. The second room was Mum and Harold's bedroom. The little chamber—as I had guessed—was to be my room. A bed and a narrow wardrobe fitted inside, and that was all. I could barely turn around in there.

'And where am I to do my homework?' I asked angrily.

'At the kitchen table,' my mother replied, trying to present an aura of carefree cheer, which came across as completely fake. 'You've got room, and no one will bother you!'

I really had to compose myself, else I would have burst into tears. Everything was so much worse than I had imagined. Not that I was spoilt. On the Beckett farm the bedrooms were small and dark, the house was run-down, and my bedroom—if I am to be honest—was only marginally bigger than the small room here. But on beautiful days the sun flooded in through all the windows and you had a view out over an endless expanse of meadows until they blurred into the sky on the horizon. From one of the top rooms you could see the sea behind a gap in the hills. I had the feeling of an almost limitless freedom. Here, on the other hand, I felt I was being buried alive, walled into a prison.

'I'm at the docks all day,' said Harold, which I took to be an attempt to make me feel better. 'And your Mum isn't home either, because unfortunately she still goes to clean for people, even though there's no need for her to. So the whole flat is yours.'

'We can use the money I bring in,' said Mum.

'We'd get by without it too,' replied Harold.

I had the feeling I was listening to a long-established argument. Obviously Mum's cleaning was a hot potato.

'Things would get tricky,' she said.

I began to ask myself why she had married this Mr Kane. He was not good-looking, and he obviously did not have money. What, for God's sake, was his attraction for my mother? I thought she was a pretty woman. She could have caught a better fish than this swollen fatty. My dead father might have been a drunkard, and completely unreliable, but he was a good-looking man. I remember that as a child I was often proud to walk around town with him and see the looks that unknown women threw him. That would never happen with Harold.

Had Mum been that desperate?

Of course, now I can understand her better. By to-day's standards, my mother, in her mid-thirties, was still a young woman. Back then she was over the hill. She was a widow, had a child and no money. She did not want to stay alone for the rest of her life, but men were not exactly running to her door, given her situation. In addition, most men her age were at the front and not exactly in a position to come courting. Mum had always been a very pragmatic person. She had seen Harold Kane as a real and possibly last chance for herself, and she had grasped it. Now she was determined to make the best of it. The only problem was that I was supposed to play along, but I was set against it.

For dinner we had potatoes and meat. The meat was so stringy that you had to keep plucking bits from between your teeth, while I found the potatoes tasteless. Mum noticed that I was not enjoying the meal.

'I'm sure the food was better in the country,' she said. For the first time since she had fetched me against my will from Staintondale she sounded a little apologetic. 'Here in town the war has brought shortages.'

I did not reply. What could I have said? Not just the food—everything was better in the country. Evening came. Around this time I would normally have run down to the bay and met Chad. We would have hugged. I would have felt his heartbeat next to mine. We would have told each other about our day, and then I would have had to listen to one of his angry monologues about the call-up he longed for...

I pushed my plate away. Thinking of Chad was too much for me. I could not eat another mouthful.

I saw too that Harold did not eat much. He more than made up for it in beer consumption. More than could be good for him. His ballooning body was probably more a result of the alcohol than the—to be generous—average cooking skills of my mother. Another drinker! At the time I did not think about psychology, otherwise I would have seen the fatal pattern in my mother's life. Her father had been an alcoholic, her first husband too, and now her second husband. She obviously had a soft spot for drunks, and was unable to break this downward spiral. I did not understand that she too was a prisoner of herself. In disbelief I simply asked myself again and again: Why? Why? Why Harold Kane?

After the meal I went straight to bed. I did not even help to clear the table and do the washing up. They allowed for my tiredness after such a stressful day and did not object. However, as I got undressed in the claustrophobic narrowness of my room, I heard Harold complain to Mum in the next room: 'She can't stand me! I noticed straight away!'

'She's got a lot to get used to today,' replied Mum. 'She's grown very close to the Beckett family. Now she feels uprooted. She's rejecting everything she finds here. Don't take it personally.'

'I think it was a mistake to bring her here against her will,' said Harold. I froze, full of hope that the two of them might come to see that—

Mum dashed my dreams immediately. 'No,' she said resolutely. 'It wasn't a mistake. It was high time. She was about to become completely integrated into their family. I should have stepped in much earlier.'

'It was your idea to send her away to the country!'

'You know how it was. Bombs were raining down night after night. I didn't want to lose my own girl. But now I don't want to lose her in another way. Don't you understand? By her seeing another woman as her mother!'

'We're doing all we can so she won't be your only child,' said Harold, and in spite of my youth and inexperience I could not help noticing that his tone had changed. 'Perhaps we should try again now, what do you think?'

'I have to clean the kitchen. And Fiona's not asleep yet. She might come in any moment.'

'Rubbish. She's dead tired. We won't hear a peep out of her tonight.'

'Harold...stop it...I'm really afraid that Fiona—stop!'

A chair fell over. I heard Mum giggle. Horrified, I held my breath. They weren't going to...right now...

The sounds which soon reached my ear were unambiguous. It was just after dinner and my mother and Harold Kane were doing it in the kitchen and could not care less that I could hear everything, absolutely everything.

It was unbearable. Quite unbearable.

I did not continue undressing but crept into bed as I was, in my stockings and the flowery summer dress Emma had sewn for me. The bed linen smelt musty. I buried my face in the pillow and clamped my hands over my ears—anything to stop me hearing the disgusting goings-on in the next room. I had kept my feelings under control for the whole of this horrible, long day. I could not any longer.

I cried. I cried the hottest, most violent tears of my whole life.

9

I REALLY DID not make life easy for my mother and Harold in the following weeks and months. My anger that they had brought me to London against my will did not dissipate. On the contrary, it became even stronger. Autumn came, and with it fog and the early nights. My mood sunk to an all-time low.

Harold avoided me and I him—as much as that was possible in the tiny flat. He was indeed away at the docks (where he was a foreman after all) just about all day long, and when he came home he would pretty quickly get drunk. Then he would fall asleep on the wobbly little sofa in the kitchen. He snored and stank of alcohol. Every time I had to pass him I shivered.

'He's a *drunk*, Mum,' I said to my mother once. 'How could you marry a *drunk*?'

'All men drink,' claimed my mother, and from her perspective and experience that must have seemed like the truth.

I shook my head. 'No! Arvid Beckett for example...'

Saying that touched a raw nerve. 'Just stop talking about the Becketts!' she snapped. 'They can do no wrong in your eyes! They're normal people like you and me and Harold!'

'They don't drink,' I insisted.

'Then they've got other vices. Everyone has a vice. Believe me!'

She might or might not have been right. I could not judge. In any case, Harold's alcoholism and the sight of his bloated face disgusted me so much that all my life I have had something against alcohol and never touched the stuff. I hate it. I cannot even stand having a bottle of a *digestif* in the house.

I went to school, conscientiously did all my homework and spent my spare time writing endless letters to Chad. I described my bleak routine, the miserable atmosphere in bombed-out London, the dark flat and the scarcity of food. In my letters he was a real monster. Chad must have thought my mother had married a fat, stupid and constantly drunk ogre. I hoped Chad would console me, but he seldom replied. He let me know that he did not like to write letters and that there was a lot to do on the farm, but that he missed me and often thought of me. I had to be satisfied with that. He was a man, after all. They all seemed to find it hard to express their feelings on paper.

At the end of November I received a letter from him, in which as usual he moaned about having to sit out the war on a sheep farm instead of fighting for England. 'The Germans' luck is changing,' he wrote. 'They can be beaten, and I want to be there!' At the end of his letter he mentioned that his mother was seriously ill again. 'A cough, fever and she looks terrible. The cold, damp weather is no good for her, but we don't have the money for her to have some time in the South, and the times are not favourable. The Channel Islands would not be bad, but Hitler's gang is there. Anyway, how would we manage here without her?'

I had to think of Nobody briefly. Who was taking care of him, if Emma had to stay in bed for weeks? Maybe they would finally put him in a home. It would be best for everyone.

There was a special surprise for me at Christmas. After we had exchanged presents in the morning (I received mainly practical things like a scarf, hat and gloves), Mum revealed that I was to have a little sibling in July.

'A baby brother,' Harold added. He was sitting on the sofa and in honour of the special day had drunk his first whisky at nine in the morning.

'We don't know yet,' Mum replied.

'I know it,' insisted Harold. 'It'll be a boy. You'll see!'

'So—are you happy?' Mum asked me.

'In July,' I said slowly. 'So it might have the same birthday as me.' That was all I needed: for Harold's son, who would no doubt take after his father, to dispute my birthday with me.

'Definitely not,' thought Mum. 'The doctor said early July. Maybe even late June. You won't get in each other's way.' Her eyes were shining and her face had a soft expression. She really was happy to be having a child with this red-faced alcoholic!

I thought of something else. 'There's no room for another person here! It'll be far too crowded!' Perhaps, I hoped, they would finally see the need to send me back to Staintondale.

Mum did not think of that. 'The first year the baby will sleep in the room with Harold and me. And then we'll see. Maybe we'll find a slightly larger flat.'

'Of course we will,' intoned Harold. I would have liked to ask him how he was going to pay the higher rent, seeing as he so consistently spent most of his wage on alcohol, but I bit my tongue. It was Christmas. I did not want to spoil the day for all of us.

WE NEED NOT have worried about the date of birth or the question of space, as it all ended dramatically earlier.

In late February Mum had a bad fall on the icy street in front of our house. She dragged herself upstairs to our flat, her face contorted in pain. Once there she sank onto the sofa and whimpered softly to herself. I made her a cup of tea, but she only had a few sips.

'It hurts so much, Fiona,' she whispered. 'It hurts so much!'

'Mum, we should call a doctor!'

She shook her head. 'No. He would just scare me. I just have to lie here and rest for a bit. Everything will be all right.'

In fact her pains got visibly worse. She was moaning loudly and pressing her hands to her stomach. I was starting to be very worried. Apart from the odd cold, my mother was never sick. I only knew her as an active, healthy person. Now her face was yellowy white, her lips were bloodless and she was writhing back and forth. With great effort she stood up, to walk a few steps, in the hope the cramps would relax. I saw a large red stain on the light-coloured sofa.

'Mum, you're bleeding,' I said, shocked.

She stared at the stain. 'I know. But…that happens… that doesn't mean anything…'

'Just let me fetch a doctor!' I pleaded.

Although she could barely stand on her feet, she snapped back, 'No! On no condition! Do what I say!'

'Why not, Mum? I…'

She pressed her lips together, then gasped, 'No!', before shuffling back to the sofa and arduously sitting back down again. I was at my wits' end.

I just did not understand why she was so set against seeing a doctor. She was in pain, and was losing blood… Did she seriously believe these pains would simply vanish into thin air? I was too young to know that my mother was suffering from shock. She was losing her child and knew it unconsciously but she was fighting the realisation with all her strength. She wanted at any cost to give Harold the son he deeply wished for, and she had taken long enough to fall pregnant. Her mother's instincts were also running away with her. She clung to the unborn child, tried to protect herself and her little one from the objective and no doubt devastating diagnosis of a doctor. She refused to face reality, putting her own life in danger. I stood there helplessly, intimidated by her sharp tone into not going for help.

Towards evening she could not bear her pain any longer and finally she seemed to realise that something had to be done.

'Run to the docks,' she croaked hoarsely, 'as quick as you can! Fetch Harold. He has to come at once!'

Without a doubt it would have been more sensible to go straight for a doctor, but I was relieved to be able to let an adult take responsibility. It was not far to Harold's dock from our house, maybe a twenty-five-minute walk. That frosty February evening in 1943 I think I made it in about ten minutes. Although there were dangerous patches of black ice everywhere, I flew through the terraces, my heart hammering. I had cramps, a dry mouth and was wheezing. My panic gave me strength. My instinct was telling me that Mum could die if she did not get help. We had wasted far too long. I prayed that I would meet Harold, and that he had not already headed for one of the grotty pubs at the docks for his first drink of the evening. In that case, I knew, I would have almost no chance of finding him. Luckily I caught him, just as he was saying goodbye to his mates. He was completely astonished by my sudden appearance in front of him out of the dark. I fought for breath and bent double with the cramps.

'Mum,' I gasped. 'You have to come home at once. She's…she's in a bad way!'

Harold surprised me. Without further ado or questions, he hurried home with me. I would not have thought that this large man could move so quickly. His face was a deep red and glistened with sweat when we arrived; he had not paused for a second. We could probably say he was lucky not to have had a heart attack.

Mum lay bent double on the sofa, her arms around her stomach. Her face was gaunt and yellow. I could not understand how, but it seemed as if she had become years older and pounds lighter in the course of that afternoon. She stared at her husband with eyes like saucers.

'Harold,' it sounded like a sob. 'I think…our son… he's…'

'Rubbish,' said Harold. 'We'll have the most beautiful boy in the world, you'll see!'

He accompanied her to the hospital. For a moment I saw his face when he was not putting on a show for Mum. It did not bode well.

My memories of that evening and the following night are hazy. I think I tried to distract myself by tidying up the flat and washing the blood out of the sofa, at which I did not succeed completely. Later there was always a darker patch on it, and when Mum could no longer stand the sight of it, Harold had to have it taken away. I never found out where he took it.

Finally, when there was nothing else to do, I waited and waited. I made myself a cup of tea, sat at the table and stared at the walls. I felt terribly guilty. I had felt such a strong inner resistance to this child. I had often wished it would not see the light of day, and now it seemed as if my secret wishes were coming true in a horrible way. And on top of it all I would lose my mother. She had looked terrible, and had lost so much blood. What would happen if she did not come home? Why had I not ignored her order and fetched a doctor much earlier? I wrestled with my feelings, I cried. For the first time in my life I realised that waiting can be the worst of tortures.

It was after midnight when I heard Harold's slow, heavy steps outside. It sounded as though he were pulling himself up the banister. I raced to the door. He was standing in front of me, staring at me with blood-shot eyes and stinking of alcohol. He must have stopped off in a number of pubs on the way back from the hospital.

'Fiona,' he said, dragging out the syllables.

'What is it? Harold, how is my mother?'

He swayed into the flat and headed straight for the sideboard in the kitchen. He got out a bottle of the hard stuff. I could have hit him.

'Harold! Please! How's Mum?'

'She'll be all right. They op-operated on her.'

I closed my eyes. I felt faint from relief. Mum was not dead. She would come back to me.

'The child,' whispered Harold. He was tongue-tied. He took a long swig from the bottle and turned to face me. 'It r-r-really w-was a b-boy. My son…is d-dead.'

I have to admit that I was not particularly moved by this news. I had nothing to do with Harold Kane's son, even if he was my half-brother. I could not stop thinking: Mum's alive, Mum's alive, Mum's alive!

An enormous weight had fallen from my shoulders.

Harold, however, was in the middle of a terrible crisis. He was in utter despair. He drank more and more, moaning and complaining with an ever more mumbling voice about the unborn child. The child that they had been waiting for. The child who had meant everything to him. The child who was supposed to change his life.

In the end I could not stand it any more and said, pretty stroppily, 'For God's sake, Harold. She'll have another child. It'll be all right!'

He lowered the bottle he had been about to put to his mouth.

'Never…again,' he said. 'Never again. The d-doctor said it w-wouldn't be p-possible a-again.'

'I'm sorry,' I said awkwardly. What else should I have said? Harold stared at me and then to my horror he burst into tears. 'Oh God,' he moaned. 'Oh God!'

He swayed over to me. 'F-Fiona, F-Fiona, hold me… hold me tight.'

I immediately stepped back, until I had the edge of a cupboard pushing into my back.

'Harold!' I said sternly.

He was right in front of me. He stank terribly of alcohol. I almost felt sick. He was also scaring me. We had never hugged, even if Mum would have liked us to. I did not want to, and he had respected that. But now, here in our flat, in the middle of the night, in his extreme emotional state, drunk and in despair, he was losing it.

'Not a step closer,' I warned him with a hoarse voice.

'Fiona,' he moaned again and went to grab me.

I ducked under his hand and was now standing in the doorway. I was more agile and quick than he was. Plus I was sober. But naturally he was much stronger, and if push came to shove, I did not stand a chance. Not a chance—if what exactly would happen?

Later I came to the conclusion that Harold Kane was not planning to assault me sexually. Neither on that night or any other had he ever given any indication that he had his eye on me. On the contrary, I came to realise that he was completely fixated on my mother. He never even seemed to notice other women.

He really had only wanted to be consoled. He was in utter despair. His world had collapsed. To feel better he would have thrown himself into anyone's arms right then, whether a man or a woman. But I was very young, and touchy. I already felt such a strong suspicion and dislike of him. I was exhausted after my horrific afternoon with my groaning, whimpering mother. My nerves must have been completely shot.

'I'll scream,' I warned him. 'If you come a step closer, I'll scream so loud the house comes down!'

He stood there, confused. 'Y-you d-don't really think…?'

I did not wait for him to finish the question. I turned round in a flash and raced through the tiny hall and into my room. I slammed the door shut behind me and leant against it from the inside. There was no key, which I had often regretted, but never as much as that night. I felt completely exposed, in danger. Harold could enter at any time and I would not be able to defend myself from him. The only thing I could do was to stay awake and make assault as difficult as possible. If he were to try to step into my territory, I would fight and scream. He would not catch me asleep in any case.

So I kept watch all night, until the morning. I sat on the floor, with my back leant against the door, and stared into the darkness. I was dead tired and at the same time awake. My heart was pounding. The thoughts were racing through my head. I could not stay here. That much was certain. Harold had said Mum had been operated on. That meant she would have to stay in hospital for a while. At least ten days, maybe even a fortnight. There was no way I was going to stay in the flat alone with her drunk husband all that time. I could not bear him. I was afraid of him.

There was just one place in the world where I felt safe. I could only hope that what I had saved of my pocket money would be enough for a train ticket to Scarborough. Once I was there, I would see what came next. I did not think that my mother and Harold would simply accept me taking flight, but at least Mum was out of action for now and Harold could not tell me what to do. And the main thing was for me to feel safe.

That was the most important thing.

So I sat and waited and brooded until morning broke. I had heard nothing more of Harold. He had not tried to follow me into my room. At some point I must have nodded off for a moment, because I jumped when I heard the front door slam shut—the first noise for hours. Right after that I heard the sound of someone going down the stairs. Thank God Harold was going to work like any other day.

I stood up, feeling stiff. My eyes were stinging with exhaustion. Nevertheless, I was resolved not grant myself even half an hour's sleep. I was going to wash, get changed, pack the basics. Then I was going to head for the railway station.

I would spend the next night on the Beckett farm.

10

IT FELT LIKE I was travelling forever. My money had been enough for the ticket, and I was in Scarborough that afternoon. But from there it seemed to take an eternity: first to find out which bus I had to take from there, and then to wait for it to come. According to the timetable, the bus should have been there much earlier, but when I complained to the bus driver he just shrugged his shoulders. 'We're at war, young lady,' he said. The fact that he called me a *young lady* raised my mood no end. 'Most drivers are at the front. Us stand-ins can only do so much.' The bus soon reached Staintondale. I pressed my nose to the window, and in the last light of day drank in the images of the landscape I knew and loved so well. Although that February day was cold and grey, with fields and sky disappearing before the horizon in a foggy haze, and all the trees were bare, I wanted to hug every patch of field, every meadow, every stone wall and every crooked hedge. I knew what it would look like in a few weeks' time when the daffodils shot up, the open March sky was an unearthly blue and all the trees were in bud.

Dear God, please let me still be here then, I prayed silently, please let me stay!

The farm was quite a walk from the road where the driver had dropped me off. Although I had not packed much, the bag was still heavy. But now I was within reach of my destination—knowledge which lent me renewed strength. I had not slept in thirty-six hours, but that did not stop me from being wide awake. I would see Chad soon. Emma would hug me.

I was almost home.

THE FARM LAY in complete darkness, which rather surprised me. It was already evening. Only the western horizon was still a lighter grey. The bare trees stood out in front of it like a bizarre silhouette picture. The wind picked up, blowing in cold and salty from the sea. I was warm from my walk. Standing at the gate I looked at the house. Emma always used to have lots of lights on, because she wanted her house to give out a feeling of warmth and life. I had often been witness to the quarrels she and Arvid had had over this. He of course found her wish wasteful. In spite of his objections, she had always won out on this issue, although she normally acted rather submissively towards her husband.

Perhaps no one was at home. But where should they all go on a cold weekday evening?

I approached the house slowly. After stopping briefly at the door, I hesitantly pushed down on the door handle. The door opened. A cat, which had been sitting right behind the door, shot out of the hall and disappeared behind me into the darkness.

The house did not smell good. I noticed that immediately. It had not been aired. It smelt of old food and dust. In spite of not being well off, Emma had always kept her house clean and fresh. It had smelt of flowers or candles or the hearth fire. A house which seemed to welcome visitors with open arms. But now... Could the farm have changed this much in the half year since I had been here last? Or had I changed? Was I seeing things differently? Was I overtired, burnt out?

'Hello?' I called out. They never left the door unlocked when no one was at home.

I went down the hall and peeked into the living room. Dark. Cold. No fire in the hearth, no candles in the window.

I walked on. 'Hello?' I called out again. 'Isn't anyone home?'

When I reached the kitchen, I noticed a weak light coming from under the door. I gave a sigh of relief. Someone was home. But somehow I still felt on edge.

Something was not right.

I opened the kitchen door.

The ceiling light was turned off. Only the little light above the kitchen sink was on. It barely lit the room. It was rather cold in there too, even though the oven was lit. Arvid was sitting at the kitchen table—big, dark and silent. A cup and a teapot were on the table in front of him. There was a strong smell of lime-tree blossom tea, the one Emma liked to make in the evening before going to bed.

'Arvid!' I stepped into the kitchen, afraid he might have a shock, but he did not even blink. He must have heard me coming and calling, but he did not react. 'Arvid, it's me. Fiona.'

He raised his eyes. I knew him to be taciturn, but at this moment he did not seem to be merely his usual silent and bad-tempered self. It was as if he were…paralysed.

'Arvid, where's Emma? Where's Chad?'

He just looked at me. A cold, heavy fear took hold of me. 'Where are they?' I insisted.

At that moment I heard steps on the stairs.

Somebody was running down the hall. I turned around and Nobody shot into my arms. He was beaming and making unintelligible sounds. The only word which crys-

tallised out of his gobbledegook was 'Fiona! Fiona!' As
he said it, he stroked my face, slobbering with happiness.

I was no more enthralled by him than I had been before, but right now I was so relieved to meet someone
else as well as mute Arvid that I hugged the boy.

'Brian! You've really grown this winter!'

He gurgled and laughed. His mental development continued to lag behind his physical progress.

I turned back to Arvid.

'Arvid! Where's Chad? Please tell me!'

Something changed in his face. His eyes finally lost
their blankness and saw me. He moved his lips, but
needed two attempts before he could articulate what he
had to say. For a few seconds he seemed disturbingly like
Nobody with his babbling.

'Chad signed up for t' army Friday.'

I gulped. 'What?'

'Couldn't stop him,' said Arvid. 'Didn't want t', either.
He's a man. Has t' decide what t' do.'

'But…what…what did Emma say to that?'

She could not have given her permission. She would
never have allowed it. There was nothing she was more
afraid of than…

Further silence. Even Nobody had stopped prattling.
The silence thickened around me and in it I could hear
the truth blaring, blaring so loudly and clearly that with
horror I realised what it was before Arvid finally managed to speak.

'Emma died two weeks ago,' he said.

I HAD GONE on a journey to nowhere. That is what I felt
on that night, lying in bed sleeplessly in my old room
on the Beckett farm, even though I was completely exhausted by then. I could hear the familiar sounds in the

house—the creaking of floorboards, the quiet rattling of the windowpanes and the sighing of the trees outside when the wind blew through their bare branches. There was nothing I had dreamt of over the past months with as much longing as the moment when I would be in this house, this room again. The only thing was, I had imagined it differently. Emma should have been there to hug me, and Chad of course. I wanted to clamber down into the bay with Chad, out of breath and with my heart beating wildly. I wanted to give myself to his words, his voice and his tender hands… Instead…

Emma was dead! I could barely grasp it. Chad at the front: at least that made sense. It had always been obvious that he would go, if his mother's objections weakened for whatever reason. Chad had grasped the opportunity immediately. Without a word to me! He had not told me he was off to the front, nor that his mother had died. Where did I fit into his life? At the moment his thoughts did not revolve around me nearly as much as mine around him. I felt hurt, sad. And helpless.

I had sat for a while longer with Arvid in the kitchen. It was actually the first time since I had met him that we were having a chat. He had suddenly become a very lonely man. He was in no way up to the task of running the large farm with all its sheep on his own, even less so now that he had to do without his son's help. The Beckett farm was becoming more and more run-down, which was already visible in the house. Emma had always managed to hide its shabbiness. Arvid did not have the time, energy or—I suspected—the necessary skills.

He told her that Emma had fought a nasty bronchitis all winter, and in January it had become full-blown pneumonia.

'She refused t' go t' hospital. I were worried…'er fever

were so high, for days on end, but I didn't want t' take 'er off against 'er will. Then it all 'appened so quickly. She couldn't fight it any longer.'

I had to think of the Emma I had met for the first time that dark November evening on a meadow near Stain-tondale. She had been a healthy woman, slight maybe, but not fragile. She had fallen ill so suddenly, without any obvious trigger. Her recurring colds. The continual coughing. The previous year's pneumonia which she had so struggled to get over. And from which she had never really recovered.

Sitting in the kitchen, shivering because the oven did not give off enough heat, for the first time I had the feeling that although the Beckett farm was paradise on earth for me, for Emma it might have been a place of toil and tra-vail. A draughty, damp house. With ovens which needed to be heated every morning. To get water in the kitchen, you needed to use a pump. That was physically demand-ing. Time had stood still on the farm. Everything was as it had been a hundred years earlier, except that there was electricity and electric lights. Chad had once told me that the cable had only been laid in 1936. Doing the cook-ing, laundry and ironing—all the things which Emma did every day—required enormous amounts of time and en-ergy. She had slaved away from morning to night with-out ever complaining or expecting too much help from us children. It was more important to her that we did our homework properly and had some time to play. Without us noticing, she had exhausted herself.

'Arvid,' I finally said, after my third cup of tea. 'Arvid, can I please stay here? I don't want to go back to London.'

He rocked back and forth, uncertain what to say. 'That's impossible,' he said in the end.

'It can't be. I'm so unhappy there. I don't get on with my…my stepfather. He drinks. He's disgusting.'

'How old are yer?'

'Almost fourteen,' I said. It was still a long time until the end of July, but there was no need to be too exact.

'So: thirteen. Yer a schoolgirl!'

'I could keep house here. Cook, clean, do the laundry…I can do all of that!'

'Yer have to go to school. An' your parents would never agree. If I had a phone, I'd have t' call them now. I could get int' 'ot water…livin' 'ere alone with a young girl like yer! Nay, Fiona, I'm really sorry. I'm half way t' prison, if I let yer stay!'

'And what if my mother lets me?'

'She won't,' Arvid prophesied. 'Yer mother didn't mind me farm as long as the bombs were hailin' down on London and we were livin' 'ere as a family. Now everythin's changed. She'll raise 'ell t' fetch yer back.'

Unfortunately, as I lay in bed and tried to make some sense of everything I had learnt in the last few hours, it dawned on me that he was right. Mother had not wanted me here even while Emma was alive. It was more than unlikely that she would let me live here with just Arvid and Nobody.

The next morning some snowflakes were falling. Nevertheless I spent half the day wandering around the farmland, followed by Nobody, who gazed at me adoringly. I said hello to familiar places and cried silent tears because I was about to have to leave them again too. I climbed down into the bay and sat for a long time on a rock, looking out to sea. It was harsh and grey that day. I thought of Chad and the last summer evening we had spent there. The shrill, despairing calls of the seagulls seemed like the echo of my dark thoughts. Where was Chad? Was he

in danger, right now while I was here at our spot thinking of him? Would he survive the war? Would I ever see
him again?

I did not hold back my tears. Nobody was squatting beside me, but he did not disturb my crying or my thoughts.
As usual, he was perfectly happy just to be near me. At
some point I looked at him and realised that his whole
body was shaking and his lips were almost purple. I
probably did not look too different myself. I had not noticed how I had slowly become a stiff icicle. By now there
were thick flurries of snow and it was hard to make out
the sea. I stood up.

'Come on, let's get home quickly,' I said. 'We'll catch
our death of cold out here.'

He immediately followed me. He would have followed
me into the sea if I had asked him to.

Back in the house I got fires going in the fireplaces,
made tea, tidied up the kitchen, and gathered together
the larder's sparse supplies to make dinner. Arvid was to
see that I was more capable than any other thirteen-year-
old schoolgirl, and that it could be to his advantage to
have a female on the farm. While I swept the floor and
scrubbed down the surfaces, Nobody sat at the kitchen
table, drinking tea, eating a few rather dry biscuits which
I had found, and looking at me with shining eyes. I could
not help being worried about his fate too. He must be
around ten years old by now, but showed no sign of de-
veloping mental abilities beyond that of a five-year-old at
most—one who was unable to learn to speak and probably never would. In losing Emma he had lost a mother
for a second time in his short life. For reasons I could
not comprehend, I was his great love and no doubt in his
eyes I would, emotionally, balance out the loss of Emma.

Except that it looked as if I would not be able to stay. What would become of him?

Arvid had never wanted him, never cared for him. What was he to do with a mentally disabled boy?

A home, I thought. Now there really would be no other option but to put him in a home.

I felt uneasy at the thought of it. But what was I to do?

By evening the house was sparkling clean, the clammy air had become warm and dry. It smelt of the wood burning in the grates and of the food I had prepared. Candles were lit in the windows. In addition, I had given Nobody a bath and dressed him in fresh clothes and made myself look as nice as possible. I was at least going to make it hard for Arvid to send me away. Thick flakes of snow were falling outside. Inside two purring cats were lying on the living room sofa. Arvid *had to* notice the change when he returned, frozen, from a long, hard day's work.

When I heard his steps at the door I stood up, smoothed down my skirt and stepped out into the hall with an expectant smile. I heard him knocking the snow off his shoes.

The door opened and two men stepped in.

They were Arvid and Harold.

'Let's have a frank talk,' said Harold. He looked tired, and he was sober. I was hardly used to the latter. He seemed different.

We sat in the kitchen. Arvid had made himself cosy in the living room. I had sent Nobody to bed, although I could hear a scraping on the stairs which revealed that he was hanging around there and probably hoping to be near me again. We had eaten together. I had barely managed to eat a mouthful and had not even been able

to appreciate Arvid's praising my work that afternoon—
in his sparing way: 'House looks good. Yer food's tasty.'

He and Harold had met at the farm gate. Arvid had
been on the way back from one of the meadows. Harold
had come from the bus stop and was extremely relieved
to have found a human habitation. Arvid had probably
guessed immediately whom he had in front of him.

'I know that you can't stand me,' Harold said. His hands
lay on the table in front of him, tangled up together. 'Not
that I know why, because I haven't done anything to
you…but that's the way it is.'

I did not say a word. What could I have said?

'At a pinch I would say you could stay, if Mr Beckett
agreed, but I wouldn't see it as a good solution, and…
Well, it doesn't matter what I think. Fiona, you can't. Because of your Mum. I can't leave you here. She wouldn't
cope with that.'

'She managed for almost two years,' I said.

'There was a reason for that. You were in danger in
London. That's no longer the case.'

'The war isn't over yet.'

'It won't go on too much longer,' Harold said. 'The Germans are running out of luck. They're almost done for.'

I did not care about that right now.

Harold fished a handkerchief out of his trouser pocket
and wiped the sweat from his forehead. 'I took time off
work to come here,' he said. 'And I told some whopping
lies to your Mum, because she'll notice of course that I'm
not visiting her for two days in hospital. She can't know
that you ran away. We can't let her get worked up.'

'How did you know I'd be here?'

'I didn't know. But I guessed.'

'You didn't have to come.'

'And what was I to tell your Mum? Who is lying in a

hospital bed in pain and crying her eyes out because she has lost our child. How should I answer her when she asks why you aren't visiting her? What should I say when she comes home and asks me where you are?'

I bit my lip. I had not really thought what I was doing to my mother.

'Fiona, I'm doing this for your Mum,' said Harold, and I thought I saw in his puffy features an expression I had not seen before: resolve.

'It's not about me or you. It's about your Mum. You have to come back. Please. She'll be in the pits of despair if you don't.'

'She has you,' I said.

He made a dismissive gesture. 'You can't compare. You're her child. Her only one. And, well, as I've said, it looks like it'll stay that way.'

I could hear real pain in his voice. The loss of his son had affected him deeply. It had shaken him to his depths. He was a different Harold to the one I had known: hurt, helpless, but at the same time strong enough to not abandon himself to his woe. I had expected him to collapse in a corner and drink without any limits. Instead he was so concerned for my mother that he had got into a train for Scarborough, found me, and now was trying to encourage me to go back with him. I did not harbour any illusion that he would not soon be the same old drinker as before. But there was obviously another side to him, and I was able to see this side for a short time. For the first time I felt some respect for him.

'How do you think that would work here?' he asked. He had heard about the deep changes to life on the Beckett farm over dinner. 'I mean, you and Arvid here on your own…that's not good!'

'Brian is here too!'

'A little boy! God, Fiona! Do you think your Mum would allow this set-up for a single day?'

I crumpled. They were all against me: Mum, Harold, Arvid. I did not have a chance.

Arvid came into the kitchen. 'Can yer brew me a cuppa tea?'

I was happy to turn around and work the pump handle, to fill the kettle with water. The two men could not see the tears filling my eyes.

'She has to come back to London with me tomorrow,' said Harold.

'Aye, I think so too,' said Arvid.

I put the kettle on the hob. My hands were shaking.

'My wife…Fiona's Mum…is in a bad way,' said Harold, who for some reason seemed to trust taciturn Arvid. 'She's just lost a child. Our son. He was going to be born this summer.'

'Sorry t' 'ear,' said Arvid awkwardly.

'Yes. It was bad, very bad.' Harold wiped his handkerchief over his forehead once more. I was surprised. The kitchen was warm, but not overly so. It was only later that I realised what Harold was struggling with that evening: he was going dry. At this time of day he was normally tanking up with bottle after bottle. His body was reacting to his unusual abstinence by sweating.

'Here's a little lad for yer,' said Arvid. He pointed to the kitchen door, where Nobody was idling around in his somewhat grubby striped pyjamas. 'T' other child over there. Don't know what t' do with 'im!'

'Not your son?' asked Harold.

Arvid shook his head. 'Came from London too. Back then with Fiona. But 'e don't 'ave anyone in t' world.'

'His whole family was killed by a bomb,' I said. 'The house was hit by a bomb.'

'Relatives?'

'No.'

'Poor lad,' said Harold. He tapped at his forehead. 'A bit gaga is he?'

'Right retarded,' confirmed Arvid.

Silence. It was clear that Harold was also not that keen on Nobody.

'He should go in a home,' he said in the end.

'Aye, that 'e should. Should 'ave long ago,' agreed Arvid.

'Listen. I would take him to London for you, but I've got too much on my plate right now,' said Harold. His face was already shining with thick beads of sweat. 'My boss was pretty annoyed about the two days' holiday, my wife will ask me all sorts of questions about these two days and she can't find out that Fiona ran off. I'm…I can't…'

'Understand,' said Arvid. He sounded disappointed. He would have liked to dispose of Nobody in as uncomplicated a way as possible.

'Up here there are bound to be orphanages,' suggested Harold.

Arvid gave the impression of being at a loss. Young as I was, I understood his dilemma instinctively. He had always been in favour of *sending the other child away*, as he had always said, and now that Emma was dead there was no one to stop him doing just that. Yet it was Emma's death that stopped him. Emma had loved Brian like her own child. She had stood before him like the angel with the flaming sword and protected him. As rough and insensitive as he was, the thought of doing something she would not have ever agreed to, and doing it so soon after her funeral, caused a conflict in Arvid. He would have been able to give Brian to us and to convince himself that we would do the right thing. But to take the child by the hand and march him to the nearest orphanage himself was quite something else. The resulting situation was of course the worst possible one for little Nobody: Arvid did not want him but nor could he bring himself to give him away. It was clear things would stagnate in dissatisfaction, annoyance, passivity and frustration. Nobody would be completely exposed to the coldness and bitterness of a lonely Arvid.

When I set off very early the next morning with Harold for the main road, to catch the bus into Scarborough, the little boy clung to me, his heart as heavy as lead. Tears ran down his pale face.

'Fiona,' he cried. 'Fiona! Boby!'

I stroked his hair. I even managed to be gentle to him as I left. 'Fiona's coming back,' I promised. 'Fiona's coming to fetch Boby. Promise.'

His light blue eyes looked at me full of hope and trust. For a brief moment my conscience stirred. I was sure I would come back. To fetch him? No. I assumed that after a few weeks or months of mourning Arvid would no longer feel duty bound to his dead wife and would put the boy in an orphanage.

I was convinced I would never see Nobody again, and this conviction proved true. I never saw him again. The last image I have of him is the following. The gate of the Beckett farm on a snowy, very cold February morning in 1943. Low, grey clouds in the sky, whipped along by a biting wind. Desolate loneliness, spring still unimaginable. A little boy standing at the gate, with not nearly enough on, shivering with cold. He is looking at us. He cries, and tries to cover his tears with laughter. He waves.

I had managed to give him hope. That made the moment bearable for him: that I would come back.

He really believed it.

Wednesday, 15th October

1

SHE WAS WALKING along the harbour front, feeling angry and disturbed. Her head down and her arms wrapped around her body, she warded off the dampness which her thin wind stopper did not fully protect her from. It was early morning and fog was wafting over the bay and the land. The weather had not improved since the day before. Seagulls seemed to appear out of nowhere and to disappear again into nowhere. Sometimes a ship's foghorn sounded out over the invisible water. Although it was a normal working day, there were not yet many people out and about. Or at least you could not see them.

She had needed to get out, to walk, to distract herself, after having tossed and turned in the early hours in her bed—actually, in Fiona's bed. She had given Stephen the guest-room.

Stephen.

They had eaten and drunk wine, wordlessly agreeing not to mention the anonymous caller again. Then Stephen had tidied up the kitchen, Leslie had sat in the living room and read her grandmother's emails to Chad. It was a peaceful, cosy atmosphere. It was nice not to be in the flat on her own. She had forgotten how nice it felt.

Her reading brought her closer to Fiona, no doubt about it. She heard about things she had not known, beginning to understand certain characteristics and peculiarities of the dead woman. Gradually, however, a feeling of menace, of impending ill, took hold of her. Fiona had talked of guilt. It was still not clear to Leslie how the events were to end, but she had started to feel increasingly ill at ease, and to have a nagging suspicion that something terrible was coming, without knowing exactly what that was. She would probably have carried on reading all night if Stephen had not suddenly entered the room, nervously, his cheeks a little red.

'I have to talk to you, Leslie. Do you have time?'

She had looked up from her reading. 'What is it?'

'I've wanted to say something…for quite a while…but you never gave me the opportunity for a proper chat…'

The hairs on her arms stood up. *I don't want to know!*

Yet she said, 'Yes? What?'

He had sat down. After a few moments' hesitation, obviously considering how best to start, he said:

'Back then, when we separated, when you decided I should move out…I started a therapy. I did it for about a year.'

'A therapy?'

'The therapist was a specialist in relationship difficulties. I…wanted to know why all that happened.'

She remembered that her mouth had gone dry in a second. That always happened when she was reminded of that evening. Why could she not get over it, not finally deal with it in a relaxed way?

'Yes, and so?'

'You know what her first question was? She asked: What are the weaknesses of your marriage, Dr Cramer? And I said immediately that there weren't any.'

She had brushed her hands over the papers. The gesture was less to smooth the paper than to sooth her nerves.

Suddenly the situation felt like an attack. She had sat here reading, sunk in another world, another time. She had come closer to Fiona and in so doing had come closer to the roots of her own and her mother's story. Reality had not existed for her for one or two hours. And now Stephen appeared, confronting her without the hint of a gentle transition, with one of the most traumatic situations of their lives up until then.

I should just have thrown him out. I should have refused to speak to him. Why should I listen to the crap he has conjured up in a hundred hours of therapy?

Somehow she had known immediately the direction the conversation would take. She had looked at him, outwardly cool, inwardly shaking.

'And then you two, you and your therapist, found out after all these long conversations that there were weaknesses after all?'

'That's what you always said. Whenever I tried to make it clear to you that it was a…mistake, a slip-up, a mix of not thinking enough and too much alcohol, you kept on asking. Saying there must be more to it, that I must be dissatisfied, that it wouldn't happen just out of the blue. And so on.'

'Stephen, I—'

'And I just wanted you to know that you're right,' he interrupted her quickly. 'That's what happened. I mean, there was a reason why it happened to me.'

I don't want to know the reason. Not any more.

Why had she only thought that, and not said it? Not managed to open her mouth? Felt like blocking it out but not articulated this?

Because the shock of what happened back then still hasn't melted away, she suddenly realised as she walked through the fog as if through the billowing humidity of a washhouse. Because I'm still suffering from shock.

'I think I often felt you were very cold, but I didn't want to admit that to myself. I felt inferior, because I was the one who loved more strongly. I always feared that you would leave me, if some great, interesting, exciting man came along. I—'

Finally she was able to say something. 'And so you very kindly made the first move? You did something to provoke the separation, to sort things out nicely, did you?'

He had flinched, hearing the harsh tone of her voice. 'I was looking for some recognition. This woman…it could have been anyone. She worshipped me. She gave me the feeling of being a damn desirable bloke. It was…a good feeling.'

'Screwing her?'

'Being desired by her.'

She had got up and noticed to her astonishment that she felt unsteady on her feet.

'What's this all about, Stephen? What are you trying to say? That I should have worshipped you? Seen you as a demigod? Reassured you every day that you impress me no end, that you are so masculine and cool that I flip out when I see you?'

'Of course not. I only wanted…'

'But that's just what you've said. You went into a bar and some young thing thought you were the greatest, and that was so good for you, after suffering your wife's coldness all those years and the feelings of inferiority she caused in you, that you immediately started flirting and not much later took the girl home and got it on with her, as your spouse was, handily, off on a trip. Afterwards you felt guilty, but no doubt you're cured of that now your know-it-all therapist has convincingly shown you that your wife was to blame for it all, after all. Cold. Unapproachable. A career woman! Yes, no need for her to be surprised if she gets cheated on!'

'You've got the wrong end of the stick,' Stephen had said, and it was easy to see that he bitterly regretted having brought up the topic.

Why had his words upset her so much? She had not been able to carry on reading. To calm down, she had made herself a cup of tea, but had still only slept fitfully, and not at all from the early hours of morning. And now she was pacing through the fog because she could no longer bear to stay in the flat.

She came past the redbrick building with the blue-painted roof where the lifeboat was kept. There was a row of small shops that sold sandwiches and drinks. However, they were all closed at this early hour. She saw fishing boats and the big signs where fishing trips were advertised, and the white lighthouse at the harbour mouth. The Luna Park funfair's big wheel, rides and stalls lay silent and abandoned in the mist, as if lights had never flashed, music blared out and people screamed and laughed here. She reached the tidal harbour, stepping onto one of the elevated wooden walkways which crisscrossed it. Below her the ships were bobbing up and down. Soon they would be lying in the mud. The tide was on the way out.

She stopped. If the fog had not been so thick, she would have been able to see her grandmother's house from here. You could see it from almost everywhere in the South Bay. It was a large, shiny white building up on South Cliff.

Stephen was in the flat right now. He was probably still asleep.

She saw him in her mind's eye—him and her, in those

years they had spent together. He was right, she was the more ambitious one, the more single-minded one. She had got better marks during their studies. She had become a doctor first. She had been the first to become a consultant. She had often registered for further training courses, while Stephen had been happy with what he had achieved and had kept to his usual daily rhythms.

Significantly, it was one of her courses which had allowed Stephen the infidelity.

Was it really still a problem, now in the twenty-first century? Could a man—an educated, intelligent man—still not bear for the woman at his side to be more successful than him?

And there was something which bugged her even more. What about the accusation itself, that she was *cold*? Had Stephen imagined that, convinced himself of it, so he could close his eyes to the fact that he could not deal with her success and her career ambitions? Or was she really cold?

Last night more than ever she had realised how cold her childhood and youth with Fiona had been. Fiona had many good and admirable qualities, but one thing could not be denied: warm-heartedness and empathy were not among them. She had always felt a need when she was near Fiona, a constant hunger which was never sated. As a child she had suffered much more from this than she had realised. But how much had it marked her? To what extent was she today unable to give warmth, love and affection?

'I don't know,' she said out loud. 'I just don't know!'

'What don't you know?' asked a voice behind her, and she spun around. Dave Tanner was standing there. He had appeared from nowhere out of the fog. He was dressed in a black anorak, and had pulled the hood up over his head. He looked like he was freezing.

'I'm sorry,' he said. 'I didn't want to surprise you. I saw you from the quay, and I thought I...' He did not say what he had thought.

'Oh, it's you,' said Leslie and tried to shake off the thoughts which were crowding in on her. 'I wasn't expecting to find anyone else out as early as me in this awful weather.'

He smiled. 'Sometimes you just have to get out. Whatever the weather is like outside.'

Perhaps he was also running away from something, perhaps only from his wretched room. What would a day in that accommodation be like when the fog was rolling by outside and you had nothing to do, were alone, and had nothing to look forward to? Then she remembered something. 'Was Gwen at your place, by the way? Colin and Jennifer wondered where she was yesterday.'

He nodded. 'She was at my place. All of yesterday. And the night. For the first time.'

'She hadn't slept at yours before?' asked Leslie surprised. She thought of the black tights in Dave's room. Perhaps there had been afternoon encounters, and Gwen had always returned to the farm like a good girl in the evening. It was time for her to change things in her life, it really was time.

'No,' he said. 'Never before.'

He looked unhappy. Depressed. Worried.

Suddenly Leslie understood: he was running away from *her*! That's why he's out walking so early this morning.

As if he had read her thoughts, he asked, 'And you? What brings you down to the harbour at this time?'

'My ex. We had a little run-in.'

He looked confused. She added, 'He suddenly turned up here. He wanted to be there for me, what with my grandmother's death. He meant well. But the two of us under one roof…it just doesn't work.'

He did not say anything, but Leslie had the impression that he understood. In the end he asked, 'Have you had breakfast yet?'

And when she shook her head, he took her arm without further hesitation and started to lead her somewhere.

'Come on. I don't know how you're doing, but I'm wet and freezing. I desperately need a strong coffee.'

She followed him with grateful relief.

2

'BINGO!' SAID VALERIE. 'I knew it!'

She put the phone down. Sergeant Reek had interrupted her breakfast. Normally she did not like this at all, as it was the only meal she could eat in relative calm—her toast, a fried egg and coffee, accompanied by the news on the radio. The rest of the day she normally only had time to grab a sandwich that tasted more of its plastic packaging than its filling, and she would arrive home so late and tired in the evening that she had no desire or energy to cook.

But Reek had given her a good bit of news, raising her mood considerably.

First he had told her that Leslie Cramer's testimony had stood up to investigation: 'She really was in the Jolly Sailors at the time of the crime, and the landlord is still amazed that a woman can drink so much whisky and walk out the door!' Then he came to the actual news.

'Amy Mills didn't take her A levels at the school Jennifer Brankley taught at,' he reported. 'But between the age of twelve and fourteen she attended a different school— guess which one!'

Valerie quickly gulped down the bit of toast in her mouth. 'Jennifer Brankley's school?'

'Exactly. One of our colleagues in Leeds did some research and has just emailed to tell me.'

Valerie noted with approval that Reek obviously got to work at his computer very early in the day.

'However,' continued Reek, 'Mrs Brankley never taught Amy Mills' classes. So she was not necessarily lying, when she said she didn't know the name. It's a very big school. She wouldn't have known all the pupils.'

'Nevertheless, there is the possibility that they knew each other. If she ever stood in for another teacher, for example. Did she have pastoral responsibilities back then? If so, Amy Mills could have gone to her with any problem she had.'

'I don't know,' admitted Reek.

'Find out. But that was good work, Reek. Thanks.'

After the call she was too excited to eat any more breakfast. While she loaded the dishes into the dishwasher, she tried to calm herself down. She knew that she had a tendency to get worked up and agitated when things did not move along as quickly as she would have liked. The Amy Mills' case had been moving along at a snail's pace. She felt under pressure. She knew that her work was being observed critically by her bosses. Now that Fiona Barnes had died too, they wanted to see some progress. Without anyone telling her this, she felt that she was at a decisive point in her career, possibly a turning point. She had the reputation of being a talented, intelligent but somewhat nervous officer. This was the reason why recently her career had—as she saw it—stagnated somewhat. She had not been promoted because people were not sure whether her nerves would be strong enough to deal with higher pressures.

She had to solve the Barnes and Mills cases, which were possibly a single case, and do it quickly. But at the same time she had to keep her cool and not make any rash decisions. She should neither assume that the murders were by the same culprit, although some factors suggested this, nor should she focus exclusively on Jennifer Brankley, just because she had lost her job and seemed to be psychically fragile and bitter.

Although that wasn't all, she thought. Jennifer Brankley also knew both victims. Fiona Barnes in any case. And probably Amy Mills too. If that were the case, then why had she denied ever having heard the name, at least until it was the talk of the town in Scarborough.

She decided to drive down to the Beckett farm around lunchtime. She wanted to confront Jennifer Brankley with her new find and have a good look at how she reacted.

Her talk with Paula Foster the day before had not been that fruitful. It had only led to her crossing the girl off the list of potential victims. She felt almost one hundred per cent sure about it. There was nothing to suggest Foster would have been a killer's target, unless you were to suppose that someone was simply out to get any young women, which made Foster no more likely a target than thousands of others. Paula Foster did not know Dave Tanner or Jennifer Brankley. She had not been working on the farm for long, and was so involved with its activities from morning until night that she had not had time to get to know her neighbours. At the end of the year she would return to Devon. She had found the body of an old woman on the edge of a sheep field. It looked like this was going to be the only experience from her time in Yorkshire that would dwell in her memory for a long time.

Valerie cleaned her teeth, put on some lipstick, took her bag and left the flat. Fog outside, nothing but fog. Yet she felt positive. She had the feeling that she was finally holding in her hands the end of a thread that could unravel this giant, tangled-up case. Not that the case looked any less confusing. But the thread gave her hope that she had a way in.

3

'Is Gwen there now?' asked Jennifer. She entered the hall, followed by her two giant dogs, which she had done her best to wipe down outside with a handkerchief. Colin was just coming out of the kitchen. 'No. Goodness, you're soaking!'

'The fog,' said Jennifer and wriggled out of her coat. 'You can't see further than the tip of your nose. It's like walking through a wet wall.'

He looked at her affectionately. Her hair was damp and messy. Her cheeks were ruddy. She was wearing an old jumper covered in the dogs' hairs and her jeans were now splattered with mud. He always felt that she was most herself when she came in from outside, when she had been doing something with her dogs. Then she was simply Jennifer—relaxed, calm and resting in herself. She was cheerful in a natural, not overly excited way. She was quite different to how she used to be when she came home from school. He had tried to show her that again and again, whenever she suffered depression and saw her life as one long failure.

'You weren't happy then. You were tense, nervous. Often with too much on your plate. You were far too involved in it all, too close to everyone. You wore yourself out. You—'

Naturally, this was normally where she would interrupt him. 'Oh right, and now I'm a completely happy person?'

'I expect no one is ever a completely happy person. But you're seeing things with rose-tinted spectacles. And you're refusing to see the good things you have now.'

'There isn't much good to see, when you're a failure.'

'You aren't a failure.'

This was the way all those conversations went—round in circles. Jennifer would spiral down and down to the bottom of her melancholy and a despairing feeling of in-adequacy. It was difficult, almost impossible, to lift her out of those pits. So this time he did not mention anything about how good she looked, how much inner harmony he could see. She would have rejected it. It was as if she could not accept that—at least sometimes—she too felt good. He often had the feeling that she felt her depression was a punishment for her failure, and that she clung to it because it seemed to her like her just deserts. She could not allow herself to feel good, not after having made such a mess of her life.

So he simply said, 'Breakfast's ready.'

'I'll just change quickly and dry my hair. I'll be there in a sec.'

Colin went into the living room. Chad was sitting at the table, but he had pushed his plate to the side and, lost in his thoughts, was just stirring his cup of coffee. In the few days since Fiona's death, he seemed to have aged consider-ably. Colin had to think of what Fiona had written. Chad and Fiona had never really been a couple, but since their youth there had been a close connection between the two of them, which had lasted years and then decades, until their old age. Both of them had married other people, had their own families, but none of this had broken their bond.

Chad had just lost the person who was probably most important in his life, and in a shattering, unforeseeable way. It was typical of him that he did not talk to anyone about it, although you could see that he was suffering.

'Gwen is still not here,' said Colin.

Chad looked up. 'She'll be at her fiancé's place.'

'Does she often leave for the night?' asked Colin. Jennifer had claimed that Gwen had never yet stayed the night with Dave, and as Gwen shared a lot with Jennifer it could be true. Chad did not know.

'Don't know. Don't think so. But she's old enough. Anyroad, the two of 'em no doubt 'ave some talkin' t' do—after Saturday.'

'Hmm,' went Colin. Obviously no one cared apart from Jennifer and himself. Gwen's own father did not, and Leslie Cramer's reply had revealed a mix of touchiness and unconcern. He thought with some irritation about the call the night before. Right from the start he had not found Leslie particularly nice, and the call had only confirmed that impression.

'I know it's not right that Gwen's away an' not made breakfast,' said Chad. 'If she 'as guests, she should take care of 'em. Of course she'll take summat off the price when you go, Colin.'

'I couldn't dream of it. That's not why I mentioned it. I think of Jennifer and myself as friends more than holidaymakers. It's no problem for us to make breakfast once in a while. No, I'm just worried. It's not like Gwen to stay away all night and not tell anyone.'

'Young people are like that,' said Chad, and again Colin asked himself if Chad saw Gwen as she was, or whether she was some kind of object in his house, not all that different from the sofa or the kitchen table, which you got used to but never thought too much about. When he said, *Young people are like that*, he seemed to be talking about a teenager and not a woman in her mid-thirties. And certainly not about Gwen. For if there was one thing she was not and would never be, then that was part of the *young people's* scene. That was what was different about her, but also tragic. Her father did not seem to have noticed.

Colin sat down and reached for the coffee pot. He would have liked to talk to Chad about what Fiona had written for Chad and which had now been read by everyone in the house. But he did not dare. Chad had no idea that his daughter had been snooping around in his emails, let alone that she had passed on what she had found to other people. On the other hand, they suggested a potential which in view of the events… But Leslie would have to decide that. Once she had read it all, she would have to determine what happened next. He and Jennifer were outsiders. It was not for them to interfere.

Jennifer came into the room, wearing a fresh pair of jeans and a clean jumper. She had quickly tidied up her hair. Once again Colin thought that she could have been a very attractive woman, if only more cheerfulness were visible in her face. Her unhappiness had settled deeply into her features. Only Cal and Wotan could lift it. A person could not, not even her own husband.

'I'm off to Scarborough,' she said. 'I want to have a stroll, go shopping, maybe browse in a bookshop. I feel like spending a few lazy hours reading on the sofa.'

Colin smiled. 'And you aren't perchance going to pass by Dave Tanner's place to see if Gwen's there?'

Jennifer did not let this throw her. 'Yes, maybe. Someone has to look out for her.'

The barbed comment was aimed at Chad, who gave no

sign that it bothered him. He drank his coffee in silence. There was a tension in the air, but luckily no one wanted to push it to conflict.

'I don't know if I'll be back for lunch,' Jennifer said after a while. 'I'd appreciate it if you could take the dogs out for a bit, Colin.'

He promised he would. He was happy. It was a good sign that Jennifer was taking the initiative, even if it was driven mainly out of concern for Gwen. But perhaps she would make a nice time of it, looking round shops, wandering around town and going to eat pasta in an Italian restaurant. It was a start, at least. After she had been dismissed from her post, she had buried herself in the house for ten months, not even going outside. Colin still congratulated himself that he had persuaded her to get the big dogs. The need to take them for regular walks had led to her breakthrough.

'Are you taking the car?' he asked, although he knew the answer.

Jennifer thought for a second, but then shook her head. 'I'll take the bus. You know...'

'I know,' said Colin resignedly. Jennifer had been an uncomplicated driver. Only after *the incident* had she no longer dared to sit behind a wheel. Colin was not sure where the connection between the two lay. It appeared that she no longer trusted herself to drive. And the more time elapsed, the less likely it was that she would ever do so again.

He looked out of the window. It seemed that the fog was getting thicker and thicker. A strange day. So silent. Even the seagulls could no longer be heard.

He was restless. He did not know why.

It might have been the fog.

4

'MY LANDLADY GAVE me notice for the 1st November,' said Dave.

They were the only customers in King Richard III, a little coffee shop on the front which offered breakfast. A young man was lounging around bored behind the counter. He had brought them coffee and scones with a scowl.

'It's not particularly cosy here,' Dave had said when they entered. 'But they have scones with jam, and they're not bad at all.' From its windows they could see the deserted promenade and the masts of the yachts looming out of the mist.

The coffee was surprisingly good too, thought Leslie. Strong and hot. Just right after the cold, damp air outside.

'Is she allowed to?' asked Leslie. 'Just throw you out so quickly?'

'I think so,' said Dave. 'We never signed a contract or anything like that. I'm living at hers illegally and don't have anything in writing. How would I complain? Anyway, it's not as if I'm inordinately fond of my prestigious domicile, as you can imagine.'

'What reason did she give?'

'She claimed that the daughter of one of her friends is going to study in Scarborough and wanted to live with her. I bet there is no such friend. The truth is, of course, that she's scared of me. She's scared I've murdered Amy

Mills and Fiona Barnes and that she could be the next victim. She no longer sleeps in her own bed, but goes to some neighbour's house. And it seems she spreads terrible stories about me while she's there. Whenever I'm out on the street, I can feel a hundred eyes drilling into me from behind the windows. But I don't care. Let them think what they want.'

'As you and Gwen are planning on marrying in December anyway, it shouldn't be a problem. Just move to her farm at the beginning of November.'

'Yes,' he said. He did not sigh, but his Yes sounded like a sigh.

Leslie cupped both her hands around her mug. Her fingers tingled as the warmth spread up them. Then it seemed to flow up her arms too. It was a pleasant feeling which not only drove the clammy cold from her bones but also soothed her overwrought state. She knew that she was probably going too far, but something about the way Dave Tanner was looking at her gave the impression that he wanted to talk, and that he did not feel cornered with her.

'You're not exactly head over heels in love with Gwen, are you?' she asked quietly.

'It's pretty obvious, isn't it?'

'Yes.'

He leant forward. 'I don't love her at all, Leslie. That's the problem. And that's not because of her drab appearance. A woman could be as ugly as hell and still fascinate me—and Gwen isn't ugly. But the fascination—that's the nub of it. Nothing, just absolutely nothing about her *fascinates* me.'

'In most relationships fascination goes after a while.'

'But it's the spark at the beginning. There has to be something there, something which captivates you in the other person, something which provokes curiosity and won't let you go. You know what I mean, don't you? Why did you marry your husband?'

The last question surprised her and for a moment unsettled her. 'I fell in love with him,' she said in the end.

'With what?'

'With all of him.'

He did not let up. 'There was nothing, absolutely nothing, which annoyed you about him?'

'Of course there was.'

His passivity. His need for harmony. The fact that he often told me what I wanted to hear, that he let me and others tell him what to do. His weakness.

'But something else eclipsed the things you found annoying and let you fall in love and even marry him. And want to spend the rest of your life with him.'

'Yes. What I liked about him was stronger.'

'What was that?'

'His care and attention, his warmth,' she said. 'He made me feel secure.'

He looked at her thoughtfully. 'You had felt a lack of security? Gwen told me that you grew up with your grandmother. After what I've experienced of Fiona Barnes I could imagine that—'

'I don't want to talk about my grandmother,' said Leslie sharply.

'OK,' Dave immediately retreated. 'Of course. I'm sorry if I've been asking too much.'

'We were talking about you and Gwen. You're faced with a decision, not me. I made my decision two years ago: I left my husband.'

'But he can still put you in quite a state, I'd say. The

conversations you were having outside at that very early hour were obviously to do with him.'

She took a sip of coffee, burning her tongue as she did so. 'He cheated on me,' she said. 'Just over two years ago. With a woman he had met by chance while I was away on a training course. I would never have known, except that unfortunately his voice of conscience was so strong that he confessed in the end. After that I could no longer live with him. We've been divorced since last Monday. That's all there is to it.'

'And what had upset you so much this morning?'

'Last night he suddenly explained to me that it was all my fault. Some therapist woman had convinced him of it. He only had the affair because I was so cold and he had been the victim of my career ambitions and—as he saw it—my superiority. Apparently his confession was not down to his conscience but was a cry for help. I didn't understand that, and so to top it all, I threw him out of our flat. The poor man! It really wasn't easy for him.'

Dave looked at her, but did not say anything. Suddenly the door was pushed open and two men came in along with a gust of damp air. They seemed surprised for a moment to find other customers there, but it did not bother them. They ordered coffee, and stayed at the counter talking to the waiter.

Leslie pushed her plate away from her. She had barely touched her scone. 'I don't think I can eat anything.'

'Doesn't it taste good?' Dave asked.

'It does, but whenever I think too much about my ex, I lose my appetite,' she explained. She gave him a challenging look. 'Is it the same for you? When you think of Gwen?'

'It's not that bad.'

'What balances it out for you, Dave? You don't like the fact that she doesn't fascinate you. And yet you want to marry her and spend the rest of your life with her. Why? In your case what is it that eclipses what you don't like about her?'

He looked at her, as if wanting to find out whether she was being serious or was just out to provoke him. 'You're really asking?'

'Yes.'

He smiled tiredly. 'You know what it is. Your grand-mother knew too.'

Leslie nodded. 'So it is true. The farm. The farm is what attracts you to Gwen.'

For the moment he seemed resigned and too exhausted to try to put a nice gloss on it.

'Yes. That's it.'

'What do you hope for, living on the Beckett farm with her?'

Now he pushed his plate away. The question of his future seemed to rob him of his hunger too. 'I want to leave behind the life I'm leading,' he explained. 'I *have to* leave it. I just can't go on as I'm doing now. But I need some-thing…I can jump onto. I don't have anything to show for my life except my ditched studies and a long chain of oc-casional jobs, with which I have just about made ends meet for almost twenty years now.'

'Do you want to bring back sheep to the Beckett farm?'

He shook his head. 'That's not the thing for me. I'd like to develop what Gwen has started in a small and rather unprofessional way. I'd like to make the farm attractive to holidaymakers. Yorkshire is becoming one of the most popular holiday destinations in England. The farm offers thousands of possibilities, without sacrificing its original charm. The house needs clean, large guest-rooms. There needs to be a safe, simple path down to the bay. People shouldn't have to fight their along the overgrown gorge. There need to be bathing facilities. Ponies can be kept in the stables and offered for trekking tours. Believe me,' his voice had risen, but now he lowered it again as he noticed that the people at the counter were looking over at him, 'I have good ideas. I can make something of that piece of land.'

'And do you have the drive to do it?' asked Leslie. 'Do you have that too?'

'You doubt it?'

'I don't know you well enough. But after everything you've told me about your former life, I wouldn't say that drive and determination are your strengths. You know, I'm always a little wary of people who need something stupendous—in your case a large piece of land—in order to make something of their lives. Often they're people who are kidding themselves. They think the fact they haven't yet made it big has always been down to conditions being against them. Real success stories are different. In them people start with nothing and still manage to achieve something in the end.'

His expression did not change. Leslie could not tell whether he was annoyed with her directness or not.

'You're very honest,' he said in the end. 'But have you considered what alternatives Gwen has? She lives off her father's pension. When Chad Beckett dies—and that is unlikely to be in the all too distant future—she will be penniless. She has no income of her own. She's hardly going to live off Mr and Mrs Brankley's two or three visits each year.'

'She could sell the farm.'

'Her home? The only place she knows and where she's happy?'

'Is she happy?'

'Would she be happier without the farm? In some flat?'

'She could look for a job. She'd finally get out, meet people. Maybe she'd meet a man who really loved her.'

'Well,' said Dave. And after a moment's silence, he added, 'So are you going to try to convince her not to marry me?'

'No!' Leslie shook her head. 'I'm not going to get involved. Gwen has to make her own mind up. She's an adult.'

He looked at her.

'By the way, I didn't sleep with her last night,' he said out of the blue. 'I've never slept with her.'

Leslie thought about the black tights in his room. *It's none of your business*, she told herself.

'No?' she limited herself to asking.

'No. She wanted to. But I…I can't. I can barely manage to touch her, let alone…' He left the unfinished sentence hanging in the air.

'So, in that case,' asked Leslie, 'what do you envisage marriage to her will be like?'

He did not reply.

5

JENNIFER HAD FOUND a slip of paper with Dave Tanner's address on the pinboard in Gwen's bedroom. Although she knew that it was not right to go into her host's room when she was not there, she told herself that her worry justified her behaviour. It was not like Gwen to be absent for so long and not to tell anyone.

Today the walk to the main road seemed longer than usual, perhaps because of the humid air which made breathing more difficult. For the bus to pick you up, you had to stand beside the red phone box. Luckily it came more or less on time. Only three quarters of an hour later Jennifer got out at the Queen Street stop in the middle of Scarborough. From there it was not far to Friargate Road, where Dave lived. Nonetheless, Jennifer felt shattered by the time she finally stood in front of the little terrace house.

The landlady opened the door after she had rung twice, eyeing her suspiciously.

'Yes?'

'Good morning. I'm Jennifer Brankley. Is Dave Tanner home?'

At the mention of Tanner's name, the old woman's face turned to stone.

'Who are you?'

'Jennifer Brankley. A friend of Gwen Beckett, Mr Tanner's fiancée.'

'Mr Tanner isn't here.'

Almost involuntarily Jennifer looked past the old lady into the dark hall. 'No?'

'Listen, I was just upstairs. He's not there. His coat isn't here in the wardrobe either. He's out.'

'Do you know if he was here last night?'

Now the landlady looked at her angrily. 'I don't know, Mrs Brankley. No idea! You know why not? Because I can't sleep in my own house any more! I get on my neighbours' nerves, always pleading to stay in one of their houses, but I panic at the thought of sleeping in the same house as that man. I wouldn't get a wink of sleep! I mean, the man might have two murders on his conscience, and I'm damned if I'm going to be the third!'

'Why do you think he has two murders on his conscience?' asked Jennifer, surprised by the near certainty with which the old lady talked.

'Well, I can put two and two together! The police were here. They asked about the evening when Fiona Barnes was murdered, and about the evening when that young student was done in. And in both cases they wanted to know if Mr Tanner had been home. I'm not stupid. They think he's a killer, just can't prove it yet. And that's the way it is today. The biggest criminals walk free because apparently you can't lock them up until you have proof. And the politicians don't give a damn what happens to innocent people!'

'So I suppose you also don't know whether Miss Beckett visited Mr Tanner last night?' continued Jennifer, who was for now more interested in this question than in putting the world to rights.

'Of course I don't know!' snorted the landlady. 'And what's more, in future I won't know either! I've given Mr

Tanner his notice. He's out on the street from 1st November—and I'll feel a lot better then.'

With these words she slammed the door, leaving Jennifer standing there flabbergasted in the mist. She carried on looking at the front of the house, as if hoping to find some clue. She did not even know which window was Dave Tanner's, or whether his window looked out onto the street. Depressed, she went back down the garden path and the few steps to the street. This visit had not led anywhere, nowhere at all. Tanner was not at home (she assumed the landlady was not lying), and no trace of Gwen.

She had a bad feeling. She asked herself if there was a reason for it.

She would have most liked to return to the farm, but somehow she thought that would be a defeat. She had driven into town, but everyone would see immediately that she had only been looking for Gwen, and then turned around afterwards. Perhaps she should grasp the opportunity and really do something, to not be such a hermit. She could do what she had told Colin she would: have a leisurely stroll around town and maybe even sit on her own in a café for a cup of something.

So easy for most people. A massive step for her.

She wandered around the aisles of the Market Hall for a while. It was warm and dry in here. She looked at the art and kitschy artifacts in the tiny shops stocked with goods up to the rafters and browsed in a charity shop, leafing through old postcards and admiring a tea service which stood out as one of the few tasteful items in the shop. It would make a pretty wedding present for Gwen—if she were ever to marry Dave Tanner.

Later she walked over to the pedestrian precinct. She bought a soft woollen scarf for Colin and a woolly hat for herself. She paid for both of them with *his* money. She was painfully aware of that. She used to have her own income. Colin had never made a fuss about the fact that he alone was now responsible for everything—the mortgage on their house in Leeds, living costs, the food for the dogs and their vet's fees, and of course the holidays on the Beckett farm.

For the first time she thought it might be possible to find a job. She would not return to work in a school, but she might find something else. Then she could stop being a burden on Colin and could now and then buy something on a whim without having a bad conscience.

Maybe losing her job back then was not the end of everything. Even if she felt it was, and had felt that since it happened. She had never known how to beat the paralysis that had taken hold of her.

Maybe I will manage, she thought, looking into a shop window. Behind the panes, candlesticks and antique jewellery were on display. She did not notice. If only I could take that first step, she thought, I think I'd…

'Mrs Brankley,' said a voice behind her. She whipped round, startled because she had been so deep in her brooding thoughts. She furrowed her brow as she looked at the young woman standing behind her. She was sure she had met her before, but she did not know where.

'Yes?' she asked.

The other woman blushed slightly. 'Ena,' she said. 'Ena Witty.'

Finally she remembered. The Friarage School playground on that quiet afternoon a few days ago. The people who came out of the building had been on the same course as Gwen. Ena Witty had been one of them and Gwen had introduced the two of them.

'Oh, Miss Witty,' she said, 'I remember! Last week, at the school…'

'Gwen Beckett was there too,' said Ena. 'And Stan, my boyfriend. We talked for a while.'

'Of course, I remember well,' said Jennifer, although she remembered that Ena had barely said a word while her boyfriend chatted away. 'It was nice to meet you.'

She remembered yesterday's call. 'Oh dear, Miss Witty. My husband told me yesterday that you called, wanting to speak to Gwen. I'm sorry, but Gwen still hasn't come home yet—at least not by the time I left this morning for town. So we couldn't—'

'That doesn't matter,' interrupted Ena. 'I was wondering whether I should bother Gwen, in any case. I read about Gwen's relationship to the murdered woman in the paper—Barnes, wasn't it? Gwen has other things on her mind, it's just—'

'We are all in a bit of a muddle right now,' admitted Jennifer.

'As I said, I can well imagine that. I wouldn't have phoned up if I hadn't…I've got something pretty big on my mind, and there's no one else I can talk to about it. I haven't known Gwen for all that long. We just met on this course. But I liked her right from the start. She was really nice, and I thought…I would just talk to her a bit…and she knows my boyfriend Stan, because he always came to pick me up at the school.'

'I'm sure you'll manage to talk to her,' reassured Jennifer. She felt Ena was confirming what she had assumed in private: that Ena's problem, which she needed to talk about, was Stan. He was a domineering kind of guy. No doubt he had blown into her quiet life like a hurricane, and brought quite a few difficulties with him.

'As soon as I see Gwen, I'll tell her, and she'll call you. It would be good for her to talk of something other than just what is happening on the farm.'

Ena looked relieved, and then visibly steeled herself. 'I don't want to appear pushy, but if you…if you have time… Would you fancy going for a coffee?'

Jennifer assumed that it had taken quite some effort for Ena to pluck up the courage and ask. After all, she had taken part in the Friarage School course because things like this were hard for her normally—things like asking someone she liked but barely knew to go for a coffee.

So many people struggle along every day with all kinds of fears, shyness and self-doubt, and in many cases no one notices what torture it is for them.

She did not want to give Ena the brush-off.

With an exaggerated gesture she pushed back her sleeve and looked at her watch. It was almost twelve-thirty, too soon to go home really. And she had wanted to have a cup of coffee, admittedly on her own. She had the feeling that Ena was under pressure. Once she relaxed a little, she was likely to tell her all her worries, especially those concerning her relationship to Stan Gibson. Jennifer was not sure if she was the best person for her to talk to right now. She herself had so many things on her mind.

'Well,' she said, 'I think…'

Ena could see her hesitate. 'Please. I would…be really happy if you did.'

Jennifer had never been able to refuse a request for help, and suddenly she realised that the core of this situation was Ena asking for help. This was not any old little problem. Ena was pleading.

'OK,' she said resignedly. 'Let's have a coffee.' After all, she had been thinking a lot about first steps today.

For her, a first step might be to engage with people again, rather than avoiding them.

Maybe she really could help Ena Witty, even if her help was only her willingness to listen to her.

Perhaps tonight Ena would be able to sleep with the warm feeling that there were still people who cared for her and her concerns.

Jennifer decided to enjoy the invitation.

6

'YES, THAT'S A SHAME,' said Valerie Almond. 'I would really have liked to talk to your wife, Mr Brankley.'

They stood facing each other in the farmhouse doorway. Colin had not invited her in. He had only stated coolly that Jennifer was not there.

When would she be back? Valerie had asked. He had shrugged.

'I can't help you there,' he said. 'I'll tell my wife that you want to talk.'

Valerie could here the animosity in his voice. He had seen through her—he could see that she was sinking her teeth into his wife.

'I found out that Amy Mills did not always go to the school where she did her A levels,' she said. 'For two years she went to the school in Leeds where your wife taught.'

For a split second he could not hide his surprise. He examined Valerie through his round glasses. He had clever eyes. He looked like a man who has deeper thoughts than you would suspect from his rather bland appearance.

He's highly intelligent, thought Valerie. And he's not at all the friendly, unassuming man whom he appears at first glance to be.

'Did she ever say anything to suggest she had known Amy Mills at all fleetingly? Or at least by name?'

'No, Inspector. She told me nothing other than what she told you.'

Valerie turned away in frustration. 'I'll come back,' she said. She asked herself if he was blocking her, or perhaps starting to see connections.

Which connections? Which? If Jennifer Brankley had known Amy Mills, what reason would she have had for killing the young girl so horrifically?

Her phone rang as she walked back to the car. Simultaneously she saw Gwen Beckett get out of a taxi at the farm gates. She looked cold and as if she had not slept much.

So where is she coming from? wondered Valerie, immediately knowing that no one had to give her an answer, nor would they.

'Yes?' she answered the phone as she opened her car door. Time to get out of this damp cold.

It was an excited Sergeant Reek.

'Inspector, we've got news. Mrs Willerton called. You know, Dave Tanner's landlady. She's found a neighbour who claims to have seen Mr Tanner leave Mrs Willerton's house late on the evening when Fiona Barnes was killed. Around nine o'clock.'

'Nine o'clock? If so, he would have just come and gone again.'

'That's right. Of course we don't know how reliable the witness is, but I think she should be interviewed.'

'Absolutely. Do you have her address?'

'Yes. She lives diagonally across from Willerton.'

Valerie bit her lip. She had not asked for neighbours to be questioned regarding the times Dave Tanner had given. That could have been a mistake.

'Drive over there, Reek. I'll come too. And see if Tanner is at home. If he is, arrest him.'

'Right you are, Inspector.'

She sank behind the wheel, frustrated rather than electrified. *She was no good!* She got muddled up, did things in a confused way, forgot about routines. A few simple enquiries with the neighbours—why had she not thought to do that? She almost hoped that the witness would prove to be an unreliable busybody, so that she could sweep her oversight under the carpet. Better that than the woman's statement giving them a breakthrough. Then questions would be asked and she would not have a convincing answer for them.

She forced herself to calm down. She could not lose her nerve now. Drive over. Talk to the witness. Question Tanner.

Damn it, Valerie: focus. Don't lose it. It'll be fine.

She looked over to the door. Gwen and Colin were standing there talking. Gwen looked very pale, almost grey. Before Valerie closed the door, she could hear Colin say, dumbfounded, 'Does Tanner know too? Really?'

'Not so loud!' hissed Gwen.

Valerie closed the door, started the engine, turned her car with a screech of rubber, and drove off.

THE WITNESS WAS called Marga Krusinski. She was in her late twenties, was holding a baby, and talking to Sergeant Reek in broken English. He was trying in vain to stem the flow of her words in order to get to the point. Marga Krusinski had divorced her husband and come to Scarborough, but it seemed that he had followed her and would lie in wait for her, harassing her and threatening to take their child. A court had placed a restraining order on him, banning him from coming within 100 metres of her, but she doubted that he would respect it. She was obviously hoping for Sergeant Reek's support in this matter and had forgotten why he had come.

Valerie arrived a little late. She had taken a little longer than expected because of the fog. She wondered if there might really be an issue with the witness's reliability. Did she make up wild stories in order to make the police more aware of herself and her need?

Don't jump to conclusions, she reminded herself.

Mrs Willerton was sitting in an armchair in Mrs Krusinski's sparsely furbished living room with a glass of whisky in her hand. Judging by her red nose, it was not the first drop she had taken to calm her fears.

'Are you going to arrest him now?' she asked breathlessly, when she saw Valerie. 'Are you going to arrest him before he slaughters more innocent women?'

'It's not a crime for Mr Tanner to have left the house again that evening,' said Valerie. 'Of course it is strange that he didn't tell us. He will have to give a very good explanation of exactly where he was and why.'

Mrs Willerton snorted. 'He'll lie through his teeth!'

'I haven't really got very far,' interjected Sergeant Reek with some frustration.

Marga Krusinski paused. 'Can you help me?'

'First of all we need your help,' explained Valerie. 'You told Mrs Willerton that Mr Tanner left the house around 9 p.m. on Saturday evening?'

'Yes.'

'Where did you see that from?'

'From this room,' said Marga. 'From window. See Mrs Willerton's house exactly.'

Valerie stepped across to the window and peeked through the curtains. She could see Mrs Willerton's house clearly. The front door and the steps to the street were in full view. She saw the lamp which was almost directly in front of the house's garden, but she still asked: 'It was dark. How did you see?'

'Lamp,' said Marga. 'Is very bright. I saw and recognised Mr Tanner exactly.'

'You just happened to be looking out of your window?'

Marga made a surly face. 'Have just told everything,' she said, nodding at Sergeant Reek.

'Ah yes,' corroborated Reek hurriedly. 'Inspector, you heard that Mrs Krusinski's divorced husband has been causing problems. Apparently he turned up here early Saturday evening and intercepted Mrs Krusinski as she was coming back from a walk with her son. He threatened her and tried to intimidate her. Fortunately neighbours came out and he took to his heels.'

'Was he already under a restraining order?'

Reek shook his head. 'That came Monday.'

'I see. And…'

'And naturally Mrs Krusinski was still very worried all evening. She was scared that he might still be lurking somewhere near her house, so she kept peeking out, from this living room window and from the kitchen window. She planned to call the police immediately if she saw him.'

'And that's how she saw Tanner leave the house?'

'Yes,' said Reek, Marga and Mrs Willerton together.

Valerie turned to Marga. 'And you are quite sure it was Dave Tanner?'

'Now listen here,' protested Mrs Willerton. 'How many men do you think leave my house every night?'

Valerie could not imagine that any did, she had to admit.

'Was Mr Tanner,' insisted Marga. 'Have recognised him. Am completely sure!'

'How sure are you about the time?'

'Quite sure, but not to the minute. Was so restless, so I always looked at clock. One time was quarter to nine. And I saw Mr Tanner maybe quarter of hour or twenty minutes later.'

'What exactly was Mr Tanner doing?'

'Got in car and drove off.'

'Was he alone?'

'Yes. Completely. Took time for car to start. I know that already. His car not OK.'

'You didn't see him come back?'

Marga shook her head. 'I was up late that evening. Just before twelve went to bed, but couldn't sleep. Every noise scare me.'

'So until midnight he wasn't there?'

'No. Always kept looking at road, but car was not there. Only next day. I got up nine o'clock. Then it was parked there.'

Valerie rubbed her fingers against her temples. She was starting to feel a painful pounding there, saying *overlooked, overlooked, overlooked.*

Nevertheless she had to ask the question which would poke at her own wound. Sergeant Reek would notice, the two women probably not.

'So why is it that you have told this to Mrs Willerton now?'

'*I* got this ball rolling,' interrupted Mrs Willerton not without pride. 'I can't sleep in my own house, and with good reason. Anyway, today I came over to Mrs Krusinski and asked if I could sleep at her house tonight. So we started to talk about Mr Tanner and I told her that I don't know for sure whether at the time of the Fiona Barnes' murder he was at home. Suddenly she looks at me and says, But I know he wasn't home! And tells her story!' Mrs

Willerton took a long sip of her whisky. 'I'll never have a lodger again, never again, I can tell you that! I gave him notice for 1st November, but if you don't arrest him today, then I'll throw him out today anyway, I swear it! Not a day longer, not a single day longer in my house!'

'He's not at home now, I take it?' Valerie turned to Reek. He shook his head. 'No, he isn't—I've checked.'

'You could have thought of that yourselves—asking the neighbours,' said Mrs Willerton in a tone of reproach. 'Instead I have to come and solve the case!'

Valerie had a sharp reply on the tip of her tongue, but she swallowed it. She should not be stupid enough to get into an argument with this unsophisticated and aggressive woman who was desperate to be admired. Especially not about this, where Valerie had slipped up. Better not to make a mountain out of a molehill. She ignored the comment and said calmly to Sergeant Reek, 'Wait here for a while, Sergeant Reek. In the car, I suggest. If Tanner appears, bring him in for questioning.'

'All right, Inspector.'

She turned to Mrs Krusinski. 'Thank you for your statement, Mrs Krusinski. I might have to take it all down in writing again, but I'll call you beforehand. Mrs Willerton!' She shook Mrs Willerton's hand and hurried out of the house. Outside she lent against the wall for a moment to catch her breath. Her face was burning hot. For the first time that day the fog was just what she needed.

I messed up, she thought.

She forced herself to breathe in and out deeply.

It will be all right.

7

THE FOG WAS going to lift today. You could see it already. It was still there—a thick wall of wool that swallowed everything and dampened every sound. But now and then a weak beam of light cut through it as if by accident, heralding a blue sky somewhere else, and that the fog would not stay over the bay and town forever.

Leslie and Dave had left the café and were now walking along the promenade, the Marine Drive. It was a wide, paved road which went round below the castle and led to the North Bay.

On the left the jagged rocks of the hill towered up. On the right the pavement ended at a wall of light coloured stone. Blocks of concrete protected the road against high tides.

Behind them lay the sea, but they could only just see it. It was still too foggy.

They had only wanted to go for a short stroll, but the cold air in their lungs was a delight. Even the wetness on their cheeks was seductive. They walked on and on, without a thought about their destination or when they would go back.

He had asked her what her mother had been like, and she was surprised to find herself answering freely and without hesitation.

'She was always happy. She wore long, colourful

dresses. Her hair went down to her waist, and she would braid colourful ribbons into it. She was as blonde as I am, but she always dyed her hair red with henna. The henna coloured her palms too. I can only remember my mother's palms with that strange orange colour.

'I think she was always happy because she was always stoned. She travelled from one hippy festival to the next. I can see campfires, lots of men and women I didn't know, and all of them dressed like my mother. People were always playing the guitar. Joints were always going round. I think she also tried LSD and who knows what else. My mother would dance with me. Around the campfires, but also at home in our living room. She loved Simon and Garfunkel's music. She would listen to *Bridge Over Troubled Water* until I was sick of it.'

Then she paused and looked at him, puzzled that she was confiding this too. 'I still can't listen to that song, Dave. Not without thinking of her and wanting to scream, mourning her. I immediately turn the radio off and leave the room when it comes on. I can't bear it.'

His face was damp with droplets of fog. 'She was your Mum. She loved you. You loved her.'

She looked past him into the grey emptiness. 'I remember she often said I was the greatest present of her life. The greatest present ever.'

'Your father...'

She shrugged. 'She didn't know. My grandmother didn't know. Mum sometimes said that she *captured* me at a festival—that I was like a wonderful butterfly that flew over to her and stayed with her. Later I understood that this just meant she had been screwing around again madly, not yet eighteen years old, and that she had got pregnant and no matter how much she tried, was unable to say who could be the father. I don't know, Dave. I'll never know. When I was a child and even into my early teens I made up all sorts of fathers. Brilliant men who travelled the world, which was why I never saw them. Once I said that my father worked in the White House in Washington, but no one in my class believed me. After that I was picked on. They asked if my Dad was the President of the United States, and then laughed themselves silly. From then on I never spoke about my father. There's nothing to say, anyway.'

He smiled, but he still had a serious look in his eyes. 'It can't be easy. I mean, lots of children grow up without their fathers for all sorts of reasons, but they know them or at least know who they are. They have a name and a face. A job, a background, a family they come from. But not to even know *who* your father is. Without anything to hold onto…I suppose there's no way to research it?'

'No, how would I? She had a ball with whoever came along, mainly with men she didn't know, and she was always so spaced out that she wouldn't have recognised them five minutes after the sex. I was much too small to know where we travelled to, let alone who else was hanging around there. It was the late sixties, the early seventies. My mum was right in the thick of it.'

Cautiously he asked, 'She took drugs, you said. That means…I can imagine she wasn't always fun, caring, gentle. People who take drugs…'

He did not say anything else but she knew what he wanted to say.

'The crazy thing is, Dave, that when I think of her I always see and feel the wonderful moments. I see her dancing and laughing. I feel how she hugged me. I couldn't think of anything off the top of my head to spoil those impressions. But when I think back, concentrating hard…

then there is something else, and it's not pretty. I see other
things then…I see her sleeping in bed all day long, and I'm
standing there beside her trying to wake her, because I'm
so hungry. And because I'm cold. But she doesn't wake
up. And again I feel the fear that I felt when I would wake
up in the night and realise she wasn't there. I'm alone in
my house. I search everywhere, every corner, I even creep
down into the cellar… For a while we lived in London,
in a dilapidated summer house in someone's garden. She
could rent it for peanuts. The beams creaked all the time.
The window frames rattled in the wind. There was a constant draught. You could only heat the place with a big iron
stove. If someone had bought wood—if *she* had bought
wood. Did she ever do that? My grandmother Fiona later
once told me that she was amazed I survived my childhood. It had always been ice-cold at our house, she said.
The fridge was bare, and strange long-haired men would
be sitting in the corner rolling cigarettes. Well, Fiona didn't
visit much. She and my mum didn't get on. Mum had run
away from home at sixteen, spent a year in care, came
back, then ran away again before her eighteenth birthday,
got pregnant and then muddled through with a number of
little jobs which often didn't earn her much. She had to
keep in touch with her Mum, because she needed to keep
asking her for money. Fiona said she had always helped out
for my sake. If it weren't for me, she wouldn't have wanted
to have anything more to do with her daughter. When I was
eighteen Fiona told me that she had even started proceedings for custody of me. I was three at the time, and Fiona
was convinced that I wasn't being brought up properly with
Mum. Imagine that Dave, she took her own daughter to
court. She lost, but would later harp on about it, so that I
knew how much she had fought for my wellbeing and how

grateful I should be. And maybe I should be—grateful.'
To her horror she realised tears were welling up, and she
tried to fight them back.

'In the years I lived with Fiona, visiting friends of hers
would often stroke my hair and say how lucky I was to
have such a grandmother, and what a blessing it was that
things had turned out like this. What they meant was "what
a blessing that your mother died so young".' Now her tears
were falling down her cheeks. It felt like she would lose
control any moment.

'So I was grateful. And I did what Fiona hoped for. I
was a good schoolgirl. I studied medicine. I'm a successful doctor. Fiona hoped I would find a reliable husband,
so I married Stephen. We had a nice flat. We earned good
money. People respected us. And I felt good, because Fiona
showed me she was happy with me. I was making up for
what her daughter had done to her. The hippy daughter
who had died from an overdose. Now at least she had a
model granddaughter. But there was one thing I didn't do
for her. She wanted me to see Mum for who she was: an
irresponsible, careless person who couldn't cope with life.
I can't do that, Dave.' She looked at him, and her voice
trembled with a sob. Shit, she thought, I'm bawling like
a little girl.

'I want to keep the other pictures, Dave. The pictures
where she's singing, dancing and laughing. And where she
says I'm the greatest present she's ever had. She loved me.
She could love. Fiona couldn't. Never did.'

She cried as if she would not ever stop. Suddenly she
thought, How could this happen? What did he do to make
me tell him? How did he make me cry? I've never told it
to Stephen like this. I've never cried with Stephen.

She let him hold her close. Somewhere a seagull cried,

muffled in the fog. She stood there with her face hidden on a stranger's shoulder and cried. She was crying for her dead grandmother, crying for her mother. Crying because she was freezing. And because she had been freezing all her life.

8

'I'M AFRAID TO make a mistake,' said Ena. 'Or that I'll come to regret my decision terribly sometime. I've been alone so long, you know. And then when Stan came... But somehow... It's not working. It's not like it should be.'

They were sitting in a little café in the town centre. On the small round bistro table in front of them stood two empty coffee cups and two glasses of water. The café was full of people seeking shelter from the inclement weather and smelt of wet woollen coats. Every time someone went in or out the damp air rushed in. Ena looked worried and unhappy.

Jennifer leant forward. 'What *mistake* are you so afraid of making?'

Ena breathed deeply. 'Breaking it off. I'm afraid that'd be a mistake. I'm also afraid it'd be a mistake to stay. I want to do the right thing.'

'What do you do for a living?'

'I work for a lawyer here in Scarborough.'

'And do you have the day off today?'

'I took the day off. To think about things. Because...I can't concentrate. I can barely sleep at night.'

Jennifer signalled to the waitress to come over and ordered two more coffees. They would be there a while, as she had rightly guessed.

'How long have you and Stan been together?'

Ena did not need to think. 'Since 20th August. A Wednesday. He invited me out for a glass of wine after the course and told me that he…that he was in love with me.'

'Did that take you by surprise?'

'Gwen had said the whole time that he had been eyeing me up. Gwen and I had become friends by then. And from the start of August the construction firm had been working in the school. They were moving walls and enlarging rooms in almost all the buildings, so it wasn't a quick job. Stan was always there, even after all the others had gone. And he always had some flimsy excuse to do work near the room our course was in. He would look at me…yes, I had noticed that. That was something new for me. For a man to look at me, I mean.'

'But you were only there on Wednesdays. He can't have seen you too often before he revealed his feelings for you.'

'No. That's another reason why I was sceptical. But Stan believes in love at first sight. He says that he knows immediately if he loves a woman. It either happens in the first second or not at all. And with me…it was the first second.'

'You don't believe him, do you?'

'I do,' said Ena, looking uncomfortable.

The waitress brought their coffees. Jennifer stirred her cup, although she had not added milk or sugar. She drank hers black. She needed to do something with her hands.

'But…what's eating you up? Why do you look so… unhappy, disheartened? Why are you thinking of splitting up?'

Ena hesitated, before saying, 'I can't breathe any more. He doesn't give me any space. He decides everything. What we eat, what we drink, whether we go out or not, what we watch on the telly, when we go to bed, when we get up, what I should wear, how I should comb my hair—

everything. Do you see? There's nothing left for me to decide. Unless he's at work. Then I can do things like this—just sit here with you and drink a coffee. But tonight he'll want a detailed report of everything I've been up to. He knows I'm not working today. It would have been impossible to hide it from him, because he often calls me at work. So often that it annoys my boss. But when I told him he got angry. He said I should look for a new job. He'll carry on calling me as much as he likes.'

She stopped for a moment and then carried on, more quietly. 'At the same time he cares for me. So then I feel bad again, and ask if I'm just imagining things. Maybe I just need time to get used to having someone in my life. Maybe he's quite normal and I'm being hysterical because I'm so odd that I...' She did not finish her sentence.

Jennifer had a hunch. 'Is that what *he* says? That you are hysterical and odd? And that he's acting quite normally?'

'That's what he suggests, yes.'

Jennifer tried to choose her words carefully. 'Ena, I barely know you. Nor do I know your boyfriend. So I shouldn't pass judgment, and frankly, I do feel like I'm being drawn out of my depth. But what you said...well, my feeling is that he's extremely domineering. He might mean well enough, but he doesn't pay enough attention to what you want, and to what kind of a person you are. Maybe you don't have to end the relationship immediately. But get some distance. Ask for a time-out. See what you feel if you don't see him for a few weeks. That will also give him the chance to think about it. To change his behaviour. Maybe he doesn't realise he's suffocating you.'

Ena looked doubtful. 'He won't agree to that.'

'He'll have to accept it,' said Jennifer.

Ena nodded, sunk in her thoughts. Then she suddenly

turned to Jennifer and there was a determination in her eyes that Jennifer had not seen before. 'Jennifer—could you do a big favour for me?'

'If I can…'

'There's something else. Something which is worrying me more than the rest. That's why I have to talk to Gwen. I have to talk to someone, otherwise I'll go mad.'

'Ena, I…'

'I don't have anyone. I need someone's objective opinion, else it'll all be too much for me. I can't calm down.'

Worried at the force of her words, Jennifer asked, 'Is it to do with Stan?'

'Yes. But not our relationship.'

'I don't think I understand…'

Ena reached into her handbag, which was hanging off the back of the chair, and fished a set of keys from the side pocket. 'Here. The keys to his flat. I can come and go as I wish. He's not home now. Would you go there with me?'

Jennifer felt very uneasy. She had not had any real contact to either Ena Witty or Stan Gibson. She did not know them. She had a very bad feeling about going into a stranger's house behind his back.

'Can't you talk about it with me here in the café?'

'No, I have to show you something.'

'I don't like the idea,' said Jennifer.

'Please. It won't take long. Ten minutes. Can you spare the time?'

It was half past one. The next bus to Staintondale went at a quarter past four. Jennifer knew that she would still need to hang around for ages, not knowing what to do. By doing Ena Witty the favour she asked for, at least she would fill the time in a useful way.

'I've got time,' she said after a pause. 'But I…OK, I'll

come with you. I'm not going to stay in the flat longer than ten minutes though.'

Ena's relief was palpable. 'Thank you. Thank you so much. Stan lives just round the corner. Just by St Nicholas Cliff.'

'Then let's go,' said Jennifer and got her purse out. 'Are you sure that he doesn't come home around lunchtime? If he did, it could be embarrassing.'

'He's at a site in Hull today. He won't come. Anyway, Stan said that his house is my house. You're a long-time friend of Gwen's. He wouldn't mind me bringing you in.'

They paid and stepped out into the street. It had now started to rain. The fog was thinning, but the sun was not about to shine through just yet.

'We have to go down Bar Street,' said Ena.

Why am I always the person people turn to when they need help? Jennifer asked herself. And why can't I shake off the role, although it has already cost me my job, my self-confidence and my independence?

She followed Ena down the road.

9

'TO MY PLACE or yours?' asked Dave.

They had climbed the steep steps from the harbour to the town itself, and now they stood up there in the pouring rain. It seemed to be getting heavier with each passing minute.

Leslie hesitated.

'I don't know how you feel,' continued Dave, 'but I find it pretty unpleasant out here. And I don't fancy sitting in some overcrowded café that smells of wet coats, where you can't hear yourself think.'

She looked into his eyes. He had beautiful, intelligent eyes. They had a liveliness she had never found in Stephen. He was not in control of his life, and yet he did not have the look of an eternal loser. You could see he faced life with too much energy for that. Dave Tanner was a man who attracted her, as she suddenly realised in shock.

In the next moment her shock disappeared and what took its place was the recognition—just as unexpected and yet strangely elating—that Dave was the answer to the question she had been asking over and over for the last two years: the question of *what next*, of life after Stephen. What did life hold for a woman on the verge of her fourth decade, who was divorced, and who in spite of her successful career was privately afraid of a lonely future? She was afraid she would return to a dark flat every evening and eat breakfast alone every Sunday morning. Then watch television on her own every Saturday evening, drinking more than was healthy in the long-term. And do that for the next thirty, forty years?

Suddenly she thought: of course there's a future! Of course I'll have another relationship! Not now, with Fiona barely dead. Not with Dave. He's Gwen's fiancé. But there are other men. And I'll be able to open up to them.

It was as if Stephen's infidelity had put her under a glass jar. Because it was transparent, she could see the world. But as it was hermetically sealed, she could not take part in anything or let anything touch her. She had done her job, she had had the energy and self-control to get on with her life, but inside she had been cold, distant from people, and alone. She had been unable to recognise other people's feelings or to accept them.

Something was changing. Here she stood in the rain in Scarborough and was capable of finding a man attractive. She responded to him. She had cried in his arms.

Only a week ago she would have dismissed such a possibility.

Dr Leslie Cramer had thrown herself into the arms of a man she barely knew and bawled out her feelings about how cold and lost her childhood and youth had been. She was so annoyed with herself that she almost laughed, a helpless rather than happy laugh, but she stopped herself in time. Laughter did not fit the moment.

'I was thinking of having a cup of tea,' said Dave. 'Talking, maybe listening to music. Just that.'

What was the harm in it?

'My flat, well—Fiona's to be precise—is not a good idea, unless you want to meet my ex.'

'Not particularly,' admitted Dave.

'So—to your place.' Leslie did not want to think what Gwen would say if she knew about this date at Dave's. She did not have the feeling she was playing with fire. She felt both she and Dave Tanner were too bound up in this confused and disturbing situation, and shocked at the crime which had entered their lives without warning. Neither had a clear idea of how things were to pan out in their lives.

Yet Gwen did not need to know about their meeting. And what happens in his room is in my hands, decided Leslie.

They walked there on foot in harmonious silence. They were both so wet by now that the walk did not make any difference.

Friargate Road looked sad and empty when they got there. Rainwater ran down the windowpanes, splashed from gutters and drained away in the tiny front gardens. Blaring music came from one of the houses. In front of the Market Hall a few youths had gathered. IPods on, they drank beer, kicked around empty cans and looked half-frozen. They shouted out obscenities at Dave and Leslie and then cracked up laughing, showing how drunk they already were.

When they came past Mrs Willerton's house, a man got out of a car on the other side of the road. Leslie had not noticed the car at first. The man quickly turned up his coat collar and rushed over to them in the rain. His face looked familiar to Leslie, but she could not place him at first. He stopped in front of them and blocked their path. He held out his ID.

'Sergeant Reek,' he introduced himself. 'Mr Tanner?'

'Hello, Sergeant,' said Dave in a friendly way.

Reek put the ID back in his coat's inner pocket.

'Mr Tanner, I have to ask you to accompany me to the

station. Detective Inspector Almond has some questions to ask you.'

'Now?'

'Yes. Right now.'

'As you can see, Sergeant, I've got a visitor and—'

'Right now,' replied Reek forcefully.

Dave brushed a few wet strands of hair from his forehead. He did not look uneasy, instead annoyed. 'Does that mean you are arresting me?'

'Mr Tanner, it's just a few questions that we urgently need you to answer. Considerable doubts have arisen about your statement concerning Saturday night. It would be in your interest to clear them up as soon as possible.' Reek's tone left little doubt that in spite of his politeness Dave had no other choice but to do as he had been asked.

Dave looked down at his clothes. 'Can I just put on some dry things? I'm soaked through, and I don't really want to catch a cold at the station, Sergeant.'

'I'll come up with you,' said Reek.

Dave turned to Leslie. 'I'm very sorry. As you can see, there's nothing I can do.'

'What could they have against you, Dave?'

He shrugged. 'No idea. It'll probably be easy to clear up. But I want you to know, Leslie, that whatever they accuse me of, I didn't murder your grandmother. Nor Amy Mills. I don't run around at night killing women. Don't doubt me, please.'

She nodded, but he seemed to feel her uncertainty, because he raised his hand and touched her face briefly with a gesture which was both helpless and tender. 'Please,' he said again.

'I don't doubt you,' she said obediently, and asked herself why she wanted so much to make the situation easier for him.

'Mr Tanner,' chimed in Reek impatiently, who was getting more and more wet in the rain.

'Just coming,' said Dave. The two men went to Mrs Willerton's house. Leslie stood in the rain and watched them go in. She watched the scene which seemed so strangely unreal to her, saw how Dave found his key, opened the door, how he and Sergeant Reek stepped inside and the door closed behind them.

Dave Tanner did not look round one last time.

10

'STRANGE THAT JENNIFER isn't home yet,' said Colin.

He stood in the study doorway. Gwen was sitting at the desk and had turned the computer on. She was moving the mouse around, concentrating on something.

She looked up. 'Why?'

'It's almost two. The weather's terrible. What's keeping her so long?'

'She's sitting in a café and waiting for the rain to ease off so she can reach the bus stop with more or less dry feet,' said Gwen, with a pragmatism which she certainly possessed, but which other people did not often see in her. 'Also, if she missed the one o'clock bus, then she has to wait until a quarter to four for the next one. We're really out in the sticks here, Colin!'

'Hmm,' went Colin.

Cal and Wotan were standing behind him. Wotan whined quietly.

'The dogs miss her.'

'She'll be back soon,' said Gwen distractedly.

Colin stepped into the room. 'Where's your father?'

'He's having a lie-down. He doesn't feel well. I think he's taking Fiona's death hard.'

'Well...' said Colin.

Gwen and he looked at each other across the desk.

'You said earlier...Dave Tanner knows the whole story?'

Colin asked quietly. Chad could come down the stairs at any moment.

She took a deep breath. 'Yes.'

'Did you give it to him to read?'

'Yes.'

'How did he react?'

'He hasn't said anything about it yet.'

'The bad opinion he held of Fiona is hardly going to have improved after he read it.'

'Probably not,' agreed Gwen. She looked very tired, Colin noticed. Tired and down.

The twenty-four hours she had spent with her fiancé had not been exactly spine-tingling, he thought.

Seeing how frustrated she was, he would have liked to leave her in peace, but he had a burning question.

'Don't you think that this whole story, about your father and Fiona, should be handed over to the police?' he asked cautiously.

She looked at him. She was neither shocked nor worked up, just sad. 'Then my father would know that I've read Fiona's mails to him. And that I printed them out and gave them to you and Jennifer. And Dave. He would never forgive me.'

'Maybe he won't care who else knows the story. Chad seems pretty wrapped up in his mourning for Fiona. I don't think that anything apart from that is going to upset him much.'

'Still. I don't want him to find out, so the police can't find out either.' Gwen sounded more decided than normal. Colin knew how close to her father she was. She would have found a lingering row with him difficult to bear. Nor did she want to dirty his reputation, by opening up his past to the police and then possibly the public at large.

The same was true regarding Fiona. Her memory would be brought into disrepute and she had been like a mother to Gwen for many years. It would have broken Gwen's heart to see these two people at the mercy of the full force of public opinion, when they could no longer defend themselves—Fiona because she was dead, and Chad because he was so self-absorbed.

'Gwen…' said Colin slowly, but she interrupted him in a tone which for her was surprisingly sharp:

'There's something else the police should know, Colin. Something which seems more important to me than these old stories.'

'What?'

'Jennifer,' she said.

He did not understand. 'Jennifer?'

Gwen did not look him in the eye. 'I've been struggling with this these last few days. That Saturday night. You know we were asked, Colin, what we did and where we were at the time of the crime.'

'I know. What's the problem?'

She seemed to be struggling with herself. Later Colin thought that she would never have said what she said next if she had not felt her back was up against the wall. She had to stop him from insisting she give Fiona's story to the police. She did it with the only option she had: she focused his attention on another person. Yet strangely, he did not doubt for a minute that what she said was true.

'Just after we heard about Fiona's death, Jennifer came to me. She said I could get in trouble, because I might have had a motive to kill her—after all, she had practically driven my fiancé away from the farm. She said things could get tricky for me.'

'Tricky…with the police?'

'Yes. And she was right. There were really only two people that evening who had a real reason to be angry with Fiona: Dave Tanner—and me.'

'Yes, but…'

'She offered to give me an alibi.'

'What?' asked Colin dumbfounded.

'She said I should say I'd been out at the bay with her and the dogs. She would confirm it. I was…so confused and afraid that I agreed.'

He was appalled. 'So, really, you weren't…?'

'No. I wasn't down in the bay with her. We sat in my room for a long time, and she consoled me, but then…she went off on her own. I stayed here. All night long. There are no witnesses for that.'

He shook his head. 'Gwen, do you know what you're saying?'

'I'm just telling you,' Gwen replied. 'I wouldn't tell anyone else, but…I think about it all the time, that…Jennifer was walking around outside at the time it happened. Even at the time, I had the thought that it could have been the other way round, you know.'

'The other way round?' he asked reluctantly. He was taken aback.

How could Jennifer have been so stupid?

'Maybe she wasn't so much wanting to give *me* an alibi. Maybe she needed one. I don't mean that she…I don't for a second think she could have murdered Fiona. Why should she? But it's strange, isn't it, Colin? Why did she lie to the police? Why did she take the risk? Why did she want to be sure she was covered?'

11

THE BIG HOUSES on St Nicholas Cliff all looked a little shabby, including the Grand Hotel whose façade seemed to have suffered particularly the wind and salt of the last few years. The house Stan Gibson lived in was at the top end and seemed very run-down. On the ground floor there was a shop for women's clothing, which to judge from the displays was aimed at middle-aged women of slender means. The flats above it had small windows. Even from the outside, you could see that they did not close well or let much light into the rooms.

All in all, thought Jennifer, it's not exactly a building I would like to live in.

Feeling uneasy, she followed Ena up the dim stairwell. Steep, creaking stairs. A terrible flowery wallpaper. A musty smell.

'It will get better,' said Ena. 'He has a really nice flat.'

Jennifer had a hard time imagining it.

On the third floor Ena stopped at a door and unlocked it. 'He renovated it himself. The landlord agreed. I think he's done a good job.' She let Jennifer in.

Stan had indeed made the best that could be made out of it, as Jennifer had to admit. She supposed that the flat had once consisted of many small rooms. Stan had knocked out the dividing walls and made a single large room. It looked cosy, and the remaining columns were nicely joined with wooden shelving. The kitchen was part of the room. Its stainless steel and black granite shone. There was also a generously sized corner sofa facing a nice brick fireplace. The Scandinavian furniture looked inexpensive but bright and friendly. A white-painted door led to the bedroom, and beyond that there was a bathroom too.

'Newly tiled, with a great shower, a big table and lots of mirrors…'

At least she likes Stan's flat, if not him. Better than nothing, thought Jennifer.

She walked across the room and looked out one of the windows. As the flat was so high up, you could see the sea from here. Below the house was the wide street and on the opposite side a few residential houses and the Grand Hotel. Not a bad place to live, thought Jennifer, revising her initial estimation.

She jumped—Ena was suddenly next to her.

'Linda Gardner lives in the house opposite,' said Ena.

The house looked a little like a long thin tooth which had a bit broken off its side.

'Who's Linda Gardner?' asked Jennifer.

'The woman Amy Mills was babysitting for. The student who—'

'Oh yes, I know,' interrupted Jennifer. 'A terrible affair. Horrible.'

And so similar to our own, she thought.

'That's the house she left on that July night,' said Ena. 'She went over that bridge and then into the Esplanade Gardens. Her last trip. Mrs Gardner's flat is on a level with Stan's, by the way.'

Jennifer looked at the windows. They were dark holes framed by the frilly curtains.

Suddenly she shivered, but that might have been because of the rainy atmosphere outside. She turned from the window. 'You wanted to tell me something, Ena. And show me something.'

'Yes,' said Ena. 'That's what I wanted to show you. The house opposite. The flat. And this here.' She pulled a tripod from the corner. A black telescope was attached to it. She put it at the window.

'He watched her from here.'

Jennifer did not understand. 'Who? Who watched whom?'

'Stan. He watched Amy Mills. On the evenings when she was over there. You can see everything in the flat with this lens. At least in the evening when the lights are on. And it was always evening when she was there.'

'What?' asked Jennifer. She understood what Ena was saying, but was hoping that there was something she had not understood. 'What are you saying, Ena?'

'It's not some absurd idea of mine, Jennifer. He told me. A few days ago. Stan told me that he used to watch Amy Mills over there, and he showed me how well it works. We could see Mrs Gardner and her daughter. She read to her and—'

'He told you that he used to watch Amy Mills?'

'Yes. For months. He acted as if he was…really proud of it. *The girl who's dead now, I knew her pretty well*, he said, and then he brought out this thing. I was completely shocked, but he did not notice. He bragged about his great telescope and that he even…even knew what colour her panties were. You can see into the bathroom too, you see.'

Jennifer put a hand to her temples. She felt a pounding starting. 'That is…indeed a little disturbing,' she said in the end.

'But that's not all,' said Ena. You could see it was doing

her the world of good to tell someone about this. 'The day before yesterday I found something which... And since then I've felt awful, and known I couldn't keep it to myself...'

She pulled Jennifer over to a little chest of drawers, and kneeling down she tried to open the lowest drawer.

Jennifer turned nervously towards the flat's front door. She was shivering even more, and she knew it had nothing to do with the cool day. 'Are you quite sure he won't suddenly come in?'

'He wouldn't come back from Hull just like that,' said Ena, but she did not sound completely convinced.

'Quick, have a look,' she insisted.

She had finally managed to pull out the drawer. It was full right to the top with photos—photos of all sizes, black and white as well as colour photos, framed in wood or paper sometimes. Ena grabbed a pile and pressed them into Jennifer's hands. She was squatting down next to Ena. 'Here!'

All the pictures showed a young woman. Most of them were grainy snaps, obviously taken at a great distance. They showed the young woman on a cliff-top walk. At the beach. Walking down a road. Coming out of a supermarket. Eating in McDonald's. Inside a flat. Reading. Watching television. Staring out the window.

'Who is it?' asked Jennifer, although she knew. Her voice sounded hoarse.

'Amy Mills,' replied Ena. 'I know because her picture was in all the papers after she was murdered. It's Amy Mills in just about every possible situation. You can see for yourself,' she motioned to the open drawer, 'the pics fill the whole drawer.'

'Most were taken with a telephoto lens,' said Jennifer,

'and it doesn't look as though Amy Mills knew she was being photographed.'

'He must have been following her all the time,' said Ena. 'At least each weekend, when he wasn't working. And on his days off. Evenings. He was constantly taking her picture.'

Jennifer swallowed. Her throat was dry. She looked at the door again.

'Did he show you these too?'

Ena shook her head. 'No. Like I said, I found them. And I didn't talk to him about them. You know, I really didn't like the thing with the telescope, and I had tried to convince myself it was just a coincidence that Amy was his target. I said it was just because she happened to go to the flat opposite his, and that it was a terrible coincidence that she was later the victim of a crime. But the pictures… I mean, it looks as if…'

'He was obsessed with her,' said Jennifer. 'What this is, Ena, is stalking. Even if the victim didn't know about it.'

'Stalkers aren't necessarily murderers,' replied Ena.

The word *murderers* reverberated awkwardly in the air. It stood out like a penetratingly bad smell. It shook Jennifer out of her paralysis. She got up, with the photos in her hand. 'Is *that* what you wanted to talk to Gwen about?'

Ena stood up too. 'I wanted to ask her what to do. I couldn't work it out on my own.'

Jennifer did not let go of the photos. Her eyes drifted back to the door. 'We have to get out. If he finds us here…'

'Do you think he…?'

'I don't know. I don't know how far his involvement in the crime goes, and I don't know how dangerous he could get with us, but I don't want to know that, in any case. Come on. We have to go.'

'And then?'

'I'm taking these photos with me. And we're going to the police. You have to tell them everything you've told me, Ena. The police *have to know*.'

In an instant it seemed as if all the energy which had carried Ena through the last half hour disappeared. Suddenly her arms hung limply at her sides.

'And what will happen to me? He won't want to be with me any more.'

'Do you want to be with someone who…'

'What?'

'Who might have committed a serious crime?'

'And what if it wasn't him?'

Jennifer waved the pictures around. 'This here just isn't normal! The telescope's not normal! The guy is, at the least, disturbed! Anyway, you aren't happy with him, as you just told me at some length. Please, Ena, let's hurry. We shouldn't stay here this long!'

Finally Ena snapped out of her torpor. She bent down and closed the drawer. 'Right. OK. I just want to pack a few things. I've already got some personal things here and I don't know if I will ever…' Her voice was trembling.

'Hurry,' urged Jennifer.

She stepped over to the window while Ena rushed around the flat. Rain. Rain. Rain. And across the road the dark windows of the flat where Amy Mills had spent her Wednesday evenings. Dark windows which when lit up would allow you to have a good view in.

Stan Gibson—a peeping Tom? A stalker?

Or a murderer?

Rain.

Suddenly she knew why she was so uneasy. Why she

kept looking at the door. Why her heart was pounding so loudly and fast.

It was pouring down. You could not work on any building site in rain like this. And it did not look as if it would stop soon.

She turned to Ena, who had just taken two pictures down from the fireplace and was stowing them in a plastic bag.

'Ena. I bet he'll come home early today. Are you ready? *We have to go!*'

'Soon,' said Ena.

Jennifer looked out again and checked the street.

Her voice trembled. 'Now, Ena, now!'

12

STEPHEN WAS NOT in the flat when Leslie came back. At first she thought he might be out walking or wandering around town, keeping himself occupied. But the guest-room door was ajar and peering in she saw that his travel bag was not there. It had been on a chair by the window until then.

She stepped inside the room. The bed had been made. The wardrobe's open doors showed that it had been cleared out. No question about it: the room's guest had gone.

Leslie found a note on the bedside table in Stephen's tiny scrawl:

Dear Leslie,

I have the feeling that I'm a nuisance to you. I'm sorry if my visit overwhelmed you. I didn't want to make you feel worse than you already feel because of Fiona's death—that really wasn't my intention! On the contrary, I just wanted to help you and be there for you, in case you needed someone you know well, and I think that in spite of everything I am still that: a person you know well.

My offer stands—to be there for you and to be ready for any kind of conversation. But I think a little distance would do us good. I've taken a room in the Crown Spa Hotel. I'll stay there for a few days, but I won't bother you. If you need me, just come over.

I would be happy to see you.

Stephen

Typical Stephen. Considerate, understanding. Putting his own needs last, but in so doing subtly creating feelings of guilt. In his presence you always felt you were the bad person. Leslie suddenly realised that after his affair it had been the same. She felt like a scoundrel for ending the relationship, although he was the one who had taken a girl he pulled in a pub screwed in into his marriage bed for a screw.

She scrunched up the letter and threw it into a corner.

The pouring rain outside made her loneliness in the large building all the more apparent to her. Normally the view outside made up for everything else. There would be either blinding sunlight on the blue waters of the bay or powerfully wild cloud formations in the sky. The South Bay retained its charm in stormy as in good weather. Only the leaden, rainy bleakness of a day like today could not convey anything except its own bleakness.

No one else could be heard in the house, as so often. Nowhere were doors slamming, windows being opened or closed, nor was there a toilet being flushed. Most flats were empty, and that would not change all autumn and winter. The house exuded a cold emptiness.

For an intensely overwhelming moment Leslie could feel the loneliness her grandmother had lived with. It filled her with an almost physical pain. Fiona had experienced many days like this over the last few years: grey, cold and oppressively quiet. She had survived the days, somehow, and she had never complained. But she had suffered. Leslie suddenly knew that, although she could not have said how she knew. Perhaps her grandmother's energy was just so strong within her four walls that it was impossible to ignore it.

She went into the kitchen and put the kettle on. She asked herself uneasily what the police might have against Dave. Doubts about his statement regarding last Saturday night?

It wasn't him. He hadn't killed Fiona. She could have sworn it, although she had nothing more to go on than her instinct, and there too she had little experience of judging other people's criminal tendencies—to be precise: no experience. Dave had claimed he had gone home to bed. If that was not true, what motive might he have for hiding the truth?

She put a bag of ginger tea in a mug, added some honey and poured on boiling water. While the tea brewed, she looked out of the window above the sink. It looked out on the well-tended little park which gave the end of the Prince of Wales Terrace, where it met the Esplanade, a picturesque look. In spite of the bad weather an old woman was dragging herself along the muddy pavement. Was she lonely too? Could she also not bear to stay in her flat and so had fled outside, risking a flu or even bronchitis? There are people who say that loneliness is the worst disease of them all, worse even than death. Was Fiona one of those people?

Leslie turned away from the window. Her gaze fell onto a small metal board which hung near the fridge. You could fix notes to it with little magnets. There was a shopping list in Fiona's familiar stiff handwriting, which had not yet become at all shaky. She had noted *sugar*, *lettuce* and *grapes*.

Next to it hung a postcard which Leslie recognised as the one she had sent the previous year on holiday. She had gone on a walking holiday in Greece with two colleagues. You could see a sunny bay surrounded by rocks, and an almost kitschy blue sky above it. Next to it was… Leslie stepped closer. The programme invite to a Christ-

mas party down in the Spa Complex. Christmas Eve with
a ventriloquist and a garish puppet. Leslie turned over the
flyer, the front of which was decorated with a Christmas
tree. The *Hey Presto Dancers* and *Naughty Oscar,* who
was going to show his extra special tricks. Fun for the all
the family, the flyer proclaimed, on the most exciting and
magical evening of the year.

The programme was from last year.

Why was it still hanging here? Had Fiona gone? Leslie
knew that nothing in the programme would have amused
or excited her. Silly tomfoolery. Nice for kids perhaps,
who did not know how to fill their time until Christmas
morning arrived when they could unpack their presents.
But for a well-read, critical old woman who found fault
with every comedy programme on television?

She had been lonely and had not known how else to survive Christmas Eve. That was Leslie's only explanation.
Christmas was the giant, problematic obstacle which people living on their own had such trouble negotiating each
year. Such a dark and scary obstacle that people preferred
to flee to any old silly entertainment than to sit at home.

Why had she not told me? thought Leslie.

She remembered last Christmas. It had certainly not
been plain sailing for her. To make sure she did not get
down in the dumps, she had volunteered to be on duty in
the hospital. The evening before she had celebrated with
two much older colleagues of hers in a pub. One of the
two women was a widow, the other was single. All things
considered, she got through the difficult days pretty well.
Now she asked herself guiltily why she had not thought
of her grandmother. What could have been more natural than to drive up to Yorkshire for a week, to celebrate
Christmas with her?

She was such a tough old cookie, Leslie thought, that you just didn't think she could have trouble with Christmas. You just didn't think that she could find anything problematic or frightening or shattering. Perhaps she too had felt grief and worry and fear, but why had she never shown the slightest trace of those feeling?

There had obviously been no evening on the Beckett farm, else she would have gone. But probably Chad with his taciturn, strange nature had not even thought to invite her, while Gwen for her part almost never made a decision herself, and Fiona was certainly too proud to ask.

Perhaps she had hoped up to the last minute that her granddaughter would come?

The phone rang and startled Leslie out of her guilty brooding. She picked up the receiver and simultaneously thought: Hopefully not another anonymous call!

'Yes?' she said.

It was Colin. This time he was looking for Jennifer, and you could hear how difficult he found it to come to Leslie a second time with a Missing Person query.

'She wanted to go shopping and perhaps have a bite for lunch. I know that the last bus went at one and the next one goes at four, but…'

'So what's the problem?' asked Leslie. 'It's half past two. You can probably only expect to see her in over two hours' time.'

'The weather,' said Colin. 'That's my problem. It can't be much fun in town with the rain, so I thought I could fetch her, if I knew where she was. But…she obviously hasn't gone to your place?'

'No,' confirmed Leslie. 'She's not here. And by the way, Colin—Gwen, who you spent yesterday ringing round about so frantically, did spend the night at Dave Tanner's. As I thought.'

'Gwen's home now,' said Colin. 'And I admit I was too worried about her. But my wife wanted to visit Dave Tanner too, and that…well, concerns me.'

'What concerns you?'

'You can imagine,' Colin replied.

Was he alluding to the still present suspicion that Dave was involved in Fiona's murder?

Out loud to Colin Leslie said, 'I met Dave this morning at the harbour, and until three quarters of an hour ago we were in town together. If Jennifer had been hoping to see him at home, then she won't have managed to.'

'Hmm,' said Colin. It was not clear whether this information put his mind at rest or not.

Leslie sighed quietly. 'Colin, you've got some issue with letting the women around you—'

'I don't have any issues,' said Colin sharply, 'but my wife does, so I'm worried.'

'It'll be all right.'

'Goodbye,' said Colin stiffly and hung up.

Leslie took her tea and walked into the living room. Talking about Dave Tanner had reminded her that he might be in some difficulty. Perhaps he needed help. Perhaps there was something in Fiona's notes. She had to finish reading the computer print-outs.

She sat down on the sofa, sipping her tea. She was very tired. She would lie down, just for a couple of minutes.

She put her cup down and stretched out on the sofa, falling asleep before any more thoughts came to her.

13

IT WAS NOT an interrogation. At least Valerie did not want to create that impression for now. She had invited Dave Tanner into her office and asked him to sit across the desk from her. Reek brought them both coffee. When she had to get tough with people, she used another room with bare walls and furnished with only a table and a few chairs. She was not at that point with Tanner. Maybe it was because he was not her favourite suspect, even if she would never have expressed that to anyone. All her instincts pointed her in another direction. Nevertheless she shouldn't, she thought, ignore the contradictions of Tanner's statement about Saturday night. She shouldn't make her mind up too soon. She shouldn't let the impatience she felt coming from her bosses push her to hurried conclusions.

She shouldn't, she shouldn't, she shouldn't…

She asked herself briefly if she would ever reach the point where she didn't just repeat the guidelines for investigating officers like a schoolgirl. When wouldn't she use half her energies in just controlling herself, and in keeping her unease in check.

Don't think about that now, she ordered herself, focus on Tanner!

She looked at him. He was just taking a sip of coffee. He grimaced, because it was scalding hot. It did not look to her as if he had a guilty conscience, but he certainly did not look comfortable. That did not mean he had anything to be guilty about. Most people would prefer to spend their time doing almost anything other than being questioned in a police station.

'Mr Tanner, as Sergeant Reek has already told you, there are some…inconsistencies regarding your statement that you drove straight home on Saturday night and went to bed immediately… We have a statement from a neighbour…'

He put his cup down and looked at her intently. 'Yes?'

'A lady who lives opposite saw you leave your landlady's house at around nine p.m., get into your car and drive off.'

He groaned. 'Mrs Krusinski, wasn't it? She spends her whole time, day and night, watching the street, because she lives in fear of her ex. Do you think she's a reliable witness?'

'That's not the question right now. I just want to hear what you have to say concerning the statement.'

She could see in his expression how his thoughts were racing. He had expressive features, she realised. She thought she even saw the moment when he caved in.

'It's true,' he said. 'I drove off again that evening.'

'Where to?'

'To a pub in the harbour.'

'Which one?'

'The Golden Ball.'

Valerie knew the pub. She noted it down. 'Were you alone? I mean…did you arrange to meet someone?'

She could just see his hesitation.

Valerie leant forward. 'Mr Tanner, you should tell the truth. This is not a game. We're investigating a murder. Because of what happened on Saturday at your engagement party you are one of the main suspects. The fact that you gave a false statement doesn't exactly count in your favour, as you no doubt realise. Don't make everything worse for yourself. Don't hide or change anything from now on.'

He snapped out of his paralysis. 'I met a woman.'

'Whom?'

'Does it matter?'

'Yes. She will have to confirm your statement.'

'Karen Ward.'

'Karen Ward?' asked Valerie surprised. She had spoken to her twice in connection with her investigation into Amy Mills' death. Not that much came of it. Karen Ward had not known Amy Mills well and had not been able to help the police.

Small world, thought Valerie.

'She's a student here in Scarborough,' she said. 'She lives in a shared flat in Filey Road, if I remember correctly. On the corner of Holbeck Road.'

He nodded. 'Yes. I know you've met her already. Because of—'

'Amy Mills, yes. Carry on. So, you met Miss Ward?'

'I called her on her mobile. She normally works behind the bar in the Newcastle Packet on Saturday nights. That's—'

'I know the one. Down at the harbour, too. A karaoke bar.'

'Yes. She was very tired and said she'd already spoken to her boss and he was fine with her going at nine. The bar was practically empty. I suggested that I pick her up and we go for a drink. She was up for that. So we ended up in the Golden Ball's bar.'

'At around a quarter past nine, twenty past nine, I'm guessing?'

'Yes.'

'We'll talk to Miss Ward, Mr Tanner, and with the staff at the Golden Ball. I have to ask what your relationship to Karen Ward is.'

His reply sounded a little too casual. 'We used to go out. For about a year and a half.'

'You were a couple?'

'Yes.'

'And the relationship ended when you met Gwen Beckett?'

'A little after, yes. But our relationship had already lost its spark. At least to me.'

'Right. But after the messed up engagement party you absolutely had to see her?'

He pulled a face. 'Not "absolutely". It was just that the evening had been downright unpleasant and I suddenly realised I wasn't going to be able to sleep. I just wanted to go out. Karen and I are good friends, so I called her up.'

'You are good friends? Three months after you left her for another woman?'

He did not say anything.

'Does Miss Ward know that you are, let's say, engaged? Does she know about Gwen Beckett?'

'She's heard rumours.'

'But you didn't tell her?'

'I didn't deny it either. It was…God, Inspector, what's this all about? About my love life?'

'About your credibility.'

He made a dismissive gesture. 'My situation…my private life is…difficult right now. But that doesn't make me a murderer!'

'I suppose you kept in with Miss Ward the whole time?

For times when you felt frustrated? Because Gwen Beck-ett is not exactly the woman of your dreams?'

'Am I being judged on morals here?'

'Why didn't you say from the start that you were in the Golden Ball with an old girlfriend?'

'Because it would cause problems with Gwen, if she heard.'

'Really? Is she that jealous? To make life difficult for you when you openly meet an ex for a drink in a pub?'

'I didn't want to risk any trouble.'

'Where did you go after the pub?'

He looked at her cautiously. 'After?'

'Well, you must have left the pub at some point. Our witness was looking out at the road until late in the night, but your car didn't reappear. The Golden Ball isn't open all night!' She was bluffing. Marga Krusinski had only mentioned midnight. A pub visit could have lasted that long. But Tanner need not know the details of the witness statement.

He shifted uneasily back and forth on his chair.

'All right, Inspector. I almost don't care now. I did go to Karen's flat with her.'

'And you stayed until...'

'Until about six in the morning. Then I drove home. I didn't want my landlady to know I had been out, so I chose a time when she was still asleep. I showered, dressed and later went for a long walk. The weather was beautiful.'

'So you spent the whole night with Karen Ward.'

'Yes.'

'And she was fine with that, although you are about to marry another woman?'

'Of course she was fine with it. Otherwise she wouldn't have taken me home.'

The situation seemed clear to Valerie now. Fiona Barnes had hit the bullseye with her accusations. Dave Tanner's interest in Gwen Beckett was calculated only to get hold of the Beckett farm property. At the same time he would meet his ex, a young student who Valerie had noticed was exceptionally attractive and better suited to the worldly Dave Tanner than the bland, inexperienced Gwen Beckett. His ex knew about Gwen and was no doubt in agonies about it, but clung to the hope that she would win Dave Tanner back and so she let him do as he wanted with her.

And Valerie realised something else. Dave Tanner had certainly not given up on his intention of marrying Gwen Beckett. After all, Karen Ward offered a sure alibi as to his whereabouts at the time of the murder, and yet in spite of his precarious situation he had not used his alibi—out of fear of losing Gwen. A lot rested for him on the chance of a new life. Perhaps too much.

She would check his statement, although she was almost certain that he was telling the truth.

She got up. 'All right, Mr Tanner. You can go now. I don't have any further questions right now. We'll talk to Miss Ward and with the barman at the Golden Ball. I expect they will confirm your statement.'

Dave got up too. He did not say anything, but she knew the question going through his head.

'Mr Tanner, I don't see any need for me to tell anyone you know about this chat. If what you say is true about the night of the crime, then you will be taken off the list of suspects. Of course I'll write a report, but it will be an internal one.'

Now he smiled. His smile was warm and alive. Valerie thought that although Karen Ward was stupid to let herself be used by him, she could understand that a woman would find it hard to let this man go. When was the last time she had been smiled at by a man like this? Too long ago to be able to remember. She quickly brushed the thought aside.

'Thank you, Inspector,' said Dave and held out his hand. She shook it.

'Of course I have no right to judge you morally, Mr Tanner. But one word of advice: decide on something and take that path. Consistently. Anything else…doesn't work in the long-term.'

To her surprise his face became serious. 'I know. And once again, Inspector: thank you. For everything.'

He left the room.

Her eyes followed him for a little too long. She ordered herself: Stop it, Valerie! That kind of man makes women unhappy. As sure as rain. Now, concentrate on the case.

Reek had to go to the Golden Ball right away. Then try to contact Karen Ward.

And then Dave Tanner would be out of the investigation.

Her phone rang. It was Sergeant Reek.

'Inspector, I've got Jennifer Brankley on the other line. Can I put her through. She says it's urgent.'

Brankley calling her? What did she want now?

'Of course,' she said. 'Put her through!'

Maybe things were moving, finally.

14

'THESE PICTURES ARE indeed…suspicious. Very suspicious,' said Sergeant Reek.

He had gone through the contents of the drawer from Stan Gibson's flat meticulously. However he had not found anything which threw a light on the murder of the young woman. The photos were definitely of Amy Mills. And it was just as certain that the young woman had been followed by Stan Gibson—if he had taken the photos. He must have spent all his free time trailing her and taking pictures of her whenever he had an opportunity. Added to that, Ena Witty had claimed he had watched Miss Mills in Linda Gardner's flat with a telescope.

Since Jennifer Brankley's call Valerie had felt breathless with excitement. It could not be a coincidence. A man who lived opposite the flat where Amy Mills had spent the last evening of her life. He had also told his current girlfriend that he had spied on Amy Mills in her most private moments during her weekly babysitting. And one of his drawers was full of photos of the dead girl.

Just let someone try and say he was a harmless peeping tom!

It still had not been easy to get a search warrant.

She had visited Ena Witty and Jennifer Brankley in Witty's flat. Ena Witty was as white as chalk. She seemed to have been thrown off balance by the realisation that her boyfriend might be guilty of a serious crime. It was enough, as Valerie knew, to throw much more self-confident and tough women than Witty. At least Jennifer Brankley was obviously holding her nerve. She was also the one with the presence of mind to take a pile of photos from the suspect's house, so that Valerie had something to hand, literally, which she could show the judge.

'It all happened so quickly,' Jennifer explained. 'I was scared silly that Gibson could walk in any minute. I grabbed these pictures, Ena packed a few personal items, and then we cleared off.'

Valerie had not pressured Ena Witty. She was itching to obtain as much information as she could as quickly as possible, but the young woman seemed so shattered that it seemed sensible to treat her with care.

'He said that he watched Amy Mills with a telescope, when she was babysitting for Linda Gardner?'

'Yes. He often said that. He showed me the telescope too. It's in his living room. He was proud that he could see her so well!'

And the photos…Valerie knew she had to get into his flat. If possible, before Stan Gibson knew the danger and removed the incriminating evidence.

'He didn't come back while you were there?' she checked. 'Or did he see you leave the flat?'

'Not that we noticed,' replied Jennifer. 'I think he would have talked to us if he had seen us. You know, I was afraid because of the rain. Ena says he's working on a site in Hull. But as it's tipping it down, they might have stopped work. I thought he might come back any moment.'

'We'll find out where he is,' said Valerie. 'He has to be somewhere. Miss Witty, I'll need to talk to you later today. Are you going to stay in your flat?'

'Of course. I…I don't know where else I should go. I'm scared. He'll be so angry, Inspector. Maybe he didn't have anything to do with Amy Mills' murder. He'll never forgive me for going to the police…'

'There was no other option, Ena. I told you that,' said Jennifer gently. Valerie realised that she had Jennifer Brankley to thank for the fact that Stan Gibson's extremely strange behaviour had been reported to the police. Ena Witty would never have plucked up the courage to do it on her own. She would have hummed and hawed until Stan Gibson had noticed she was disturbed and perhaps put the photos in a safer place.

'I'll stay with Ena for now,' said Jennifer quietly, as she accompanied Valerie Almond to the door. 'I don't think she should be on her own.'

The situation seemed to have reinvigorated her, thought Valerie. The challenge is good for her. She's not as tense as before, but seems calmer and more in control.

The judge was none too pleased when Valerie appeared with a request for a search warrant for Gibson's flat. It was past four o'clock, and he should have been going home, not dealing with some tiresome problem. If Gibson was just a harmless citizen with a screw loose, the media would scream *Basic Rights Violated* if they got wind of it.

'Don't you have anything more than this suspicion?' he had asked, disgruntled. She pointed to the photos spread out on his desk. 'That's more than suspicion! These photos are facts! He followed Amy Mills for weeks, secretly taking pictures of her.'

'As long as the victim doesn't complain, then it doesn't concern us as a crime.'

'The victim can't complain. She's dead.'

'Inspector…'

'He spied on her with a telescope from the flat opposite. He was obsessed with her. It's patently obvious that his life was completely taken up by this. Maybe in his fantasies she was meant to be his. When she didn't care to share that opinion, perhaps he murdered her. The crime was done with ferocious hate. That's just what you would expect when a man, who has...' she pointed to the photos, 'lived in such a strange fantasy world, is rejected.'

'That's guesswork!'

'And maybe I can back it up, if I can get into the flat.'

'Why don't you arrest Gibson first?'

'He can't be found right now. Sergeant Reek contacted the construction firm he works for. He was assigned to a site in Hull today, but work stopped at midday because of the rain. No one knows where he went next. The foreman says some of the men wanted to go for a drink and he might have gone with them.'

'Not a crime.'

'No. But when he gets home he'll get in touch with his girlfriend straight away. He'll notice something is wrong, because the young lady is completely distraught. I want to search the flat *before* he destroys everything which could be evidence!'

The judge growled, 'Hmm...' The law permitted a house to be searched when there was a good probability that evidence relevant to a crime would be found. Moreover, a house could be searched without the resident's knowledge if there was a reasonable suspicion that informing the resident would lead to the materials in question being destroyed.

Valerie played a trump card. Nothing conclusive, but a nice piece of the puzzle. 'Sergeant Reek found out something else. The firm that Gibson worked for is the firm which was doing the building work down in the Esplanade Gardens. Gibson was working on that project. That is the building site where the two fences were moved, blocking Amy Mills' shortest way, forcing her to go through the darkest and most deserted part of the park.'

'Any passer-by could have moved the fences. Any stupid kid. Any homeless person. You don't have to work on the site to access the fences.'

'No. But if you work on the site, and see the fences every day, the idea might come to you that you can direct Amy Mills in the direction you wish. Sir, all of the points on their own are flimsy, I admit that. But put them together and they do throw a suspicious light on Stan Gibson. I think a search warrant would be justified.'

She had got her piece of paper. Maybe she had only got it because the judge wanted to go home and he knew that he would not get rid of the officer quickly any other way. She could be very insistent, especially when she was under pressure and finally, *finally*, saw a lead that could help, that could even be the breakthrough.

Not that it looked like that in Gibson's flat right now. They had found the tripod and telescope as described. They had found about five hundred more photos. That was all.

Not enough to accuse someone of murder, thought Valerie.

It was already getting dark outside. The day was almost over. The rain was letting up.

Four officers had gone through Gibson's flat with a fine-tooth comb—without finding anything conclusive. Valerie felt like crying out of frustration. She had had to cross Dave Tanner off the list of suspects today. And now it looked as if she could say goodbye to the next challenger for the crown of chief suspect. Even before he had really come on the scene.

'That's just not nearly enough for a murder charge,' she said dully.

Reek had to agree. 'Not even for an arrest warrant, if you ask me,' he added.

She dismissed the idea with a gesture. 'Arrest warrant! If I go to the judge for that, he'll throw me out! He'll be annoyed he let me talk him into the search warrant.'

'We have to question Gibson. Our hand is not that strong, but we have a few cards up our sleeve. He stalked a woman, invaded her privacy, and that woman was then brutally murdered in a park at night. He has a little explaining to do!'

Valerie looked grim. 'For example, I'd like to know where he was on Saturday night. When Fiona Barnes was murdered.'

She heard a laugh behind her and turned around. Reek looked towards the door too. The man who had appeared looked young for his age. He was wearing jeans and trainers, and had to be the flat's tenant. Stan Gibson.

'I can tell you that,' he said. He smiled in a friendly way, which seemed extremely strange considering the chaos in his living room and the presence of the police officers. 'I was in London. From Saturday morning to Sunday late afternoon. At my parents' house. With my girlfriend Ena Witty. I introduced them to each other. Both my parents and Ena Witty can confirm that.'

Valerie took a moment to recover from her shock and surprise at the absurdity of the situation. Then she approached the stranger.

'Stan Gibson, I take it?' she asked in a sharp tone. 'Do you have any ID?'

He fished around in his jeans' pockets. Finding his wallet, he showed Valerie a card.

'Happy?' He was still smiling. 'And…um… *Ma'am*, do *you* have any ID?'

She flashed her ID and waved the search warrant at the same time. 'Detective Inspector Valerie Almond. And this is the judge's warrant to search your house.'

'All right. It would be great if you could tell me what this is all about.'

'Happily. But I'd ask you to please accompany me to the station. We will need to have a long chat. About Miss Amy Mills. And her murder.'

'Are you arresting me, Inspector?'

'It's just a chat,' replied Valerie politely. Inside she hissed: Happily, you bastard! You don't know how much I'd like to arrest you this instant, you and your revolting perma-grin!

The man was obviously not quite right in the head. When you come home and find your flat turned upside down by the police you don't smile as fixedly as that. At least, not if you are innocent. Stan Gibson had a skeleton in his cupboard, she was sure of it. He was grinning like a Cheshire cat because he thought he was safe. He found the situation amusing. He was looking forward to a little game with the police.

Just watch out, she thought.

'You can have a lawyer with you.' She reluctantly made him aware of his rights.

After a moment's badly acted consideration, Gibson shook his head. 'No. Why should I? I don't need a lawyer. Come on, Inspector. Let's go!'

He looked as if he had just invited her to go for a pint, like a cheery mate.

Don't let him get to you, she told herself, as she went downstairs with him and Sergeant Reek. That's just what he wants, and it won't work. He'd better be prepared. He'll soon stop grinning.

She had always claimed she had a nose for psychopaths.

She would have bet anything that she had one in front of her now. The worst kind of psychopath.

One that was exceptionally intelligent.

11

It was a long time, a very long time, until I saw the Beckett farm again. The rest of the war and one further year. Why? My mother. She came back from hospital a different person. She was never the same as before. I had known her to be an energetic, resolute woman, sometimes rather hard and brusque, but also cheerful and confident. Someone who took life by the horns, as we say. But after she had lost the child, the son which Harold had wished for so keenly, her optimism and forward-looking nature evaporated. She not only looked worse, thin and grey, but she also seemed deeply sad. She often burst into tears for no apparent reason. She would sit at the window for hours staring out. Everything was too much for her—the war, the bombed-out city, the badly dressed people and the rationed food. The shocking thing about her depression was that she had been someone who did not let things throw her.

'Could be worse,' she used to say *before* it happened.

Afterwards she said, 'Life was never as hard as it is now!'

And yet there was more and more to be hopeful about. The Germans were running out of steam. They would lose the war. Everyone was sure of it by now, even the worst pessimists—except my mother. The only thing that puzzled people was why the Germans had not given up yet.

The Nazis' fate was sealed on 6th June 1944, D-Day,

when the Allies began Operation Overlord and the armed forces of many nations landed on the beaches of Normandy in their thousands.

France would soon be free, everyone said so, and then things would move swiftly. A powerful Russian army was pushing in on the German borders from the East. Listening to the BBC, you asked yourself why Hitler did not throw in the towel immediately.

Instead he used his soldiers as cannon fodder. Apparently he was set on not surrendering as long as there was a single soldier in his army who still had his head on his shoulders.

'A madman,' Harold often said. 'A complete madman!' Not that Harold had any real understanding of politics, but I thought he was right in his estimation of Hitler. Admittedly, you did not need to be particularly intelligent to recognise the madness of the *Führer*.

While everyone waited for the war to end and made hopeful plans about what would come next, my mother could not find a single positive thought in her.

'Yes, perhaps the war will be over soon,' she would always admit in the end. 'But who knows what will come next? Maybe things will only get worse. Maybe only terrible things will happen and one day we'll say that the 1940 bombing wasn't as bad as what came later!'

In view of her deep depression I had given up fighting to be allowed to return to Yorkshire, or at least: I put it off for now. Even when the Nazis made one last attempt after Operation Overlord to fight back and started bombing London with their infamous V2 rockets, I never once considered fleeing the city. It was clear that Mum needed me, the child she had left. I could not leave her in the lurch. She clung to me nervously if I came home from school half an hour late or if I was longer than usual doing the shopping. I accepted how she was. I was not happy about it, but what could I do?

In any case, were I in Staintondale I would not have had Chad, as he was at the Front. Our correspondence had trickled out. I had no address to send a letter to, and he...well, he had never liked writing. Later I heard that he had taken part in the Normandy landing. With hindsight I was glad we had not been in touch over that period. I would have gone mad with fear, as we heard in the news how many soldiers had to pay with their lives for the invasion. Of course, later, when it all ended happily for him, I was very proud that he had been at that decisive event.

I no longer suffered as much from living in London, probably because Mum's mental condition forced responsibilities on me. There seemed to be a reason for my stay in London.

And Harold changed. He did not change fundamentally, of course. But Mum's weakness drew out his strength. He was no longer just hanging around drunkenly. Instead he helped me with the housework when he got home from work. Only once that was done did he get drunk, which was a step in the right direction. I saw him differently too, because the whole miscarriage and my flight to Yorkshire had showed me that he really loved my mother and wanted, in his own way, to make her happy. It was important to him that she was not hurt in any way. So I kept to our agreement. Mum should never hear about my lightning trip up to Staintondale in February 1943. Until her death in 1971 she never heard a word about it.

In May 1945 the war ended and people danced in the streets. Winston Churchill appeared on the balcony of Buckingham Palace with the royal family and thousands of people cheered them, singing *God Save the King* and

Rule, Britannia. I was there, tears pouring down my face, as we all held hands and sang the most popular, patriotic—and sentimental—war-time song:

There'll be bluebirds over the white cliffs of Dover… Tomorrow, when the world is free…

Many families were mourning their dead, and whole streets were still in ruins, but we were looking to the future, clearing the rubble, and starting the work of reconstruction. Everyone was happy to know that husbands, sons and friends were out of danger now, that we need not fear air raids or tremble at the thought of Nazis occupying our island.

The nightmare was over.

I left school in 1946, and had no idea what was to come next. My happy, even euphoric sense of a new start at the end of the war had collapsed, swallowed up by the realisation that I had to get a grasp on my life, although I did not know what path to take. What had I been thinking about the past years? I had been dreaming about Yorkshire. Apart from that I had just been trying to cope with each day as it came. I had usually seen my future in a sunny light, but that was all. I had not come up with any plans I could put into action.

'Do something with children,' suggested my mother when at the end of July we were having coffee and cake on my seventeenth birthday. (We used beaten egg whites instead of icing for the cake.) I had been moaning about not knowing what to do next.

'I think being a nurse on a children's ward is a wonderful job!'

Since she had lost Harold's baby she thought constantly about children. Without asking for any payment she looked after children in the neighbourhood, took them for walks, read to them and helped them with their homework. Harold and I were starting to get fed up with it, but we did not say anything, as her behaviour was obviously a kind of therapy for her. I myself felt no connection to anyone under fourteen, and immediately rejected her idea. 'No, Mum, no. I can't deal with children, you know that!'

'I think you should learn bookkeeping,' said Harold. 'They are always looking for people for office jobs, and you can work your way up.'

That sounded deadly boring.

'No. I don't know…oh God, I think I won't ever find the right job!' I looked darkly at the wall. Bookkeeper. Children's nurse. I might as well let them bury me alive.

Then a suggestion came which surprised me, and from my mother of all people. 'Maybe you just need to get away from London for a bit. From us. You're like someone who is running around in a little cage and can only see its bars, not the world behind them.'

I looked at Mum in astonishment. She had hit the nail on the head.

'You enjoyed Yorkshire so much during the war,' she continued. 'Perhaps you should go and visit for a few weeks. Walk by the sea, breathe in the fresh air. Sometimes a new place is all that's needed to see a new direction.'

Harold and I looked at each other in surprise.

'What was the name…of that lady who took you in? Emma Beckett, wasn't it? Maybe she would let you visit? Of course you would give her something to help with the extra expense, but we'd scrape that together.'

As Mum knew nothing about my flight up to Yorkshire, we had also not told her that Emma was no longer alive. And no doubt it was better that she did not know. I was not sure she would let me stay with Chad (if he had survived the war), Arvid and Nobody.

'Mum, are you serious?' I asked.

She was astonished. 'Why ever not?'

I looked at Harold again and saw that he would keep quiet about Emma's death.

My heart began to pound. The day had looked dark and without hope. Now everything ahead looked brighter.

I was going to see everything I loved. Chad. The farm. The sea. Our bay. Yorkshire's wide, rolling fields.

And all of that with Mum's blessing.

12

I ARRIVED IN Scarborough in August 1946. No sooner had I stepped onto the platform than I knew I was home again, and would never leave. I had needed to trick my mother a little. She had wanted to contact Emma, but I had claimed to be corresponding with the Becketts and that they invited me again each time they wrote. As Emma's affection for me at the time of my stay had not escaped my mother, this seemed plausible to her. We did not have a telephone, nor did the Becketts, and the post was extremely slow and unreliable in those post-war times. If she wrote to the Becketts, my mother could expect to wait a long time for an answer, assuming her letter arrived in Staintondale. In the end she had allowed me to travel more or less into the unknown, and I had breathed a sigh of relief when I was finally sitting in the train. Right until the end I had feared that she might reconsider.

But I was a little nervous. More than three years had passed. Who and what would I find? Was Chad still alive—and if so, had he returned to the farm? What had become of Arvid? Perhaps a bitter, lonely old widower, who would not be at all happy to see me? He might have become an alcoholic and be in a worse state than Harold in his glory days. Only Nobody would not have changed. He must be about fourteen years old by now. Yet the fact that at forty he would still act like a small child made him someone you could depend on, in a way.

I had to wait a long time for the bus and it was already evening when I finally arrived in Staintondale. Fortunately it was not getting dark early, as it was August. Nevertheless, when I walked across the fields to the farm from the main road the light was already dim. The day was cool and sunny. I carried what I owned in a rucksack on my back. It was not much. I felt free and happy. Horses, sheep and cows grazed around me.

And above me seagulls screeched.

Once I could make out the farm in the distance, I began to run. I was not only running out of a joyful anticipation, but also out of nervous fear. I wanted to finally know how things were on the farm.

The summer evening presented the farm in the best possible light, but I was still horrified at how dilapidated it had become. The farm gate was hanging on broken hinges and could obviously no longer be closed. It would never be repaired again. I was always amazed that in over half a century no one had found enough energy and resolve to deal with the problem.

All kinds of scrap equipment were strewn around the farmyard. In among these items, chickens pecked around. In the past they had lived in their own separate chicken run. The sheep pasture fences were in desperate need of repair, and so many stones had fallen out of the walls that the animals could easily climb through them. The house looked dark and almost uninhabited. Weeds grew almost to the front door. The bench was missing where Emma had loved to sit in the evening sunlight. It had probably been turned into firewood. The windows were thick with dirt. It was not likely that you could recognise much of the splendid landscape, when you looked out.

But the air smelt just as it always had, and the sea

would be the same, as well as the bay and the particular light there in the evening.

The thought of the bay crystallised a decision in me. I suddenly knew where my first walk should take me.

I put my rucksack down in the nettles by the front door. Freed from its burden, I set off with a spring in my step.

As soon as I had plunged through the dark gorge and stepped onto the twilit beach, I saw Chad. The sun had disappeared behind the cliffs, and the sea was an opaque night-blue. The beach, normally so wide, was just a thin strip of sand, but the tide had passed its height and the water was gradually retreating.

Chad sat on a rock, his face in his hands.

I stepped up closer.

'Good evening, Chad,' I said in the end.

He gave a little jump, looked up, and then leapt up. He looked completely confused. 'Fiona! Where d'yer come from?'

'From London.'

'What…I mean…just like that?'

He did not sound as excited as I would have hoped, but nor was he unfriendly. He was simply surprised.

'Well, looks like you survived the war,' I said, not thinking of anything more witty. I added, 'Not that I could have known this happy situation from your lively correspondence with me!'

He ran a hand through his hair. It was a gesture which reminded me of the fifteen-year-old boy he had been when I met him, the boy who—I could see this even in the rapidly diminishing light—was now a distant memory. He was twenty-one years old, and he had changed completely. At that moment I would not have been able to put into words exactly what the change was, except for the obvious fact that he was four years older than the last time we had met. But of course I had expected that. I think what amazed me was that he had aged much more than I had expected. More than the furrows and wrinkles on his face, it was in his expression. He did not look like someone who was twenty-one. He could have been thirty or forty.

When I had time to think about it in the following weeks I realised that war had speeded time up. These men, who had still been boys really when they reported for duty, full of patriotic fervour and a naive idea of what was awaiting them at the Front, had experienced more things, and harder things, than others experienced in a lifetime. They had seen mates fall and the possibility of their own death was a constant presence. They had killed in order not to be killed. They had held out in ice-cold trenches, enduring hours of nerve-shattering gun-fire, and had been forced to listen to the sharp screams of the dying. Nothing remained of their earlier lives in which they had often not had a care in the world, and had been safe. The Allies had vanquished Hitler's Germany. This knowledge remained for men like Chad, giving all they had endured a meaning. It did not change the images they would carry inside them for the rest of their lives. It did not change anything about the unsparing brutality to which they had been confronted from one day to the next—a side of life that none of them would have imagined beforehand.

By the way, Chad never talked to me about his war experiences, not then or later. Years later I discovered a revolver on a shelf in his study on the farm. It lay between a couple of files. When I asked him about it, he said, 'Me gun. From t' war.'

'Why are you keeping it?'

'Just am. In case we get burgled.'

I held it. 'It's heavy,' I realised.

'Put it back!' he ordered. 'Don't want t' have t' do with all that any more!'

I had understood. I never mentioned his gun again, nor dared to ask him about that traumatic part of his life.

Right now what he said was, 'I'm sorry. I shoulda written. It were all…too much.' He made a gesture of something billowing up.

'How's your dad?'

'He's not copin'. He barely does anythin' on t' farm. Just sit at home starin' at t' walls. He never got over me mam's death.'

I was not surprised. As an eleven-year-old girl I had intuitively understood that Emma was the soul of the Beckett farm, and that it was she, much more than her husband, who had the impulse to grasp the nettle. Without her, Arvid had become a hollow shell. It fitted in with the image I had of him.

'I try t' do me best,' said Chad. 'But it's hard t' get a farm goin', when it's totally run down. In these times…'

His eyes bored into me. 'Yer a right young lady,' he said, changing the topic abruptly. I felt myself blush.

'I've left school,' I said. 'I didn't know what to do next. Mum thought some distance to my life in London might do me good. That's why I'm here. I'd like to stay for a while…if I may.'

'Of course. Could do with another pair of hands,' said Chad and grinned.

He was kidding me. I smiled.

And suddenly, in a split second, he was the Chad I had known, the boy who had responded so tenderly to my infatuation. He opened his arms and let me fall into them. I felt secure with him that evening on the beach, although the feeling was later to prove to have been illusory. Whether because of the war or the example of his silent father, he was already starting to become the clammed-up man who in the end would be unable to show feelings.

At the time I did not know that this change had already started. I was too young to understand it, and too blissfully in love to think about the future. The bitterness and weight of the last few years evaporated. London, the war, my depressive mother, Harold—suddenly that was all far away and unimportant. Finally I had arrived at the place where I belonged. Close to the man I loved.

That was the extent of my romantic thoughts on that darkening beach. Soon night fell. The sound of the sea changed as the ebb tide sucked it further and further out. The sky was clear and full of stars. August nights have a particular magic to them. Perhaps a falling star or two even fell into the sea. Who knows. In any case, that's how I imagined it, after the first time that we made love in that stony bay in Staintondale.

It sounds corny, I admit. A warm summer night, stars, the sound of the sea, two young people and first love. An overwhelming feeling of happiness after years of doing without. It might sound too perfect, but I have to say that it felt just like that. No doubt I saw things with rosy spectacles, as you do when you are young. Today I can imagine that the pebbles were uncomfortable, that it stank of seaweed, and that clouds drifted across the sky concealing the stars. I can imagine that there was not a single falling star, that it was rather cool and that we started to shiver with cold. But back then I did not notice any of that. It was like a dream which was not disturbed or tarnished by anything. The complete intimacy with Chad, the way we melted together, seemed to make it the most wonderful moment of my life and—naive as I was, in spite of everything—I was sure that we would be inseparable.

Chad had cigarettes. Afterwards we cuddled close together for a while on the rocks and smoked. I did not say that this too was a first for me, in order not to look too childish. I dragged on the cigarette as casually and naturally as I could, and thankfully I did not cough. Chad had put his arm around me. For a long time he did not say anything.

In the end he said, 'I'm cold. Shall we go back t' farm?'

That was when I realised I was freezing too. I nodded, which he must have been able to see, because he got up and, holding my hand, helped me up too. Hand in hand, we silently felt our way back through the gorge. At the top, I breathed a sigh of relief. Now the stars and the moon lent us a little light.

Chad carried my rucksack into the house. It was dirty inside. I saw that at a first glance. And it did not smell good either. It smelt as if food was rotting somewhere in the kitchen. It was clear that inside the house the process of decay was also far advanced. It was no longer the cosy nest which Emma had made of the simple and poor house. It was cold, damp and a mess. Even I, who was ready to see the Beckett farm in almost any condition as paradise on earth, had to admit that you could no longer feel at home here. I resolved to start to make everything beautiful and homely the very next day.

Chad turned on the light in the kitchen. Dirty dishes were piled in the sink. The remains of dinner stood on the table.

'Looks like Dad's gone t' bed,' said Chad. 'Unfortunately 'e don't normally even tidy up 'is meal.'

Disgustedly he looked at the salami sausage and bread which had been bitten into rather than cut in slices, and at a cup half full of coffee. The coffee had globules of fat on the surface. 'It get worse every day!'

'I'll tidy it up,' I offered immediately, but he held me back.

'No! I don't tidy up after 'im, and I don't want you to either! 'E ain't sick, just lettin' 'imself go, and I ain't got any patience no longer.'

'It will go off, and it stinks. Just let me put the sausage in the fridge.'

The farm had an old-fashioned icebox which regularly needed a new block of ice. It turned out that no one had ordered an ice delivery in a long while. The icebox was as warm as the rest of the room. Inside it there were a few indefinable items that stunk and should have been thrown away long ago.

Chad looked slightly embarrassed. 'T' farm takes up all me time and energy. Dad should look after t' house, but…' He did not finish his sentence. It was obvious that his Dad did not look after anything.

In the end I put the sausage and bread in the pantry. It had no windows, was dark and a few degrees cooler than the house.

'Tomorrow we have to order ice,' I said, as if I were the housewife on the farm.

Chad agreed. 'Will do. Promise.'

We stood there looking at each other. I thought, Now say you love me. Say that I should stay forever! Please. Don't let what was so special tonight just disappear.

However, he could not stop casting angry glances at the table. He was angry with his father. That was clear to see. Perhaps he was no longer thinking about what had just happened down at the beach.

And I suddenly knew what had been irritating me the whole time.

Something was missing. Something which should have seen us coming and appeared by now.

'Where's Nobody, by the way?' I asked.

Chad lowered his gaze. Suddenly it was creepily quiet in the kitchen. I heard something rustling in the pantry. A mouse, I thought.

I asked again, almost afraid.

'Chad! Where's Nobody?'

13

'WELL,' SAID CHAD SLOWLY. 'Couldn't go on like that.'

We were sitting at the kitchen table, right under the light. It made Chad look tired and grey, me no doubt too. Chad had opened a bottle of beer and offered me some, which I had refused. I was serious about not touching a drop of alcohol.

The evening—the night—had changed. There was the kitchen with its rotten smell, the clammy air in the house and the feeling that something threatening was coming closer. I shivered. I suddenly felt terrible.

'What do you mean, *Couldn't go on like that?*'

Chad stared into his glass. 'He were no longer t' boy you remember. He suddenly shot up and were enormously tall fer 'is age. Don't know how old 'e was, but I'm guessin' he were fourteen or fifteen. Not much longer and he'd be a man.'

I thought of the lanky, young blond boy. Only three and a half years had passed since I had last seen him, but of course he could have changed a lot in that time. I just found it hard to imagine.

'Yes…and?'

He looked up at me. 'Fiona, his mind don't grow with his body. He still think like a child, and always will. Me Mam always claimed he'd wake up one day. Rubbish. Nobody's mentally disabled, no gettin' away from it.'

'That's nothing new,' I said.

'You knew 'im as a child. He 'ad 'is limits, but were 'armless. That changed. He...' Chad stopped.

'What?' I asked. I was feeling more and more worried.

'March this year a young lass appeared on t' farm. We didn't know her. She was lookin' for work, and askin' at all t' farms round about. We had enough work, but no money. Anyroad, we 'ad t' send her away. But just as she were goin'...Nobody came out.'

I waited.

'Like I said, the lass was young. Not twenty years old. She had beautiful long blond hair.'

I could guess what was coming. 'And Nobody...?'

'He ran over, grinned at 'er an' grabbed 'er 'air. He were makin' those incomprehensible sounds he always make when he talk. The woman were frightened half t' death. She tried t' get away, but 'e kept hold of 'er 'air. Then 'er breasts. He were slobberin' over her. He were...first time I've seen 'im like that...'e were all excited. Then she starts screamin'. I could drag Nobody off 'er and she ran off, fast as she could. I shouted at 'im, but 'e just grinned. Soon as I let go, 'e rubbed 'is hands frantically over 'is crotch. Disgustin'. *He* was disgustin'.'

I gulped. 'That...that doesn't sound nice.'

Chad leant forward. 'It'll only get worse. He's got sex on t' brain like a man, but t' mind and maturity of a child. So 'e can't control his lust. He don't even know what was happenin'. He's a menace t' every woman 'e meets. And Dad and I couldn't watch 'im all day.'

I thought I knew what was coming next, and relaxed a little. After all, it was something we had often talked about.

'So you put him in a home,' I said. 'I'm sure that was the most sensible thing you could do.'

Chad looked down at his glass again. 'A 'ome...right,

we thought 'bout it, Dad and I, but…there were some problems.'

'Really?' I asked.

'By gum, Fiona, don't be so daft! You can't just bring a young man like Nobody int' home an' say, Hello, this lad's been livin' with us the past six years but it can't go on, now you take him. I mean, we'd have trouble. Weren't proper, right from start. Nobody shouldn't have been with you evacuees. Mam shouldn't have taken 'im in. He shouldn't have grown up with us like our family secret.'

I remembered the dark November evening in 1940 and the field opposite Staintondale's little post office. The frightened children crouching and waiting…

'But the evacuees' escorts agreed Emma could take him with her,' I said. 'They didn't know what to do with him themselves. They wanted to check with someone higher up and then get back to her. But they never did. That's not our fault.'

'But Mam should have told someone, when she saw they'd forgotten. She had no right t' keep Nobody. He weren't 'er child or even a foster child. He were just *t' other child*, like Dad called him. You were here officially, not him though. She shouldn't have just let the years pass like that.'

'She wanted to protect him. She meant well with him.'

'My Dad should have done summat, at least when she died. I don't know why he didn't, whether it were his laziness which put everythin' off, or loyalty to Mam. Don't matter which. Then t' war was over, I came back. I didn't do nowt. Somehow…didn't think to. We were used to Nobody, he didn't bother us. Until…well, that incident. Then I noticed 'e were a tickin' time-bomb and we could get in right trouble. The woman could've taken us t' court. Lucky she didn't.'

I leant forward. '*Where's Nobody?*' I asked slowly, emphasising each syllable. I was starting to fear they had drowned him the bathtub or chased him out into the sea

'An opportunity came up,' said Chad. 'My Dad wanted t' sell his old plough, an' I told everyone around here. A farmer from Ravenscar came by. He saw Nobody, who were about like usual.'

'And?'

'He asked who 'e were. My father told 'im a bit 'bout 'im. A lad evacuated t' our farm in t' war. With no parents or relatives. Someone we didn't rightly know what to do with… The farmer—Gordon McBright, by name—said 'e could do with a pair of hands on his farm. We warned 'im of course. That you couldn't use Nobody for nowt, that 'e never understood you, and mainly was more trouble than 'elp. Dad also pointed out 'is enormous appetite, which was out of all proportion to the 'elp he could be. But this McBright didn't let up. Said 'e could use Nobody. So Dad and I agreed.'

I could not help asking, 'And Nobody…I suppose he didn't go willingly?'

Chad stood up abruptly. This part of the story seemed to agitate him more than the rest.

He stood with his back to me as he answered. 'No. He didn't go willingly.'

He must have struggled, screamed, fought. The Beckett farm was his home, probably the only place he felt safe and maybe even secure. Chad and Arvid had put him in the hands of a complete stranger and sent him off. I knew Nobody and his violent emotional outbursts. I only had to look at Chad, who was no longer able to look me in the eye, to know.

He must have made a terrible scene.

I swallowed. 'But…'

Chad whipped around, and now his face was distorted with rage.

'Damn it, now don't be a prig!' he hissed at me although I had said nothing except for a cautious *but*. 'You got us into this! You brought 'im here! You weren't 'ere for years, you don't know what it were like t' see yourself lumbered with this big 'alf-baked lad! And no one were goin' t' blame you. You were a child then, only seventeen now. You got out of it all just fine. But me Dad and I, we coulda got in a right pickle. Nobody shoulda been in a school for kids like him. A 'ome. He shoulda been cared for by people who knew. Instead 'e grew up 'ere like a wild animal. We coulda been in 'ot water 'bout that. Even been dragged t' court!'

His voice lowered. 'Look around, Fiona,' he said bitterly. 'We're strugglin' t' survive. Me Dad's done all but nowt since Mam died, and I were at t' Front. All broken and abandoned 'ere, and we've got debts left, right an' centre. I work like a dog from morning t' night. I just can't be 'avin' any trouble, any investigation, where I might need to get a lawyer—God knows I couldn't pay one— just because I put Nobody in a home, and people 'eard of 'im. So should I wait for 'im to rape a lass? Should I wait for 'im to kill someone, because the person 'ad summat he wanted? What should I tell t' police then? Easy to raise your eyebrows now, Fiona, but what would you've done?'

I stood up and came over to him. I wanted to show him that I understood him, that I was not against him. After all, I loved him!

'I'm sorry,' I said. 'I didn't want you to think I was judging you. How could I? You didn't do it lightly.'

He shook his head. 'No, I didn't.'

We stood close to each other. I could feel Chad trembling. I wanted to ask a question, although I was afraid that it would lead to another angry outburst, as it started with another *but*. I still asked it.

'But…why did this Gordon McBright agree? He could get in trouble too, if he took on Nobody.'

Chad shrugged. 'We told 'im. But 'e said it wouldn't worry 'im.'

'He can't just lock him up. Or chain him up.'

Chad shrugged his shoulders, and bit his lip. I suddenly had the impression that this was just what Chad's unspoken fears were, that Gordon McBright would do just that: lock up Nobody, or keep him chained up when he needed him for work. Keep him like a slave.

'What's…this Gordon McBright like?' I asked nervously.

'Don't rightly know,' replied Chad, looking out of the window into the night.

'But you met him.'

It was clear that Chad just did not want to answer this question.

'Don't matter.'

'Where does he live?'

'Near Ravenscar. Outside t' village, on a farm on its own.'

Ravenscar was not too far from Staintondale, just up the coast towards Whitby.

'I could visit him,' I suggested. 'Nobody, I mean. And meet McBright.'

'Don't! Nobody will go crazy again, seein' you, and McBright…'

'Yes?'

'He'll put 'is dogs on you, or face you with a gun. He get irate if someone just approach 'is farm. He don't get

on with other people. I doubt he'd let you within a thousands yards of 'is land.'

'How do you know?'

'I asked a few people in Ravenscar 'bout him,' murmured Chad uneasily.

How had he and Arvid given Nobody to such a man?

I did not dare to ask this question out loud, as I was
afraid I would make Chad angry again. He felt cornered
by me, needing to justify himself and yet—that was obvious—he himself had a bad conscience when he thought
of what had become of Nobody. I shared that feeling. I
could scarcely hide my horror. I had never exactly been
close to Nobody, he had been a pain in the neck, but
somehow he had been part of life on the Beckett farm.
With my new maturity at seventeen I felt that I too shared
responsibility for the helpless boy.

I resolved to visit him at his new home, even if Chad's
warning scared me. I told myself that Gordon McBright
could hardly kill every harmless walker who arrived at his
farm—else he would have been put in prison long ago.

'I'm tired,' said Chad. 'I 'ave to get up early tomorrow.
Think I'll get to bed.'

I had thought—hoped—he would ask me to sleep
with him. I had thought we would spend the night holding each other tight. But he did not say anything else. He
just left the kitchen. Then I heard him going up the stairs.

I drank some more water, then turned off the light and
went upstairs. Nothing had changed in my old room, except for the thick layer of dust on all the furniture and
the bed linen. The sheets were the same set I had used
in 1943. The bed had obviously not been stripped. The
sheets smelt musty. I quickly opened the window and
let in the fresh, cool night air. I pressed my hands to my
hot face.

It was all too much. The magical hours at the beach. And then the sudden change of mood when we talked about Nobody. And the painful distance between us which had come with it. It hurt me as much as seeing the Beckett farm so run-down, dirty and bleak.

And I understood something else. I was disappointed in Chad, and that hurt the most. I had always forgiven him everything: the dismissive way he had treated me at first, the fact that he had not told me about the death of his mother and his signing up for the army, that he had barely ever answered my letters, that he had left me in the dark as to whether he had survived the war. I had not taken any of that personally. I knew him, after all. He was not a communicative person, he never would be. I could live with that. However, the way he had got rid of Nobody horrified me. That evening I did not yet realise the full extent of my feeling. Poison had trickled into our relationship, and it would work slowly. Chad had told me his motives, and I had understood them. I could see why he did it. I still did not think they were reason enough to do to a person what he had done to Nobody.

I consoled myself with the thought that perhaps everything looked bleaker to me than it was. Of course, there was also the possibility that everything was worse than I could imagine.

I could not sleep that night. I brooded.

I was sad.

14

THE NEXT DAY I set off for Ravenscar. I made a point of not getting up when I heard Chad banging about in the kitchen early in the morning. I did not want him to ask me what I was going to do, as I would have had to lie. So, although I was wide awake and nervous, I stayed in bed and only got up when I had not heard any noise coming from downstairs for a long time.

Chad really had gone already. The all-terrain vehicle was no longer in the yard, which gave me the hope that he was some distance from the farm and might not come back too soon. I could not see Arvid anywhere either. He was probably still asleep.

I did not dawdle over breakfast, but was soon running over to a shed where Emma used to keep her bike. It was still leaning against a wall, and even still carried the basket in which she used to put her shopping.

My eyes became moist. I suddenly missed Emma terribly.

The tyres were a little flat, but I hoped they would get me to Ravenscar and back. I could not see a pump anywhere, and did not want to waste time rummaging around. After all, I did not know when Chad would return.

It was a cloudy day, a northerly wind had picked up overnight. The air was cool and dry. It was just right for a bike trip. The dirt track was not easy to ride down, but once I got to the narrow road I was much quicker. My mum had packed chocolate in my rucksack. I had not touched it. I put it in the basket for Nobody. He would like it, and I would promise to visit him often and always bring something nice for him. That would be sure to cheer him up, if he was down at all. I might find him a contented boy.

I felt more positive in the daylight. Although at night I had painted a dark picture of Nobody's fate, that morning the whole thing did not look too bad. He would be better off with Gordon McBright than with Arvid, who was obviously letting himself go completely, and with Chad, who would not have a moment to spare for Nobody. At least he would have something to do on McBright's farm, and even if the man were a tough nut, like most farmers round these parts, that did not mean he was necessarily inhumane and cruel.

Ravenscar is only a cluster of houses. At the time it was not much smaller than it is now. It has a lovely location on the crest of a hill, with a wonderful view down to the nearest bay and across the rolling green hills. Here and there you can see a farm, a blotch of another colour in the green. Of course I did not know which one belonged to McBright, but I had decided to ask around.

Someone would be able to tell me.

'McBright?' asked the woman standing behind the counter of a roadside stall, where she sold lettuce and beans she had grown. 'What do you want with *him*?'

'I want to visit someone,' I said truthfully.

She looked at me as if I had lost my mind. 'You want to visit Gordon McBright? Dearie, you'd be better off not. He's...' She tapped at her head.

I did not find that encouraging, but I still got her to tell me how to get to his farm. I went the wrong way the first time, and had to ask at another farm. There too they could hardly believe me.

'You're a brave lass,' said the farmer, amazed.

'I just want to visit an old friend,' I murmured, before turning away and getting back on my bike. I had secretly hoped that someone would ask me about Nobody. He had been living for almost half a year at McBright's place, so someone might have known he was there. It would have been an immense relief to hear someone reply to my *visit an old friend* with, 'Oh, you mean that nice young fellow who lives with Gordon! A little touched, the lad, but doing fine. Great help on the farm. Almost like a son to Gordon!'

How naive I was to wish that! How hard I was trying to twist the facts to something I could live with. Nobody was *a little touched*. He was so *touched* that he could barely be used for any work at all, not even simple menial tasks. Even for those he needed to have some understanding of what he was being asked to do. The only way I could imagine getting the Nobody I knew to work was through physical violence, which would break the resistance of his clouded mind. But of course I did not want to imagine that.

And...*like a son to Gordon*? To the people of Ravenscar, Gordon McBright seemed like a kind of devil. No one was on talking terms with him. No one seemed able to believe that I would really want to visit him. And yet he was to find a place in his heart for Nobody of all people?

I would really have liked to turn back. I was afraid— of McBright himself, but also of the condition I would find Nobody in. What if I had the impression I should go to the police? I loved Chad. I wanted to marry him. If I decided to save Nobody, our love would not survive my action. Chad would never forgive me if I got him into trouble over this. He had looked so exhausted, so laden with cares. He was fighting to keep his parents' farm going, and it was clear he was struggling. *I just can't be 'avin' any trouble*, he had said last night in his dirty kitchen. There had been something desperate about the way he said it.

Was I, of all people, going to bring him the trouble he so feared?

In spite of my doubts I rode on, pushing down harder on the pedals of the old bike whose tyres were losing air. It was becoming more and more of a struggle to ride. I tried to numb the tortuous thoughts in my head with the physical exertion. For the first time in my life I was faced with a difficult question of conscience. I suddenly wished I had not come to Yorkshire.

I COULD SEE the farm from a long way off. It was far out of Ravenscar, buried deep in the countryside and a good way from the sea. The buildings were on a little hillock above a wood. There were no other signs of human settlement near or far. It was a place of loneliness and isolation.

The day was not sunny. A blue sky only peeked through holes in the clouds occasionally. Nevertheless it was still a bright August day. A beautiful day. The wind bent the blades of grass and raced over the stone walls. The day smelt of sea and summer. The atmosphere could have been beautiful, even romantic in a wild and elemental way. Yet it was not. The farm looked dark and threatening, although I could not have said why exactly. Even from a distance it looked somehow desolate, even though it was not more run-down than the Beckett farm. Nevertheless, it seemed to exude a cold horror. I shivered. Or was I affected because of everything people had suggested?

I approached hesitantly. The path was stony and overgrown with thistles. I found it hard to not fall off the bike. When the path started to go uphill, I had to get off and

push. I stopped many times. I was hot, and felt myself
sweating all over my body.

I came up to the farm gate unchecked. Behind it was
the farmyard. Stables and sheds formed a semi-circle
around the farmhouse, encircling the farm like a fortress.
Thistles and nettles were shooting up between the rusty
equipment scattered around the yard. A car was parked
right in front of the front door. It appeared to be the only
thing which was regularly moved around here, as it was
not surrounded by weeds.

I could see all of this when I got up on my tiptoes
and peeked over the wooden gate. I had just dropped
my bike in the grass at the side of the path. I could hear
my own heart beating loudly and fast. Apart from that I
could not hear anything.

I cannot say that anything really happened. Nothing
dramatic or terrible. No dog rushed at me with bared
teeth, nor did Gordon McBright appear with his gun at
the ready. I was not shouted out, not chased away. I just
stood there, looked over the gate, and nothing happened.

And yet in some way which is difficult to describe
this 'nothing' was worse than a raging McBright would
have been. If he had appeared in person I could have
had a good look at him, could have made my own mind
up about him, confronted him. As it was he remained
a spectre.

And the eeriest thing was that I could feel that he was
there. I could feel that people were there on that godforsaken and apparently dead farm. There was even a clue:
the car's tyre tracks crossing the yard. They could be seen
in flattened grass and weeds, which had not had time to
straighten up again yet. I guessed that the car had parked
an hour ago at most. And how would anyone leave here
except by car?

However I did not actually need that proof. I simply knew that I was not alone. I could feel that eyes were trained on me behind the windows. I could feel that the silence here was not the silence of an abandoned place, but of horror and evil. Even nature held its breath here.

Years ago I had read a sentence in a book: *A place which had fallen out of God's hands.*

Now I knew what its author had meant.

And in that warped and frightening silence I heard Nobody scream. I did not hear him with my own ears. Nothing broke the silence. But I could perceive him with all my senses, I swear I could. I could hear him screaming for help. I could hear him calling for me. I could hear his despair and extreme fear. The screams were the painful, tortured screams of an abandoned child.

I picked up the bike, jumped into the saddle and tore down the hill as fast as I could. Twice I almost fell off the bike, as I was almost riding on the rims now. I just wanted to get away from this place and the screams which seemed to pursue me. I knew now that Nobody had landed in hell. Whatever happened to him on this farm, it was torturing him almost to death. He was completely helpless and Gordon McBright could kill him without anyone knowing. He could bury the body in a shallow grave in a field and no one would notice. In a horrific way the name which Chad and I had carelessly, and not without hate, given him proved to be only too appropriate: Nobody. This boy did not exist. A chain of unfortunate incidents had allowed Brian Somerville in the confusion of the war years to fall through the cracks in the care system. He had become nobody. He had no protection at all. Because of his disability he was unable to protect himself. He was at the mercy of anyone whose hands he fell into, for better or worse.

Three people knew of him and his fate: Chad, Arvid and I. The three of us should have done something to help him.

We did nothing. We had our reasons, the main one being fear. I know that is no excuse. What we did—or rather, did not do—is unforgivable.

I have paid for it, mainly with the image which has haunted me in waking and sleeping moments for all the decades of my life: the last image I have of Brian Somerville. The small, shivering boy is standing at the gate of the Beckett farm in the February snow and looking at me go. He wants to cry, because I am leaving, but he is trying to smile behind the tears because he believes that I will come back and fetch him.

He is trying to smile because he trusts me.

Thursday, 16th October

1

SHE HAD NO wish to carry on reading. She stood up and looked out of the window. The night was dark and overcast, without the moon or stars. A few lights shone in the harbour. The sea was a black, turbulent mass.

She went into the kitchen and, looking at the clock, saw that it was already past midnight. She opened a bottle of whisky, put it to her lips and took a few swigs. She wiped her mouth with the sleeve of her jumper. Suddenly she started to cry.

What had happened to Brian Somerville, the *other child*?

The images raced through her head in a confused jumble: her grandmother as a seventeen-year-old girl, Chad Beckett as a young man with too much on his plate, the dilapidated farm not far from total collapse. The war just over.

Try to understand her, a voice in her head said. Try to forgive her.

Her crying grew louder. She put the bottle to her lips again. She could see the little boy who had been a victim from the first day of his life and had remained one, because…Fiona had neglected to protect him. Because, given the choice, she had chosen to protect Chad Beckett, the man she loved.

Or at least: the man she thought she loved.

As if Fiona Barnes had ever loved in her life.

She felt dizzy. She had not eaten for a long time, filling herself only with strong alcohol.

Why was I always, always freezing as a child? Why did my mum become drug-addicted?

She had to find out what had happened to Brian Somerville. She only had a few more pages to read. It was obviously not about Fiona's whole life. She supposed it contained some clue as to Brian's fate.

'I can't face it now,' she murmured.

She was drinking the whisky like water. That was the next question: *why have I become an alcoholic?*

Of course she had not really become an alcoholic. She just drank a little too much, a little too often. Particularly when things got difficult.

She knew that she needed to stop doing that urgently.

She stood in the kitchen with the open bottle and looked around at the familiar objects. The coffee maker and the shelf with the mugs which she knew from her childhood. On the table, the clay ashtray decorated with flowers. She had made it for Fiona at school. At least her grandmother had kept it and used it. That was already a lot from a woman like Fiona.

She put the bottle down on the sideboard, but then immediately reached for it again, taking another few swigs. She was going to get drunk now. She was going to get so plastered she knocked herself out. Then—if she could still manage it—she was going to sway over to her bed and sleep until late the next day. When she would finally wake up, she knew she would feel terribly sick, but the headache would numb her thoughts, she knew that from experience. A really bad hangover was just what was needed to switch off from the world around her. The furry, dry mouth, the urge to vomit and the stabbing pain at her temples would push everything else into the background. She longed to be sick, to lie in bed and be able to moan, and pull the blanket over her head.

She wanted to be a child and for someone to console her.

Except that no one was going to. Not a mother or a grandmother. Fiona had never been good at that in any case. Stephen had moved out. He was a few houses further down the street in his bed in the Crown Spa Hotel no doubt, sleeping peacefully.

She was alone.

Hey, Cramer, now don't drown in your own self-pity, she thought as the tears rolled down her cheeks.

And at that moment the doorbell rang.

IT WAS ONLY after she had buzzed the visitor in, and was waiting upstairs at the door to the flat, that she realised it wasn't particularly safe to open the door after midnight. Maybe it was because she had been drinking, or because she felt so lost, but she remained in the stairwell and listened to the footsteps of someone coming up the stairs. The light had come on automatically, and its very bright white light made Leslie blink. She was still holding the open bottle in her hand. Her make-up must have been smeared and her hair messed up.

She did not care.

Dave Tanner appeared in front of her with a big suitcase in his hand. He stopped.

'Thank God,' he said. 'You were still awake?'

She looked down at her clothes. She was wearing jeans, a jumper and trainers.

'Yes, I was awake,' she confirmed.

He appeared relieved. 'I was afraid you might not open

the door,' he said smiling. 'You really should use the intercom to ask who it is! It's half past midnight!'

She shrugged.

'Can I come in?' asked Dave.

She moved aside and he stepped in, putting down his suitcase with a sigh.

'Goodness, it's heavy,' he said. 'Almost everything I own is in it. I had to walk, because my car finally gave up the ghost just now. Listen, Leslie, could I sleep here tonight? My landlady has just thrown me out.'

Leslie tried to get her drink-addled brain to follow him. 'Thrown you out?' she asked slowly. 'Can she do that?'

'No idea. But she was completely hysterical. She was screaming for the police, raging… There was just no point in staying. I tried to reach an old friend, but her phone is turned off. She works in a bar down in the harbour, so I waited there from ten to a little before midnight, but she didn't come. Then I walked up here, hoping you'd be in and could grant me asylum. In all honesty, Leslie, I can't walk another step.' He paused, and stared at her. 'Is everything all right?'

She could not help starting to cry again. 'Yes. Well, no. It's about Fiona. She is…' She wiped her eyes. 'I need some time to come to terms with everything.'

He carefully took the bottle from her hand and put it on a chair in the hall.

'I can smell the alcohol on your breath a mile off, Leslie. You'd better stop. Otherwise *you* might be dead tomorrow morning.'

'Maybe that would be for the best.'

He shook his head. 'No.'

Like a little child she objected, 'It would!'

He held her by both shoulders, steered her into the kitchen and forced her gently but insistently to sit down.

'I'm going to make a nice warm cup of tea for you now. With honey. Do you have honey?'

She was too tired to struggle against his attention. Maybe, she thought, I don't want to struggle.

'Yes, honey's somewhere. No idea where.'

'OK, I'll find my way around.'

She looked at him blankly as he moved around the kitchen. He put the water on to boil, took two mugs from the shelf, opened this cupboard door and that one until he found where the tea was kept. He found a jar of honey on a shelf above the oven. Leslie watched him as he poured the golden liquid into the mugs. The water was boiling. Dave made the tea and put both mugs on the table, seating himself opposite Leslie.

'What's wrong?'

She shook her head and carefully took a sip. The whisky had left her feeling sick.

Too much, too quickly on an empty stomach. She jumped up and ran to the bathroom, reaching the toilet just in time.

Retching and coughing, she threw up. Not much other than stinking bile came up.

Dave had followed her. He brushed her hair from her face and put a hand on her sweaty neck.

'It's all right,' he said. 'Good for it all to come out.'

She stood up, swayed over to the sink and filling her hands with cold water rinsed her mouth out.

'I'm sorry,' she mumbled when she was done. She looked at the chalk-white face staring at her in the mirror with its messy hair, smeared make-up and trembling lips.

'When did you last eat?' asked Dave.

She tried to remember. Everything from the last few days seemed so distant.

'Breakfast with you,' she said. 'At the harbour.'

'One bite of a scone, if I remember rightly. Great.' He shook his head. 'What's wrong, Leslie? Why are you sitting here in the middle of the night pouring whisky down your throat like there's no tomorrow? Where's your ex?'

'Stephen moved out to a hotel. He just left a letter.'

He looked at her observantly. 'Did that throw you so much?'

'Of course not!' She was aware that she had protested a little too much. Had she been upset about Stephen's silent departure? Had it brought to the surface the pain which had been gnawing away at her since he had cheated on her and so cut the ground from under her feet?

'I didn't even want him to come here, so how could his going throw me?'

The dizziness was abating. She walked unsteadily back to the kitchen and collapsed onto a chair, reaching for her tea. It smelt of vanilla and honey. Calming and familiar.

'Why did your landlady throw you out?' she asked Dave, who had followed her back.

He sat opposite her again. 'She thinks I've murdered two people. The fact that the police were waiting for me when I came home confirmed her opinion. She didn't want to let me stay another minute under her roof. Nor did she consider that if the police had anything against me they would hardly have let me go. I can sort of understand her.'

'Why did they need you at the station?'

He waved the question away. 'There were conflicting reports about where I was last Saturday night. I've cleared it up. If I hadn't, I wouldn't be here now.'

He convinced her. Of course he was fine. The police did

not let murderers just wander about—at least not if they had already taken them into custody.

He leant forward. He asked her again, 'What's wrong, Leslie? What happened? You look exhausted. What's troubling you?'

He looked concerned, like someone she could confide in. A friend who was worried about her. For a moment Leslie was tempted to tell him everything—about the war, Brian Somerville, Fiona and Chad, and the fateful thing they had done. But then she decided against it. Her wish to protect Fiona was stronger than her need to tell someone.

So she only said, 'I think I'm just caught up with my own life. I don't know what comes next. So much has happened.'

'Do you want to keep the flat here? I suppose it belongs to you.'

'I don't think I'll keep it. I've never felt comfortable here. This big cold house is always half empty…I think I'll sell it. And what I'll do with the money—no idea. Maybe I'll buy a little flat of my own in London. Make a little nest, just for myself. Perhaps then I'll have the feeling I have a home. A harbour to retreat to.'

'You don't have one?'

'Where would I? I'm almost forty. My marriage broke down. My last living relative is dead. I'm successful enough at work, but that's hardly keeping me warm and cosy.'

'A little flat of your own,' he repeated. 'That sounds… lonely. Nothing about a husband, children, a big dog— whatever, something warm and cosy.'

She laughed, but it sounded forced and—as she noticed with alarm—rather desperate. 'No, it doesn't. But do you think I can just click my finger and the man will appear who suits me, who will marry me and with whom I'll have three wonderful children and go for walks at the weekend with our big dog out into the country? You don't find men like that lying around. I don't, anyway. Actually…I'm in the same bloody situation as Gwen. Alone and desperate.'

'But you aren't Gwen. You are successful and active, you have drive. Unlike Gwen you know how things work. There's only one thing you have in common with her: you both think about the past too much. And you don't realise how much that is blocking you.'

'I don't think I—'

He interrupted her. 'Look at Gwen. She sits there on her farm, clinging to a bygone era. An era when a woman did not train for a career, when she lived with her parents until she became old and grey, unless a man came along who would take her to his home. A man she would idolise and obey. Why do you think she's had no luck? Because no man wants a woman like that today. Because men want a partner, an independent woman, someone capable of leading her own life.'

'She hooked you.'

He was silent for a moment.

'You know how that happened,' he said finally.

'It won't work, Dave.'

'I know,' he said quietly.

She leant forward. 'I don't think about the past too much, Dave.'

'You do, and how you do, Leslie. Just differently to Gwen. You let the past rule your present. You brood about who your father was. Inside, you are still struggling with your mother, wanting to be fair to her. And you still have a quarrel with your grandmother. You are torn between the feeling that you should be grateful to her, and a rage you are more and more aware that you feel about your youth with her. You told your husband to go to hell after he cheated on you, but you are constantly thinking about him, analysing him, analysing yourself, asking yourself how it could have come to this. You aren't free, Leslie. Free for a new life.'

She could feel tears welling up again, and she fought hard to stop them.

'So how should I be? I can't act as if I don't have the past I have!'

'But you can just let it be. You can't change it, so accept it. Accept yourself and your feelings. You'll never know who your father is. You'll have to live with the fact that your mother flipped between being an angel and being neglectful. You can be grateful to your grandmother for her support and be mad with her for being such a hard old lady who did not make the effort to see into the soul of the girl who was suddenly in her care. And, for God's sake, just forget Stephen! He cheated on you. Do you need a man like him? And do you think that one fling would have made you throw him out if everything else really was hunky-dory between you? A strong relationship would survive something like that. But in other relationships a one-night stand is just the final straw. I expect that was the case for the two of you.'

She smiled, tiredly, her eyes blurry. 'And you're an expert on relationships, are you? A life coach?'

He stayed serious. 'I'm a total loser, in every way. In relationships as much as the rest of life. But someone who can't get their own life in order can still have a clear understanding of other people's lives. The two don't always go together.'

She drank her tea in little sips. The warmth did her

good, and the honey calmed her stomach. She thought
how good it was that Dave had appeared in the middle of
the night. In the frame of mind she had been in, she might
have drunk herself senseless. She was thankful not to have
to be alone. It was the right moment, she thought, gradually feeling more aware, at peace and ready. She lifted her
head and met his gaze.

She did not evade either what she saw in his gaze or
Dave himself when he got up and came round the table.
He took both her hands and slowly pulled her to her feet.
She let him enfold her in his arms, which were tender and
consoling. It was what she needed at that moment. She
wanted to lean on him and be protected, just for the night.
She wanted to feel another person's heartbeat. She wanted
to forget Fiona and everything she had read about her.

His lips brushed her forehead. She raised her head and
her mouth met his. She kissed him with a mixture of des-
peration and anger, and he responded gently and softly.
She could not be doing this. It was out of order, definitely
wrong, maybe fatal. He was engaged to another woman,
and a suspect in a murder case. But she had not let herself
fall for so long. And she liked him. He was so different
to Stephen. He was a man whom her grandmother would
never have accepted for her. He seemed opaque and strange
to her on the one hand, perhaps unpredictable. He was so
different to all the men she had ever known. But on the
other hand, as contradictory as this felt to her, she could
understand him perfectly. He was a gifted student, an ide-
alist who wanted to change the world, someone who had
wasted his life, whose entire worldly possessions fitted inside a single suitcase. Suddenly he seemed to her to be the
exact opposite of Stephen. Stephen had finished his studies, become a doctor, earned good money and had a safe

job; he was respected and looked like the perfect partner, and then he went and discharged all the years of repressed frustration with a ridiculous affair. Now she understood why it would never have worked with Stephen. He was too unassuming for her. Too conservative. Too predictable even when he did the unimaginable and cheated on her. In that too he was a square, who lost his bottle after a single night and had to confess to it, because he could not live with his shocking deed, or at least not with the fact that he had not been caught.

He was just a phase in her life. Nothing more.

Dave's hands slid under her jumper and she closed her eyes as his fingers cupped her breasts.

'We shouldn't do this,' she murmured, simultaneously asking herself if she really meant that, or whether she was trying to appease her conscience by at least showing a few moments' resistance.

'Why not?' asked Dave.

It would be so easy, and she felt such a longing to give in to her desire for warmth, protection and security, to escape into the physical union with a man and forget everything which weighed on her mind.

To lean on someone. She needed that much more than sex. She needed to find a home, as she had for years, perhaps for her whole life.

It was hardly likely she would find that home by having sex on the kitchen floor or elsewhere, even if the man without a doubt exerted a strong sexual fascination on her. She was in a moment of physical weakness, plagued by hunger and feelings of sickness, and in an instable mental state because she had found out things about Fiona which had shaken her to the core.

The feeling that her body was being taken over by lust changed. Reason regained the upper hand.

She tried to take a step back, but was immediately up against the wall. 'I can't,' she said.

'Why not?' he said again. His tongue touched her lips. She liked the way he kissed, she liked the sensation of his hands on her body. But she was afraid. Afraid that the emptiness afterwards would be greater than before.

She turned her face to the side.

'I really don't want to, Dave,' she said with sudden vehemence.

He stepped back and raised both hands. 'I'm sorry!'

'It's all right. Fine.'

He was annoyed. 'Leslie, I thought you…'

'I what?'

'That *we*,' he corrected himself, 'wanted the same thing a minute ago.'

'Yes. A minute ago. But now…I can't.'

He looked at her thoughtfully. 'What's the problem, Leslie? Or—who is the problem? Gwen?'

'Yes. Gwen too. But also the fact that I feel very fragile right now. I don't want to sleep with someone I barely know, because I'm very fragile.'

He looked at her intently, and she saw in his eyes that he understood. 'Sometime you'll have to come out of your shell. You're so afraid that you'll be hurt that you don't dare to live. That's…after a certain point that's a downward spiral, Leslie. Get out before you no longer have the strength to.'

'Don't worry. I've got my life under control.'

He did not reply, and that annoyed her. She did not think he had the right to analyse her and her life like that—not from where he was standing, suspected by the police, thrown out by his landlady, no doubt with nothing in his bank account, and a worthless engagement... How dare he tell her about her life?

'When men don't get what they want,' she said aggressively, 'then they often say a lot of things which would be better left unsaid. Maybe you should find another way to compensate for not getting any.'

He smiled, not scornfully, but with resignation. 'Believe me, I can live with *not getting any*, as you call it. What I said was not to let off steam. I just wanted to explain how I see you and your situation. But you're right, maybe I overstepped the mark.'

'That's how it felt to me,' she replied.

'I'm sorry,' he said.

They stood there, with a sudden distance between them. Everything had been said. Nothing had happened.

Leslie felt tired and lonely. 'I'm going to bed,' she said. 'You can sleep in the guest-room. Stephen doesn't need it now.'

'Thanks. And of course I'll look for somewhere else to stay tomorrow morning.'

'Take your time.'

She watched him leave the kitchen.

She thought she should be feeling relief at having done the right thing. Instead she felt dejected and unsure. She sat down and, taking a packet of cigarettes, she lit one.

She had reacted wrongly again. She had raised a wall high around herself, blocking herself off even more. Why had she not just done what she felt like doing? Without worrying about what would come afterwards. Was she really scarcely capable of living?

She sat enveloped in her thoughts and the rings of

smoke which spread out in the brightly lit kitchen and filled the room.

She would find it hard to sleep this night.

2

ALTHOUGH VALERIE HAD gone to bed late, she got up early. No sooner was she up and out of the bathroom than her mobile rang. With a towel wrapped around her body, she ran over to her bedroom, where her mobile was plugged in to charge.

'Yes?'

It was Sergeant Reek, who always seemed to start work before seven. 'Am I calling too early?' he asked hesitantly.

'I'm just having breakfast,' lied Valerie. 'What's up?'

'Nothing you'll be pleased to hear, I'm afraid, Inspector. I managed to get in touch with Stan Gibson's parents in London late last night. They said their son had spent last weekend in London with them, together with Miss Witty, whom he introduced to them as his partner. And I expect Miss Witty will confirm that. Gibson isn't stupid enough to lie to us about something that easy to check up on.'

'Unfortunately Gibson is not at all stupid, Reek. That's one of our many problems. Do his parents seem trustworthy?'

'Yes. They are in shock, but they wouldn't lie. They are too confused to do that. They can't imagine that their son could have committed a crime. They describe him as a nice boy, reliable and willing to help anyone. However, he has had a lot of short relationships, for which his mother naturally lays the blame at the door of the women who are unable to appreciate his qualities. In my opinion, no one can bear to be with him for too long. Miss Witty can no doubt give us more of an insight into that. But—'

'—that doesn't help us with our case,' Valerie finished his sentence for him. 'Not for Amy Mills' murder.'

'We obviously can't hold him responsible for Fiona Barnes' death,' concluded Reek.

'Doesn't look like it,' agreed Valerie with a sigh.

'I'm going to drive back out to Filey Road and try my luck with Karen Ward again,' said Reek. It sounded as if he wanted to say, Chin up, we still have other irons in the fire! 'She didn't go home yesterday evening, but maybe she got home sometime during the night.'

'Did you go to the Newcastle Packet?'

'Of course. But she didn't work there yesterday. Her flatmates didn't know where she was either. Something that could be of interest though: her flatmates said that Dave Tanner tried to phone Miss Ward twice at the flat that evening. And he appeared in the Newcastle Packet and asked after her, as they told me in the pub. He seemed quite intent on talking to her.'

'Not surprising. He still has a close relationship to her.'

'Anyway, I won't cross off Tanner until I have a statement from Ward matching his. I also went to the Golden Ball yesterday, where they remembered the two of them. However, they were only there briefly. About ten they left the pub. So that statement is neither here nor there.'

Valerie was thankful she had such an invaluable colleague. Reek put in a hell of a lot of overtime and she had never once heard him complain about it. 'You're doing a great job, Reek,' she said. She could practically hear him beam down the connection.

'I'll get onto the case with Ward,' he said briefly and said goodbye.

Getting dressed, Valerie realised how heavy and tired her movements were. She felt the opposite of her colleague: wide-awake, ready-for-action Sergeant Reek. Was it just the disappointment? That she had not solved the two cases in one go?

Had she even solved *one* case? She crept into the kitchen and turned the coffee maker on. Just a coffee, that was all she wanted. She did not even fancy her breakfast today, and that was usually sacred to her.

She had sat talking with Stan Gibson for almost two hours the previous evening, without once managing to put a crack in his good mood. He had answered every question politely and patiently with a smile, not showing the slightest sign of irritation or annoyance.

Yes, of course he had heard and read of Amy Mills' death. It was the only thing people talked about all summer in Scarborough. Horrible, a horrible thing. That someone could do that! Of course he had felt personally involved. Amy had meant a lot to him, although he had never had the courage to talk to her. He did not seem to Valerie like a man who was shy with women. She should not be deceived by appearances! He had never tried to talk to Amy.

Yes, his telescope. The pictures! Of course he knew that you should not really do something like that. But nor was it exactly prohibited, was it? He had thought she was so pretty. When had he seen her the first time? He had to think. It must have been January. He had just spied on the flats opposite for a little fun, and that's when he had seen her in Linda Gardner's flat. She had been doing something with the child, and her wavy hair had looked like a halo to him. He had started to become interested in her, he had. Was he being accused of that?

Obsessed? He couldn't say. OK, he had often followed her secretively, as much as his scarce free time allowed. She had gone on many long walks on her own. She had always seemed so lonely to him. She had rarely gone for a cup of coffee or a chat with a fellow student. Normally she kept to herself.

Had he approached her? Been rejected by her? Had that made him angry? No, no, no. Inspector Almond was barking up the wrong tree. He had never talked to her. He had said that already. So she couldn't have rejected him. Anyway, he could live with rejection. He didn't beat to death women who chucked him. Although he had to admit that he had never been chucked. Never! He had no problems with women. Particularly not with pulling them. Indeed, if he were honest, he didn't know what rejection felt like.

And so he continued the whole time, smiling continuously. And everything in Valerie, all her nerves, her intuition, her experience, her gut feeling, whatever you like, they all told her that he had done it. That this grinning bloke had Amy Mills on his conscience.

While she waited for the coffee to percolate through, Valerie asked herself what evidence she had.

Nothing, if she was brutally honest.

Nothing, except for the initial clues which had put her onto Gibson, and her intuition, which screamed *murderer*, and a vague hope. A hope based on the impression she had of Gibson.

The coffee was ready. She sipped it, looking out of the window. It was still dark but she thought she could make out that the rain had stopped. Nor did it look like the fog had returned.

Gibson might show himself to the world as a nice, friendly, smiling young man, the dream of every mother-in-law, but he could not fool her, Valerie. She had seen that his smile was pathological, and seen the madness in his eyes. She knew that he had an enormous problem, and although she did not know him well enough, nor know the details of his life history, she could see that his relationship to women was the catalyst which could turn his problem into something horrific. Into hate, revenge, murderous anger and unbridled brutality. Amy Mills' body had been clear enough evidence of that.

In her opinion, his problem was rejection. Gibson had kept on about how a woman had never turned him down. He had stressed that, and she had seen the expression in his eyes as he said it. She suspected that this was the reason why Amy Mills had been killed, and why her death had come with such violence. Gibson had been obsessed with her, all the photos he had made of her showed that, but she had not wanted him. At some point, either in the days before she was murdered or at the latest in that night in the park, she had told him no. Valerie was convinced that Gibson could not deal with rejection from women.

She knew what Sergeant Reek would say. 'Facts, Inspector, facts! Don't get carried away just because you want to find the culprit. Just because you want to wrap up the case. Stick to the facts!'

Or was that not Reek? Was it her own voice of caution?

She had woken up several times that night and wondered why it had started to go so smoothly. For months there had not been any clues or leads, nothing. And now suddenly Ena Witty had appeared, trembling with fear and reporting her boyfriend's strange behaviour. Suddenly there was a suspect, photos that proved his obsessive attachment to the murdered girl, and a telescope that pointed into the flat where Amy Mills had started her last journey.

In the dark silent night she had asked herself if this was not all a little too pat. It looked as if her suspect was being handed to her on a plate. It looked like the culprit had been pulled out of a magician's sleeve like an ace. It was impossible that Amy Mills' apparent murderer would just materialise like that in front of her. Life or—not to get too philosophical—her job did not provide such solutions normally.

Now in the early hours of the morning she knew the answer to all of her sceptical questions. The culprit had appeared so suddenly because he had wanted to appear right then. Stan Gibson had wanted all of what happened: the police in his flat and the questioning which he had prepared himself for in advance. He had known that his perma-grin would irritate no end the investigating officer. Because he had wanted all of this, he had told Ena about his telescope and placed the photos where she was bound to find them at some point. He had known that alarm bells would ring for Ena from that moment. It was only a question of time until she either went to the police herself or told a friend who would take that step for her.

He had planned his appearance, and it had all gone like clockwork.

And Valerie realised one more thing. He had made sure that she would not be able to prove anything. He had not been surprised by the investigations, and so he had thought it all through in advance. He would not have let the police have all the clues they had if any of them presented a danger to him. He was clever and rational. Valerie could turn the whole world upside down, she would not find the evidence to put Gibson behind bars.

There was no such proof.

If there had been, then Gibson would not have given himself up. And he would not have played the grinning game at the station.

She poured herself a second cup of coffee and drank it quickly, as if she could swallow her bitterness and frustration with the coffee, before they became too much for her.

Yet she could feel a spark of hope, a macabre, almost cynical hope, which sprang from the pleasure she noticed Gibson felt during their conversation. He had been enjoying the situation immensely. It was the ultimate kick for him. It made him euphoric. He was already addicted to it. *She* had done that to *him*, and so she was one step ahead of him, although he did not know it. She had also come to two realisations of immeasurable importance. He was really sick. And he would want to do it again. He would want to repeat the deed and his cat and mouse game with the police.

She was ready to swear an oath on it.

She poured the rest of her coffee down the drain. It was no good. She had to face the day. She had to check Dave Tanner's statement, and she hoped Reek managed to find Karen Ward as soon as possible. She would also talk to Ena Witty once more. Hopefully she had calmed down by now and might remember one or two important details from the short time she had been together with Stan Gibson. Not that she was going to provide the key that unlocked the case. Valerie had no illusions about that. But she had to do her work, the day-to-day routine of the job she had learnt. And going beyond that, she had to try to get close to Gibson. To find out everything about him that she could.

You've got a bloodhound on your heels, Gibson, she thought. I'm going to be there when your smile freezes on your face and you realise you're up shit creek without a paddle!

She took her bag and car key, folded her coat over her arm and left her flat.

15

Dear Chad,

I am going to write the end of our story as a letter to you. I have told most of it by now, and the only thing remaining is my need to explain why I wrote down our story at all.

I know you as a taciturn and pragmatic man, who only sees the value in things which have an obvious and clear use. And I know what you will think after reading all this about us: Superfluous scribbling! Our story—so what? As if I didn't know it already!

So what was the point?

Our story always made me so sad, Chad. For many reasons. Above all because of Brian Somerville, of course. Perhaps I was closer to the young boy than you, although you spent more time with him. He lived in your house for years, even after I had left.

But he left London as a young, orphaned boy holding my hand. He always wanted to be close to me in Scarborough. I was the only one he called by name. Did you notice that I was the only person he ever called by name? Not even Emma, who loved him more than anyone else. Who, in fact, was the only one who loved him. But he had chosen me, from the first moment of that November morning in bombed-out London, next to the smoking ruins of his family home. And although I never responded to his affection, and continually betrayed his trust, he stayed loyal to *me. Sometimes I think that no one else in my life has ever been as true to me as Brian Somerville.*

The second reason why I am always dejected and almost melancholy when I think about the two of us is due to the direction our paths took. In other words, to the fact that we did not take the same path, as I had dreamt we would. To this day I am convinced that we were meant for each other. I was not happy with the man I later married, and nor were you happy with the woman you finally decided to marry at quite an advanced age. I am convinced that our relationships were not blessed because they were not our destiny. That is why we both experienced disappointments with our children. Your Gwen became a gauche old virgin who is now about to marry a charming con artist who is only interested in her property and will—I would bet on it—cheat on her even before they marry. And my daughter…well, you know.

Hippy communes, hash and LCD, never a proper career, screwing around in everyone's bed, and worst of all: the irresponsible way she brought her daughter into the world. I was not surprised that she died of an overdose of drugs and alcohol. I even saw it coming. Of course I wished a different life for her.

Without a doubt there is a connection between Brian Somerville and the fact that we did not forge a life together. Although we could not see it at the time, our story was decided on that August day in 1946. I pedalled away on your mother's bike with its flat tyres to Gordon McBright's ghostly, barren farm, and understood that something terrible had happened and we had to intervene. You will remember that I brought it up that evening in our bay.

It was not the romantic atmosphere of the previous evening, which had been full of happiness and light as we reunited, loving each other. That first evening I had seen our

*future lit up brightly ahead of us. On the second meeting
we started to argue. I told you about my trip, and you re-
sented my visit there. You started shouting so aggressively
that I burst into tears. I could not understand what had
made you so angry. Of course I can see now that it was
your fear. Fear that I might take further steps which could
put you in the difficulties you were so afraid of. You reacted with dismissive scorn when I tried to explain how
palpable the horror and evil had been in that place. I even
dared to tell you about Brian's screams which I had heard
in my head.*

*You did not want to accept that. I saw something close
to hatred in your eyes. At that moment I was like an enemy
to you. And a threat.*

*You let me know that we would not exchange another
friendly word if I did not forget the Somerville affair. You
said that the Beckett farm would be closed to me. In short,
that there would be no more contact between us, ever. It
would be the end not only of our love and friendship, but
you would act as if you had never known me.*

*I am not reminding you of that evening to put the blame
for Brian Somerville's fate on you. Even admitting that at
the time I was only seventeen, in love, inexperienced and
helpless, too deeply involved to ignore the threatened consequences and do the right thing, I still had many opportunities to be brave in later years. I could have looked into
it again, done something. I was not seventeen forever. I did
not always have the excuse of being young and helpless.*

*At some point my conscience should have been stron-
ger than…well, than what? I have thought long and hard
about what always blocked me from acting. Was it the fear
of losing your friendship? As important as you were to me,
and still are, I do not think that fear was enough on its own
to silence forever the little voice which often reminded me*

of Brian. I do not think that the only explanation, or even justification, for my silence is that I was once in love with you. Not even that I, perhaps, have loved you all my life.

No, the explanation is much more banal. It is almost like a law of nature. The further we go down a path, the harder it is to go back, and the more consequences the U-turn would involve. There is always a point when we can shout No! and refuse to go on. If we miss it, each later moment is more complicated and brings with it the need to explain why we did not say no earlier. And then there comes a time when we no longer dare to. We have gone so far that it is impossible to turn back. At least, it is impossible to turn back without losing face completely. So we grit our teeth and march on, whistling and humming as we go, so as not to hear the voice of our conscience. That is what I did.

Maybe you did too. I don't know. Sometimes I fear that your conscience did not prick you nearly as much about Brian's tragedy as mine did me. I could never work that one out. The few times I tried to talk to you about Brian and our role in the drama, you torpedoed my attempts. You just did not want to talk about it. Full stop.

That summer I went back to London just a few days after I had arrived in Yorkshire. Everything had changed. I could not bear your aloofness. You were so cold. And the fact that you always avoided me, that you made it obvious you wanted to avoid contact with me. There were no more evenings in the bay, no more conversations, certainly no more tender displays of affection. Brian Somerville and the threat he represented to you stood between us. You could no longer approach me. I think you were extremely relieved when I finally packed my rucksack and left the farm.

I no longer know what I told my surprised mother and gobsmacked Harold. Something or other. I expect they *figured the rest out for themselves. I never spoke about my feelings for you, but at least Mum would have suspected something, and now assumed it had not worked out, that I had left Scarborough in such a hurry because I was disappointed in love. That was not completely wrong, although she could not guess any of the complications and events which had led to the situation.*

I went to the borough office and asked about the Somerville family. I gave their previous address and said they were acquaintances whose current address I was looking for. Such queries were absolutely normal back then, just one and a half years after the war ended. Men had not returned from the Front. Families had been evacuated from the major cities and then disappeared. There were still children who were looking for parents, parents searching for children, wives for husbands and fiancés, husbands for wives, and so on. The Red Cross hung up long lists of missing persons, and people who had given up hope were still finding each other in this way.

The shadow of war still hung over the country.

As for the Somervilles, I was told, as I had expected, that the whole family had been killed in November 1940 in an air raid.

'All of them?' I asked the young woman behind the counter who had looked at the files for me.

You could see her heart go out to me.

'All of them, I'm afraid. Mr and Mrs Somerville and their six children. The house collapsed and they were trapped in the cellar.'

'They were all found in the rubble later?' I had to ask.

'Yes. I'm sorry that I haven't got any better news for you.'

'Thank you,' I mumbled.

Back then half London had burnt down. The injured and dead had been dragged out of the rubble. No won-

*der that in this case it had no longer been possible to as-
certain whether all six children had died in the cellar of
a collapsed house with their parents. I can still remember
the words of poor Miss Taylor on that November morning:
'They dug them out…at least, what was still left of them.'*

*Perhaps there had been a leg here, an arm there… Who
would have had time in the midst of the inferno that had
raged night after night in the city to carry out extensive
post-mortem tests?*

*Now I knew for certain. Officially Brian Somerville had
been dead for almost six years. Nobody really had become
a nobody. He no longer existed. There had been a note
about him on a Red Cross nurse's notebook once, but that
had obviously been lost somewhere on its way through
the organisation. So no one had asked about Brian, nor
would anyone. Something had happened which seems impossible today in our networked, computer-driven world:
someone had just slipped through the cracks. He was there
in body, but not officially. He would never have to go to
school, nor pay taxes. He had no national insurance, and
no right to vote.*

*And he was not in the least protected in the way a ci-
vilised society protects the people in it.*

*I crept home and wrote a letter to you, telling you what
I had found out. I don't know if you remember that letter. In any case, it was one of the few times you replied to
me—and without delay. I expect you were rather relieved
to hear about Brian's official 'death'. Now you could be
sure that the authorities were not going to ask questions.
As long as I kept quiet, you had nothing to fear.*

*You thanked me for my letter and told me not to worry.
After all, I did not know that Brian was as badly off as I
had believed in the heat of the moment (I remember your
expression word-for-word!). And I should consider what*

the alternative was: a care home—that was the only other option—was probably no picnic for a boy like Nobody. The patients there were strapped to their beds and left to vegetate. Lying helplessly in their faeces, they were washed down with cold water. Often there was abuse and unexplained deaths…

You painted such a gruesome picture of it that Charles Dickens could not have done better. Even today, looking back on it, I have to admit that you were probably not far wrong. In the forties care homes for mentally disabled people were not comparable with what we have today. And even today we are regularly shocked by scandals where a reporter uncovers sick and old people being got rid of.

However…now I am almost eighty years old, Chad. As my own death approaches (it won't be all that long now), I no longer want to lie to myself and other people.

The path we chose was not right. And since Semira Newton uncovered the scandal at the start of the seventies, not even you can actually believe that it was, in any of its twists and turns.

It was a horrific, irresponsible, unconscionable path to take. Selfish and cowardly. Yes, perhaps that is our defining characteristic: cowardice.

Simply cowardice.

16

WHAT CAME NEXT? I did what I had rejected before. I went to secretarial college and learnt typing and shorthand, and then worked in a number of offices in London. By the way, as I remember now, my mother once asked about Brian in that time. It came out of the blue one Sunday morning over breakfast.

'What happened to that other child?' she asked. I choked on my tea in fright. 'You know…the little…what was the name of that family? Somerville, if I remember rightly. The boy you took up to Yorkshire with you…'

'He was put in a care home long ago, Mum. Years ago,' I replied, dabbing at the tea I had spilt on my jumper. 'You know, he was rather…' I tapped at my forehead.

'Oh yes,' said Mum, and that was that. She never mentioned him again. That settled it for her. After all, it had just been a question that had shot through her head briefly. She had never really been interested in the answer.

In August 1949 I married the first boyfriend I had after you. Oliver Barnes was a nice history student in his last term. I met him during a temporary job at the university library. I think I was besotted with him, but it was not real love. Perhaps at twenty you are not old enough to know what is. I married him because he was nice and because he adored me. He still lived with his parents, but he had his own basement flat in their large house, so I could move in with him. That was how I finally escaped the confined conditions with Harold and Mum. I was certainly taking a big step up the social ladder, something which impressed Mum immensely. She liked Oliver and until the end of her life she was convinced that he was the love of my life. I let her believe it, why should I have got her worried?

I was barely twenty-one when my daughter Alicia was born. And I was twenty-eight when my husband, who by now was an assistant lecturer, was offered a post at the University of Hull.

Was it chance or fate? I was heading back to Yorkshire.

I have no wish to bore you with all the subsequent years.

The catastrophe had occurred in our lives. At the all-important crossroads we had chosen to go in different directions, and we could never undo that. For me that was, and still is, tragic. I don't know if you feel the same. I can't talk to you about such things. Over the years you became more and more of a loner. You retreated more and more into your shell. It was left to me to keep our contact intact, to visit you, and to try to draw you out of your shell. That was still true after you married, at forty-five, a woman who was twenty years younger than you and who wilted visibly with your inability to talk. It makes perfect sense to me that she, although she was so much younger, died before you. She reminds me of a flower which, denied water, dries up and then disappears.

Gwen has also suffered from your character, but she is your daughter. Since the day she was born she has only known a father who practically does not speak and who withdraws completely from his family. Someone who is there and at the same time not there. She was able to develop mechanisms that allowed her to survive in the desert. Although your wife was young, she was too old to do that. You wore her down. In the end she died of worry

*and frustration. The tumour in her breast was simply the
physical expression of this unhappiness.*

*Why am I so merciless in telling you this? Because I
have been merciless in putting myself in the dock too. I
have asked myself if I too carry the blame for your having
been so distant from your family, for your taking so little
part in it and, although officially husband and father, for
your not taking on those roles in reality?*

*I insisted we live in Scarborough, although Hull would
of course have been much easier for Oliver. As usual, he let
me have my way. Back then we did not live in the Prince
of Wales Terrace, but in a charming little house further
up, in Sea Cliff Road. The road looks like it ends in the
sea. It is lined with trees and its houses are spacious with
pretty gardens. We could have been a proper happy family, and I could have thrown myself into that life. Instead
I was always going back to the Beckett farm. For a long
time I was not aware of how much time I was spending
there, but then there was an ugly scene with my daughter Alicia. She was twenty or twenty-one, and already a
mother to little Leslie. She was living a dissolute, messy life,
and I tried to tell her how much more she could make of
herself and her life.*

*'You had everything!' I exclaimed. 'You aren't deprived,
like some other young people can claim. Did you ever lack
anything?'*

*Her skin was already an unhealthy yellow colour by
then; she had continual problems with her liver and gall-
bladder because of her drug-taking and her completely
deficient eating habits. I remember how the sick colour
deepened as she replied violently, 'Anything I lacked? My
mother! I always had to do without my mother!'*

I was frankly astonished. 'Me?'

'Unfortunately I don't have another one.'

'But I—'

'*You were never there,*' *she interrupted me.* '*You were always hanging around on that farm, tagging along after Chad Beckett. Practically every day when I came home from school, all I found was a meal you had made earlier and a note that said you were at the Beckett farm and would be back later. I wish I had kept those notes. I could have filled a shipping container with them!*'

Now I know that she was right. I never let you go, Chad. However reserved and difficult you became in the end, to me you were still the wild, handsome war-time boy I used to sit with in the bay in the twilit hours of evening, who wanted to go to war and save the world. The boy I idolised, and whom I believed was going to be everything to me. I had woven a whole world around him in my dreams— without realising that it was only in my dreams, and not in yours. For decades I had romantic thoughts about you, and romanticism is not something you could normally accuse me of. I pulled the wool over my own eyes. I convinced myself that someone—I!—had to help you. After your father died, you were alone on the farm for many years. You had to work off the debts. You were over-worked and had your worries. I cooked for you, I took your laundry away to wash it. I talked to you about harvest problems and falling prices for grain. I knew more about your life on the farm than about my husband's life at the university, which did not interest me in the slightest. Above all, I lost touch with what was going on in my daughter's head, soul and life. I knew the price of a kilo of sheep's wool. I did not know the date of the school show in which she was a solo singer.

And after you married, and became a father, I was so used to that strange life with you that I did not manage to stop. I was unable to let go of you, just because there was now another woman. I persuaded myself that I needed to support her too. She was young, inexperienced, and had too much on her plate. I was ready to help and always there in an emergency. Except that was never the case. The family had no insoluble problems. Probably the only real problem was me.

Chad, sometimes your wife must have been sick to death of me. But she was a submissive, fearful kind of woman. She suffered in silence.

The strange thing is that we never had an affair.

Physically, we never cheated on our spouses. Perhaps an affair would have made everything easier, at least clearer. Perhaps Oliver would have asked for a divorce if he had found out. Perhaps your wife would have had the strength to leave, if she had found us together in bed. But as it was, no one really knew what to accuse us of. Especially as I was acting in the guise of a good Samaritan.

My recurring question is whether everything would have turned out differently without Brian. Whether we would have married, had a few lovely children and been happy. Or am I deluding myself there too? Perhaps our relationship would have survived the whole incident with Brian if we had really been made for each other? It is both depressing and fascinating to think that the lives of two people, and so also the lives of their later spouses and children, could be decided by a chance event. If my mother and I had left for the station earlier or later on that morning in November 1940, we probably would not have met Miss Taylor and Brian. And some things would have happened differently. Maybe everything.

We survived the 1970 scandal better than was to be expected, in spite of the storm thrown up by Semira Newton, the police and the press. Surprisingly, no one blamed me, because I had been a child when the decisive incidents occurred, and because people assumed I knew nothing of

Brian's horrific later fate. I was not hounded in the press, only mentioned in passing occasionally, and normally not by my full name. In your case there was a willingness to blame your parents and not you. It was generally assumed that your father alone had given Brian to Gordon McBright. You did nothing to deny that. Of course, that was not so much because you wanted to lay the blame on your father, but rather because your general approach was not to talk to people. Not just in this case. You had started at that point to avoid almost any communication with those surrounding you.

The case caused quite a commotion. The forgotten child was one newspaper's headline, another's was The child with no name. Naturally the press had a field day, but thanks to how young we had been, we got away lightly. Public opinion blamed Arvid Beckett, the man who had never wanted Brian and barely shown any interest in him. You and he did it together, and indeed Arvid was a sick, at times even confused, old man, who probably did not realise the full extent of what he was doing.

But who would it have helped, if I had gone public and put ourselves and our families at risk?

I know you well, Chad. Perhaps better than any other person I have met in the course of my life. I know that if you have even read all of this, or at least skimmed it, you will be sitting there now with a furrowed brow asking, So what? I still don't know why she's dishing up this old story…

I am not sure my reason will convince you, but I will try to explain.

I wrote it all down because I wanted to face the truth, and I can only do that completely clearly and unsparingly if I write it all down. Thoughts get interrupted, fly off at tangents, lose themselves, are not taken to their logical conclusions. In writing there is nowhere to escape to.

Writing forces you to concentrate and to express precisely what cannot be said. You finish your sentences, even if your mind twists and turns and your fingers would rather not touch the keyboard. You want to run away, but you write it down.

That is how it was for me.

And why have I sent it all to you?

Because you are part of my story, Chad, and part of my truth. Because our and Brian's fates are intertwined. The direction each life took is not imaginable without the other two people's lives. I feel connected to you two in a beautiful, sad and certainly very special way. So it would not have seemed right to keep our story to myself.

Maybe there is also a certain wish for fairness behind my sending you these chapters. Chad, it was not easy to face the truth. Maybe it just seems fair to me for you to have to do it too. Of course I cannot force you to read all of this. Perhaps you will just press the delete key, as soon as you see what this is about.

Perhaps you will protect yourself and not make yourself read it. I could understand that.

But I want to share my life with you. If not in one way than at least in another way.

Fiona

LESLIE WONDERED WHY she felt so rotten. It could not be the whisky, could it? She could hardly have thrown up more than she did last night. Perhaps she had not slept enough. Two hours at the most. And she had read too much that burdened her. Things had not become any clearer, instead they had seemed to become ever more hazy.

What had happened to Brian Somerville?

And who was Semira Newton?

She left her bedroom. It was slowly growing light outside. A bright red strip glowed above the sea between dark banks of cloud. The sun was rising, but Leslie doubted that it would show itself today. It was going to be a grey autumn day.

She went into the living room where, to her surprise, she found Dave Tanner already dressed and just picking the phone up from its cradle. He jumped and put the phone back down. He obviously felt bad being caught making a call.

'You're awake early,' he said.

'You too,' replied Leslie.

'I didn't sleep too well,' admitted Dave. 'Too much on my mind…' He did not go into details, but Leslie could guess.

'You don't know what to do with your life.'

He smiled unhappily. 'That's an understatement. I'm

at a dead end and have the feeling I can't go backwards or forwards. Talk about taking a wrong turn…'

She pointed to the phone. 'Did you want to call Gwen?'

'No. I wanted to call an old friend, but she's…it's not important.'

'Ah.'

He looked at her a long time. 'You look tired, Leslie. I'd say you didn't sleep too well either.'

'Not enough, that's for sure.' She did not want to tell him about her grandmother's files and that she had spent hours reading them.

She pushed aside thoughts of Brian Somerville and Semira Newton, whoever she was, and tried to concentrate on Dave.

'Why did the police not believe your statement about Saturday night?' she asked. She had been in too much of a state the night before to go into it, but later, as she lay in bed, the question had gone round and round in her mind. He had said something about *conflicting reports* and then abruptly changed the topic.

From the changing expressions on his face, she could see that he was thinking quickly about what and how much to tell her, and that he finally, with a kind of relieved resignation, decided to tell her what he and Detective Inspector Almond had discussed.

'A neighbour saw me leaving the house late on Saturday night,' he said. 'Although *I* had said that I had not gone out again. She told the police.'

'And was it true? Had you gone out again?'

'Yes.'

She looked at him in amazement. 'But why…and where did you…?'

He could see the distrust and fear in her gaze and he

raised his hands in a calming gesture. 'I didn't kill your grandmother, Leslie. Honestly, believe me. But I did go out again, and I didn't want to mention it.'

She guessed what was coming. 'You were with another woman?'

During their conversation he had been standing in the middle of the room. Now he collapsed into an armchair and stretched out his legs. He was ready to surrender completely. 'Yes.'

'The whole night?'

'Yes.'

'Dave…'

'I know. I'm a monster. I acted terribly. I lied to Gwen, cheated on her…*I know*!'

'Who is she?'

'Karen. A student. We used to be together. I broke up with her because of Gwen.'

'Apparently not.'

'I had, actually. But now and then I've been weak. She didn't want to lose me, so she always made it easy for me… But of course, it should never have come to that.'

She stepped towards him. 'Dave. You are having an affair with your ex. Last night you wanted to sleep with me. And—'

He interrupted her. 'I'm sorry if I—'

'You didn't hurt me, Dave. At the moment you would probably bestow your favours on pretty much any woman in Scarborough who you found halfway decent. Who didn't have anything against you. I don't take it personally that I would have been one of many…'

He looked at her with affection, as it seemed to her. 'You would not have been one of many, Leslie. You *aren't* one of many.'

'I'm part of your chaotic and incurable situation, Dave. Just like Karen. And Gwen. You are in a crisis, and you're acting in a wild flap, hoping that some path will open up for you. Your plan for your life has not worked out, or rather: you can see that it was a mistake not to have a plan. That's the sort of thing people normally notice once they're about forty. And they tend to have panicky reactions.'

He smiled a little. 'Like you?'

'I'm not a murder suspect. And I don't cheat on anyone. I limit my panic attacks to myself.'

'And a lot of whisky.'

'And I bear the consequences of that too.'

He stood up, looking more tense now. 'What do you want, Leslie? You're not just giving me this little sermon because you have some time to kill. What's your point?'

She took a deep breath. 'I've known Gwen for ages. My gran and her father have been friends all their lives. I've spent a lot of time on the Beckett farm. I don't want to claim that I'm close friends with Gwen. We're too different for that. But I feel responsible for her. She's almost like family to me. I can't stand by helplessly and let her...'

'.... waste her life on a rake like me?'

'You're already cheating on her before you're married. You're horrified by the idea of sex with her. You have no connection to her at all. My gran was right: all you want is the farm. The land. Nothing else.'

He shrugged. 'I admitted that to you ages ago.'

'I can't let Gwen walk into that.'

'Do you want to tell her everything? About Karen? About...us?'

'I want you to tell her everything.'

'Leslie, I...'

'Please, Dave. Go to her. Sort this mess out. Tell her the truth. About Saturday night and about yourself.'

'She'll break down if I do.'

'If the two of you stumble into a catastrophic marriage, she'll have a much worse breakdown. Or do you think you can hide your affairs, escapades and unhappiness with the marriage forever?'

'Probably not,' he acknowledged.

'Put it behind you, as quickly as you can.'

He did not say anything. She guessed that he was weighing up the various possibilities. He was used to leading people on a merry dance, living on his wits, avoiding conflicts and twisting out of unpleasant situations. He was not used to a straight path lined with disagreeable consequences. And never before had his path crossed a murder's. Fiona's violent death had not only upset Dave's favoured mode of operation, it had also catapulted him into a situation where he could not move forward with his usual mixture of tricks, evasions and cheating. It was one thing to play off against each other the women who drooled over him, or to elegantly manoeuvre them round each other. It was quite another thing to have to explain yourself in a murder investigation. A damn sight different, thought Leslie.

'I assume you aren't giving me a choice,' Dave finally said. 'If I don't go to Gwen, then you will, won't you?'

'Before I see you marry? Yes.'

'Then I'll tell her soon,' he said.

She could tell that he had only agreed because she was holding a gun to his head. If it had just been a question of her tough demand in isolation, he would have tried to negotiate with her. He would have used his charm to convince her. He would have fought. But she could see that he was tired of fighting, that he saw the senselessness of the path he had chosen. He was willing to withdraw from the battle, because there was no way to win.

'I can drive you to Staintondale,' Leslie offered.

'That would be nice. I'll just leave my suitcase here temporarily and later I'll—'

'I told you last night: you can take your time to find a new place. Really, this flat is massive. It's not a problem for you to stay a few days. You can have a second key and can come and go as you wish.'

He appeared relieved. 'Thanks, Leslie. Shall we have a coffee and some toast before we go? I don't think I can face Gwen on an empty stomach.'

'Of course. I need a coffee too.'

They had breakfast in the kitchen. It did not seem that the difficult task ahead had spoilt Dave's appetite. He fried eggs to go with his toast, and squirted plenty of ketchup on them. Leslie could not face anything more than two cups of black coffee. She looked on in horror. She hurriedly smoked three cigarettes. Surprisingly this made her feel a little less queasy. She steeled herself for the comment she knew was coming.

'You don't eat enough,' Dave said, on cue. 'And you drink and smoke too much.'

She had heard that often enough. 'I always have. I still feel fine.'

He looked at her. Considering and doubting what she had said.

'Why were you so worked up last night?' he asked. 'Somehow I don't think it was anything to do with Gwen and me.'

Without thinking too much she asked, 'Do you know Semira Newton?'

'No. Who's she?'

'I don't know. I was asking you.'

'Semira Newton…' He thought for a minute. 'Where did you get the name?'

'She's a…a part of my gran's life. I can't tell you more right now. Have you heard of Brian Somerville?'

'No.'

Leslie stubbed out her cigarette and stood up. 'Let's go. The sooner you talk to Gwen, the better.'

Dave got up too. 'Let's go for a walk by the sea first,' he suggested.

She agreed. 'One or two more hours won't make any diference.'

He smiled with relief.

4

SERGEANT REEK HAD the impression that in the last few days his job had mainly involved sitting in his car in front of some house or other and waiting for people who took forever to turn up. The task was excruciatingly boring. He bore it with resignation, in the knowledge that it had to be done. He was also comforted by the thought that his career would soon have a different focus. At some point he would be promoted again. At some point he would be telling someone below him to do these brainless jobs. His boss's praise that morning had given him the hope that he would not have to wait forever to step up the career ladder.

'You're doing a great job,' she had said. That built his confidence.

As usual, the traffic was heavy and loud on Filey Road. Pupils and students were swarming along the pavements. Some were already in woolly hats and scarves. The air was cool this morning. At least it was no longer raining, but autumn had definitely come. The first weeks of October had still had something of an Indian summer about them. Now everything had changed. Now you could even start to think about Christmas.

Christmas! On 16th October! Reek shook his head. And yet the obligatory stars and wreaths were already up in the pedestrian zone. Maybe it wouldn't be a bad thing to start looking for presents now. Then it wouldn't be such a rush in December. He always ended up racing from shop to shop late on Christmas Eve, swearing in exasperation that he would never let it come to this again. Only to find himself in the exact same situation one year later.

He jumped. Lost in his thoughts, he had only just noticed in the corner of his eye the movement on the paved courtyard in front of the large brick house where Karen Ward lived. That was what happened when you sat planning your Christmas shopping instead of looking out. He quickly got out of his car. The young blonde woman who was making her way hurriedly to the front door could have been any of the house's residents, but his intuition said that it must be Karen Ward. She was carrying a travel bag, as if she was returning from a night away. That would fit in. They had not been able to reach her at home late last night. Throwing caution to the wind, Reek dodged his way through the road's heavy traffic and pushed open the garden gate.

'Miss Ward?' he called.

The woman turned around. She looked as though she had not slept much, as Reek noticed immediately.

'Yes?' she asked.

He came up to her and showed her his ID. 'Police. Sergeant Reek. I've got a few questions I'd like to ask you. Have you got ten minutes?'

She looked at her watch. 'I just wanted to change quickly and then go to uni.'

'Really just ten minutes,' Reek repeated.

'I've told Detective Inspector Almond everything I know about Amy Mills.'

'It's something else,' said Reek.

She gave in. 'OK. Do you want to come upstairs?'

THE FLAT WAS LARGE, bright, extremely messy and empty. Piles of dirty dishes towered up in the sink. Empty mugs, a bottle of ketchup and a jar of mayonnaise stood on the table among the crumbs. Mud-encrusted boots had been thrown down carelessly by the door. It was clear that none of the students who lived here felt obliged to tidy up, to clean or do the dishes.

Probably, thought Reek, everyone leaves it to someone else and in the end they get used to living in the chaos.

As a tidy, even finicky, person, he shuddered inside.

'I'm sorry it's such a mess,' said Karen. 'We've got a cleaning rota, but somehow it just doesn't work. Sit down. Would you like a cup of tea?'

'No thanks,' answered Reek, inconspicuously brushing a few bits of food off a wooden chair before sitting down and taking out his notebook and pen.

'So, Miss Ward, as I said, I won't keep you long. It's just to check a statement.'

She had sat down opposite him. He could see that her eyes were red. She had cried during the night.

'Yes?' she said.

'You know Dave Tanner?'

She jumped. 'Yes.'

'Mr Tanner claims to have spent last Saturday night with you. In the Golden Ball in the harbour from around twenty past nine to ten, and then here in your flat. Until six in the morning. Can you confirm that?'

Her hands closed around an empty mug, opened, then clasped it again. 'I understand,' she said in the end. 'That's why he's been calling me the whole time. The display shows at least a dozen calls from him.'

'You weren't available?'

'I saw his number and didn't answer.'

Reek did not say anything. He looked at her expectantly.

'I spent last night at a friend's house,' Karen explained. 'She lives down the road. I…I'm not doing very well right now. No one understands me in the flat, so…at the moment I'm sleeping somewhere else.'

'I understand,' said Reek, although he only had a vague idea and was not sure if he was right. 'Are your…problems to do with Mr Tanner?'

She looked as if she was about to burst into tears. Reek hoped she could control her emotions.

'Yes. I expect you've heard from him already that we were together for a long time. Out of nowhere he broke up with me in July. Apparently because the chemistry wasn't right any more. But now I know there's another woman.'

'Miss Gwendolyn Beckett.'

'Is that her name? I'd just heard she's older and rather plain,' said Karen.

Without making it too obvious, Reek had a look at her. Although she was obviously coming out of a difficult patch, and looked tired and worn out, she was a very beautiful young woman. Just the kind of girl you could imagine beside Dave Tanner. Quite different to poor Gwen.

'And why does it matter what Dave did last Saturday night?' asked Karen, who seemed to have suddenly realised that she was being asked a question about something new to her.

Reek found it very unpleasant to be the bearer of bad tidings.

'He is…well, last Saturday evening there was a…party on the farm where Miss Beckett lives. Mr Tanner was there too.' Reek could not bring himself to say the word 'engagement'. 'There was an argument between him and one of the guests. Mrs Fiona Barnes. And so the party had a somewhat sudden end.'

Karen knit her brow. 'Fiona Barnes? That's the old lady who was found murdered in Staintondale. I read about it in the paper.'

'Right,' said Reek.

He could see her dawning understanding in the expression on her face.

'Oh,' she said. 'And because Dave had an argument with her…'

'We're checking up on all the guests,' added Reek quickly.

Karen leant back. She had very expressive features. You could see that she was torn in different directions.

'Please, Miss Ward. A simple answer to a simple question. Was Dave Tanner at your place until six in the morning? Please tell me the truth.'

'The truth!' exclaimed Karen. Suddenly she stood up, wiping away the few tears that glistened on her cheeks with her balled fists. 'The truth is that I did everything for him. *Everything!* I loved him so much. He doesn't have a job, or a future, or a proper career. He lives as a lodger in that terrible room. But I didn't care! At all. As long as I could be with him. Talk to him, laugh with him, go for walks with him. Sleep with him. I wanted to spend my whole life with him. Sometimes I have the feeling that I'm dying because he left me. It's breaking me apart!'

Reek stood up too, embarrassed by her outburst. 'Miss Ward, I think you—'

'Did you know he's been using me and my feelings? I still don't really get it, but something can't have been all that fantastic with this…Gwendolyn. In any case, he always needed me now and again. To talk to. To go out with.

To fool around with. And for sex. And I was stupid enough to go along with that, whenever he snapped his fingers. And then to sit here alone afterwards, waiting and not hearing from him for days. I started to think about suicide.'

Reek knew that his words would not mean anything to her right now, but he still said them, because they were true. 'You're still so young. Someone else will come. You can be sure of it.'

She replied as was to be expected. 'I don't want someone else.'

'But,' replied Reek cautiously, 'neither do you want him any longer? You didn't answer his calls.'

She let her arms drop. Her still balled hands relaxed.

'I don't want him to drive me crazy,' she said. She sounded very tired all of a sudden. 'I just want to be rid of him. I want to forget him.'

'He met you at the Newcastle Packet on Saturday and went to the Golden Ball with you,' said Reek with a level voice, steering the conversation back to his concern. 'We've checked that. So you were willing to talk on Saturday night?'

'No, I wasn't. I had decided to break off all contact, in order not to lose my health, and my self-esteem too. Or maybe it was the other way round: my self-esteem, and my health. Yes, my self-esteem has been damaged the most.'

She stared out of the window. Reek thought that she was really almost transparent, she was so pale.

'But you went into the Golden Ball with him?'

'I let him talk me round. But I knew it wasn't a good idea. When we got there, I quickly saw what the score was. He was frustrated again, dissatisfied. Not that he was exactly forthcoming about what had rained on his parade, but it must have been to do with the argument you mentioned.

In any case, I was there to distract him. To jump into bed with him and give him a few hours of fun. And the next morning he would have got up and disappeared and not remembered me for days afterwards. That's the way it's been since July. And I can't do that any more.'

Reek held his breath. 'So you…?'

He did not finish his sentence, but Karen understood. 'Yes. So I drank a glass of wine with him, talked with him about something important, rejected his attempts to get closer, and told him I was tired and wanted to go home. Alone.'

'He didn't go with you?'

'No. I didn't want him to. I even refused his offer to drive me home. I know how charming he is. I didn't know if I'd manage to stick to my guns.'

'Do you know what you're saying? That Mr Tanner lied to the police about Saturday night. And moreover, that Mr Tanner no longer has an alibi for the time of the crime against Mrs Barnes.'

She remained calm. 'Maybe. I'm just telling you what happened.'

'You might have to repeat your statement under oath.'

She smiled a little. 'My statement is not my way of taking revenge on a man who has left me, Sergeant Reek. It's just the truth. I've not got a problem with testifying to it under oath.'

Reek put his notebook and pen back in the inside pocket of his coat. 'Thank you for talking, Miss Ward. You have been of great help.'

She looked at him sadly. Reek thought how bad she must feel. In spite of her resolve to end things completely, all those missed calls from Tanner might have sparked a little hope in her that a new start was possible, a change in the behaviour of the man she loved. And now she saw that he had only wanted to use her once again, to cover himself. Since Valerie Almond had interviewed him, Tanner must have been calling his ex like crazy, so that he could get her on message regarding his statement.

Bad luck, thought Reek with a certain glee. Bad luck, pal, that she's going her own way now. You're in a tight spot!

'Goodbye, Miss Ward,' he said. After a short pause, he added, 'Allow me a personal comment: Don't cry for Tanner. He's not worth it.'

5

'I HAVE TO call my boss,' said Ena Witty. 'I want to have today off too. There's no way I can concentrate on work.'

Valerie nodded in sympathy. She was standing in Ena Witty's small and cosy living room and had just refused her offer of a cup of coffee. She had poured enough of the stuff down her throat already—black, hot and far too strong. Her heart hammered too fast and almost too loudly, it felt to her. But perhaps it was just the adrenaline coursing through her veins. She was so restless, she was almost flapping around like a bird.

To her surprise it was Jennifer Brankley who had opened the door to her. Jennifer's face was crumpled and her hair messy. She still looked sleepy.

'Are you *already* or *still* here?' Valerie had asked.

Strange how she did not manage to suppress a certain aversion to Brankley.

'Still,' replied Jennifer. 'Ena wasn't doing well yesterday evening. She couldn't bear the idea of having to sleep here alone. So I called my husband, explained it all to him, and stayed here. Gwen Beckett's coming to pick me up any time now. She just wanted to do a bit of shopping and then give me a lift back to the farm.'

'Did Mr Gibson come over last night or this morning?'

'No.'

Ena was pale and sitting at the living room table with a

piece of toast spread with butter and marmalade in front of her. She was obviously not feeling able to eat it. 'Was it him?' That was her first question when she saw Valerie. 'Did he do it? Did he murder Amy Mills?'

Valerie could only evade the question. 'We don't know. He denies it, and we don't have any firm evidence.'

Ena looked as if she was not sure whether to be happy or sad. 'So, he might be innocent?'

'At the moment anything is possible,' replied Valerie. She shook her head when Jennifer offered her a cup of coffee, but then sat down opposite Ena.

'If you are taking the day off today, perhaps you could come to the station at lunchtime. We still have lots of questions.'

Ena nodded apprehensively.

'Where were you,' asked Valerie, 'last Saturday night? Can you remember?'

'Yes. Of course. We were in London. Stan and I were. We left early Saturday morning, and Sunday evening we got back to Scarborough. Stan wanted to introduce me to his parents. Why?'

'It's about Fiona Barnes, isn't it?' interrupted Jennifer.

Valerie nodded. Her check was a pure formality. Neither she nor Reek believed that Gibson had lied. He was definitely not a suspect for Fiona Barnes' murder.

'It would be great if you can recall some more details about Mr Gibson, Miss Witty. Anything could be important. His behaviour, things he might have said offhand. Things that sprang out at you…or that didn't. Everything. Don't be afraid of talking about trivialities. Often it's just these things that tell us a lot about a person.'

'I haven't known him that long,' said Ena quietly.

'Long enough to want to leave him already,' interjected Jennifer.

Valerie looked at Ena. 'Is that true? You wanted to leave him?'

'I…I thought about it, yes. I wasn't sure, but…'

'Was it related to his…obsession for Amy Mills? Or were there other reasons?'

'I couldn't bear his domineering nature any more,' said Ena. 'Everything always had to go the way he wanted it. Always. He was charming and attentive, if you went along with his plans, but he'd quickly get angry if you contradicted him. Then his voice, his facial expression—everything—changed.'

'Were you afraid of him in those moments?'

Ena hesitated. 'Not exactly,' she replied in the end. 'But I could imagine that I would be afraid sometime. He seemed to be getting worse. The first time I refused to do what he said—it was about something negligible—he had his reaction under control. The next time he was less able to control it. The next time even less. You know…I wondered where it would all end.'

'Did you argue a lot?'

Ena pulled a face. She looked depressed. 'Inspector, I'm not a woman who often says no. That's why I went on the course where I met Gwen Beckett. I had never really learnt to stand up for myself. I think that's why Stan chose me. So: no, we didn't often argue. That's why I was so surprised about how angry he got on those few occasions.'

'Can you imagine that he could lose control completely? That he might get violent, if a person—a woman—went against his plans and desires?'

'I could imagine that,' said Ena.

Valerie nodded. The picture she already had of Stan

Gibson was filling out. The pieces fitted together. But none of this brought her a step further as far as evidence went.

She stood up. 'Thank you, Miss Witty. That was an important point. Please come to the station at two o'clock. And please make a note of everything that occurs to you before then.'

Jennifer accompanied her to the door.

'Do you think it was him?' she asked.

Valerie would have liked to give a clear yes, but that was impossible given the scarcity of evidence. 'What I think is not important,' she said. 'What's important is what I can prove. And at the moment that's all just hazy.'

'Goodbye, Inspector,' said Jennifer.

Valerie nodded goodbye. Stepping outside, she noticed Gwen Beckett getting out of a car on the other side of the road. She was wearing a warm anorak and had her standard plait up in a bun this time. She had not seen the policewoman. After a second's hesitation, Valerie crossed the road and went over to her.

'Good morning, Miss Beckett. You've come to pick up Mrs Brankley, I presume?'

Gwen jumped. 'Oh...I didn't hear you. Good morning.' As always when someone started talking to her unexpectedly, she went red.

Poor thing, thought Valerie.

'You're up and about early.'

'Yes. As you said, I've come to pick up Jennifer. Crazy affair, isn't it? I could scarcely believe it when Colin told me.'

'I was just upstairs. I think Miss Witty is much more stable now, and she can be left alone.'

'Good,' said Gwen. She seemed a little undecided. She locked her car and put the key in her handbag. 'I really did

dare to come here by car,' she added, almost apologetically. 'I don't like to drive, you know, but I really wanted
to fetch Jennifer. The bus is so infrequent…and I could do
a bit of shopping. Colin lent me his car. I can park better
with his than with my Dad's.'

'Is Colin…Mr Brankley on the farm?'

'Jennifer wanted him to stay with the dogs. She's always worried about them.'

'She'll see them soon. Listen.' Valerie decided to grasp
the opportunity she had. 'Since I have you here… Did you
know Stan Gibson?'

'More in passing than anything.'

'How well, exactly?'

Gwen thought about it. 'Not that well. He worked for the
construction company that was doing work at the school,
and he always managed to have something to do in front
of the room we had our course in. It was pretty obvious he
had his eye on Ena. And it didn't take long for the two of
them to get together. Sometimes the three of us would walk
the same way for a bit after the lesson—I'd head towards
the bus stop and Stan and Ena into town. Those were the
only occasions I had to get to know him—if you can call
that *getting to know him*.'

'What was your impression of him?'

'He was…well, he was obviously very keen on Ena. He
was charming and paid attention to her. He brought her
a red rose once when he fetched her. But he was also…'

'Yes?' prodded Valerie, when Gwen stopped.

'He was very assertive,' said Gwen. 'Nice, friendly, but
he never let anyone doubt that everything had to go according to his plan. He always had the evening or weekend planned, and he never asked if Ena might want to do

something else. You had the feeling that he could react quite strongly, if you contradicted him.'

'How could you tell?'

'I don't know…it was just a feeling I had.'

'Did Ena Witty ever contradict him in your presence?'

'No. But often she did not seem happy. Once or twice I realised that he was trying to discourage her from continuing on the course. He said it was all rubbish, and why did she want to be more self-confident anyway. He made disparaging remarks along the lines that this stuff would only lead to ridiculous women's libbers…something like that. And he laughed in an almost insulting way when he heard about the role-plays from Ena.'

'Role-plays?' asked a confused Valerie.

Gwen wriggled. She seemed embarrassed by the topic. 'Well, yes…we used to practice difficult situations. Role-plays.'

'And what were considered *difficult* situations in the course?'

'Situations which…well, everything which people like us have trouble dealing with. Going to a party on your own. Going to a restaurant on your own. Approaching someone. Letting a shop assistant advise you in a shop and in the end not buying anything. That kind of thing. That might seem silly to you but—'

Valerie shook her head. 'Not at all. On the contrary. You have no idea how often I've bought things I didn't really want, just because I didn't know how to make my excuses to the shop assistant. I think most people have problems like that.'

'Really?' asked Gwen in surprise.

I've just destroyed her picture of the all-powerful policewoman, thought Valerie. She answered drily, 'Really.

So Miss Beckett: he made fun of that. He ran down the course, or at least its usefulness. He had no interest in his new girlfriend learning to be a more independent and self-confident person, did he?'

'No interest at all. That's what I always thought: Stan Gibson wants a submissive woman. He's a man who can't bear to be told no.'

'Interesting way of putting it,' said Valerie. 'What do you think he was capable of doing to a woman who rejected him and his advances? In other words, someone who clearly said no to his approaches?'

'I don't know,' said Gwen. 'But I'd be afraid of having to say no to him.'

'I understand,' said Valerie. She held out her hand. 'Thank you, Miss Beckett. You've been a great help.' She turned to go.

Gwen stopped her. 'Inspector, is he…I mean…Stan Gibson…did he kill Fiona too?'

It was of course the question which would occur to anyone who knew the whole story.

'We still don't know if he had anything to do with the crime against Amy Mills,' said Valerie. 'We really are just starting to investigate Mr Gibson.'

Valerie said goodbye and walked to her car. No sooner had she got in and started the engine than her mobile rang. It was Reek, and his voice had an edge of happy excitement.

'Inspector, get ready for this—I've got something for you. I've just come from Karen Ward's house. Dave Tanner has got some explaining to do. Ward confirms that they met in the Golden Ball, as we already knew. But listen to this: after that she went home *alone*. And stayed alone.

That means there are no witnesses as to Dave Tanner's whereabouts after ten p.m. And it means he's lied again.'

Valerie gasped. 'Is she reliable?'

'Yes.'

'Well, well, well. He's really trying it on!'

'And he's been calling her again and again since yester-day,' continued Reek. 'To get her to say the right thing, I suppose. Unfortunately—for him!—she had just decided to make a clean break from him. So she hadn't answered his calls.'

'I'm just in front of Ena Witty's flat,' said Valerie. 'I'll be at Tanner's place in five minutes.'

'Me too,' said Reek and hung up.

6

AT FIRST SIGHT the Beckett farm looked almost deserted. Chad's old car was parked by a shed, but no one was to be seen. As Leslie got out of her car, she noticed that the wind, which that morning had been blowing in from the sea, had abated. The day had taken on a strange immobility. Nothing seemed to move. The clouds hung leadenly in the sky.

Dave got out too. He seemed tense. They had gone on a long walk, had sat on the cliffs and smoked cigarettes, had spoken, sometimes even laughed. It was noon by the time they left for Staintondale. In the end Dave himself had pushed for them to get going.

'I just want to get out of this whole thing,' he had said. 'I want to sort it out, finally.'

Suddenly it seemed that he could not wait to get rid of Gwen, to free himself from his web of lies.

'It doesn't look like anyone is at home,' said Leslie. 'The Brankleys' car isn't there, in any case.'

They went over to the house and knocked. They could not hear anyone move inside, so Leslie put her hand firmly on the door handle. The door was not locked.

'Hello?' she called out.

A shadow appeared in the kitchen door opposite—a large, stooped man who had trouble walking. Chad Beckett.

'Leslie?' he asked.

'Yes, it's me. And Dave. Is Gwen home?'

'Drove off this mornin' to pick up Jennifer. An' she wanted t' do some shoppin'. Probably two of them 'ave gone somewhere to eat. No idea.' His gaze fastened onto his almost-son-in-law, who had popped up behind Leslie. 'Day, Tanner. Police were 'ere askin' after you.'

'When?' asked Dave in irritation.

'Two hours ago, perhaps. Don't know what they wanted.'

'I'll get in touch with them,' said Dave. 'But first I'd like to talk to Gwen.'

'You'll 'ave to be patient.'

'Why is Gwen picking Jennifer up? And where?' asked Leslie.

Chad's brow knitted. 'Jennifer went t' police yesterday, with a friend of Gwen's, if I 'eard rightly. Seems the lass's boyfriend 'ad summat to do with t' murder of that student back in July. The lass found out and turned to Jennifer.'

Dave and Leslie stared at him. 'What?'

It was clear that Chad was not particularly interested in the story and had probably not been listening carefully enough to know many details. 'Ask Jennifer yourselves. She'll tell you better than me. I just know what Colin told me after she called. She stayed t' night with Gwen's friend. Apparently she were near to breakin' down, couldn't be left alone. Anyroad, Gwen wanted to fetch 'er today.'

'I can't believe it,' said Leslie in shock.

'Does that mean they know who murdered Amy Mills?' asked Dave.

Chad seemed as unfazed as ever. 'Maybe.'

'At least I'm not a suspect any more then,' said Dave.

'Where's Colin?' asked Leslie, who harboured the hope that the younger man might have more information. She asked herself what all who heard the news asked themselves: if Amy Mills' murderer had been found, did that mean that Fiona's murderer had also fallen into the police's hands?

'Colin's out with their dogs,' explained Chad.

At the moment it did not seem they were going to find out more. Leslie rubbed her hands on her temples, trying to focus. She had just heard something completely crazy, but as she could not talk to either Jennifer or the police right now and ask them the hundred questions she had, she should remember why she had come.

'Chad, can I talk to you for a minute?' she asked.

Chad agreed. 'Come in t' kitchen. I've just made meself summat to eat.'

'I'll wait outside,' said Dave. 'I need some fresh air, anyway.'

Leslie followed Chad into the kitchen. A pan with pale yellow, rather slimy scrambled eggs was on the table. He had sliced a few pieces of fatty sausage and added them to the pan. They lay on the top and were probably cold.

'I'm sorry to disturb you at a mealtime,' said Leslie.

Chad made a dismissive gesture and sat down on the bench. He took one of the plates which had been piled on the table since breakfast, wiped the crumbs off it and shovelled his unappetizing meal onto it. 'No fun eatin' alone. Want some?'

She felt queasy. 'No thanks.'

He looked briefly at her. 'You're too skinny.'

'Always was.'

He made an unrecognisable noise. Leslie sat down opposite him, opened her bag and took out the pile of paper which Colin had put in her hands only a few days ago.

'Do you know what this is?'

He looked up, munching. 'No.'

'Print-outs of computer files. The files were attached to emails which my gran wrote you. Over the last half year.'

Chad went rigid for a moment when he realised what she held in her hands. He lowered his fork. 'Where d'you get them?' he asked sharply.

'Doesn't matter.'

'You were at your grandmother's computer?'

Leslie thought that it would be simplest if he believed this for now, so she did not contradict him.

'It contains lots of things I already knew. And some things I had no idea about. I had never, *ever* heard about Brian Somerville.'

Her voice rattled as she said the name that now hung, strangely clear, hard and unavoidable, in the air.

'Brian Somerville,' repeated Chad. He pushed his plate away. As untouched by everyone and everything as he always made himself out to be, this did seem to have ruined his appetite.

'Yes. Brian Somerville.'

'What d'yer want to know?'

'What happened to him?'

'Don't know. I don't even know if he's still livin'.'

'Don't you care?'

'I've finished with it.'

'About sixty years ago, if I'm to believe what's written here.'

'Aye. 'Bout sixty years ago.'

They looked at each other across the table. In silence. In the end Chad said, 'If you've read it all, you know we had no choice in the matter. I'd've never brought Brian here. I had no responsibility for 'im. I made sure 'e found somewhere to stay. A roof over 'is 'ead. He couldn't stay 'ere.'

'You should have informed the authorities.'

'You know why I couldn't. Easy to come here now and…' He interrupted himself, stood up and went over to the window. He looked out at the motionless scene.

After a while he added, 'Course, it all looks different lookin' back.'

'I can't understand that you weren't interested in finding out what happened to him.'

'Then don't understand.'

'Who was Semira Newton?'

He turned around. Leslie saw that a vein on his forehead was pulsing. He was more upset than he let on. 'Semira Newton? She…discovered 'im back then.'

'Brian?'

'Aye.'

'1970?'

'Don't know exactly. It's a long time ago. Sometime… aye, coulda been 1970.'

'She discovered him? What do you mean?'

He turned back to the window. 'What I said. Discovered. Made a right old fuss. Police. Press. The lot.'

'She *discovered* him on Gordon McBright's farm?'

'Aye.'

Leslie got up. She was shivering although it was not cold in the kitchen. 'What exactly did she discover, Chad?'

'She found 'im—Brian. She saw 'im and 'e wasn't…in the best state. By gum, Leslie, what the 'eck d'yer want to know?'

'Everything. What happened. The things that Fiona's letters don't talk about. That's what I want to know.'

'Ask Semira Newton.'

'Where is she?'

'Believe she lives in Robin 'ood's Bay.'

Robin Hood's Bay. The fishing village half way between Scarborough and Whitby. Leslie knew it. It was small enough that you could find someone just by asking after them in the village.

'So you don't want to talk to me about it?' she persisted in asking.

'No,' said Chad. 'I don't.' He continued doggedly to look out the window.

'Aren't you at all afraid?' she asked.

'Of what?'

'That something terrible has happened, Chad. You can't make it go away by not talking about it. You and Fiona, you were in this up to your necks. Have you considered that Fiona's death might not be unrelated to this whole thing? And that, if it is, you could be in danger too?'

Now he turned around, genuinely surprised. 'Fiona's murder? But they've got their man now. Man's got nowt to do with Brian Somerville.'

'The suspected killer of Amy Mills?'

'That's 'im. Colin said he's some psychopath. Snoops on women an' then kills them. Completely loopy. No idea what 'is problem is, but it's nowt to do with Fiona and me.'

'Maybe. But who's to say that Amy Mills' murderer is the same as Fiona's?'

'Police seem t' think so.'

'Are you sure they still do? I wouldn't be too sure of this theory, if I were you,' said Leslie. She crammed the pile of paper back into her bag. 'Be careful, Chad. You spend a lot of time on your own out here.'

'Where you goin'?

She rummaged around for her key. 'I'm driving over to Robin Hood's Bay. To Semira Newton. I'm going to find out what's been going on, Chad. Count on it!'

7

'WE'VE COME UP against a brick wall,' said Valerie. She leant on the door and looked unhappily at Sergeant Reek. She had just accompanied Stan Gibson out of the door. Cursing silently to herself, she had to let him go after she had talked to him for two more hours..

'He hasn't put a foot wrong.'

'And are you sure it was him?' asked Reek. 'That he murdered Amy Mills?'

'Absolutely sure, Reek. The way he grins at me, because he knows that I know, and because he knows that I can't do anything. He is enjoying his game with me. He's polite, patient. Even helpful. And inside he's laughing away.'

'And your chat with Miss Witty didn't help?'

Before her talk to Stan Gibson, Valerie had talked to Ena Witty for an hour. Nothing new had come up. 'No. She just confirmed again that he had been in London at the time of the Barnes crime. Apart from that she repeated what she had already said about Gibson's daily life. She's afraid of him, Reek. Or at least, she was on the point of being afraid of him. Gibson really does have a screw loose. She was increasingly aware of that—me too. The man is very dangerous, but he hides it perfectly. Behind his polite smile there's a highly disturbed psychotic. I'd swear my life on it.'

'A screw loose, psychotic, your sworn oath—the judge will brush that aside in a second.'

'I know. I've got nothing on him.'

Cautiously, Reek said 'You are—' before tactfully correcting himself: '*We* are at our wits end with this case, Inspector. A horrific murder and then no lead for months. We shouldn't get fixated on someone just because we...'

She laughed sadly. 'Oh, Reek! Say what you think! That I'm clinging to Gibson because I've finally got a possible culprit? No. That wouldn't be logical. Gibson has got everything perfectly covered. It would be stupid of me to waste time on him if I weren't convinced he was the right one, because I won't get a conviction. Not now. Not for this crime.'

Reek rubbed his eyes. All the overtime was making itself felt. 'What are we going to do?'

'I'm going to dig out every millimetre of soil from around him,' said Valerie. 'Figuratively speaking. Question everyone who knows him, no matter how distantly. His boss, his work colleagues, the people who live in the same house as him, all his acquaintances, relatives, friends. I'm going to sift through the sand in the hope that I find a nugget of gold somewhere.'

'Although you are already convinced that you won't be able to get a conviction?'

'He's too clever. Canny. But he's human. He'll make a mistake one day. And then I'll be close enough to get him.'

'What kind of mistake?' asked Reek.

Valerie went over to the window, and looked out. She did not know if Gibson had come by foot or car. She certainly could not see him in the car park. Maybe he had already left, probably whistling merrily all the way home.

'He'll do it again, Reek. For two reasons. He'll want

another woman. Not Ena Witty. He'll keep clear of her because he knows we're watching her. No, someone else. And at some point that woman won't want what he wants. And then he'll have a problem. And that's what he can't deal with.'

'And the other reason?'

'He's sick enough to not be content with this one success. It won't be enough for him to have given the investigating officer an ulcer because she can't pin anything on him. It's a massive triumph for him. He's almost high on happiness right now, Reek. He'll need to feel that again sometime.'

'A dangerous game, Inspector.'

She turned around. Reek was startled by the anger burning in her eyes. 'Yes. It's a shitty game, Reek, you're right. But there's no other way. Except waiting, and then getting him. It's my only chance.'

'That doesn't clear up Amy Mills' case. At least not officially, and not for her relatives. Her mother and father might not see the guy convicted who has their daughter on his conscience.'

'Maybe not. And believe me, Reek, I find that as tough as you do. But shit happens. Again and again. We don't get them all. We don't get them all for what they have done. We can't always satisfy the need for justice that the family of the victim feels. It's terrible, but true. In Gibson's case it's just about getting a highly dangerous individual safely behind bars. To prevent any further crimes.' Suddenly Valerie felt exhausted. She guessed that she looked it too. 'A case which cannot be officially closed. Not exactly satisfying.'

And not good for her career, she thought to herself, before feeling embarrassed for her thought.

'That's just the way it is sometimes,' said Reek. He could see how down his boss was.

'Still, Inspector, Stan Gibson's conviction wouldn't have helped us with Fiona Barnes' case. So at least we don't need to worry about whether we've just sent a murderer of one or two people home.'

'Although Gibson's not Fiona Barnes' murderer, we'll probably never know whether he has another murder or a rape or two on his conscience,' said Valerie. 'And in the Barnes case we are just as much in the dark as we were at the start. Not exactly comforting. And still no sign of Tanner?'

That morning they had arrived almost simultaneously at the house in Friargate Road. There they had learnt from the landlady that she had thrown Tanner out the previous evening.

'I wasn't going to have a murderer in my house any second longer!' she had screamed, still bordering on the hysterical. 'I threw him out. Him and all he owned. I've got no wish to be the next one, have I?'

'It's almost certain that he has nothing to do with the murder of Amy Mills,' Valerie explained. 'And in the Barnes case there is no evidence against him either.'

'But he crept out on Saturday night, we know that now,' said Mrs Willerton triumphantly. 'And he claimed something completely different!'

Yes, and unfortunately nor was that his only lie, thought Valerie, but of course she did not share this with the excitable Mrs Willerton.

'Do you have any idea where he might have gone?' she asked. 'I mean, he needed somewhere to sleep.'

'No idea. To his fiancée I suppose. If she still wants

him. You wouldn't feel your life was too safe with a guy like that. When I think about the danger I was in…'

Yet he was not to be found on the Beckett farm, which they tried next. After what Reek had found out that morning, it did not seem likely that Karen Ward had taken him in.

'Still no trace of him,' said Reek. 'I've posted an officer at the Friarage School. Tanner has a Spanish class there at six tonight. But somehow I don't think he's going to turn up. Perhaps we should put out a warrant for him?'

'He's not on the run. He's been chucked out of his room, and had to find a place to stay for now. He has no idea we're looking for him,' said Valerie.

'He lied to us about his whereabouts on the night of the crime—twice,' added Reek.

Valerie looked at her watch. 'It's a quarter past five. We'll wait for an hour. If he doesn't appear for his Spanish course, then we'll take things up a notch.'

They looked at each other.

'That's when we'll put out a warrant,' said Valerie.

8

As LESLIE HAD SUSPECTED, it was not difficult to find the house in Robin Hood's Bay where Semira Newton lived. She had asked in a gift shop and the shop assistant had nodded immediately. 'Of course I know Semira. She owns the little pottery shop down the road. You can't miss it.'

Leslie had walked down the steep village street. Robin Hood's Bay clung to a steep hillside, winding down almost to the bay. Although the village had become a tourist destination, full of gift shops and boutiques, it had retained its original charm with its low, small houses, its cobblestones and the little stream which purled down through the village towards the sea. Tiny gardens in which the last flowers of the year bloomed. Small terraces with painted tables and chairs placed close together, telling of lazy summer evenings out in the open. And the smell of salt and seaweed wafting over everything from the sea.

Leslie had quickly found the pottery. It was just above the place where the road widened and opened out onto the beach. The house was as small and crooked as most of the other village houses. It had whitewashed walls and a door of shiny black wood. Beside the door there were two windows in which Semira Newton's wares were displayed: mugs, cups, plates and bowls in glazed clay. They were thick, sometimes unsymmetrical, but certainly unique and highly original. Not one of them was colourfully decorated. Depending on the glaze used and the firing temperature, they varied in tones of brown between light beige and a dark brown, but that was the limit of their variety. Leslie, who had no love of crockery decorated with flowery motifs, liked the simplicity of these pieces.

Unfortunately Semira Newton was not home, at least not in the shop. A note on the door read *I'll be back around four o'clock!*

Leslie looked at her watch. Just before two.

Nevertheless she knocked on the door, and looked up at the upper windows in the hope that she might see a stirring there. Nothing moved behind the white curtains. Obviously Semira was really not home.

Leslie went down to the beach. There were barely any tourists at this time of year. Armed with drawing pads, a class of about twenty eight- or nine-year-olds sat on the long flat rocks at the top end of the bay. Their teacher was reading a book, while the children painted, deep in concentration, often with their tongue between their lips. The sea, the sand…Leslie glanced at a few of the drawings as she passed.

Nice to come out here for the art lesson, she thought.

Two elderly women were walking along the mudflats and collecting stones and shells. A man was leaning against the wall which supported the houses at the edge of the village nearest the bay. He looked thoughtfully into the distance. Another man was throwing a tennis ball for his dog. The dog bounded up and down the beach, barking enthusiastically. Leslie watched him for a while, then she sat on a rock and wrapped her coat more tightly around her. She was not actually all that cold, but she was still shivering. She knew why: she was afraid of the upcoming chat with Semira Newton.

Perhaps she should just drive back to Scarborough, she thought. Let sleeping dogs lie.

Perhaps it was already too late for that. The mystery would pursue her. She could leave the past alone, but would it leave her, Leslie, alone?

The beach slowly emptied of people, because the tide was coming in. The man disappeared with his dog. The class packed away their pads and pencils. The two elderly women turned round to go home. When Leslie set off for the pottery at four, only the lone man was still standing at the wall. He continued to look out over the sea at a spot on the horizon which he and no one else could see.

In spite of her promise to be back by four, Semira Newton was nowhere to be seen, not by a quarter past, and not by half past four. Walking up and down in front of the house, smoking cigarettes, feeling increasingly cold and depressed, Leslie was about ready to read it as a sign: their meeting was not to be. There was no point to it, it served no purpose. Perhaps she was being given the chance to not meet Semira, and if she did not take it, one day she would wish she had.

At ten to five she decided to leave Robin Hood's Bay. Just then she saw a figure coming down the road. Instinctively she knew it was the woman she had been waiting for all afternoon. A little woman, who found it difficult to walk and used a Zimmer frame. The steep street did not make it any easier. She walked slowly. It seemed that every step required her determination and concentration. She was wearing beige trousers and a brown anorak. In other words, she was wearing the colours of the pottery she sold. Her dark skin, black hair and coal-black eyes showed her to be an Indian or Pakistani.

Leslie's heart was pounding like crazy. She went to-wards the old lady.

'Mrs Newton?' she asked.

The woman, who had been looking down at the street the whole time, looked up. 'Yes?'

'I'm Dr Cramer. Leslie Cramer. I've been waiting for you.'

'I took longer than expected,' said Semira. It did not look like she was prepared to apologise, although she did explain her lateness. 'I always have a massage on Thurs-days, from a friend here in the village. It's important, be-cause my frame,' by which she meant her body, 'is so bent and crooked. Today we had a cup of tea too and chatting we lost track of time.' She had reached the door to her shop. Awkwardly, she fished out her key out of her anorak pocket and opened up. 'Not often that someone comes at this time of year wanting to buy something. Busy as anything in the summer, but now... Didn't expect to find someone wait-ing.' She entered slowly, turning on the light. 'Do you want to buy something, Dr Cramer?'

The sales room was very simple. Wooden shelves with the displayed pottery lined one wall. A lead box on a big table stood in the middle of the room. Probably it was her cash box. A door led to another room. Leslie assumed her studio lay behind it.

Semira moved laboriously around the table, sinking onto a chair with a sigh. She kept her Zimmer frame to hand.

'Excuse me for sitting down at once. But walking and standing are very tiring for me. Although I should do them more often. My doctor always tells me off, but, well, he can't feel how much it hurts!' She looked at Leslie. 'So, you'd like to buy something?'

'Actually I've come for another reason,' said Leslie. 'I…
would like to talk to you for a little, Mrs Newton.'

Semira Newton gestured to a stool in the corner. 'Pull
it up, and sit down. I'm sorry I can't offer you anything
more comfortable.'

Leslie put the stool on the other side of the table from
Semira Newton. 'It's fine,' she said.

'So?' asked Semira again. Her eyes were focused on
her visitor. Leslie saw that they were clever, lively eyes.
Semira Newton might move like an eighty-year-old, but
mentally she was still agile.

She forced herself to start. 'I'm Fiona Barnes' granddaughter,' she said. 'Her maiden name was Fiona Swales.'
She waited for a reaction, but none came. Semira remained
impassive.

'You know my grandmother, don't you?' asked Leslie.

'I met her a few times, yes. But that's an eternity ago.'

'She was…murdered last Saturday night,' said Leslie.
She had trouble saying this. It sounded so odd.

'I read about it in the paper,' replied Semira. 'Do they
know yet who did it? And why?'

'No. The police is still in the dark. At least that's what I
gather. They haven't suggested in any way that they have
a hot lead.'

'I read recently that many crimes remain unsolved,'
said Semira casually, as if just in passing. Leslie could
see the woman was withdrawn. It was not going to be an
easy conversation.

'Yes, that's true,' she agreed. Then she looked earnestly
at Semira. 'You can imagine why I'm here, can't you?'

'Tell me.'

'I never knew everything about my grandmother's life.
Some things I only heard about by chance after her death.

There are names I hadn't heard before, like Brian Somerville for example.'

Semira froze. Not a single muscle in her face moved.

Leslie persisted. 'You know who I'm talking about, don't you?'

'Yes. And you do too. What do you want from me?'

'From a letter which my grandmother wrote to Chad Beckett a few weeks before her death I gather that there was a scandal in 1970 around Brian Somerville. She wrote that there was a real storm in the press. She wrote about police investigations...and about you. I take it you set things off.'

Semira smiled wanly. She did not look tense, tired instead. Like a person who has to deal with a topic which has been part of her life for decades, and which she barely has the energy for now.

'Yes,' she said slowly. 'I did set it all off. I told the police and the press. At least, that was after I narrowly escaped death and could do something.'

'You told the police and press because you...found Brian Somerville?'

'It was a December day,' recounted Semira, her voice remaining monotonous and her face immobile. '19th December to be precise, in 1970. A Saturday. Bitterly cold. Snow was forecast. My husband and I lived in Ravenscar back then. My husband was the cook in an old people's home. I was unemployed. I had been a social worker in London, but we moved to the North because my husband had finally been offered a job here after a long time out of work. I was also hoping to find work at some point, but back then in a rural area like this one...I didn't have the best of chances as a Pakistani. There were still lots of prejudices. Not that I was unhappy. John—my husband—

and I loved each other. We were hoping to have a baby.'
She paused, and seemed to be remembering the time for a moment.

'Anyway, at the beginning of December the children of one of John's fellow workers told me something,' she continued. 'They had been wandering around the countryside and had ended up near Gordon McBright's farm. And, by the way, all the parents had strictly forbidden their children to go near it. Barely anyone ever saw McBright, but there were any number of rumours about him. Apparently he was unpredictable, brutal and dangerous. Some saw him as the devil incarnate.'

'Gordon McBright...'

Semira Newton looked past her visitor and out of the window. The October day was turning to twilight. 'It exists,' she said. 'Evil. More unimaginable, merciless and sly than most of us ever guess. In any case, I was then twenty-eight, and although I had certainly not only seen the sunny side of life in my time as a social worker in London, I didn't then know *real evil*.'

She was skirting around the topic, Leslie could see that. She found it difficult to return to that December day almost forty years ago.

'Do you know what I read a few months ago?' asked Semira. 'I read how a lot of people get rid of their dogs in Spain. They hang them up on trees. But not in a way that lets them die quickly. They hang them up so that the claws on their hind legs just scrape the ground. That delays death. The dogs struggle for hours before dying.'

Leslie swallowed.

'And do you know what they call it?' asked Semira. 'The Spanish?'

'No,' said Leslie. Her *No* was a barely intelligible croak. She cleared her throat.

'No,' she repeated.

'They call it *playing the piano*,' said Semira. 'Because in their desperate attempts to keep the tips of their paws on the ground, to avoid the slow strangulation, the dogs pitter-patter from side to side. Just like the movements of a pianist's fingers on the keys.'

Leslie did not say a word. She was horrified.

'Yes,' continued Semira. 'That was what shook me. Not that fact that they do it. But the name they gave to the cruel show. Maybe we feel the full power of evil most when we aren't faced with simple brutality. But when the brutality is accompanied by cynicism. Because then we see that the rational faculties are involved. And isn't it unbearable to know that *rational* people do things like that?'

'Yes, it is,' said Leslie.

'But that's not why you came, to chat with me about the evil in the world,' said Semira. 'You came about my particular story, about which I've thought so much over the years. About Gordon McBright, and Brian Somerville.'

'And my grandmother?'

Semira laughed. 'Oh, you want to know if I murdered your grandmother last Saturday night? You want to know if I have a motive? Yes, Dr Cramer, I did. But I'm going to have to disappoint you. If I had wanted to kill Fiona Barnes, I wouldn't have done it a couple of days ago. And spared her the troubles, hardships and loneliness of old age? Why would I have been that nice? And also—look at me. I read that your grandmother was beaten to death and thrown into some kind of gorge by a meadow. In the middle of the night. Do you think I could have done all that? Stuck as I am in this wreck of a body?'

Leslie shook her head. 'Hard to imagine.'

'Impossible. I'd have trouble killing myself. Someone else? No. I'm afraid not.'

'I didn't want to suggest that you—'

'No, I know you didn't, my dear. You just want to understand a few things, I understand. You know, I always hated your grandmother. And Chad Beckett. The innocent couple—they made things easy for themselves. They would do anything to save their own skin. At the end of the day, my messed-up life has a lot to do with their selfishness, cowardice and egotism. I can tell you about it, Dr Cramer, if you like. I can tell you how Gordon McBright beat me so badly I became an incurable cripple. I can tell you everything he did to me, and it won't be like anything you've experienced in your life, Leslie. I don't imagine life is easy for someone whose grandmother is Fiona Barnes, but it's nothing compared to my suffering. You can bet your life on it.'

'I'd like to hear about it,' said Leslie.

9

'BUT WHY DID you do that?' asked Colin.

He stood with his back to the little window of the garret they had always stayed in since they spent their holidays on the Beckett farm. And although he was not a particularly wide shouldered man, he covered almost all the pane and blocked off the late afternoon light.

Jennifer was sitting on the bed with Wotan and Cal at her feet. Both dogs had put their noses on Jennifer's knee and were looking up at her, their eyes pleading for her to stroke them. She scratched their heads absentmindedly.

'I don't know,' she said to Colin in the end.

'Well, Jennifer, really…' He shook his head. 'You gave a false statement to the police. In a murder investigation! You could get into real trouble for that. And you say you don't know why you did it?'

She acted unaffected by his words. 'Maybe I was a little too impulsive. I just felt it would be better…to have an alibi. That policewoman, she's like a bloodhound. She wants to see this case solved however she can, even if the person she'll present as the culprit isn't guilty. I wanted to avoid any problems.'

'And so you claimed that you and Gwen spent the whole evening together, even though it wasn't true?'

'What's so bad about that?'

He put his face in his hands. This was not the Jennifer

he knew. She was acting so naive and yet stubborn. 'It's a *false statement*. There'll be hell to pay if it comes out.'

'How should it come out?'

'Well, Gwen told me. Obviously she's wondering why you thought it was necessary to knock together this story. Then she'll talk to Dave about it. Then maybe her father. And Leslie Cramer—it'd be good to tell her too. In the end, you can bet on it, the police will hear. Jennifer, how could you count on Gwen? She's a little girl, who always needs someone's advice. You've known her for years!'

'So what? So the police will hear about it. Colin, my conscience is clear. Let Inspector Almond think what she likes, she won't be able to pin anything on me. Because I haven't done anything. I haven't murdered Fiona Barnes, have I?'

'You're not making sense. First you say you want to avoid any problems, so the policewoman can't stick anything on you. But now that you might have got them properly interested in you by lying about an important fact—now you act as if none of it matters and they can't do anything to you anyway. Why the change?'

Jennifer did not stop scratching the dogs' heads. They were starting to drool with joy. 'She was already suspicious of me. Because of what happened back then. It doesn't matter what else comes up. She's been out to get me from the start.'

'And so you go and give her plenty of reason to be suspicious.'

'Maybe it will become clear somehow that it was Gibson. Then the whole thing is settled anyway.'

Colin moved away from the window. He drew up a chair and sat opposite Jennifer. 'Jennifer, you yourself told me he wasn't anywhere around here at the time of the crime.

That's even in the statement of the woman who reported him to the police, and she has absolutely no reason to cover for him. So the two of us are still suspects, like it or not.'

'We would be even if I hadn't agreed anything with Gwen.'

'Yes, but you wouldn't have put yourself in such a risky position. No one, not even Inspector Almond, can seriously consider what happened back then with your pupil as the basis for a murder charge. It doesn't help her. Your false statement does.'

'Gwen's in it just as much as me.'

'But it wasn't Gwen's idea, it was yours. We were all in shock after Fiona's murder, and I expect it wasn't hard for you to convince our inexperienced Gwen that it would be best to accept your suggestion. Well, now she's starting to think about it, and I got the feeling that she is getting more and more uncomfortable with going along with the lie. Jennifer, the longer the investigation goes on, and the more thorough it becomes, the more her discomfort will rise. And even if she doesn't spill the beans to one and all, at some point she will buckle when questioned. Unfortunately, I'm completely sure of that.'

'I can't do anything about it now,' replied Jennifer. She sounded resigned, as Colin realised with some apprehension, as if it were no longer of importance to her.

'Go to DI Almond,' he asked her. 'Go and explain what happened. Tell her what you told me: that you were afraid, because you had been out with the dogs and so were an immediate suspect. That you wanted to avoid any problems and so you reacted as you did in a thoughtless panic.'

'Then she'll ask why I panicked. Colin, it's almost like admitting I'm guilty!'

'But it'll be worse if she hears it from Gwen. Or from someone else. Much worse.'

They looked at each other. The dogs felt the tension in the room. They pricked up their ears and looked attentively from one master to the other.

Jennifer said quietly, 'I think I'd like to go home.'

'We have to leave on Saturday anyway. My holiday is over by Monday.'

'I want to go today.'

'Now? Today?'

'Yes.'

'In my opinion, we shouldn't do that.'

'The police have our names. They have our addresses. We live an hour and a half drive from here. I don't think it'll be a problem.'

His eyelids hurt. He was sure he looked just as tired as his wife and asked himself where this crippling tiredness came from which enveloped the two of them and filled them with an indeterminate sadness.

'I think you should go to the police,' he insisted.

'I can call them from home.'

'Will you?'

'Of course!'

He had the impression that she was ready to promise whatever he wanted to hear at the moment, as long as he agreed to leave the Beckett farm with her right then. He reached out and took her hands in his. 'What's happened, Jennifer? Why this sudden flight? Is it…because of yesterday? It shook you deeply. It wouldn't be surprising if it had disturbed you. Maybe we should have another chat. About today, about the man, about your fears. About how you have had to be strong the whole time and support this woman, when maybe you yourself needed someone to support you.'

'It's not just the whole thing with Stan Gibson which is on my mind. It's…everything. The farm. Gwen. Dave Tanner. The police. Everything on this farm is grey, have you ever noticed? Lifeless. Chad is lifeless. Gwen's life is no life. Tanner is a parasite, not a ray of light. Can you imagine the three of them living here together—Chad, Gwen and Tanner? Without even Fiona's sharp tongue to stir things up?'

He could not believe his ears. 'Everything grey on this farm? Lifeless? *You* always wanted to come here, Jennifer. *You* were fond of all of this. The landscape, the sea, the house, Gwen. I had the feeling that…the Beckett farm was everything to you. And now…you're telling me this?'

'Yes,' she replied. 'Now I'm telling you this.' She stood up with a strange mixture of sadness and newfound resolve.

'We're changing, Colin. All of us. I've changed in the last few days.'

He got up too. 'In what way?'

'Hard to describe. I don't know when it started, either. Maybe when Almond dug up what happened back then and thrust it in my face. When I felt pushed into a corner again because of it. But I only understood what I felt yesterday. When I saw how scared Ena Witty was of Stan Gibson. And her hesitation. Should she split up with him or not? Did he have anything to do with Amy Mills' death? Was she just imagining his strange behaviour to her? Back and forth it went, and the only thing that came across was her uncertainty, weakness, lack of courage and inability to make a decision. I spent the whole of yesterday afternoon with her. The evening. The night. This morning. And at some point I just wanted to go. To get away. I couldn't bear her any more!'

'That poor woman? You couldn't bear her any more?'

'She made me so angry. So terribly angry. Her submissiveness. Her fear. Her whining. Everything she had told me about the weeks with Gibson. How could she have taken that crap from him? How could she make herself so weak and let him be so strong? I felt ready to explode. I could explode now!'

'I understand,' said Colin in a calming voice, although he did not really see what she was trying to tell him.

She looked at him with an expression which was almost scornful. 'I don't think you do understand me, Colin. It's taken me a while to understand it. Because you see, I wasn't actually angry with her, but with me.'

'With you?'

'I saw awful Ena Witty and had to think of Amy Mills—of what the media said about her. She must have been just the same. A victim. Stan Gibson likes women like that. Women who lie down and turn over. Who let a man like him be their lord and master. And what's worse: he can find them. They exist. And there are plenty of them.'

'It does seem so, unfortunately. But you…'

Now she was avoiding his gaze. She was staring at some invisible spot on the opposite wall. 'I'm like that too. I could have been. A victim. The victim of a person like that.'

He was confused. 'But you aren't! You have your issues, but I certainly wouldn't describe you as a completely shy, submissive person.'

'I'm different from Ena Witty. And Amy Mills. But I'm eaten up by self-doubt, Colin, you know that. The only reason it's not too obvious is because I've withdrawn almost entirely from normal life. For long periods you and the dogs are my only company. I find it difficult to mix with people. I can't even drive a car, because I don't dare to. So many fears stop me living my life. Maybe I'm just better at hiding it than some others.'

'But someone like Stan Gibson would sniff it out?'

'I'm convinced of it. He's a master of it. If I didn't have you, I'd be a lonely person. Plagued by all kinds of neuroses. And probably I'd be ready to make any number of allowances, just to get someone to care for me.'

He could think of nothing to say which would contradict her theory. 'Oh, Jennifer,' he said helplessly. Then he added, 'But you do have me. You'll always have me.'

But that was not the point. That was not what she had meant. And he knew it.

'Why do you think Inspector Almond had her sights set on me?' continued Jennifer, ignoring Colin's interjection. 'Without any real reason, in a flash, I became a victim again.'

'Well, you have to admit—'

'She did not let him finish. 'I'm so angry, Colin, so damn angry. I think I'm going to get more and more angry every day. I'm angry about the way they forced me out of my job back then. About how this policewoman has tried to use my past against me. About how I've hidden away all these years. How I've stopped living. How I felt—injured, overwhelmed and under attack. And angry about the deeper reason why I always came back to the Beckett farm: because they aren't really alive here. Gwen and her father are just existing like the living dead. That's why I felt comfortable here. I fitted in here, because I was lifeless too, paralysed. I don't want that any more. I don't want to fit in here any more in this isolated house near the sea.

The only thing they do here is keep the world far away. I want to be part of the world again. Not its victim.'

Thinking about the start of their conversation, Colin was tempted to say: And so you put yourself in the role of the victim again by making up a dodgy story with Gwen?

But he did not say anything. It was not appropriate. Jennifer had made a mistake, but a finicky criticism of her ill thought out action would only have put a damper on the new direction she was deciding to take. She had bigger and more important things to think about than who had murdered Fiona Barnes and whom the police might have their eyes on. Even if they suspected her, it did not seem to be what she was thinking about now. So he smiled, more with resignation than happiness, but it was a smile to reassure Jennifer that she had his support.

'Good,' he said. 'Then let's pack and get going. And leave this room behind us forever, right? I don't think we'll be seeing it again.'

'No way,' said Jennifer.

10

'So, as I was saying,' said Semira. 'The children of one of my husband's fellow workers came to me about it twice. They had been at McBright's farm and noticed something strange and unsettling…a child cowering in an abandoned shed. He had an iron ring around his neck and was chained up. He could barely move, and was shivering with cold.'

'And you didn't report it to the police immediately?' asked Leslie. She herself felt ice-cold, down to the tips of her toes. She kept her coat on, not wanting to freeze completely.

'I thought about it,' replied Semira. 'But John advised me not to. The kids were known to make up all manner of crazy stories and tell them to people. John said I'd make myself look like a real fool if I went to the police about it. He said I shouldn't take it seriously. A child on a chain! That just doesn't happen!'

'But you couldn't get the story out of your mind,' prompted Leslie.

'That was it. Unlike John, who has always worked as a cook, I wasn't sure that there are *things which don't happen*. Especially when it comes to what people are capable of doing to each other. As I said, I had been a social worker in London. I had experienced any number of cases of serious domestic violence. I was six years younger than John, but much less naive than him.'

'You looked for the farm.'

'After all the humming and hawing, I thought I'd better see the farm for myself and then tell the police and youth services, if what I saw confirmed what the kids had said. I was certainly afraid. Like I said, Gordon McBright had a scary reputation in Ravenscar. Although at that point we had not been living there for long, we had already heard a lot about him. People said he was a brutal, completely asocial man, full of hate. Apparently he had been mistreated for years by his own father. I don't know if that rumour was true. It was an explanation for why he lived in a wordless fury against God and the world, showing a vicious contempt for other people. He had a wife. She was said to be a physical wreck. She had only been seen two or three times in the village in all the years she had been there. Apparently she no longer had teeth, was as skinny as a rake, and lived in patent fear of her husband. But she had never asked anyone for help, including the police. And no one had intervened on their own initiative. Everyone was too afraid of McBright.'

'It was…it seems mad to go there on your own.'

'Oh yes,' agreed Semira. 'I found that out. But at the time, although I was scared, I underestimated the danger that he represented. And you have to remember that because of my job I was used to meeting violent people and bothering them. I'd had to deal with tons of aggressive, brutal fathers already. But back then in London I'd been part of the social services, and so protected. Wherever I went, my co-workers knew where I was going. Or I took a colleague with me. Or even the police, if the situation looked really awkward. Of course that wasn't the case here.' She paused briefly and then said thoughtfully, 'My biggest mistake was not telling anyone what I intended to do. I didn't let anyone know what I'd planned. *That* was the madness, Leslie. Driving to that isolated spot, to a sick man like Gordon McBright, and not even leaving a note at home on the kitchen table, which said what I was up to.'

'You found a child?'

Semira shook her head. 'No. Not a child. I discovered a man. In a shed beside the farmhouse. He was lying on the ground with his knees up to his chin, like an embryo. That made him look a lot smaller than he was. Barely any light fell into the shed. The kids had thought he was a kid too, but that was the only thing they were wrong about. Apart from that, everything was as they'd said. The iron ring round his neck. The chain which was secured to a beam with a padlock. The dirty straw he lay in. The terrible cold to which he, almost naked, was exposed to. I couldn't believe it. Even now, talking about it forty years later, I can barely believe it. Although it changed my whole life, it still seems strangely unreal.' She looked at Leslie, and at the same time looked through her. 'I'd found Brian Somerville,' she said.

FOR THE NEXT fifteen minutes she did not say anything, just stared at an invisible spot on the wall. The clock seemed to be ticking twice as loudly as before. It became dark outside.

Leslie did not dare to break the silence.

In the end Semira said, 'He was dying,' so directly that Leslie jumped. 'He was only skin and bones. His body was covered in large wounds that oozed pus. They were marks of the mistreatment he had been subjected to. Later we heard from Mrs McBright that he had been held like a slave and forced to carry out the hardest of physical activities, even when he had still been a boy. As there had been little point in explaining things to him, as he didn't understand anything, Gordon McBright had regularly beaten him mercilessly until he was of use somehow. Mrs McBright reported that she had often been afraid that her husband would beat Brian to death. That went on for twenty-four years. For twenty-four years Brian had to live in that hell. He was rarely fed, and he was chained up in this shed every evening, and whenever he wasn't working. Mrs McBright had once brought him a blanket, but her husband had caught her doing it and she never dared to do anything like it again. In some way, as could be gathered from the hearing, Brian's presence on the farm offered some relief to her, although she claimed to have often stopped her ears so she wouldn't hear his tortured screams. Her husband hated the boy so much that he increasingly discharged his aggression on him. Mrs McBright herself suffered his attacks less frequently. Maybe that was why she did nothing to help the defenceless child right from the start. Because at first that's what he was: a child. But maybe she wouldn't have helped in any case. She was a broken woman. She had not had a will of her own for years.'

Semira shook her head, as if it were all more than she could understand, as Leslie thought. She probably knew better than most people the phenomenon of women who could not defend themselves. Or who tried too late to do so.

'In any case,' she went on, 'Brian didn't seem to have long to live by the winter of 1970. He wasn't yet forty, but he looked like someone who was at least sixty. I don't know what McBright had done to him, but it looked like he wasn't going to survive it. The man I found on the floor of the shed was still breathing but—even though I'm no doctor—I knew that he would probably not survive, not even with medical attention. And once again I did the wrong thing. Instead of running like hell immediately, jumping into my car and racing to the police, I squatted down next to him. I turned him over. I looked for a tap, because it looked like he was parched. I wanted to help him. Right then and there. And so I stayed too long in the shed. Just too long.'

'McBright found you there?'

'Not in the shed,' said Semira. 'I managed to clamber out of the window. The shed backed onto the wall around the farm, and the window overlooked a field beyond the wall. The pane had gone long ago. But I still had to walk around the property and get back to the front of the hill. My car was parked at the bottom of it. And that's when he turned up. At his farm gate. He had looked out of a window and seen my parked car. I had parked a way off among some trees, but now I know that you could see it from one of the farmhouse's upper windows. And of course the bare trees didn't conceal it properly. Suffice to say, he was suddenly standing in front of me. If I hadn't stayed with Brian for so long I'd have already been in the car by then.'

She looked down at the tabletop, tracing a few scratches with her fingers. 'I knew immediately that I was in extreme danger. The man was a sadist who knew no limits. If he realised that I had discovered his secret, he wouldn't just let me drive off. I can still recall how my heart pounded and how dry my throat was. And that my legs threatened to give way. I tried to make him believe I was harmless. That I wasn't from around here and had got terribly lost and come to the farm in the hope of finding someone who could help. He listened, but I could see he was watching me intently. He was not sure. It appeared he had not seen me go into the shed, but he suspected I'd been there. His eyes bored into me. I haven't looked into colder eyes in my entire life.' She shook her head. 'I almost thought I was going to get away safely. He made a few derogatory remarks about Pakistanis and then said I should get lost. So I turned around and started down the hill. Not too quick, so he wouldn't get suspicious. But then...he reconsidered. He called me back, looked at me, and...something told him that I knew. That I'd seen Brian.'

'You tried to run away then?' said Leslie in a voice she did not recognise.

'I ran for my life. He followed me. He was not a young man any more, but he was strong and determined, and he was getting closer and closer. I knew I wouldn't manage to make it to my car, open up and get in. There was a little copse below the farm. I turned into it instinctively, without thinking. I needed to find a hiding place, as I hadn't managed to run away. But the trees were leafless and far apart. I couldn't hide from him for a moment.'

Leslie took a deep breath. Even if Semira had not already said so, Leslie only had to look at her crippled body, and the laborious way she had walked, to know that McBright had got hold of her and taken out the full extent of his anger on her.

'I don't want to go into the details of what happened,' said Semira. 'He got me, and he was raving. I think he considered himself to be fully within his rights to do with me as he wished. I was on his property. It made no difference to him whether I'd been in the shed or in his living room with my hands on his purse. He had a completely sick character. He was a dangerous psychopath. Later he didn't die in prison but in preventive detention. Thank God no one was willing to let him out among people.'

'How did you manage...to stay alive?'

'That's a mystery to me to this day,' said Semira, laughing bitterly. 'I don't think McBright thought I would. But there too you see how disturbed he was. It would have been logical for him to check that I was really dead. And if need be, to carry on until I was dead without a shadow of a doubt. Then he would have had to bury my body, to remove all trace of the deed. And drive my car into a nearby pond, something like that. But he didn't do any of that. He didn't feel guilty, he didn't feel like a person does who can be held accountable for his deeds, and so has to make sure he isn't caught. He just did what he thought was right. He left me in that godforsaken copse and went away, not caring less what would happen to me.'

'And your husband noticed you were missing that evening?'

'Not that evening, unfortunately. He was working on the Saturday, and we'd planned to go to the cinema when he got back. He was late, and not finding me, he assumed I'd gone on my own. Or with a friend, and gone for a drink with her afterwards. I would do sometimes, when he was busy, so he didn't think any more about it. He went to bed and slept. It was only on Sunday morning, when he woke up and realised that I was still not home, that he realised that something wasn't right.'

'And the whole time you were lying in the wood?'

Semira nodded. 'Half dead and dropping in and out of consciousness. Both my jaws were broken in multiple places, my nose too, which was so swollen that I could barely breathe. He had shattered my pelvis with a heavy branch. I was in unimaginable pain, but—as I said—at least I was often unconscious. If I try to remember how it was, it all goes hazy. I know it was freezing. And wet. And dark. Now and then it became brighter. I could see the bare treetops above me and the low winter clouds. I could hear birds screeching. I remember the taste of blood in my mouth. I still know that I couldn't move, not at all. Sometimes I saw people I knew from my time in London, and animals, moving around me. I must have had a high fever. I was convinced I was dying. That didn't make me panic, just surprised me. The whole time I thought how I'd thought death would be different, although I couldn't actually imagine how it should be. Just different. Simply different.'

Leslie swallowed. 'When were you found?'

'Late on Monday afternoon. Forty-eight hours after Gordon McBright had attacked me like a madman and broken almost every bone in my body. My husband John had gone to the police on Sunday afternoon, but they didn't take it seriously at that point. They assumed we'd had a fight, or that I'd felt the need to go back to my *clan*. In describing me, John had had to say I was Pakistani. I can't prove anything, but I'm fairly sure that only left the police more disinterested. At the time people were very sceptical about mixed marriages. People assumed they couldn't work. They thought I'd run off and probably they considered John a complete fool for having got involved with me. In any case, nothing happened at first. John spent all his time calling around, asking even the most remote and fleeting of acquaintances whether they had heard or seen anything of me. As my car was not at the house, it was clear that I must have gone somewhere. But where? John racked his brains. We had not argued. It should have been a weekend like any other. No accidents had been reported to the police. Nevertheless, John called every hospital in the North of England to ask whether a young Pakistani woman had been admitted. Only on Monday afternoon did he remember Gordon McBright. He immediately informed the police of the story. They dispatched a highly sceptical officer, who told John in no uncertain terms how loathe he was to visit the isolated farm in the cold and sleet. John drove there too. Of course they saw my car immediately, and then the cogs started to turn. McBright slammed the door in the face of the policeman, who soon after that found Brian Somerville dying in the shed, and called in reinforcements. Well, and that's about it. They combed the surroundings and found me in the end. By that point I'd been unconscious for a long time. I wasn't aware of any of this. I only came back to consciousness a day later in the hospital.'

She went silent. It was a long time until Leslie could say anything again. She felt numb, in shock. Suddenly she wished she had never come. Or had never read her grand-mother's letters to Chad Beckett.

'I suppose,' she said in the end, 'that help came too late for Brian? He died, didn't he? He died because my grand-mother and Chad Beckett—'

'Probably it would have been for the best,' said Semira. 'But no, he didn't die. The doctors saved him. He must have had the constitution of an ox. He really did survive Gordon McBright's sadism.'

'And now…'

'Now he's an old man,' said Semira. 'I sometimes visit him, but it's not easy for me, because I can barely get around. He lives in a care home in Whitby. Didn't you know?'

Leslie shook her head.

'Well,' said Semira, 'Fiona Barnes did. For a long time she couldn't even hope he had died, because until a few years ago I'd always send her a Christmas card remind-ing her about him. And later, when I stopped doing that, she could easily have found out by herself. I wrote to her again and again to say he was still waiting for her. He asked after her. He barely said anything else, but every day he'd ask the carers when Fiona would finally come. She told me that she had promised him in February 1943 to return one day, and still today, over sixty years later, he still hasn't given up hope of that. But she didn't visit him a single time. And that, Leslie, is what I most hated your grandmother for. That more than everything else.'

11

OUTSIDE THE WINDOWS it was growing dark. The day, which had been so grey, so leaden and lifeless, was giving way to a quiet evening. Yet Gwen hesitated to turn the light on. She did not want to light up her face or that of Dave, who was sitting opposite her. She wondered why she held back. Maybe she was afraid that the sudden brightness would also light up the truth, and that would have been unbearable.

The truth that Dave was going to break up with her.

They had been sitting in the living room of the Beckett farm for about an hour. They had barely spoken in all that time. They could hear Jennifer and Colin walking back and forth above them. At one point the thought had flitted through Gwen's head as to what the two of them were so busy with up there. You could hear the dogs' claws on the wooden floor. They seemed to be restless too. Normally they just flopped down in a corner and slept. But then Gwen had decided that it did not matter what Jennifer and Colin were doing up there, what they had planned or what was bothering them.

In view of the fact that her own life was collapsing right now, that was of no interest whatever.

Actually she had guessed as much. She wondered if she had known from the start, the very start, that her relationship with Dave was on thin ice, was not going to last.

There had been dozens of signs. She remembered the day when she had gone to his place and asked him to sleep with her. Was it two or three days ago? He had wriggled out of it, evaded her, had got her talking about all sorts of other things. Afterwards he had left for school with obvious relief, after constantly glancing at his watch as if he could not wait for his course to start. He needed an excuse to leave his room and his future wife for a couple of hours. He came back late, spent the whole night reading, and then set off in the early morning on a walk. He had said no when she asked to go with him.

'I need to be on my own,' he had said. She had stayed in his room for a while waiting, and feeling frustrated and humiliated. In the end she had left his room and house and wandered aimlessly around town for a few hours before she got a cab back to the farm. Without having slept with him. And she had known that she never would: they would never have sex.

Because Dave did not desire her. He felt not the slightest physical attraction to her. He would probably have rather got his rocks off with his landlady than with her. It was not just that he did not love her—he was repelled by her. There was nothing which drew him to her. Nothing—except that bit of land by the sea which she would one day own.

And now he had abandoned even that idea. She had seen that as soon as she and Jennifer had arrived back at the farm. They had spent ages with Ena Witty, who had dissolved into tears again and not wanted to let the two of them go without churning up the whole Stan Gibson affair once more. When they had finally pried themselves away, Jennifer had not wanted to get home immediately, so they had strolled around for a bit and then eaten lunch at the Italian restaurant in Huntriss Row. Then they had walked down to the harbour, had a cup of tea, and Jennifer had even allowed herself two shots. Jennifer was definitely different, thought Gwen. She could not stop thinking about Stan Gibson. She spoke the whole time about Ena Witty, Amy Mills, herself and him. She kept coming back to the question of why Gibson might have found Amy Mills an ideal victim, and why some people seemed predestined to be victims, while others never got close to being one. It was not that Gwen had no interest in this theme, but she had other worries racing around her head. What was to become of her? What future would she have?

Dave had been sitting in the living room with Colin. The dogs were lying on the rug between the two of them and snoring. Someone had lit a fire in the grate. Gwen found it a nice welcome home, at least apparently so. But the situation was temporary, and so of considerably diminished value. The dogs jumping up, waving their tales and panting happily; the two men who came over to the two women; the warmth of the fire; the cosy moment—all of this was not going to last, just a short glimpse of what could have been. A loving husband, children who greeted their mother happily. Instead everything would remain as it had always been. The rare trips she took to Scarborough would always lead her back to a cold house, with no one waiting for her apart from her old father who knew little of her life and concerns. There would be no one else.

Colin and Jennifer had withdrawn, and as so often Chad was nowhere to be seen. After they had looked at each other in silence for a while, Dave had said quietly, 'I have to tell you something, Gwen...'

He had not said much more than that, because Gwen had replied, 'I know.'

And he: 'Yes. Then there's not much more to be said.'

And she in reply: 'No.'

And then they had sat again in silence, a silence in which much changed and happened. A silence in which a relationship between two people ends, a relationship which, as Gwen thought, had probably never been what it should have been, and yet which in a strange way had been a relationship. On his side there had been a calculation, on her side hope. Perhaps it could have worked somehow, if the two of them had made an effort.

Perhaps...but what that *perhaps* might have looked like, she would never know.

Neither of them had noticed that the fire had died down, but it had become unpleasantly cool in the room, rousing them from the private thoughts each had pursued.

'It'll be half past five soon,' said Dave. 'It won't be light much longer. And I've got quite a long walk back to the bus stop...'

'You can stay here for the night if you'd like.'

'I think I'd better be getting back to Scarborough,' Dave said, standing up. 'I don't even know when the last bus goes. If there is still one.'

'And if there isn't, are you going to walk?'

'No idea,' he said. She knew: he just wanted to get away. He does not care what comes next. If he has to hitch a lift, so be it. As long as he gets away from me.

She got up and thought: it can't end like this! With him just getting up and going. And never coming back.

'I...please, don't go yet. I can't bear to be alone yet.'

His reluctance was easy to see, as were his feelings of guilt. 'You're not alone. Jennifer and Colin are here. Your father—'

'My father!' She made a dismissive gesture. Lord, he

knew her father! 'And I don't want to talk about all of this with Jennifer right now. Later. But not now.'

'All right,' said Dave. 'OK.'

He looked out the window. He remembered his Spanish course, but it was too late in any case. And he doubted that he had the energy for it today.

'I'll drive you in later,' said Gwen. 'But please stay for a little while.'

It was terrible to think that he would give in to her plea out of pity, but at the moment she did not have the energy to be proud and do without his sympathy.

The alternative was a deeply painful loneliness. However much she had to humiliate herself, it still seemed like the lesser of the two evils.

12

'YES,' SAID SEMIRA. 'And of course it caused an almighty scandal which the press pounced on. I had found a man who was almost forty, was mentally disabled and kept in a shed, a man who had almost died from the abuse dished out to him, and had just scraped through alive—and no one knew who he was. The police had assumed at first that he was McBright's son, and that his existence had been kept a secret because of his disability. Gordon McBright would not say anything at all, and Mrs McBright needed weeks of psychological support before she could be questioned. She explained that she had never had children. One day shortly after the war her husband had come home with a boy of about fourteen and said he had arranged a farm-hand. They had called the boy Nobody. That was the name her husband had introduced him by.'

Leslie remembered how this name had appeared over and over in her grandmother's letters. She and Chad had baptised the boy Nobody in their childhood cruelty. But it was hard to imagine that Chad Beckett had also handed Brian over to his torturer with that name. *Here's our Nobody. You can have him.*

And yet that is how it must have been.

'Gradually the whole situation became clearer,' continued Semira. 'Nobody's trail could be followed back to the Beckett farm. I still don't know today how Chad Beckett managed it, but in the eyes of the public the responsibility for the whole tragedy remained largely with his dead father. I don't think Beckett would have talked much to the police or the media, he's not exactly Mr Eloquent, but from the little he did say the story could be filled in. Arvid and Emma Beckett had decided to take the boy in without telling any of the authorities. And they didn't try to find any special needs help—admittedly, there wasn't much help available back in the forties. The final report stated that Beckett had returned traumatised from the war, and had not been able to deal with Brian, who was now older and more difficult. He apparently had thought nothing of it that his father was sending the boy to a farm where no other children lived. None of that is of importance now, but then, in 1970, someone like Chad Beckett who had taken part in the Normandy landings was highly respected. Much time had passed, but people still credited their courage against Hitler. By some completely twisted logic, the fact that he had voluntarily enlisted to go and fight while still practically a child, in some way absolved him of possible later mistakes. The press did not really dare to attack him, so everyone ranted about the father for a while, and then nothing more was heard about it.'

'And my grandmother?' asked Leslie. 'She pretty much got away scot-free too, didn't she?'

'They did establish, of course, that Brian Somerville had left London by her hand, as it were. But she was eleven at the time! Not even sixteen when the war ended—and by then she'd been back in London for ages. Who would seriously have criticised her?'

'How is it then that you obviously saw things differently, right from the start?' asked Leslie. 'You certainly hold Chad Beckett and Fiona Barnes responsible!'

Semira's hand flitted around the table. She was a very nervous woman, Leslie realised. It just took a while to notice. She had been tortured for decades by a body which caused her pain and continual problems. She had obviously learnt self-control, but when she was too exhausted it started to crumble. It was clear that Semira Newton was exhausted now. From sitting on the wooden chair for so long, from reconstructing her trauma in such detail. Her fingers trembled.

'Look, my life's been marked by this thing,' she said to Leslie. 'It changed me. When Gordon McBright almost killed me in his copse, on top of everything else I suffered shock. At least, that's what the psychologists have told me. Years later I spent a good bit of time in a clinic. Because of my continuing depression. That's where I learnt pottery, by the way. Creativity as therapy. I don't think it did anything for my psyche. But I can earn a little bit extra to add to my pension. That's not to be scoffed at. Afterwards I was never able to work again, and I divorced in 1977. As the victim of a crime I've been given some compensation. Not a lot, but I don't need a lot. But now and then the few extra pounds from these crooked bowls and cups comes in handy.'

'Did your divorce—'

'—have anything to do with the Somerville affair? Yes, it did. John had married a cheerful, energetic, self-confident woman. Someone in the thick of things. Now the woman beside him was a broken being, a woman who could not stop talking about her experience on 19th December 1970, who was always brooding about where evil came from and what to do about it. A woman who wanted to take care of Brian Somerville and could not get over the fact that nothing had been done to the culprits, that they could go on living as if nothing had happened. A woman who needed a number of operations, was in constant pain and often a little confused in the head because of all the medicines she was taking. I was not the same Semira he had fallen in love with. Today I don't hold it against him that another woman took my place in his heart and life. He fled from me. We've never been in contact since.'

That was understandable, Leslie thought. And yet horrific.

'In any case, as I said, my life's been marked by this drama. Unlike the doctors and psychologists I've seen, I don't think the trauma was set off by the attack on me—but by the view of Brian chained up in the shed. I could never forget the story of the helpless boy (and later man). I couldn't deal with it. I couldn't close the chapter. So I went looking for the people who were connected to it: Fiona Barnes and Chad Beckett. Again and again. I wanted answers. I wanted to understand it—and be free of it. And for that I had to understand how it could have happened. And in talking to them I came to be completely convinced that the two of them were not at all innocent. Rather, they knew what they had done. They were responsible for what had happened to Brian Somerville. And indirectly for my destroyed life.'

'Chad Beckett spoke to you personally?'

'Rarely. And not much. A fish would talk more than him. But sometimes Fiona agreed to meet me. She told me quite a bit. I think she too was looking for a way to deal with it all. But then she found me a bother and at some point did not want to have anything more to do with me. Since 1979 she has hung up without a word whenever I have called her. We never saw each other again. But I already knew enough. And unlike the media and the police,

I did judge Barnes and Beckett—from the depths of my heart. What they did cannot be forgiven.'

Ideas rattled round Leslie's head.

Semira had a motive. Of all the people Valerie Almond had as suspects, including Dave Tanner, Semira had the motive that was clearest and easiest to grasp: revenge. For two lives destroyed, Brian Somerville's and her own.

Leslie looked at the small dark-skinned woman with her smooth black hair flecked with much grey, and with her big brown eyes, which revealed a little of how pretty she must have once been. She did not look like someone who would hesitate and let herself be eaten up inside by hate and a need for satisfaction. But was that something you could always recognise in someone? Or was it not often surprising how harmless and even inconspicuous dangerous criminals and unpredictable psychopaths could appear on photos?

There was one burning question Leslie had to ask. She leant forward. 'Semira, excuse me for asking, but I need to know something… Did you ever call my grandmother? Although she refused to have any contact to you? Did you call and just…not say anything?'

'You mean, have I ever harassed her with anonymous calls?' asked Semira. 'Yes, I have. But only in the last week or two. The last time I did was on Tuesday, before I read in the paper that she was dead. Sometimes I felt I was going to explode. The calls allowed me to let off steam. Sometimes when I'd seen Brian Somerville and his wretched life again, or my body was torturing me, or depression had me in its grip again, then I'd think, why should she have it good? Why should she be able to carry on cheerfully without a thought for what she's done? And yes, frankly, it did help to hear her voice asking again and again who was on the other end of the phone. With each question she sounded a little more frantic and shrill. Afterwards I felt a little better, and I'd think: Now I've got you worried, wondering whether the old affair you'd so like to forget has come back to haunt you. After that my day would brighten up.'

'I see,' said Leslie, and she really did understand. Semira Newton's life was full of troubles and hardship. A poor, lonely life. Robin Hood's Bay was an enchanting place, but it was very quiet in the autumn and winter, and she knew that in November and December the fog could sit like lead on the coastline for days, swallowing up all voices and sounds into its dull colourlessness. Then Semira was alone in this crooked old house, making pottery which no one was going to buy until the spring… Or she would be on the bus to Whitby, off to visit a man who was extremely disabled mentally, and who was still waiting for the person who had promised to come over sixty years ago yet would never come. What was her mood like when she returned from these trips to her dark little room?

Leslie shivered to think of it.

She got up. Her limbs were stiff after sitting on the uncomfortable stool for so long.

'I have to go,' she said and held out her hand. 'Thank you for having given me so much time, Semira. And for having been so open.'

'Oh, it's not like I have a whirl of a social life,' replied Semira smiling. The hand that shook Leslie's was as cold as ice. 'Nice to have someone come by. And to be able to talk.'

'I can't undo what my grandmother did,' said Leslie. 'But…I am sorry. I'm deeply sorry about everything that happened.'

'Can't be helped now.' Semira got up with difficulty. 'Nothing you can do about it! I just wonder why all the fuss now. Why suddenly there's so much interest in the old story.'

Leslie, who was about to turn to go, paused.

'What do you mean, so much interest?'

'Well, it's strange. No one wanted to know anything for decades and now two people appear in two days, wanting to know everything.'

Leslie held her breath in surprise. 'Who else?'

'A man...what was his name? He came here late yesterday afternoon. Mr Tanner, I think, something like that.'

'Dave Tanner!'

'That's it. Dave Tanner. A journalist. He already knew a lot. He'd looked through all the old archives, he said. But he hoped to hear some new facts from me. I talked to him for a long time. Of course, it's good for me if the media latch onto the story.'

'What paper was he working for?'

Semira thought about it. 'I'm not quite sure,' she admitted. 'I mean, he did tell me, but I was not really listening. Is it important?'

'And I suppose you didn't ask to see his press ID?'

'No.'

'Dave Tanner isn't a journalist. You mustn't be so trusting, Semira. People aren't always who they say they are. Don't let everyone in. And don't tell people everything you know.'

Semira looked at her in consternation. 'But then who is Dave Tanner?'

Leslie dismissed the question. 'Doesn't matter. What's important is knowing why he came here. But I'll find that out.'

'But you…you told me the truth, didn't you? You are Fiona Barnes' granddaughter, aren't you?'

'Unfortunately I am,' said Leslie, and stepped out into the dark steep street.

She could hear the sea roaring very near to her.

The tide had reached its height.

13

SHE SAT IN the car trying to sort the thoughts racing wildly
through her head. What game was Dave Tanner playing?
She had asked him this morning if the name Semira Newton meant anything to him. With an ingenuous look he had
completely denied that it had.

No. Who's she?

It was now just twelve hours since he had sat with her
in Robin Hood's Bay, asking her all kinds of questions.
And he had apparently already known a good many details, which probably meant that he had also read Fiona's
letters to Chad. Had he got hold of them secretly? Had
Gwen given them to him?

Gwen! Leslie smacked the steering wheel with her
palm. Typical Gwen. To poke around in her father's emails,
find an explosive story which was obviously not meant to
be shared in public, and then to show it to practically everyone she knew.

She was so immature. Not at all grown up.

Don't be unfair, Leslie, she told herself. Gwen couldn't
cope with what she read. She had to speak to someone
about it.

With Dave?

He was after all the man she was going to marry. At
least, that is what she had assumed at that time. Could you
hold it against her that she had shared something with him

which had thrown her into turmoil, played on her mind? The image she had of her father must have been damaged immeasurably.

She had also shown the print-outs to Jennifer. Then Colin had been given them. And Colin had shown them to her, Leslie. It had not taken long for the distribution network to kick in.

She was driving without another car in sight on the main road between Scarborough and Whitby. It was dark and the road was lined with silent woods. The beams of her headlights took in the sides of the road. At one point the eyes of an animal shone in them. She thought it was a fox. She realised how fast she was going and decelerated. No one should die, just because she was so nervous.

When she saw a wide dirt track heading into the woods to the left, she quickly decided to turn onto it and stop. She needed a moment's calm, to think.

She leant back in her seat and breathed deeply. Dave had read the notes, or Gwen had told him what was in them, and then he had wanted to take a closer look for himself and had visited Semira Newton. Just like her. He had lied about who he was. That too was understandable, as he had no way of knowing whether Semira would talk to him if he did not seem to be someone important. It was not a bad idea to present himself as a journalist to a woman who—he could imagine—found it hard to bear the lack of attention people had paid to Brian Somerville's tragedy.

And why did he lie to me?

Because I'm Fiona's granddaughter. Because he could not guess what I do and what I don't know. Because he didn't want to be the person to tell me things about my grandmother's character which would shock me.

She closed her eyes. She saw Semira Newton's face

behind her eyelids. It was slightly bloated, revealing that she had taken far too many medicines for far too long. Her body must have been a wreck when she was found. No doubt some days she feels pain in every bone and muscle of her body. And every movement is torture. She thought of Gordon McBright, the man who had left his half dead victim in the wood like any old rubbish, the man who had died in preventive detention.

Fiona and Chad had handed Brian Somerville over to a man who not even the most well meaning of psychiatrists had later allowed to live in freedom again. She opened her eyes. The images were too horrific to bear.

Two people had a clear motive to kill Fiona Barnes and throw her body into a wooded gorge: Brian Somerville and Semira Newton. One of them must be between seventy and eighty years old, mentally disabled and living in a care home in Whitby. The other one was in her mid-sixties, and could only move with difficulty and the aid of a Zimmer frame.

'Neither one could have done it,' said Leslie out loud in the darkness. But they could have paid someone to do it —at least Semira Newton could have.

Dave Tanner?

But Dave Tanner had only visited Semira the day before. Many days after Fiona had been murdered.

Apart from that: would the Dave Tanner she knew kill for money?

Not the one she knew, if she was honest. She liked him. But she did not know him. For a moment she realised in astonishment that it did not follow that he did not know her.

One thing was transparent to her. It was no longer all right to keep what she knew about what had happened to herself. She had to let Detective Inspector Almond know, as quickly as possible.

Otherwise I'll be guilty, she thought. Again she had the thought that had come to her once before: Chad Beckett could be in great danger.

She turned on the inside light and rummaged around in her handbag. She found DI Almond's card in a side pocket.

The policewoman had given it to her after their first conversation. In case anything occurred to her regarding her grandmother's murder, however trivial it might seem…

'And what I have for you, Inspector, is not at all trivial,' she murmured to herself.

She keyed the number into her mobile. Reception was not great out here in the wood, but she had a couple of bars. DI Almond answered after the fourth ring. She sounded out of breath. 'Yes?'

'Inspector? Leslie Cramer here.'

'Dr Cramer! I wanted to call you this evening.'

In the background Leslie could hear car horns, the sounds of engines and voices. Valerie Almond seemed to be walking through town.

'I have to speak to you urgently, Inspector,' said Leslie. 'It's about my grandmother's murder.'

'Where are you right now?'

'I'm on my way back from Robin Hood's Bay, near Staintondale now. I could be in Scarborough in twenty minutes.'

'I'm just on the way to a pizza place,' said Valerie, adding with a little embarrassment. 'I haven't eaten yet today. Do you want to meet me there? In Huntriss Row.'

'Yes, of course. I know where it is.'

'By the way,' said Valerie. 'Did you know we have a suspect for the Mills case? Did Mrs Brankley tell you?'

She remembered Chad's rather confused description that morning. 'I heard from Chad Beckett, yes.'

'The investigation is tricky, but we can already exclude the possibility that the suspect is Fiona Barnes' murderer. He has an alibi for the time.'

This did not surprise Leslie overly.

'Inspector, reception is bad here, I'll be there soon and—'

'One more thing,' interrupted Valerie. 'Do you know where Dave Tanner could be?'

She could have answered: *Yes, this morning he was at the Beckett farm and if you don't find him there, then he's probably already in my grandmother's flat.*

Instead she just asked cautiously, 'Why?' Perhaps she felt a kind of loyalty to him, but she was also loathe let the policewoman know that Tanner had found temporary accommodation with her. It could have looked compromising.

'We've got a warrant out to find him,' explained Valerie. 'His statements about where and how he spent Saturday night were false. We have to talk to him urgently.'

For a moment Leslie could not reply. Her mouth felt dry and she tried to swallow.

'Can you hear me?' asked Valerie.

'Yes, yes, I heard you. But it's difficult…I'll be right there, Inspector.' With that she turned her mobile off and put it back in her bag.

She could feel her heart beating wildly.

She knew the story he had dished up for Valerie Almond. It was the one he had told her that morning: the night of love with his ex. It was a story which everyone would understand why he had hidden until then, as it put his relationship to Gwen at risk. Only when the situation had got difficult for him did he pull the ace out of his sleeve. And now what? Was his ex refusing to play ball? Something must have happened that meant Valerie no longer believed him. And had even put out a warrant.

He had lied again. He had lied when she had asked him about Semira. He had lied about where he had been at the time of the crime. He had lied at the start when he claimed to have spent the whole night peacefully in his bed.

He lied whenever he opened his mouth.

And she had taken him to the Beckett farm. Had left him there alone with Chad Beckett, the man whom a few minutes ago she had thought might be in real danger. Chad, a slow, old man who was physically no match for Dave Tanner.

She started the engine. The wheels spun on the sandy track as she put her foot down. Then her car shot out onto the road with a screeching of tyres. She gunned the engine to the maximum, driving much faster than the limit. When she came to the small country road that led to Staintondale she did not stay on the main road to Scarborough. She turned off. She had to be sure.

Detective Inspector Almond would have to wait a little longer.

14

THE FIRST THING she noticed was that the Brankleys' car was still not in the yard, just like at lunchtime. Could it be that Jennifer and Gwen still had not returned from town? It was just after seven now. What on earth had they spent the whole day doing?

She parked and got out.

There was not a single noise and she asked herself why the silence annoyed her, until she realised that she had been used to the barking of the dogs over the last few days. Jennifer's Great Danes. They always made a racket when someone arrived at the farm. They had not at lunchtime because Colin had been out walking with them. Was he out walking with them now too?

In the dark?

She could not see any lights on in the house, although of course she could not see the back windows from the yard. She knocked on the door, out of habit, and then stepped inside.

She turned on the light.

Somehow the house seemed strangely deserted to her. As if no one in it were breathing, and no heart beating.

The dogs, she thought. It's really the dogs which are missing. When you expect two giant, lively Great Danes to jump up and try to lick your face, then of course you feel like you've entered a mausoleum when they're no longer there.

She asked herself why she had thought of a mausoleum just then, but quickly brushed aside the thought. She could not get carried away dreaming up horrors now.

'Dave?' she called. Her voice sounded far too quiet. She cleared her throat.

'Dave?' she called more loudly. 'Chad?'

Nothing and no one could be heard. She walked down the hall, peeked into the kitchen, and turned its light on. Empty. A mess. As chaotic and dirty as usual. It did not look as if someone had prepared dinner.

The living room next to it was empty too. The smell of burnt wood revealed to Leslie that a fire had burnt in the grate earlier. She saw that a few of the embers were still glowing. Then she found two empty cups on the table and she found that somehow calming. Two cups of coffee and a fire—that suggested a normal atmosphere, something which the last few hours had taken her far away from.

She went out of the living room and noticed the light coming from under the bottom of the study door. She breathed out contentedly. Someone was home.

She knocked and went in. Relief coursed through her veins as she saw Chad sitting at the desk, staring at the monitor. It was icy cold in the room, but the old man did not seem to notice the cold, even though he sat in a much too thin cotton shirt and had no socks on his feet, just a pair of open slippers. He was so focused on the computer screen that he jumped when Leslie spoke to him. 'Chad?'

He seemed to return from another world. He stared at Leslie with incomprehension and then only said, after a few seconds' silence, 'Oh, you, Leslie.'

'I'm sorry I gave you a fright. I called and knocked, but...'

'I were far away,' said Chad.

She could not see what he was reading, but she could guess. 'Fiona's letters?'

'I read them again,' said Chad. 'Before I delete them. It wouldn't be good if...other people read them.'

She stopped herself from telling him that everyone around him already knew everything in them.

'I visited Semira Newton today,' she said, looking at his face as she said her name. It was as if a mask went up immediately.

'Oh, aye?'

'A woman who has suffered a great deal.'

'Aye,' he said.

'Did you know that Brian Somerville is still alive?'

'I reckoned so.'

'Don't you think you could...I mean, I could drive you...'

'No.'

She looked at him. He did not avoid her gaze, but he was distant.

'Are you all on your own?' she asked after they had just looked at each other for a moment. 'Where are Jennifer and Colin? Where's Dave? Gwen?'

'Jennifer and Colin took off. Mighty sudden. This afternoon.'

'Why?'

'Probably weren't exactly the holidays they'd 'oped for. Understandably.'

'Does DI Almond know?'

'No idea.'

'And Dave?'

'They wanted to go for a walk. He and Gwen.'

'It's already pretty dark outside!'

He looked out of the window. He seemed to only now realise that night had fallen. 'True,' he said in surprise. 'How late is it?'

'Quarter past seven.'

'Oh, already?' He rubbed his face with one hand. He had red eyes from tiredness and the strain of reading. 'Then they've been away ages. I think it were 'bout half-five when they set out.'

'That's almost two hours ago. Was everything fine, between them?' She wondered whether Dave had done it: told Gwen he would break it off. Or had he kept the news for the walk? Or had he backtracked from the plan?

'I don't know,' said Chad, unsure. 'I think…well, what weren't to be fine?'

She looked at him and thought, Gwen could die before your eyes and you wouldn't notice. You don't understand that her life is a mess, because to you your daughter is not even worth spending a moment's thought on. You were not even interested in getting to know the man she wanted to spend the rest of her life with. The man who might be—in every way—very dangerous for her. You don't notice. You never notice anything! You never deserved the love she has showed you all her life, a daughter's crazy love for you, her father and—after her mother's early death—her only living relative.

'Chad, you told me at lunchtime that the police had been here asking about Dave Tanner. Now I know that there's a warrant out on him. He doesn't have an alibi for the time when my grandmother died. He lied to the police.'

Chad just looked at her. His lethargy drove Leslie to a fury.

'Chad! The police are looking for him! They came here too! And you let him just wander off with your daughter and two hours later you aren't even asking if everything is fine?'

'But what reason is there to suspect Tanner?' asked Chad.

Now she did not hold back. 'His lies. For one thing. That's what the police know. And something else that only I know. Dave Tanner knows the whole story about you and Fiona. And Brian Somerville and Semira Newton. He knows everything that's in your computer.'

At least now she had managed to pierce his indifference. He seemed irritated.

'How? Have you given it him to read? Or Fiona?'

'That's not the point now. He's been to see Semira Newton. He seems to be taking great interest in the whole story.'

She could guess that similar thoughts were swirling around in his head as in hers. She could also see that he immediately brushed them aside as *ravings*. 'What reason'd Tanner 'ave to dig up this old stuff?'

'He's clever,' said Leslie. 'And he needs money. Urgently. Maybe he doesn't care how he gets hold of the money.'

'You think he killed yer gran and was paid by Newton to do it?' asked Chad.

'He only went to see her yesterday. So that theory doesn't seem to tie in with the actual timing. But maybe there's an explanation. I don't know what to think any more, Chad. One thing's for sure. The guy who most probably killed Amy Mills is not Fiona's killer. Valerie Almond said he has an alibi. Unlike Dave. His was a lie.'

'Then call t' police now,' said Chad. 'Tell them to come here, look for Dave an' Gwen an' do summat.'

She weighed up the options briefly and then shook her head. 'I'm going to go outside first and look around. If I don't come back in half an hour, call Detective Inspector Almond, OK?' She pulled the inspector's card out of her bag and handed it to Chad. 'Here you go, her number. And be careful. You'd better lock the doors.'

'Why should I—'

'Because,' she snapped, 'you're in danger if this is about revenge! That's why! Like Fiona, you're certainly not as innocent as a lamb, accept it!'

He pulled a face in annoyance, but she had the impression he was acting calmer than he was. He did not like the situation either, although in his case it was probably not out of fear. He did not enjoy being roused from the lethargy and self-absorption of his own world. Under a week had passed since Fiona's murder and in that time he had been obliged to talk to more people than he had in the last ten years. Something new was always happening. Someone was always wanting something from him. He must feel harassed and cornered. He was an old man who had no wish to change his way of life, let alone have his lifelong friend murdered on a meadow, his own life in danger, and his daughter off in the dark with a shady character. Leslie could see that her request to wait half an hour before calling the police already seemed unreasonable to Chad. He lived in his own routine and had decided decades ago not to let himself be diverted from it. His father must have had a similar bent, and perhaps Chad could not help his almost autistic way of dealing with things. It was what he had grown up with.

It would have been a miracle if he had taken care of Brian Somerville, thought Leslie. He doesn't do that kind of thing. He can't put himself in other people's shoes enough to do anything for them. 'Do you have a torch I could borrow?' she asked.

He got up, lumbered into the hall and took a torch from a shelf full of dusty scarves, hats and gloves.

'Here. This one must still work.'

Luckily he was right. The batteries still had juice.

'Right,' said Leslie. 'Then I'll have a look on the farm and round about. And like I said: lock the doors!'

He growled something or other but after she had stepped out, she could hear him turn the locks behind her.

Something wasn't right. As she followed her beam of light over the yard and towards the former stables, she asked herself why she had not called Valerie Almond immediately. The policewoman was now sitting in the pizzeria and would soon start to worry what was keeping Leslie. Wouldn't it have been better to tell her immediately? Just as it would have been right to give her a straight answer about Dave Tanner. So why didn't she?

She knew the answer, and that it would not sound convincing to anyone, perhaps not even herself: because she liked Dave Tanner. Because she considered him a friend, at least since the night before. Although he had lied to her twice. She did not want to denounce him. She wanted to talk to him, and ask why he was incapable at any point in this messy affair of trying to be truthful. And ask him to go to the police of his own accord.

Of course he'll do that if he's Fiona's murderer, she thought. Maybe Gwen was in extreme danger, while she was wasting valuable time here.

Just another half hour, maximum, she resolved.

She had reached the stables. She shone the torch inside. It was empty, except for the piles of slowly rusting junk.

No one was about, nor did it look like anyone had been. There were no footprints in the years-old dust and dirt.

Leslie had to cough. Then she turned away. She looked back at the house. The light was out again. Chad had probably withdrawn to his study to delete Fiona's letters in the mistaken belief that he could delete the guilt from his life. Just a click of the mouse and everything was sorted.

After a second's deliberation, Leslie decided to widen her search beyond the immediate environs of the farm.

She struck out towards the beach.

15

THE CLOUDS BLOCKED out the moon's light, but the torch Chad had lent her shone brightly. Leslie could walk along the well-trodden path without difficulty. She knew that Gwen loved the beach and that she went there whenever she went walking. Perhaps she and Dave were still down there, squatting on the large rocks and talking. Although it was rather cold now. Maybe they were wrapped up warmly. Maybe they were so engrossed in their conversation that they did not notice the cold and the unpleasant clamminess.

At one point Leslie stopped, got out her phone and lit the display. There was no reception, as she had expected. Never mind. Another ten minutes, then the half hour would be up and Chad would call Valerie. The police would swing into action. So she had given Dave a chance of thirty minutes. Anything more would have been irresponsible.

She did not meet anyone as she raced over the hilly meadows. Once some grouse flew up from a bush, but apart from that it felt like she was all alone in the world. What was to say that Gwen and Dave were still anywhere near the farm? Chad's car had been in its usual space, but the two could also have taken the bus. Maybe they had driven to Scarborough, found a pub and were now each nursing a pint of Guinness to get through the terrible time. But would Dave really do that if he were trying to break off the engagement? Would he take the unhappy fiancée into town, seeing as he would then have to bring her home again? And then she had another thought: what if Dave had been back in her place, Fiona's flat, for ages? And Gwen was wandering around out here, alone, despairing of life, at her wits end and deeply hurt? Leslie cursed quietly that she had not thought of calling Fiona's flat to check. She flipped open her mobile without any great hope, and indeed: no reception.

She crossed the wooden suspension bridge. It seemed to be wobbling more scarily than usual, but she knew she was just imagining it. It was because of the gaping black hole below her and the darkness which made the gorge look like it went down forever. In spite of the torch, what she was doing was still dangerous. The bridge's planks were not even and predictable. The gorge was deep and rocky. And she had not been here for a long time, so although she had a rough idea of the lie of the land, she did not have the sleepwalker's certainty she had once had here when she was a child. Back then she had visited the Beckett farm almost every day with her grandmother, and had played in the gorge and on the beach with Gwen, while Fiona…well, did what exactly? What had Fiona and Chad and Chad's wife done all those long hours? As a child she had never asked herself that. She had just taken as normal the fact that she and her grandmother spent more time with another family than at home. Later the topic had not interested her any more. And now she would probably never be given an answer. Chad's wife had been dead a long time. Fiona was dead now too. And Chad was not the kind of person to ever give an answer.

She had reached the end of the hanging bridge. Now the descent into the gorge began. She remembered how she used to spring down like a mountain goat. Now she moved more like an old woman, cautiously and laboriously. Had it been this steep back then? Had the rocks, which made a kind of ladder, been so far apart that you could not step from one to another with a single step but had to lower yourself carefully from one to the next? In the end she sat down and slid on her backside to the bottom, using both her hands to help her down. Not the easiest thing to do while holding a torch. At one point it slipped out of her hand. Luckily it fell only to the next rock step. Trembling with the shock, she tried to calm herself down. She sat down and thought about everything. What she was doing here was crazy. She did not have the faintest idea if there was any point to it at all. If she lost the torch, she would scarcely have a hope of finding her way back, at least not without putting herself in serious danger of spraining her ankle, or even breaking it.

Leslie decided she had better go back.

The police might already be at the farm. If not, then the officers would turn up any minute. They should continue the search. They were equipped for it.

She started the climb back up. It was extremely difficult, as she only had one hand free. She was breathing heavily and bathed in sweat when she reached the bridge. A glance at her watch told her that almost an hour had passed since she had set off from the farm. She had lost loads of time with the climb.

She walked faster across the bridge than she had before, as if she had got used to its swaying and to the apparently endless chasm below her. In reality it was fear that drove her on, a fear that had grown stronger because the images in her head were becoming more frightening and insistent. There were only two possibilities, and both were horrific. Either Dave Tanner was behind the crime against Fiona and had now disappeared with Gwen. In that case things did not look good for Gwen. Or he had not done anything evil—*in which case why the constant lies?*—and he had returned to Scarborough after breaking off the engagement. That would mean that Gwen was wandering around outside in the night, despairing and alone, perhaps tempted to something terrible. Leslie could not tell whether Gwen was the kind of person who could entertain the thought of ending her life. But she knew that the end of a love relationship, with feelings getting hurt, was one of the most common reasons for suicide. And who really knew what Gwen was thinking? Who ever had?

She made progress more quickly across the meadows. If she had hurried before, now she was running. She heard the thud of her steps on the ground and her own panting breath. She was horribly out of shape, she knew that, and although it was irrelevant right now, she resolved to go jogging regularly. The idea surprised her, but she told herself it was perhaps quite normal to latch onto something banal when fear was threatening to turn to panic. She wondered whether her jogging bottoms were still somewhere in her cupboard. The thought offered her some relief. Everything else she could have thought about concealed horrors.

She stopped when she saw the farm below the hill she was standing on. It was dark, completely dark. She could dimly make out the farmhouse roof, and beside it the roofs of the stable buildings and the shed. Nothing was moving down there. Where were the police? Cars, headlights, torchlight moving this way and that, spotlights, a voice roaring over a megaphone…

God, Leslie, did you seriously believe they would send a squad out here just because Chad calls Valerie Almond

and says that his daughter and her fiancé disappeared a
couple of hours ago?

But there was a warrant out for the fiancé. One officer,
at the least, should have turned up. Maybe Valerie herself,
especially as she was waiting for Leslie to meet her. Was
she taking her time over her pizza before getting into her
car and roaring out to Staintondale?

Leslie ran down the hill, through the gate and into the
yard. She could see the dark shadow of her car parked near
the drive, and Chad's Land Rover much further on. Apart
from those two there were no others. Neither the police,
nor Valerie Almond or anyone else.

Perhaps Chad had called later than agreed. Or he had
not called at all and instead, as soon as Leslie went out the
door, had forgotten what he had been asked to do. That
would be just like him.

She ran to the front door. Threw it open. Why wasn't
it locked any more? She herself had heard Chad turn the
key in the lock. 'Chad?'

No answer. The hall was dark and empty.

She had left the light on when she left. She knew that.
But perhaps Chad in his economising way had turned it
off.

She turned it on, and walked down the hall. The door
to Chad's study was ajar. Cautiously she opened it and
peeked in. Empty. The desk lamp was on, the computer
too. She could hear its quiet hum.

'Chad?' she asked again.

She went into the kitchen, turned on the light. The light
should be on. She felt a little safer if the house was not
completely dark.

Why wasn't Chad answering?

Something was wrong. Chad did not just leave the computer and lamp on and go to bed. Chad was so thrifty it could drive you mad. He must be around here somewhere nearby, and there was no reason for him to hide from her.

'Chad?' she called out again, realising that her voice sounded almost fearful.

She stepped into the living room, turning the light on there too—and saw Chad lying on the floor in the middle of the room. He was on his stomach, his head turned to one side so that she could see his chalk-white face. His eyes were closed and his arms were down by his sides.

She stared at him. For a moment she was too shocked to do anything. Snapping out of it, she rushed to him. She knelt down and felt his pulse, an automatic reflex. It was very weak, but at least it was still there. She carefully turned him to face her.

'Chad! What happened?'

His eyelids flickered. Leslie felt that she had put her hand in something warm and sticky. She lifted her right hand. It was red with blood, and now she could see the blood on the floor too. It had spread over the stones and trickled into the cracks. Chad's thin blue shirt was soaked in blood. As far as Leslie could see, the bleeding had stopped now, so there was no need for her to provide first aid assistance for that. She guessed it was a knife or bullet wound. In other words, he had been attacked after she had left him.

Whoever had done it might still be nearby.

She forced herself not to react hysterically and run for her car. She had to call an ambulance and the police, and she could not leave Chad alone. His condition was critical. He had lost a lot of blood and she had no idea what his internal injuries were.

She touched his cheek softly. 'Chad! It's me. Leslie. Chad, what happened?'

His eyelids began to flicker again, and this time he managed to open his eyes. His eyes were cloudy and wandered unsteadily. He was in shock. 'Leslie,' he whispered.

She held his head in her lap. 'It'll be all right, Chad. I'll get help. We'll get you to a hospital…'

He focused on her. 'Dave,' he whispered. He was finding it extremely difficult to speak. 'Dave…he…'

'Yes, Chad, you…'

'He…is…still…' His gaze went cloudy again and although he seemed to want to say more, his tongue refused to cooperate. He could only babble incoherently.

But Leslie had understood what he wanted to say. Dave Tanner was here. He was still somewhere on the farm. He had given Chad life-threatening injuries and now he was probably looking for her. Her car was parked in plain sight in the farmyard. He knew she was there. He knew how dangerous she could be to him.

Had he searched the house for her and was now outside, a silent shadow moving between the shed and stables, perhaps with a torch to shine in hidden corners, guessing that she was trying to hide from him? Or was he still in the house? Upstairs perhaps, in one of the bedrooms?

She knew that you could barely move upstairs without making the floorboards creak. It was almost impossible to creep silently through the rooms. She listened out, but could only hear the roar of blood in her ears.

She had to do the right thing now. She could not take any risks.

She lowered Chad's head to the floor carefully, stood up and shot to the door of the room. She closed it and turned the key, then leant against it with a sigh of relief. A little bit of security, a chance to win some time. She had no doubt that Dave could break down the old door. But it would take him some minutes. Minutes which could be the difference between life and death.

She turned the light out. If Dave was creeping around out there, she did not want to present herself to him on a plate. Especially as he might be in possession of a gun.

She got out her phone. No reception. Reception in Staintondale and the Beckett farm in particular could drive you crazy. She tried another corner of the room. No luck. It was not even better near the window. She knew that she might be in luck if she left the farm and headed towards the main road. But that would have meant running the risk of an encounter with Dave. He was somewhere around here. He had tried to kill one person and he would not just stand by and let her phone the police. She tried Valerie's number, but as expected it did not ring. She was about to throw the useless thing across the room, but she controlled herself just in time. Who knew when she would need it.

Her eyes had accustomed themselves to the dark. She could see Chad, as a shadow, lying on the floor. He was completely immobile, possibly unconscious. If he was not helped soon, things did not look good for him. Although she was a doctor, she could do almost nothing for him here. Even getting him into a more comfortable position on the sofa seemed too dangerous to her, as she did not know what injuries he had sustained. And she had nothing there, not even a bandage. Only a phone with no reception. And somewhere outside a madman was lurking and would stop her from getting help. Why was he doing that? Why Chad? Why—most probably—Fiona too? Was he really working for Semira Newton, who in turn was looking to satisfy her desire for revenge (in spite of her claim that she had no wish to spare Fiona the troubles of old age)? Or had Dave killed Fiona on his own initiative, and had then suggested to Semira yesterday that he could also give Chad the punishment he deserved? Or was what Semira had said not true, perhaps Dave had visited her much earlier? Perhaps the whole story of his presenting himself as a journalist was not true? Were Dave and the old lady from Robin Hood's Bay a much more sophisticated and cunning pair than Leslie had imagined? But then why had Semira said that he had visited her? It would have been more logical for her not to tell anyone.

And what if Semira was not behind it? What if Dave had done it on his own? Leslie looked at Chad, who was not moving. He was the man who stood between Dave's desire to own the farm and the fulfilment of that desire. Was that the key? Dave was ready to marry a woman who meant nothing to him in order to have better prospects for his future. Yet the property would only be available to him when his father-in-law had kicked the bucket. Had he not wanted to wait? Had he murdered Fiona, so that she could not ruin his plans with her sharp tongue, and Chad, so that his future path was smoothed immediately? But where on earth did Gwen fit into the story? It was unlikely that he had shot her dear father in front of her eyes. On the other hand, he could not do anything to Gwen herself, because he needed her and their marriage in order to get what he wanted.

Where was Gwen?

Not the moment to think about it, she decided. Not the moment to solve the mystery.

She had to phone. That was the next and absolutely necessary step. Nothing else.

The landline was in the study. The question was whether

she could risk leaving the living room, where she felt more or less safe for the moment, to rush across the hall and barricade herself into the study to make the call. If she encountered Dave she would be lost. She had no illusions: he could not let her live. She represented the greatest danger to him. He had to eliminate her. She had no doubt that he would do it without hesitation. Even if she had not managed to suss out his motives, she was sure that he was playing for high stakes. He had probably planned his actions well in advance and thought of all the possible consequences. Whatever he was getting out of it, he would not let it be snatched away in the home straight. He was dangerous, cruel and amoral. His continuous lies were only the tip of the iceberg. Leslie's alternative was to stay in the room and hope that help would arrive—but she had no idea when that would be, if ever. What would Valerie Almond do when Leslie did not turn up as agreed in the pizzeria? She would probably try to reach her by phone, and that would not work. Maybe she would drive to the Prince of Wales Terrace and ring her bell like crazy, and no one would open the door. Would she be worried? And would she think to drive to the Beckett farm?

The Brankleys had gone. She had no idea where Gwen was. So there was little hope of help. And very little chance that Chad would survive. Even if Leslie had not been a doctor she would have seen that Chad did not have much longer to live. He would not survive the night if he were not taken to a hospital as soon as possible.

She crept to the door and silently turned the key, then slowly opened the door with bated breath. She had almost expected to see Dave standing in front of her, but the hall was bright and empty. She could still not hear any noise anywhere.

He's either outside, or he's standing around somewhere in here, holding his breath and waiting for me to make a mistake.

Her heart was beating like crazy. And the blood was pounding in her ears. She had not known until now what real fear was. She knew the fear of an exam, of being alone, of an unpleasant conversation, a visit to the dentist, of divorce proceedings. A thousand fears, but what she felt now was a fear of death. That was new. Leslie had never experienced it before. In those moments she came to know this extremely physical fear: she kept breaking out in a sweat, on her whole body. She had a buzzing in her ears. Her mouth was completely dry. She could not swallow. Yet she still felt her way bravely along the hall. As in the living room, there was a stone floor here. She managed not to make the slightest sound.

Just a few yards, perhaps three or four. They seemed infinite to Leslie, and the minute it took Leslie to cross them seemed an eternity. Each second she expected a hand to rest on her shoulder or a voice to speak at her. But nothing happened. Nothing broke the silence.

She reached the study and slipped inside. Nothing had changed. The lamp on the desk was still on. The computer was humming.

She closed the door quickly and froze, realising there was no key in the lock.

Gathering all her courage, she opened the door once more and looked on the outside. But there was no key there either. She was sure the study had one normally. Never mind, she had no choice but to make the call here with the door unlocked—as quickly as she could, praying no one would find her. She picked up the phone.

'I wouldn't do that,' said a voice behind her. 'I'd put the phone down now and slowly turn around.'

Leslie started to shake with fear, horror and surprise.

She turned around, her eyes open wide in astonishment.

Gwen was standing in the door.

She was holding a revolver in her hands and aiming it at her friend. Her hands were steady.

The expression on her face was that of a madwoman.

16

NICE TO BE home again, thought Jennifer. The house smelt a little strange after their two-week absence, but Jennifer opened all the windows and let fresh, autumn air flood the rooms. Colin was working his way through a mountain of post, which their neighbour had conscientiously fetched from the letterbox and put in a pile on their dining room table. Cal and Wotan had been given their evening meal and had now happily occupied the corner of the living room where their blankets lay. The television was on quietly in the background.

What am I doing tomorrow? wondered Jennifer. She was standing in the open door to the kitchen and looking out at the dark garden, which smelt of autumn leaves, dying grass and the damp. She liked autumn. She loved its dusky afternoons, early evenings and all the things that heralded the approach of the Christmas period. Going for long walks with Cal and Wotan over misty fields, returning to a warm house with a crackling fire and candles in the windows. The inner warmth that the atmosphere created had always done her good. But there needed to be something more in her life. She needed communication with other people, its stress and irritations, but also the happy moments which arose with other people. What she needed was to take part in life. That was what she should look for.

So—a job. That was the first thing. That was the

starting point for everything else. She would look in the papers. Maybe even put in an ad herself. After all, she was a teacher. She had studied English and Modern Languages. So she could offer private tuition. And perhaps she could teach an adult education course like the ones on offer in Friarage School. She would enjoy teaching a French class two or three evenings a week. Maybe she would even make new friends.

Thinking of Friarage School made her think of Dave Tanner. On the drive back to Leeds from Staintondale there had been something at the back of her mind, some question, but she was so absorbed in her plans for the future that she had not tried to tease it out.

Now she remembered the images of yesterday afternoon. Dave Tanner had been sitting in the living room with Colin when she and Gwen returned from town. They had exchanged a few banalities and then Jennifer had hurried upstairs. She had wanted to be on her own, with Colin, to tell him about her thoughts and plans. Nothing else had interested her.

She closed the kitchen door and walked over to the dining room where Colin was studying some official letter with a frown.

'The contributions for our pensions—' he began, but she interrupted him.

'Colin, why did Tanner come to the farm today? He seemed so self-absorbed when the two of you were sitting by the fire…'

'The boy's finally come to his senses,' said Colin without looking up from the letter in his hands. 'I mean, that idea of marrying Gwen…no one liked it, and no one had a good feeling about it.'

Jennifer could feel the hairs rising on her arms before she knew why. 'And?' she asked.

'He wanted to tell her,' said Colin. 'And of course he felt pretty uneasy about it, the poor guy. Well, I came along at the right time, to help pass the time.'

'What?' said Jennifer. 'What was he going to tell her? And who is "her"? Gwen?'

'Of course Gwen. Who else,' replied Colin, finally glancing up. 'He wanted to tell her that the idea of a future together no longer made any sense to him, and that it would be better if they would go their separate ways. Something like that. I think it's only sensible. She never was his great passion, and she had just created a fantasy which would never have stood the test of reality.'

The tingling on Jennifer's arms could not be ignored. 'God,' she said quietly.

'Better a horrible end than a horror without end,' suggested Colin. 'It's hard for Gwen, but don't you think she's already had an inkling for a while? She's not insensitive. I can hardly imagine that all of this will come out of the blue.'

'But the decisive moment is always...' She did not say anything else. The fear rising up in her threatened to overpower her.

Keep calm, she told herself. Maybe you're just seeing things.

'I think I should give Gwen a call,' she said.

Colin did not think so. 'She has to get through this on her own. You can't do everything for her.'

'In a situation like this we all need someone,' replied Jennifer. She took the cordless phone off its dock on the dining table and dialled the number of the Beckett farm. She waited nervously. No one answered.

She tried again. Still no answer.

'Strange. They must be there. Chad at least. And Gwen too, actually.'

'You know Chad. He's a loner. He might not feel like answering the phone right now. And Gwen is probably bawling her eyes out.'

'She could still answer the phone.'

'She'll get by without you. She has to. After all, there's nothing you can do for her.'

'I've got a very bad feeling.'

'She's not going to commit suicide, not Gwen. She might be a fragile creature, but she has good, down-to-earth farming blood in her veins. She'll cope.'

'I wish I was there,' said Jennifer uneasily.

'Why?'

'So I could be sure that everything was all right.'

'And what wouldn't be all right?'

She stared past him out of the open window. 'If Dave told her that he was breaking it off—'

'—then life goes on somehow for Gwen,' said Colin impatiently. 'Jennifer, all of us have had to come to terms with a situation like that sometime. You think the world's collapsing and then afterwards you realise that it goes on as reliably and stably as ever. Gwen will see that.'

She still was not looking at him. 'I'm not worried about Gwen,' she said in the end.

Colin frowned. 'Who then?'

She turned to look at him. He saw that she was as pale as a corpse.

'I'm worried about Dave Tanner,' she said.

17

THE PHONE HAD rung a number of times. Relexively, Leslie's
hand went to pick up the phone, but Gwen's voice had cut
in on her action. 'No! Leave it! No one's in!'

They were standing facing one another in the little
room. Leslie was by the desk and Gwen in the doorway.
The lamp was on, the computer still hummed. It could have
been an absolutely normal situation: two women meeting
in a study at the end of the day. If one of the women had
not been aiming a revolver at the other.

This is a nightmare, thought Leslie, an absurd nightmare.

She tried to understand what on earth was going on, but
she felt like someone who had lost the thread of a conversation and is suddenly faced by a phrase that is completely
unintelligible to them. It was as if Gwen, the Gwen holding the revolver, had suddenly dropped into the scene from
the heavens. Someone, an invisible director, should shout
Stop! The plot had escaped him and now it was high time
to try to wrest control of it again. But no one called *Stop!*
No one stepped in. Leslie was faced with trying to make
sense of what was happening on her own.

'Gwen, what is it?' she had asked after the first horrific
seconds, and Gwen had smiled.

'What do you think it is? I'm taking my life into my

own hands. I'm doing what all of you have always told me to do.'

'What we told you to do?'

'Why are you hanging around here, anyway?' Gwen had asked. 'Looking for Dave? You like him, don't you? Attractive man. You thought you could get him to bed with you, now that he doesn't want me, did you? There's been an empty space next to you for ages!'

At that point Leslie had still not understood. The mention of Dave made her recall the words Chad had stammered out.

'Gwen, your father warned me about Dave. He's dangerous. He's almost killed him. He…' She stopped then, because realisation started to dawn.

'Did *you* shoot your father?' she asked instead.

Gwen smiled again, a strange smile which contained no happiness. 'Clever, Leslie! You always were clever. Leslie, our super-clever girl! You've got it in one! I shot my Dad. And if he said anything about Dave, then he was probably wanting to let you know that he could do with your help. He's down in our bay. Shot. It'll be dicey for him when the tide comes in the morning. But that's not my problem.'

The phone rang before Leslie could answer. By then she had been cured of all doubt that Gwen would make use of her gun, so she obeyed her former friend's order and left it. When the phone began to ring again after a few seconds' silence, Leslie's fingers stayed absolutely still.

'Well, the question is, what am I to do with you?' wondered Gwen. 'Pretty stupid of you to come here, Leslie. Oh yes, we haven't got to the bottom of that, have we. It was because of Dave, wasn't it?'

'Not in the way you think. I thought Dave had done it. That he had murdered my grandmother. And I feared for

Chad. I thought that Brian Somerville could be the motive. For him and Semira Newton. So Chad would be in danger too.' She looked carefully at Gwen as she mentioned the two names, but Gwen's smile was frozen onto her face.

'Charming,' she said. 'Taking such care of good Chad! Did he give you Fiona's emails? Or Jennifer?'

'Colin did. He gave them to me.'

'I managed to get the story round,' said Gwen smugly. 'I thought somehow that it would spread if I told Jennifer. The story will reach the police too. And then it'll be clear who killed Fiona and Chad.'

'Semira Newton?' asked Leslie. 'Who can barely move even with her Zimmer frame? Or perhaps Brian Somerville? From what I've heard he's gormlessly heading towards eighty in a care home, with the mental age of a preschooler. You seriously think you could hang two murders on them? And you expect someone to believe you?'

'Ever heard of contract killings?'

'Yes. But only Semira would have the intelligence to do that. And apart from the fact that she barely has enough money to live on, and so you'd wonder how she could pay the unknown killer, she's just not the type. No way. Valerie Almond would quickly see that too.'

'Oh, Valerie Almond,' said Gwen scornfully. 'She's simple-minded. She has no idea of psychology. She got the wrong idea about me too.'

Like all of us, thought Leslie, shivering involuntarily. Out loud she said, 'And how does Dave fit in? Shot or drunk, however he'll be found. And me? If you plan to bump me off too. How do I fit your theory about an old lady's belated acts of revenge?'

Gwen appeared for a moment to be unsure of herself,

but then quickly pulled herself together. 'You two got in the murderer's way.'

'Dave down in the bay and me here? Gwen, you…you're going postal. This isn't going to end well for you like this, believe me.'

'This isn't going to end well for *you*,' replied Gwen. 'That's how you should see things, my dear.'

'I find that hard to believe,' said Leslie, although she was not sure if she should believe herself. 'We've always been friends, Gwen. We've known each other since we were little. You wouldn't just go and shoot me.'

'I know my Dad longer than I've known you,' replied Gwen, 'and Fiona. Didn't bother me. Not at all.'

Leslie gulped. 'Why, Gwen? I just don't understand—why?'

'Of course you can't understand. How should you? Your life has been a dream. You have no idea how people feel who don't have it as good as you!'

'My life has been a dream?' asked Leslie amazed. 'How can you say that? I'm divorced, lonely and frustrated. I spend my weekends on call or with too much alcohol in front of the telly. No one cares about me. My work colleagues and my old university friends, who I regularly call up to try to arrange to meet up, are all busy with their family life and have no time for me. That's what my dream life looks like, Gwen. Nothing else.'

'You could change it at any time.'

'How?'

'Men are queuing up for you. It didn't work with Stephen, so marry the next guy. It's not a problem for you.'

'I'm afraid I haven't noticed the queue yet.'

'Because you don't want to see it!' Gwen fumbled

around impatiently with her gun. 'Dave, for example. He had the hots for you. And don't tell me you hadn't noticed!'

Leslie was forcibly reminded of the night before in her grandmother's kitchen. She did not reply, but Gwen might have seen some change in her expression, because Gwen laughed triumphantly. 'Well then. You know exactly what I mean. And he's not the only one. And Stephen would practically kill himself to put himself back in your good graces. You'd just have to snap your fingers. You have a number of directions open to you, and whenever you come out of that paralysis which Stephen's little unscheduled screw has put you in, then you'll walk off happily into the sunset.' She paused, and glanced at her gun. 'That is, you could have. But of course it's all going to be different now.'

'You need help, Gwen.'

Gwen laughed once more, this time it did not sound triumphal. There was something hysterical in it. 'Fantastic, Leslie. Truly fantastic! I need help? In the last minutes of your egocentric and completely self-centred life, you suddenly realise that good old Gwen needs help. Too true. Damn right I do. I need help. I needed help years ago. But none of you cared then.'

'Whenever we saw each other...'

'Which did not happen all that often, did it? Twice a year? Busy Dr Cramer would rarely come from London more often than that to see her grandmother. And yes, each time a duty-bound visit to the Beckett farm. *I'll just come by for a quick coffee, Gwen!* Quick! Always with a time limit so I wouldn't get any idea of asking for more from you than you were ready to give—which was never much. You found the farm boring, and you found me boring! I never had much to say. What should I have told you about? About my struggle not to break down? Of my ef-

forts to get by with my Dad's meagre income? Of my attempts to attract paying holidaymakers and yet only ever
getting Jennifer and Colin, who I could no longer bear to
see, but who I had to pamper so they didn't leave too? Riv-
eting stuff, isn't it?'

'You could have just said the truth. That you weren't
doing well. That you needed help.'

'Couldn't you see that? Did you seriously believe that I
could be happy with the life I led? Here at the back of beyond? With my aging Dad who barely speaks? And then
with your overbearing grandmother on top, who was always hanging around here and made it plain that she found
me an insignificant old maid and was only here for the
company of my Dad, the love of her life? Did you think I
was doing well? Without friends or a social life? Without
any men taking an interest in me? Without any hope of a
normal life with marriage, children and my own home?
Did you think I didn't want all that? That I had no dreams
of my own? Did you *really*, Leslie?'

Leslie closed her eyes for a second. 'No,' she said quietly. She opened her eyes again and looked at Gwen.

'No. I knew what you dreamt of. I knew what you
longed for. But—'

'But what?'

'But you always showed a smiling and calm face. You
were so fond of your father, and saw Fiona as a second
mother. Somehow…you seemed so secure in that life. You
were…different to other people. I should have…'

'Yes?'

'I should have looked more closely,' said Leslie.

Neither of them said a word.

Dear God, thought Leslie, let me get through to her.

'I'm sorry,' she said in the end, but Gwen just shrugged.

'In your shoes that's what I'd say too.'

It went quiet again. Leslie could feel her racing heart-beat slow down a little, not that the tension and fear she felt had gone. She was able to think more clearly. It seemed to her as if Gwen were not happy with the situation. She had obviously shot Dave and her own father. She had felt no qualms in leaving both men to their fates, which almost certainly meant death.

But now she had been standing in the doorway for a good half hour, aiming her gun at her former friend, and she had not pulled the trigger. She seemed not to harbour the same nameless hatred for Leslie which she had for Chad, Dave and possibly Fiona. Nor had Leslie been part of her plans for the evening. She had just turned up unexpectedly. She should not have been here. Gwen might look like a warrior, but inside she was undecided about what to do next. Leslie sensed it was her chance, although she had no illusions: Gwen's uncertainty about what to do might make her feel she was out of her depth, and then she might make a hurried decision.

Talk to her, that was the only thing that came to Leslie's mind.

'Where did you get the gun?' she asked.

'It's my Dad's army revolver. He had it in the war. That might be a long time ago, but if you want to know if it still works, just look at Chad. And Dave in the bay.'

Leslie remembered a passage in her grandmother's notes. One time she had found Chad's army gun on a shelf in the study. She had tried, and failed, to use it to get him to talk about his experiences at the front. Probably the gun had not been moved. In all the years. For what reason would Chad have seen to put it somewhere safer?

'You...practised shooting?'

'I thought, who knows when I might need it,' Gwen said casually. 'And somehow I was spot on. I really need it now.'

'Gwen…'

'Actually I wanted to shoot Fiona too. But since everyone was talking about the student's murder, I thought I could cause more confusion if I killed Fiona in a similar way to how the poor girl died. Smart of me, wasn't it? I could have died laughing when I heard that incompetent inspector pondering what the connection could be between Fiona and the young woman.'

'You've changed, Gwen,' said Leslie. She thought how grotesque that sentence sounded to her. As if Gwen had just got a new haircut or lost a few kilos. Instead she had mutated into a serial killer. Gwen—with her flowery cotton skirts, her fearful clinging to a withdrawn life on a lonely farm…she had gone and trained as a markswoman with her father's ancient revolver. She had procured ammunition and hatched her plans. She had found Fiona's letters to Chad and seen the chance to construct a motive for the murders of Fiona and Chad. She had obviously spread the letters intentionally. It was not her naivety, as everyone had assumed.

'Did you send Dave to Semira?' she asked. 'To divert suspicion onto him?'

'Did he visit Newton? I almost thought he would. I didn't send him to her. No, but I noticed how curious he had become, and I thought: I bet he goes to Newton! When I visited him two days ago I gave him a second print-out of the files. He read the whole thing that night. He was happy to have something to hide behind, so that he didn't have to go to bed with me. The timing of the plan had changed. Dave should have heard about the Somerville affair before Fiona died. But after the argument which you all saw, the opportunity was too good to miss. From the stairs I heard that she wanted to walk to the cab. I followed her and…well, the rest was easy. I had the revolver with me, and used it to force her to walk along the footpath. When we were a good distance from the road I grabbed a stone and smashed it against her head. Again and again. Until she no longer moved. A day later I threw the stone into the sea from a cliff.'

Leslie fought against a rising feeling of dizziness. What kind of person was she facing? And how could she have been so wrong for so many years? 'So Jennifer lied when she said that you went out walking with her and her dogs?'

'Good old Jennifer. She was worried I could be a suspect, so she covered for me. Her need to help people is sick. It's all she does. Well, it certainly was good for me. Later I told Colin that Jennifer had forced me to accept the story. You should have seen his face. His wife's strange behaviour certainly got him thinking.'

'You…you've been very clever,' said Leslie tiredly, 'in every way.'

'I have, haven't I? I casually let drop to Colin that Dave also knew the old story. I made sure that later, when he would be arrested, no one would believe that he had only heard the story *after* Fiona's death. I could feel how shocked Colin was, and that he thought I was a real gossip. I split my sides laughing inside. He was no better than me. After all, he told you everything.'

'Dave denied knowing Semira Newton when I asked him. He denied ever having heard of her.'

'Of course. He was the main suspect anyway. He knew that this could be used against him. He would have been an ideal candidate for Semira to get to carry out her revenge on Fiona Barnes. So he acted as if he had no idea. Not all that clever of him, because it was obvious it couldn't be hidden forever.'

'When…when did you have the idea to…kill Fiona and Chad?' asked Leslie.

Gwen seemed to take a moment to think carefully about it, but Leslie had the impression that she already knew the answer and was only looking for a way to say it that would make it sound less banal than it might otherwise.

'Always,' she finally answered.

'Always? As a child? A teenager? *Always*?'

'Always. Yes, I think so. Always,' said Gwen, and it seemed she was being sincere. 'I always dreamt of it. I always imagined it. And over the years the desire became stronger and stronger. And now I've done it.'

She smiled happily.

Leslie realised in horror: for years she's been a time bomb. And none of us noticed.

18

JENNIFER DIALLED THE number of Fiona Barnes' flat for the third time, but again the answering machine came on.

'She's not there!' she said in despair.

Colin was sitting at the wheel and driving them, pushing the legal limit, back in the direction they had come from just hours ago. He asked again, 'And you're sure you don't have Leslie Cramer's mobile number?'

'Yes, I am. Unfortunately.' Jennifer knew that Colin was thinking to himself that she was mad. He did not understand what was happening.

'Why are you so worried about Dave?' he had asked at home, confused.

Jennifer had replied, 'I'm afraid that Gwen will go crazy when he tells her the relationship is off. She won't accept it.'

He had not seen the problem. 'Good Lord, Dave Tanner is a big strong man. What's to fear? That Gwen will scratch his eyes out? He can defend himself!'

'I've got a bad feeling. A really bad feeling, Colin. The fact that no one on the farm is answering the phone… seems odd to me. I wish, oh I wish I could just check everything's OK.'

Although Colin had felt sure his wife was in danger of becoming hysterical, he had suggested they call Leslie. 'She could do us the favour of driving over to the farm to take care of Gwen—or Dave Tanner, if he really needs protecting.' Yet Leslie was obviously not home.

'I'll drive to Staintondale,' Jennifer had said in the end, picking up the car key from the kitchen table. 'If I don't, I won't have any peace until I do. Call me crazy, Colin, but I'm driving there now!'

'It's almost an hour and a half's drive! We've just come. I do find that a little crazy, Jennifer!'

She had put on her coat and marched out the door. After refusing for years to drive a car, she now seemed resolved to drive off just like that. Colin had followed her, cursing, and in front of the garage had taken the key from her hand.

'OK. But let me drive. You haven't driven in years. For God's sake, Jennifer, what's up?'

She had not replied. But he had seen in the light of the street lamps that she was feeling really bad. She was highly worried, and Colin asked himself—not for the first time— how many secrets his wife might be hiding from him.

'If you are so worried about Tanner,' he said, 'perhaps you should call the police. Rather than racing through the night and depriving us of our sleep!'

'I didn't say you should come!'

'In the state you're in, I couldn't let you drive on your own. Jennifer, what are you afraid of?'

She did not look at him, but pressed the side of her face against the glass. 'I don't know exactly, Colin. That's the truth of it. I just know that Gwen could snap if Dave breaks up with her.'

'What exactly do you mean by "snap"?'

She did not reply.

Colin pressed her. 'Jennifer! What do you mean by "snap"?'

She seemed to be struggling with herself. 'She's wound

up so tight,' she said in the end. 'She's eaten up with hate and despair. I don't know if she'll be able to brush off this failure.'

'Hate? Gwen?'

Now she turned to him. He looked over at her briefly, before he concentrated on the dark road again. Her eyes were wide open and full of fear.

'I can't call the police,' she said. 'Because then I'd draw their attention to Gwen, and that might put her in a situation she can't get out of. But I know that Gwen has hated her life for years. She sees herself as someone who has had only misfortune. She's really angry about it. She never told me directly, but I can feel it. I just know, Colin.'

'Are you aware of what you're saying?'

'Yes. But that doesn't mean she killed Fiona.'

'But you don't exclude the possibility?'

Jennifer again said nothing.

Colin took a hand from the wheel and rubbed his forehead. His skin felt cold and damp. 'The alibi,' he said. 'The stupid fake alibi. You didn't want to protect yourself, but *her*. You had an inkling, and instead of telling the police you made sure you got Gwen out of danger as quickly as possible. That's crazy, Jennifer. That's really crazy.'

'She shouldn't suffer any more.'

'But she might have killed someone!'

'But we don't know!'

'And it's the police's job to find out. It was your duty to tell them everything you know. All hell will break loose now. Do you realise?'

Instead of answering, she asked, 'Can you drive faster?'

'We have to call the police now, Jennifer.'

'No.'

With a loud curse Colin put his foot on the accelerator pedal. Breaking the speed limit hardly mattered now.

19

'YOUR FATHER WILL die if no one helps him soon,' said Leslie. She could barely stand. She did not know how much time had passed. She felt that Gwen did not know how to get out of the situation she had put herself in. The minutes were ticking away and Chad's chances of surviving were trickling away. Dave Tanner's too. And there was nothing she could do. She had to stand opposite this madwoman and hope she did not panic and pull the trigger.

Gwen shrugged. 'Let him. That's the point. Fiona dead, Chad dead. He blocked my life, and she helped him do it. And what's more, the two of them have my Mum on their consciences. Because Fiona refused to let go of my Dad, and because he was unable to show Fiona her place, my mother got ill. Or perhaps you think she enjoyed having your gran here on the farm day after day? Your gran even cooked for my Dad, took care of him when he was sick, shared his worries. Sometimes the two of them acted as if neither my Mum existed nor me. We just weren't there. That's how Mum got cancer. And I…' She stopped there.

'You became mentally ill,' said Leslie. She weighed her every word with the utmost care. 'And I can understand. I'm so, so sorry not to have paid attention, not to have seen how things were. You had a horrible childhood and youth, Gwen. But why didn't you leave, later? When you were eighteen? Why did you stay?'

'I wanted to leave. You have no idea all the things I tried! You thought I was reading those stupid romance novels and living in dreamland. Instead I was…'

'Yes?'

'I think I answered over a hundred personal ads. Met I don't know how many men. Over the internet too, in the last few years. I know all the matchmaking sites. I know all the systems. I've spent hours each day at the computer. And many evenings on dates with men.'

Leslie would never have guessed it, but by now little could surprise her. 'You didn't meet the right man,' she suggested lamely.

Gwen laughed shrilly. 'You're too much, Leslie! You've always got a wonderful way of describing the shittiest things! *You didn't meet the right man*… Nice way to put it! Thanks for your tact! No, I didn't meet the right man. The man who would have wanted someone like me. The horrific truth is there was never a second date. They saw me, they tortured themselves through an evening with me, maybe they paid for the meal, which they had wasted on me, and then they made off. Relieved it was over. And they never wrote again. Didn't even reply to my mails. Let alone try to see me again.'

'I'm really sorry.'

'Yes, it's sad, isn't it? Poor, unfortunate Gwen! But the evenings when they struggled to keep a conversation going with me were good days. Do you know what often happened? Imagine you're in a restaurant. You're nervous. You're waiting for the man who might—*might!*—be Mr Right. You've made an effort to look good. You know that you aren't pretty and that you're not good at doing yourself up, but you've done your best. You're trembling with anticipation. And then the door opens. The guy coming in doesn't look bad. Nor unfriendly. You know it's him. The man you've been chatting to on the internet for weeks. You slowly get a feel for it, you know? You don't need any sign, a red rose or a particular paper under your arm, anything like that. You just see. And he does too. His gaze wanders round the room and fixes on you. He recognises it's you, just as you recognise it's him. And you see he's startled. Because you aren't at all what he had hoped for. In a flash he feels queasy at the thought of having to spend the evening with you and that he'll have to fork out for it, too. And you immediately know he won't have the decency to stick around for the evening and then make a graceful exit later.'

Leslie knew what was coming next. 'So he acted as if he were in the wrong place, and left.'

'Lovely situation, isn't it?' said Gwen. 'You've just told the waiter you're waiting for someone. Now you have to explain to him somehow that the person can't unfortunately make it. You pay for the glass of water which you've been holding the whole time, get up and leave. You feel the staff's pitying looks. They understand too and feel sorry for you. You creep back home. Humiliated. Rejected. And your hatred grows. It becomes stronger than anything else. It even becomes stronger than your pain at some point. The time comes when you have the feeling that you are nothing but hate. And you think that you're going to explode, unless something happens.'

Leslie understood. She understood what had been building up in Gwen. She knew that hate which is hidden behind such a smooth and smiling surface for so long becomes a tornado, highly unpredictable. Yet she felt compelled to question the logic which Gwen saw and based her actions on.

It might not be sensible to raise objections to a mentally ill woman who is facing you with a revolver, but she did it anyway. An instinct told her that one thing should not happen in any case: the conversation should not be interrupted.

'Two things, Gwen, that I don't get,' she said. 'First, why blame Fiona and Chad for all of that? And secondly, why didn't you ever think of trying to find a way out of your situation, apart from finding the perfect man? Why not an education? A job? Your own money and independence? That's the direction you should have taken.'

Gwen looked at her in astonishment. 'I could never have done that,' she said and seemed really surprised that Leslie could have such an idea. She was so astonished that Leslie understood now. It was impossible to quickly make Gwen realise that she was intelligent and capable, and that she could have learnt a career like any other person and gone her own way. Probably months of effort could not do it. It would certainly need a very well trained psychologist. Decades of Gwen's life would need to be worked through too, starting with her earliest childhood, and if it were not clear whether even that would be of help.

'Oh, Gwen,' she said gently. She did not insist on an answer to her question. The answer was now clear to her. Gwen's hatred of Fiona and Chad, and her blaming of them, had led in the end to the murders. The self-doubt that ruled her life, her fear of really living and her inability to take responsibility for herself and her future—these were at the bottom of her hatred. Her life was pure pain, uncertainty and a feeling of constant inferiority. Her experience was of being rejected constantly. She was clever enough to realise that her life had been determined in her childhood by her indifferent father and by Fiona, who had destroyed her parents' marriage over the years. Add to that the death of her mother, which she probably rightly attributed to the unconsummated and therefore unending affair between Chad and Fiona. In casting blame, Gwen was not mentally ill. The reasons for blame seemed completely right to Leslie. But the course of action that Gwen chose, that was sick. Yet for someone like her, who had felt like her back was against a wall for all her life, it was the only way out, however bitter it was.

Gwen had not been able to bear it any longer. And she had begun to fight back.

'As I said, I spent many hours at the computer,' said Gwen. 'And so I came across the mails your gran sent to my Dad. I could barely believe what I read. And yet what happened to poor Brian Somerville was just like them. It fitted my Dad's autism, and Fiona's almost sick selfishness. If you couldn't defend yourself against them, you'd go under. That's what they were like. What they were always like.'

'And you thought you could use Brian and Semira for your plan,' stated Leslie, not without bitterness. It seemed particularly tragic to her that these two people, who each in their own way had suffered so much, were then used as pawns by a mentally ill murderer.

'It was a perfect opportunity,' said Gwen.

'Did you plan to frame Dave right from the start?' asked Leslie. Dave had certainly, she thought to herself, done a fine job of making himself look suspicious. Panicking that he could be found guilty, he had tangled himself up in ever more lies. At first he had not said that he had left his house a second time on the night of the crime, and when that story was blown, he had only made it worse by making up the night spent with his ex. It had been easy for Gwen to put him in a rather suspicious light.

Gwen shook her head energetically. 'No. Only after I gradually realised that he...was not serious about me. I'm not stupid you know. I bet you all asked yourselves how I could be presumptuous enough to think that a guy like Dave would really be interested in me. Probably each of you urged another one to open the eyes of the poor, naive girl that I am! You were all worried about me, and about the rude awakening that I would have one day... But, frankly, Leslie, I'm not half as stupid as you all took me to be. From the first moment I could see that Dave wasn't the typical guy to be courting a woman like me, and I watched him closely. I didn't need your gran's help to get the idea that he might just be after my property. More and more things suggested it. And that hurt. Because you know, in spite of all my scepticism and reservations, I had fallen in love with him. It was a wonderful time with him. His attention and his efforts—even if they weren't really done for me—were something special. I hadn't ever experienced anything like it. It was beautiful. There were moments I could really enjoy. They were out of a dream.'

She sounded sad. Leslie could glimpse the old Gwen, the one who was always a little melancholic and willing to please.

And Leslie thought: we didn't see that she was mad. But why didn't we at least notice how sad she was?

'Why did you shoot him?' she asked. 'It puts paid to your plan to frame him for the crimes against Fiona and Chad.'

'There was nothing else I could do,' said Gwen. 'Sitting in a room with him, having to say goodbye and feeling how he was straining to get away from me, seeing that he was only sitting out the few hours out of decency, while inside he was quivering to go, because he couldn't stand me any longer, because he wanted to get away, away... It hurt so much. It hurt so bad. I couldn't let him go. I wouldn't have been able to bear it.'

'You persuaded him to walk down to the beach with you?'

'I said I had to go out. I asked him to come too. He didn't want to, but I think he felt sorry for me. So he came. I think his only concern was to end things decently. And part of that was not leaving me on my own after breaking off the engagement. He wandered down to the bay in complete resignation. I had stowed away the gun. I didn't know what I would do, but I knew I wasn't going to let him walk away.'

'Are you sure he's still alive?' asked Leslie.

'No idea. He was alive when I left. Either he'll bleed to death or the tide will take him. I don't care either way. It doesn't matter any more, does it?'

She said it with a resigned voice. Leslie grasped the opportunity. 'It does matter, Gwen,' she said urgently. 'Your father is still alive. Dave might still be alive too. Let's call for an ambulance. Please. You can still save both of them. It's— then it wouldn't be two murders which you—'

Gwen interrupted her with irritation. 'No, just Fiona's murder and two attempted murders. Do you think that'll help me much? Do you think prison will feel nicer like that? Rubbish, Leslie. And you know it!'

Leslie could see that Gwen was a complete contradiction right then. On the one hand she had a good understanding of her situation. She knew she would end up in prison, and she was resolved to try to prevent that. At the same time she did not seem to grasp the mess she was in. Did she seriously think she could get out of this untouched? Shoot down her father, Dave, Leslie, and then carry on as if nothing had happened, without any police suspicion alighting on her?

Everything she had done revealed two sides. On the one hand, she had calmly made sure people around her knew about Brian Somerville's story, ensuring a motive for the murders of Chad and Fiona was getting around and would sooner or later reach the police. She had also thought carefully about how to increase the suspicion which was in any case already falling on Dave. And then she had suddenly sabotaged herself, by losing control of her emotions and shooting Dave, unable to accept and bear his leaving her.

She was more sophisticated, knowing and tactically clever than anyone had given her credit for, but she was not as calm and untouched as she would have liked to be. She remained unpredictable to others—and to herself.

That made her, as Leslie realised with a shiver of fear, a terrifying and highly dangerous enemy. You could never foresee what the next moment would bring.

'I left Dave lying there and came back to the farm,' said Gwen indifferently, as if she were recounting some minor occurrence. 'And then I saw a torch beam roaming around. You were going towards the bay, but I thought: who cares, even if she finds Dave, she'll have to come back here. You never get reception on your mobile, which has its up sides, as we can see. My father had locked the front door, just as you asked him to I imagine, but of course he opened it when he heard my voice. Well, and after I had put him out of action, I just had to wait for you. I sat at the top of the stairs. I took the precaution of taking the key out of the study door. I thought you'd try to call from there.'

'Very clever, Gwen,' said Leslie. 'You really thought it all through in advance.'

'Yes, stupid, naive little Gwen. You all underestimated

me. For thirty years. You should all have kept a sharper eye on me!'

Leslie wondered what to say to that. Should she recognise their guilt, although it was no justification for Gwen's actions? In any case, she had the feeling it would do no good. Gwen was not in her right mind. It was not a question of making amends and showing understanding. Gwen had edged herself into a dead end. In her skewed perspective there was only one way out, and it chilled Leslie.

Gwen seemed to be having just the same thought. Thoughtfully she said, 'What am I to do with you now, Leslie? We can't just stand here all night and chat. After all, we never had much to say to one another. Nor do we now.'

'I arranged to meet DI Almond,' Leslie said. 'I was supposed to be there hours ago. She'll be surprised I didn't come, and look for me.'

Gwen smiled. It was a cruel smile that seemed to take pleasure in the idea of pain.

'Then it's time I came up with something for you,' she replied.

20

VALERIE ALMOND'S BAD feeling was increasing with every minute of the evening. She had waited in the pizzeria for a long time, had tried repeatedly to reach Leslie on her mobile, but Leslie was unavailable. In the end she drove home, but she could not switch off. She called Fiona Barnes' flat several times, but no one answered there either. By about half past nine she could bear it no longer. She jumped in her car and drove over to Prince of Wales Terrace. She thought it unlikely that Leslie would be there, for there was no reason for her not to answer the phone, but she just wanted to check.

A simple reflex, she thought as she manoeuvred her car into a space. I feel helpless, so I'm just doing something. Because it's better than sitting around.

She got out. She felt anxious because she had not heard from Leslie, who had wanted to tell her something urgent to do with her grandmother's murder. She had sounded nervous, and had said she would be at the pizzeria in twenty minutes' time. She knew Scarborough well. She had grown up here. So Valerie could be sure she had not got lost. And if she had, why wouldn't she have called?

Something wasn't right, thought Valerie.

There was still no sign of Dave Tanner. And now Leslie seemed to have disappeared too.

A man was standing in front of the entrance to the enormous building. Valerie wondered why he was hanging around here at night. Not that he looked like someone up to no good. Instead he looked rather bewildered.

She stepped past him and rang the doorbell by Fiona Barnes' name.

'No one's there,' said the man behind her.

Valerie turned around. 'No? Did you also want to go to the late Mrs Barnes' flat?'

'I've rung three times, but…' The man shrugged. Then he introduced himself. 'Dr Stephen Cramer. I wanted to see my wife…my ex-wife. Leslie Cramer. But she doesn't seem to be there. There's no light on up there.'

'Detective Inspector Valerie Almond,' said Valerie, holding out her ID. He glanced at it briefly. 'I wanted to see Mrs Cramer too.'

He looked worried. 'I looked around,' he said. 'Her car isn't here.'

'You don't have a key to the flat, do you?'

'No. I'm staying at the Crown Spa Hotel, a little down the road. I haven't seen Leslie for two days now.'

'Is that unusual?'

He hesitated. 'Well…she knows where to find me. But maybe she doesn't see any need to. But where is she now? At this time of night?'

Valerie had the impression that Leslie's ex was still brooding on the divorce. No doubt he had spent the last two days in his hotel, hoping and waiting for his former wife to appear—something which she had obviously not considered doing for a minute. Now unable to bear it any longer, he had come to snoop, and the fact that she was not sitting at home like a good girl was the last straw for him.

Poor boy, thought Valerie.

He suddenly became aware that it was not usual to meet

a senior police officer late at night outside his ex-wife's door, and that the police officer had to discuss something with her that could not wait until the next day. 'Has something happened?' he asked in alarm.

'Do you know where Dave Tanner is?' asked Valerie.

Stephen frowned. 'Dave Tanner? Gwen Beckett's fiancé? No idea, why?'

'I'd like to talk to him,' replied Valerie vaguely.

'And you think he might be here?'

'No. No, I'm just concerned about Leslie. She called me about seven and wanted to meet, to tell me something important to do with her grandmother's murder. We agreed to go to a pizzeria. But she didn't come, nor call me, and I can't reach her on her mobile. It just seemed strange, so I came here.'

'That is rather odd,' said Stephen. 'Where was she calling from?'

'She was in her car. Somewhere just before Staintondale. She said she was on the way from Robin Hood's Bay. Any idea what she was doing there?'

'No. Like I said…we haven't spoken recently.'

'Something stopped her coming,' murmured Valerie.

'Could she have gone to the Beckett farm? Since she was so near?'

'Why should she? But I'll give them a call. You don't have the number, do you?'

Stephen had it saved on his phone. But no one answered at the farm either.

'That's even stranger,' said Stephen. 'As far as I know, old Chad Beckett practically never leaves the house! Why isn't he there? I wonder if…' He stopped.

'Yes?' prodded Valerie.

'Leslie didn't tell you about the letters yet, did she? Which Fiona Barnes wrote to Chad Beckett?'

'No. What letters?'

'Emails,' said Stephen uneasily. 'Gwen found them and gave them to the holiday guests, the couple, to read. They gave them to Leslie. I don't know exactly what's in them, but Leslie told me that Chad and Fiona got mixed up in something years ago…that there was a dark story in their lives which no one knows about. It unsettled Leslie.'

Valerie stared at him and then gasped for breath. 'I can't believe it! I can't! Why don't I know about this?'

Stephen looked even more nervous than before. 'I tried to get Leslie to give you the papers. I was convinced that she shouldn't keep what she had found to herself. But she… waited. Fiona, her grandmother…came out of it all in a rather bad light. She didn't feel happy about letting other people read what she had read.'

'Her grandmother was *murdered*, for God's sake. Everything, absolutely everything to do with this old woman should have been told to me!' shouted Valerie. 'I can't believe it! This may…'

'Yes?'

'Chad Beckett may be in danger too. In any case, there seems to be some complicity, if I understand right.' She got out her car key. 'I'm driving to the Beckett farm now.'

'Please, can I go with you?' asked Stephen. She hesitated and he added, 'Otherwise I'll go in my car. You'll have me there one way or another.'

Valerie gave in. 'OK. Get in.' She was already running to her car.

Stephen followed her.

He saw that Valerie was calling as she jumped in.

She was calling for backup.

21

THEY SAW LESLIE's car immediately. It was parked in the middle of the yard. There was a second car beside it. Valerie recognised it was the Brankleys' car. The light was on in the house and the front door was open.

Scarcely had Valerie stopped when Stephen sprang out of his seat, ready to rush in. The police officer held him back.

'No. You wait here. Who knows what's up. I'm going over to the house.'

He obeyed, but once he saw that she had reached the front door, he followed.

Valerie stepped into the bright hall. 'Mr Beckett? Miss Beckett? Inspector Almond here. Where are you?'

She heard a male voice. 'In the living room! Come quick!'

She ran along the corridor. Reaching the living room door, she saw Chad Beckett lying on the floor. Colin Brankley was kneeling next to him, brushing Chad's thin grey hair from his forehead again and again, and calling his name.

'Chad! Wake up, Chad! What happened?'

'Mr Brankley,' said Valerie.

He turned around. 'We found him like this, Inspector. He was lying here. I think he's been shot.'

'Where were you in the last few hours?' asked Valerie,

kneeling down next to Chad. The waxen pallor of his face and his complete motionlessness were not good.

'We were in Leeds. Jennifer suddenly wanted to go home this afternoon. But…'

He could not say anything else. Stephen appeared and pushed him aside. 'Let me see him, I'm a doctor.'

He felt for a pulse.

'You had no permission to just take off,' said Valerie in a sharp tone.

Stephen raised his head. 'He's dead,' he said. 'Bled to death. From a gunshot wound, as it appears.'

'Oh God,' said Colin, shaken.

'No one touch anything here from now on,' said Valerie.

Stephen stood up. Valerie saw that he looked desperate. 'Where's Leslie?' he barked at Colin.

'She's not here. We just found Chad. No one else is here,' replied Colin. Then he knotted his brow. 'Who are you?'

'Stephen Cramer. Leslie's ex. Leslie's car is outside. She must be here somewhere.'

'Where's your wife, Mr Brankley?' asked Valerie.

Colin looked about, confused. 'She was here a minute ago. Maybe she's just looking around the house again.'

'You two: stay here,' Valerie ordered the men. She got out her gun and released the safety catch. 'I'm going upstairs.'

'No one is in. We were in every room,' said Colin.

'I'm just going to check for myself,' replied Valerie.

After she had gone, Colin and Stephen looked at each other over Chad's body.

'What's happening?' asked Stephen quietly. 'Fiona was killed. Now Chad. God, who's sick enough to do this?'

'I don't know,' said Colin.

'It's about the story, isn't it? With Fiona and Chad. The two of them did something damn stupid and got someone so mad with them that he's knocked them both off.'

'You know the story?' asked Colin.

Stephen shook his head. 'I just know that the two have got into a real mess. That's all Leslie told me.'

Colin said nothing.

Valerie came back to the living room. 'No one there.'

'But Jennifer must be somewhere!' said Colin worriedly.

He wanted to go out into the corridor, but Valerie held him back. 'Mr Brankley, who was here when you and your wife left?'

'Chad,' said Colin. 'And Gwen. And Dave Tanner.'

Valerie inhaled sharply. 'Tanner?'

'He was waiting here for Gwen. He wanted to tell her that he was ending it. I thought that sensible of him. But that was why Jennifer wanted to come back as soon as we got to Leeds. She panicked when I told her what Tanner planned to do. I thought at first she was worried about Gwen, that Gwen would not bear the break-up. But then she said she was worried about Dave Tanner. I didn't get that at all.'

'Did she elaborate on that?'

'No. I asked, but she said she'd tell me later. I've rarely seen her that worked up. Then we got here, found Chad dead—or as we hoped: badly wounded—and saw Leslie's car. We searched all the rooms, but didn't find anyone. Then you came…' He looked around helplessly. 'Where's Jennifer?'

'Where's Leslie?' asked Stephen.

'Maybe Jennifer is outside, looking around the outbuildings,' said Valerie. She tried to convey a calm exterior, but the situation seemed like a nightmare to her. A killer was running around; no one knew who it was; one man was lying dead on the floor; a further man and three women had disappeared; it was night, and neither literally nor figuratively could you see what the situation was. She prayed that backup would come soon, and that she could keep the two men calm until then. They were very worried and wanted, as she could see, to rush off and look for their wives. Valerie was horrified by the idea that the two of them might disappear into the dark too.

'Jennifer was here a minute ago,' said Colin once more.

'Stay with Chad,' ordered Valerie again, making sure her tone was clear and decisive enough to keep the men obedient for a while at least. 'I'm just going to have a look around.'

'When are your people coming?' Stephen wanted to know.

'Any minute now,' reassured Valerie.

She knew that it would be more sensible to wait. It was also what guidelines recommended. It was highly risky to creep around out there on her own. But she knew that she could not expect Colin and Stephen to remain calm if the three of them just sat with Chad's body in the room and waited. The two men would flip within minutes and go outside.

'I'll be right back,' she said.

22

JENNIFER RAN THROUGH the night. She had gone for walks with Cal and Wotan so often late in the evening or early on dark mornings that her eyes worked quite well in the dark. Nevertheless, she was guessing more than seeing her way. The overcast sky hiding the moon and stars did not make it easier for her. Out here in the open she was making quick progress. It would get more difficult on the other side of the hanging bridge. Without moonlight, it would be complete madness to go down into the gorge without a torch, but she decided not to think about it yet. She would decide what she should do when she got there.

Her heart was pounding, her lungs hurt. She was fit, but she was not used to going this fast, uphill too. Strangely, she had no doubt that she was heading to the right place. She knew Gwen. Gwen had always been drawn by the bay.

Gwendolyn Beckett.

She felt the guilt weighing on her like a millstone. She would have burst into tears if she could have afforded to cry right then. If it turned out that Gwen had left this bloody trail behind her—killed Fiona and shot her father, and was the cause why Dave Tanner wasn't to be seen on the farm, and why Leslie had also disappeared—then she Jennifer was to blame, at least partly.

Why hadn't she said anything?

Not that she had suspected something the whole time.

If that had been the case, then she would probably have gone to the police in the end. It had normally seemed completely absurd to suspect Gwen. Was Gwen to have gone and murdered an old woman she had known all her life, who had played a part in her upbringing, and who was the only person apart from her father whom she was close to?

And then there were all the print-outs which Gwen had given her at the start of her holidays. 'Read it, Jennifer, please. There are things…I don't know what to make of them…I don't know what to do!'

After Fiona's murder Jennifer had clung, almost in relief, to the idea that the letters were the answer to the riddle. The other child, the one who had come to the farm during the war years. Fiona and Chad bore the guilt for his fate, if not directly, then at least through negligence.

Gwen had also told her about Semira Newton. 'I looked on the internet. Semira Newton found Brian Somerville years ago. On a godforsaken farm. Half dead. The farmer, a madman, caught her and attacked her, leaving her maimed for life.'

And later Gwen added, 'She's still alive. That old woman. In Robin Hood's Bay. I found her through the electoral roll. It must be her. I don't expect there are too many Semira Newtons around here!'

It all seemed so obvious. Naturally, Jennifer had brought up the police. Gwen had almost burst into tears. 'That will just stir things up again. It's almost forty years ago. No one remembers the story any more. Do you want to dish the dirt on Fiona? And my Dad…he's an old man, his leg is always causing him trouble…can I do that to him?'

Colin had also wanted to go to Valerie Almond immediately. He had held back because Jennifer had asked him to, for Gwen's sake. She suspected that in his confusion he had told Leslie. Each of them had passed on the responsibility to another. None of them had done the right thing and told the police. Gwen's feelings about her father and Fiona should not have been decisive in this situation.

And the whole time Jennifer had been thinking: come on, it wasn't Gwen. Gwen had nothing to do with it. I know that.

But her doubts had never gone completely. The same doubts had led her in the first terrible hours after they heard about the murder to provide an alibi for Gwen.

Better to make sure she's safe, Jennifer had thought. After all, she had a motive, after what Fiona did earlier in the evening, and it was better to take precautions now.

Jennifer stood still for a moment, bending over forwards, her hands at her sides where she felt the cramp.

Breathe deeply, she told herself, otherwise you'll collapse.

She looked back at the farm, but could only see the dark night. Colin did not seem to have followed her. She had used the moment he was still kneeling in horror next to Chad to shout that she was going to look for bandages. Then she left the house as quietly and quickly as possible. He would never have let her go, or he would have wanted to come with her and have demanded explanations. What could she say? That the intuitive fear that Gwen could be a killer, which had been lodged in her like a tiny poisonous sting from the beginning, had been growing larger and more painful over the last hours? And that in the minutes since their arrival at the farm the poison had spread throughout her whole body, leaving her breathless? That she was afraid of what might happen to Dave Tanner and Leslie Cramer and that she was not going to wait until the police came. Colin could tell them what was happening. He would fetch an ambulance for Chad. She was not needed now at the farmhouse.

She ran on, gathering her last reserves.

She knew she was the only one who had seen behind Gwen's mask, practically from the first summer she and Colin had spent on the farm. She had not just seen the nice, friendly, rather homely and naive woman, who seemed to have settled into a life without any major ups and downs and was satisfied with what she had around her—the wonderful wide-open landscape, the sea in its always changing colours, the sky which often looked higher and wider than anywhere else, the wild cliffs and, somewhere between the rocks, the little bay which she liked to retreat to. And the father whom she loved and cared for. The rundown but comfortable house. A life far away from the world. What people looked for when the stress of their everyday lives, its worries, bustle and problems became too much. Gwen had made all that her own. Whoever did not look closely could even envy her it.

But Jennifer could see more deeply. She often could. It was part of the marked ability to empathise with which she was blessed—or cursed. She herself often did not know whether to accept it or fight it. She saw the anger in Gwen. The sadness. The nameless rage. The pain. The despair. She saw the withering life, which had never blossomed. She saw the suffering which came of it, and she saw the innumerable unshed tears which were dammed up in her, faced as she was with everyone's indifference. The loved father who did not notice, because he was not interested. And Fiona, who could not leave the little family alone, and whose care concealed an obsession to cling to Chad. Gwen had seen through her long ago. Fiona was not interested in Gwen either. Jennifer even thought it possible

that Fiona's attacks on Dave Tanner during the engagement party had less to do with the thought that he might
be a misfortune to Gwen than with her concern about what
would happen to Chad if a much younger, more ambitious
man started to take control of the farm. Whatever Fiona
had said, Jennifer had never believed that she was really
thinking about Gwen's future.

And sometimes Jennifer had thought: what would happen if everything which has been hidden inside Gwen for
decades, all the anger and hate, finds a way out?...What
would happen when the pressure becomes too great?

And that thought had always made her afraid.

Nevertheless a murder was so unimaginable, such a
crazy idea, that Jennifer had repressed the fear with all
her strength. And her need to protect others had grown
with each meeting with Inspector Almond. She had known
that the inspector would seize on every little scrap thrown
to her, like a starving dog. Here too she had seen further
than Colin and the others. Almond might look energetic,
competent and sure of herself. But behind the mask there
was a woman plagued with doubts and fears. She was a
nervous officer who could gain no confidence from her
career progression. She was driven in an unhealthy way by
ambition to move up the career ladder. She feared deeply
that she would fail to solve the Barnes' case. Jennifer had
felt that. The woman was at the end of her tether.

If Jennifer had given her Gwen, the inspector would
have latched on to her and never let go, whether or not
Gwen was involved or not.

And I can't do that to Gwen, she had told herself.

Perhaps her silence had now led to tragedy.

She reached the highest point of the wide hill. From
here it was no longer far to the hanging bridge and the

gorge. The most difficult part was still ahead of her. She could no longer just aim to go as quickly as possible. She also had to think about her own safety. It would not help anyone if she broke her ankle.

Immediately she thought: A broken ankle… As if you didn't know that something much worse could happen.

She had always felt sorry for Gwen. She had always wanted to protect her. But she was realistic enough to know that Gwen had never really repaid her affection. To Gwen she was always a paying holiday guest. Someone who brought some variety into her life now and then. But Jennifer had never felt a friend's warmth in Gwen. She had never felt any warmth in Gwen. The nice smile had never come from her heart.

Jennifer followed the path that led down the hill towards the steeply sided rocky gorge. Then would come the bridge; then the uneven steps hewn into the rock with their unpredictable variations in height and distance. She would have to go down almost blindly.

She still had not reached the end of the path when she saw a beam of light shining out of the darkness ahead of her. She could not see exactly where it was coming from, but she had the impression that it was either from beyond the gorge or from the other end of the bridge. The light was not moving.

Jennifer stopped. Tensely, she strained to make something out in the darkness. She could not recognise anything. She was too far away. She had to feel her way closer to the object. She assumed it was a torch. But why was it not moving? Had the people up ahead—and it could only be Gwen or Leslie or Dave, or all three of them—already got to where they wanted to be? Or had they noticed they were being followed and were now waiting?

But then they would have turned off the light, thought Jennifer.

She crept closer, holding her breath.

When she had reached the bridge, she could see everything. It confirmed her worst fears. The torch was on a rock on the other side of the gorge. It bathed the creepy scene in its bright, almost searing, light. Leslie Cramer stood almost at the far end of the bridge. Her back was against the bridge's railing of plaited rope. Gwen was in front of her, pointing a gun at Leslie. The two women were staring at each other silently.

Suddenly Gwen said, 'Hurry up and jump!'

And Leslie replied, 'No. I'm not jumping. You're crazy. I'm not going to do what a crazy person tells me to.'

'I'll shoot you,' said Gwen. 'Then throw you down there. I'd think about it, Leslie. If you jump, you might have a chance.'

'If I jump down there, I've got no chance,' replied Leslie.

Gwen raised her arm. In the silence of the night the quiet click of the safety catch being released was audible.

'Please,' begged Leslie.

Jennifer took a step forward. 'Gwen,' she called.

Gwen spun around. She looked in the direction from where she had heard her name, but she did not seem to be able to see who had called her.

'Who's there?' she asked sharply.

Jennifer stepped onto the bridge. She knew that the bridge's swaying would betray her approach, but she also knew that Gwen would not be able to pick her off easily. She was protected by the dark.

'It's me,' she said. 'Jennifer.'

'Don't come a step closer!' warned Gwen.

Jennifer stopped. She was now close enough to be able to see Leslie's face, rigid with fear, in the torch's beam. Gwen's face was hidden in shadow.

'Gwen, be sensible,' asked Jennifer. 'Colin's on the farm. He's calling the police. Soon the place will be swarming with officers. You don't have a chance, so let Leslie go. She didn't do anything to you.'

'She let me down just like you all did,' said Gwen.

'Shooting people you have a problem with doesn't solve anything. Please, Gwen. Put down the gun, come over here.'

Gwen laughed. It was a horrible but also sad laugh. 'You'd really like that, Jennifer. My advice to you is to get lost—else you'll be next! Don't poke your nose in what's none of your business. Go back to Colin and your curs and carry on with your smug, easy life. Just leave people alone who have it worse than you!'

'My life has never been easy and smug, you should know that after all these years. And Leslie is not who you obviously think she is. Other people have problems too, you know, Gwen. Even if you can't imagine that.'

'Just shut up!' hissed Gwen.

Jennifer thought the gun in her hand had trembled a little. Gwen was nervous and unsure of herself. She had obviously hoped that Leslie would jump off the bridge when she threatened her with a revolver. She did not seem to be finding it easy to just shoot her one-time friend. And now someone had turned up, and was lurking in the shadows—an invisible threat. Gwen was acting like someone who feels driven into a corner, and that could cause the situation to escalate.

'Gwen, whatever you feel right now, Leslie and I have

always been your friends, and we still are,' said Jennifer. 'Please. Put down the gun. Let's talk.'

'I don't want to talk to either of you!' shouted Gwen. 'I want you to leave me alone. I want you all to finally bugger off.'

Leslie moved and Gwen immediately spun around and aimed the revolver at her once again. 'You're about to die!' she warned.

Jennifer dared to step closer. 'Gwen. Don't do it.'

Now Gwen whipped around to face Jennifer. The gun was pointing right at Jennifer's chest. 'I can see you,' she said triumphantly. 'I can see you, Jennifer, and I'm warning you: one more step and I'll shoot. You can bet your life on it.'

'Gwen,' beseeched Jennifer.

She took another step towards her.

The next second the shot rang out.

Everything happened at once. Leslie screamed. Jennifer clutched at the railing, because suddenly the bridge swayed wildly. She waited for the pain, sure it would cut into her like a knife. She waited for her legs to give way, to collapse. She waited for the blood which would start to flow.

And she saw Gwen fall, slowly, almost in slow motion. She sank down onto the wooden bridge, falling like a supple dancer glides into a new position. The gun slipped out of her hand and lay right by the edge of the bridge. With a little more momentum it would have fallen off.

Leslie knelt down next to Gwen, grabbed her arm and felt her pulse. Jennifer saw that too, and was still surprised to find herself standing and not in pain.

Then she heard a voice behind her.

'Police. Don't move!'

She turned around. A shadow appeared from the darkness, walking along the bridge. Jennifer recognised Valerie Almond. She was holding a pistol in her hand. And Jennifer understood that the police officer had shot—at Gwen.

She realised that she herself was uninjured.

And that she did not have to wait for the pain.

Saturday, 18th October

THE WEATHER WAS grey and windy, and it was colder than the previous days. Thick, angrily massed clouds raced across the sky. The wind over the treeless moors was icy. A few sheep huddled together at the bottom of the hills. Nothing had remained of the golden October in which the week started, but nor had anything remained of the foggy and rainy Novembery last few days. The day seemed bathed in a curious emptiness. It was just grey. A nothing day.

Maybe that's just me, thought Leslie. Maybe I'm just seeing my own emptiness out there.

She was in her car on the road to Whitby. And she felt cold and lonely inside.

She had called Semira Newton and asked about the care home where Brian Somerville lived. After a few minutes' hesitation, Semira had told her.

'Don't hurt him,' she had asked.

Leslie did not think that just her visit was going to disturb the old man.

I can turn around any time, she thought, as she saw the first of the terrace houses on the edge of Whitby. A large cemetery stretched out on the left. The road led down steeply to the right towards the town centre. Leslie could see the famous abbey up on one hill.

She hardly knew how she had spent the past day.

She had been in Fiona's flat, had smoked and stared

out of the window. At some point she had gone for a walk of an hour or two, along the beach over to North Bay and back again. Then she had bought a ticket for the funicular railway up from the Spa Complex to Prince of Wales Terrace. Five of them had sat on a wooden bench in the carriage being pulled up the tracks. Leslie remembered how she had felt that she had nothing in common with the people who were in such close proximity. Too many terrible things had happened.

Chad was dead. She knew that he had still been alive when she had left the house with Gwen. She had heard a quiet groan from him. By the time Valerie Almond and Stephen arrived, Stephen had only been able to confirm he was dead. He had bled to death. He could have been saved if help had come sooner.

Gwen had been shot in the leg by DI Almond. She was in hospital but would soon be well enough to leave. She was to face charges of two murders and one attempted murder, as well as deprivation of liberty and coercion. The question was whether a psychiatric report would pronounce her of sane mind or not. Leslie thought it likely that Gwen would not be put in prison but in a psychiatric institute. Perhaps forever.

She had spent all of yesterday with the image of the bridge scene in front of her. The torch's glare; Gwen collapsing at her feet; Jennifer Brankley a shadowy figure some distance away, who obviously could not move after the shot rang out. And Valerie Almond, who appeared out of the dark to save them. She calmed them down, saying, 'She's not badly injured. Don't worry. I've just injured her a little.' She meant Gwen. And Leslie remembered that she had jumped up and shouted, 'We have to go down to the bay! Quick! Dave Tanner's down there. She shot him! Quick!'

She kept saying that, and in the end Valerie Almond had put her hand on her shoulder, looked her steadily in the eyes and said with a clear voice which would not allow for contradiction, 'We'll look after him. OK? You aren't going down there now. My officers are just coming. Don't worry.'

The memory of her sitting at the Beckett farm afterwards was more hazy. Ambulance men and the police had been swarming all around. Someone had wrapped a blanket around her shoulders and pressed a mug of hot, sugary tea into her hands. To her surprise Stephen was there, and he was also the one to tell her the news that Tanner had been rescued injured but alive.

'He'll survive. He's been lucky. He was unconscious. The tide would have taken him in the early hours.'

Some time late at night Stephen had taken her to Fiona's flat and stayed there himself too. She had not tried to refuse. She had felt too weak to ever stand up to anyone or anything. He had asked if he could read Fiona's letters. She had nodded. Everyone was going to find out now, so why not him? Later she herself had told him about Semira and about Brian, and how although he lived so near to Scarborough, Fiona had never brought herself to visit him.

In the afternoon she had talked to Valerie Almond for a long time. The officer came straight from the hospital where she had talked to Dave Tanner.

'He was really lucky. He could have bled to death or drowned. He's escaped this whole affair by the skin of his teeth.'

Dave was now free of all suspicion, but Leslie still wanted to hear for herself. 'So, where was he then? That Saturday night, if not with his ex?'

'The two of them were in the pub together,' Valerie explained. 'That much was true. But then she went home alone and Tanner drove around aimlessly. He parked somewhere, had a smoke and a think. About his rather worrying future. By the time he got home it was well past midnight. As he was scared that no one would believe him, he made up the night with Miss Ward—sure that she would play along. But he made a big mistake there.'

'He shouldn't have lied so much. He just made everything worse.'

Valerie Almond's eyes narrowed. 'A good number of people shouldn't have lied so much. Omitting to mention important facts is also considered a lie. At least in a murder investigation.'

Leslie knew at once what she meant. 'But what happened to Brian Somerville wasn't Gwen's motive, Inspector,' she said. 'The little boy who became a helpless man—he hadn't touched her heart at all. She just saw it as her chance to give in to her hate and throw people off the right scent.'

'I should still have been told,' Valerie had said. 'Your silence could even have legal consequences for you, Dr Cramer. The same goes for the Brankleys of course. Maybe even for Dave Tanner.'

Leslie had just shrugged.

Now too she tried to shake off the threat in DI Almond's words and to remember Semira Newton's directions.

Cross the river, left at St Hilda's Catholic Church. The station on the right. Follow the signs to the home.

She reached the port. That was in Semira's directions. She breathed more easily. At least she had not gone the wrong way.

'Right opposite the home you'll find a big car park,'

Semira had said. 'You have to get a ticket, but at least you don't have far to walk.'

She saw the car park and turned in. It was busy, but there were still spaces. She parked and got out.

When had the wind turned so cold? It must have been overnight. She shivered, pulled her coat tighter round her body and looked around.

She thought that area might look nicer on a day that was not as cloudy and grey. The view of the port facilities was ugly and depressing: the big black cranes, the long warehouses and the ships on the dull grey waves. And above it all the constant presence of the seagulls with their piercing cries.

She turned away. So this was where Brian Somerville would die. With the view of this port every day. Did he like it? Did he look at the ships? Did the cranes fascinate him? Perhaps, she thought, he sees the movement and life of it all.

She hoped so. The bleakness of the grey day weighed on her. Across from the port rose the hill where the abbey stood, but you could not see the impressive building from here. A row of houses ran down the road below her. The Captain Cook Memorial Museum. A hairdresser. A teashop. An Italian restaurant. A pub.

The nearby redbrick building must be the home.

Leslie gulped. She went over to the ticket machine, got a ticket and put it carefully behind her car's windscreen. Her movements were slower, so much slower, than usual. She knew why. She was dragging out the moment before she visited the home.

She would meet a very old man who, if you believed Fiona's writings and Semira's words, had the mental age of a child. She found it hard to imagine him. Would he be playing with building blocks? Would he just be staring apathetically in front of him? Or would there even be days—beautiful, sunny, special days—when a nurse would take his arm and accompany him on a walk, maybe even inviting him to a cuppa and a piece of cake in the teashop?

She breathed in deeply and crossed the road.

WHEN SHE STEPPED outside less than an hour later, she saw Stephen. He was leaning against her car with his hands buried deep in the pockets of his coat. His shoulders were hunched up against the cold. He looked out over the harbour. Nothing had changed in the time she had been inside. Not the cold wind, and not the almost aggressively bleak day.

Stephen turned around when he heard her steps approaching. He looked completely frozen.

'What are you doing here?' she asked by way of a greeting.

He made a vague gesture. 'I thought…you might not want to be alone.'

'How did you know I was here?'

'You suddenly disappeared. I just guessed. You said that Brian Somerville lives in a care home in Whitby, and using Directory Enquiries the rest was easy. There are only two possible homes in Whitby. I was just lucky on my first try. I saw your car parked here and…well, I decided to wait for you.'

She smiled wanly. 'Thank you,' she said quietly.

He was looking at her attentively. 'Everything OK?'

'Yes. Yes, I'm OK.' She looked past him and fixed her gaze on the top of a crane. Its dark metal stood out against the clouds in the sky. A seagull sat up there and looked down with concentration at the water far below. Somewhere in the distance a ship sounded its horn.

'He's still waiting,' said Leslie. Her voice sounded strange, and she knew it was because she was struggling to remain calm. 'He's still waiting, Stephen, and he's convinced she's going to come. He's been looking forward to her visit since February 1943. This old man asked after her and I…I couldn't bring myself to tell him…' She had to stop.

'You couldn't tell him that she's dead,' Stephen finished her sentence. 'You couldn't tell him that she'll never come.'

'No. I couldn't. All he has is his hope. It's carried him through his whole terrible, horrific life. It will be with him until he dies, and perhaps…the most merciful thing we can do for him is not take it away.'

'Thank God,' said Stephen. 'Thank God, that was what you decided.'

'How about walking a bit?' asked Leslie. 'It's so cold.'

They left the car park, strolled down the road and went up the little cobbled alleyways, which crisscrossed the harbour like a spider's web. Souvenir shops, pubs, all kinds of small shops with nautical equipment. Stephen had taken Leslie's arm. She let him.

'Gwen used his story,' said Leslie. 'I just can't believe how coldly calculating that was. It's as if now at the very end of his life he's been taken advantage of once more. Just to quench the hate and thirst for revenge of a woman who felt hard done by—and a failure. How could she do that?'

'How could Gwen do any of it all?' asked Stephen. 'Kill Fiona, kill Chad, then try to kill Dave Tanner. You too. She lost control completely. Our Gwen! The nice young lady with a friendly face. Hard to grasp…'

'We didn't really know her, Stephen. We just saw her façade. And if we're honest, none of us really made an effort to see behind it. Perhaps just Jennifer Brankley. But she obviously couldn't see how dangerous things were getting.'

'Only someone trained in those things could have,' said Stephen. 'It was too much for us.'

'Still. I wonder how I could have been so blind,' said Leslie. 'It was all so clear the night before yesterday in her father's study. When she talked to me. In that strange monotone, with no expression in her eyes. She's a person with no empathy whatsoever. Without the slightest feeling for anyone else. That can't just have been like that for one night!'

'Probably not. But she hid it perfectly. She was our gentle, good-natured, friendly Gwen. And she was a person full of hate who was out to kill. She was both people. Hard to grasp, but true. And whether or not we understand it—we have to accept it.'

Their walk had taken them to the quay. They could look out towards the open sea. Below them quiet waters lapped on a small strip of sand. Leslie took her arm out of Stephen's and leant against the railing. In the distance the water and sky merged. She found this sight soothing, although she could not have said why. Perhaps it was just a more beautiful sight than the cranes and the steel warehouses.

'I think that the whole affair with Brian Somerville has been like a poison acting on the Beckett family,' Leslie said. 'And on mine. A crime which is so thoroughly suppressed, a guilt which isn't worked through, doesn't just trickle away because you don't talk about it. You can see how powerful it was by the fact that it stopped Chad and Fiona getting together. And caused them to choose the wrong partners. And so the poison also acted on their children and grandchildren, who all lived with that jarring situation of having two people whose path to each other was blocked, and yet who weren't free for other people. Fiona kept some kind of ownership on Chad's life, and we all suffered as a result. Chad's wife got cancer so young. My mother ended up a drug addict. I had to be brought up by my grandparents. And Gwen…well, Gwen most of all. With her father closed in on himself. And Fiona meddling. For decades on the farm she had to put up with the woman who she, at first intuitively and then quite consciously, blamed for her mother's death. That can make a person sick…'

'Yes,' said Stephen. 'Probably. But…we can't change things now. We have to find our own way forwards.'

'What'll become of the farm?'

'It'll be sold, I bet. Chad's dead, Gwen will be behind bars for a long time, if not forever.'

Leslie looked at him. 'If no one had stuck their nose in, then Gwen and Dave might have married. Dave would have made something gorgeous out of the farm. And Gwen might have made her peace with life. If—'

'Leslie,' Stephen interrupted her gently. 'She's sick. She's been sick a long time. Her life has been heading towards tragedy for years. Something bad would have happened in any case. Nobody and nothing could have stopped it. I'm sure.'

She knew he was right. And realising it, the tension which she had taken to Whitby with her suddenly evaporated. Suddenly she felt very tired. Her eyes hurt. It was not just the lack of sleep last night. She was tired of everything which had happened during the last week. And during the last years of her life. When everything changed.

As if he could guess where her thoughts were heading,

Stephen asked suddenly in a quiet voice, 'And us? What's to become of us?'

She had been fearing that question since she had seen him beside her car. And yet she was relieved that he was there. He knew her. He had guessed that she would look for Brian Somerville, and he had known that she would not feel good afterwards. That was how he was and, she hoped, always would be: a friend who knew how she felt. A friend who took her in his arms and gave her his shoulder to cry on. A friend who talked to her when she needed it, and was silent with her when she could only make herself understood without words.

But not more than that. Not more than a friend.

She looked at him, and he saw in her eyes what she was thinking. She knew because of the grief that flooded his face.

'Yes,' he said. 'I thought so. No, I knew it. I just…had a spark of hope.'

'I'm sorry,' said Leslie.

For a while neither of them knew what to say, then Stephen broke the silence. 'Come on,' he suggested. 'Let's go and find a hot cup of tea. If we stand around too long we'll catch a cold.'

'There's a teashop just beside the home,' said Leslie. Then she was suddenly overwhelmed by an urge to go back, to the home where Brian Somerville was numbly approaching his death, having to look at the port day after day. To the home where he was waiting for a woman who had promised him sixty-five years ago that she would come back and look after him. Anger and despair mingled in her at the thought that she would never escape everything that had happened. That from now on, it would always be part of her life.

'I don't know how to deal with it, Stephen,' she said, and immediately knew that what she said was an understatement. She did not even have the faintest glimmer of an idea how she was to work through what she had experienced over the last few days.

'She was my gran. But she's a demon to me. Maybe I'll come to understand some things, but there's one thing I'll never get: why didn't she visit him a single time? In the course of all those years. Semira Newton kept asking her to. Why didn't she? Why wasn't she capable of even that little display of humanity?'

Stephen hesitated. He only knew one answer. It would not satisfy Leslie and not absolve Fiona of guilt, but it seemed to be the only true answer. 'Because no one likes to face up to their guilt,' he said.

They went back to the car park slowly. They stood in front of the teashop. No one was inside except for a bored looking woman who was drying a few cups behind the counter.

'And what should I do now?' asked Leslie. Stephen understood that she was talking about her grandmother. It took him a moment to dare to say what he thought.

'Forgive,' he said. 'In the end that's the only thing to do. In every case. Forgive her. Try. For your own sake.'

'Yes,' said Leslie, 'I can try.'

She looked out over the port.

She felt the wind. It stung her cheeks as it dried her tears.

She had not realised she had been crying.

* * * * *

REQUEST YOUR FREE BOOKS!
2 FREE NOVELS PLUS 2 FREE GIFTS!

✦ HARLEQUIN®

ROMANTIC suspense

Sparked by danger, fueled by passion

REQUEST YOUR FREE BOOKS!

2 FREE NOVELS
PLUS 2 FREE GIFTS!

MYSTERY ™ W❂RLDWIDE LIBRARY®
Your Partner in Crime

ReaderService.com

Manage your account online!

- Review your order history
- Manage your payments
- Update your address

*We've designed
the Harlequin® Reader Service
website just for you.*

Enjoy all the features!

- Reader excerpts from any series
- Respond to mailings and special monthly offers
- Discover new series available to you
- Browse the Bonus Bucks catalog
- Share your feedback

Visit us at:
ReaderService.com